The Saturday Supper Club

Amy Bratley works as a freelance journalist and lives
in Dorset with her husband and two children.

Also by Amy Bratley

The Girls' Guide to Homemaking

The Saturday Supper Club

AMY BRATLEY

PAN BOOKS

First published in Great Britain 2012 by Pan Books
an imprint of Pan Macmillan, a division of Macmillan Publishers Limited
Pan Macmillan, 20 New Wharf Road, London N1 9RR
Basingstoke and Oxford
Associated companies throughout the world
www.panmacmillan.com

ISBN 978-0-330-51968-7

3 5 7 9 8 6 4 2

A CIP catalogue record for this book is available from
the British Library.

Typeset by CPI Typesetting
Printed and bound by CPI Group (UK) Ltd, Croydon, CR0 4YY

Visit **www.panmacmillan.com** to read more about all our books
and to buy them. You will also find features, author interviews and
news of any author events, and you can sign up for e-newsletters
so that you're always first to hear about our new releases.

For my mum, Anne Cook

Acknowledgements

For their unswerving support during a year of blood, sweat and tears, I'd like to thank my agent Veronique Baxter and her assistant Laura West. Thanks to Jenny Geras for her brilliant editorial insight, patience and understanding, Eli Dryden and all at Macmillan for their hard work. Thanks to my best friends, Caroline, Karen, Helen and Mel and to my family, Isabel, Jo, Tony and my mum. Thanks to various friends for their anecdotes that have stayed with me and appear in this book. My love and thanks to Jimmy, Sonny and Audrey, my life. Finally, love to my dear old dad.

PART ONE

Eve's Supper Club

Chapter One

Life has a way of flinging messy, unfinished business in your face, just when you're least expecting it. Everyone knows that. I know that. It's an unwritten law that just when you're sailing happily along, life socks you in the gut and leaves you gasping for air. Even so, I was *absolutely not* expecting it that humid Saturday evening, at the beginning of June, when I opened my front door to welcome dinner guests and found all six-foot-two of my messy, unfinished business standing on the doorstep holding a dewy bottle of Chablis and a bunch of scarlet poppies.

'Oh my God!' he gasped, rocking backwards, stumbling into the dreadlocked wisteria dangling from the trellis in soft violet blooms. 'Eve?'

My hand shot to my mouth. I could not believe my eyes. I blinked. My mouth fell open. It was my ex, Ethan Miller. Ethan looked at me and I looked at him. He let out a strangled laugh while I fought a sudden urge to burst into tears. I could not find any words. I just gawped at him, the air sucked from my lungs.

But who could blame me? It had been three years since he'd upped and left without a word of warning, vanishing from my life and into nowhere like a shooting star into the night sky. Now he was here and it felt like the hands on the clock were whizzing noisily backwards, rewinding all the days, weeks, months and years since he walked away. Gathering myself, I tried to close the door, but Ethan wedged his size-eleven Patrick Cox brogue into the gap. Admittedly, I didn't put up much of a fight. I took a deep breath and let the door swing open, holding on to the handle, gripping so hard my knuckles went white.

'Christ almighty,' he said, his eyes perfect circles. 'I cannot believe this. It's been nearly three years.'

I frowned, confused and disorientated. It seemed both of us were in shock at seeing one another. My cheeks burned. I shook my head. Still, I could not speak. From behind me came the hiss of a saucepan of water boiling over onto the cooker top and a bitter smell of dark chocolate burning. My pudding, I registered vaguely, would be completely ruined.

'Eve,' he said.

'Ethan,' I said.

'I didn't—' he choked. 'I didn't know you lived here. I feel like I'm going to have a heart attack. Should I just go?'

He pointed towards the street with his sad bunch of poppies. Their scarlet petals flopped listlessly, wilting in the heat. A black cab slowed down, its diesel engine noisily whirring, but Ethan turned back. He held the flowers out towards me, a tiny tentative smile on his lips, as if remembering something that was good, once upon a time.

'No,' I said. 'Don't go.'

And even though warning bells were ringing in my head, I did what I definitely should not have done. I let him in.

Earlier that Saturday, a bizarre thing happened. I had found an old photograph of me and Ethan I'd thought was lost, tucked in the pages of a notebook. I had been standing, surrounded by the intoxicating smell of strawberries and raspberries, near a spectacular fruit and vegetable stall at Borough Market, riffling through the notebook looking for my shopping list to check I hadn't forgotten anything. I was in a bad mood because with just twenty-four hours' notice I'd reluctantly agreed to host and cook a three-course dinner party for people I'd never met, taking part in the Saturday Supper Club, a (hugely popular) dinner-party competition run by the *London Daily* newspaper.

'I'm about to ask you a massive favour,' my boyfriend Joe had said down the phone from his desk at the *London Daily* newspaper offices in Canary Wharf, where he was freelancing as a reporter. 'Prepare yourself.'

'You're scaring me,' I said warily, because I knew that whatever it was, I would have to agree to Joe's request. Joe wore the badge of Nicest Man On Earth and when he asked me to do something – as long as it didn't involve rubber gloves or galvanized chains – I did it.

'OK, so you've seen the Saturday Supper Club competition in the paper, haven't you?' he continued. 'The one where people cook dinner parties for strangers in their own homes, then mark each other out of ten? The winner gets a thousand pounds? Well, one of the contestants has dropped out of the competition tomorrow night . . .'

Joe's words trailed off almost guiltily, and I narrowed my eyes, hearing his lovely Irish accent become stronger with nerves. I could picture him exactly, his slim frame hunched over his desk while he made this private call, nervously rubbing his jaw with his free hand, blond stubble scratchy on his palm, blond eyelashes fluttering over shiny brown eyes.

'Right,' I said. 'And did you, by any chance, suggest I could take this person's place?'

I made my voice light but inside I felt annoyed. Joe knew my life was hellishly busy at the moment. I had no time to invite my friends over to the flat, let alone cook a three-course dinner for strangers that the whole of London would read about. Sensing my bad mood, Joe cleared his throat a couple of times and lowered his voice. I had to shove the phone up against my ear to hear him.

'You love cooking, don't you?' he said quickly, as if that was the issue. 'You're a brilliant cook and well, if I'm honest, if I can find someone, i.e. *you*, this will make me look really good. I can see myself getting a job here, Eve. I'll soon be in my own office.'

He paused for breath and continued in an almost-whisper.

'Imagine it, though,' he said. 'My name in gold lettering above the door, feet up on the table, smoking cigars and barking orders at underlings—'

He was trying to make me laugh, but there was a serious subtext. Joe had been freelancing for years on various publications and was desperate to get a full-time, permanent position on a well-respected newspaper. He wanted to prove he could be as good as his dad once was, not that he'd ever admit his motivation to anyone but me. I bit the inside of my cheek. I was going to have to agree.

'And the editor says she's happy for you to talk about the cafe and will even credit it,' he added. 'Publicity like that is worth a few quid, you know? This paper is read by over six hundred thousand people. What if they all came in for a coffee and a slice of cake? You'd be a millionaire!'

I sighed. The cafe was my very raw nerve. I was supposedly opening a new place in eight weeks' time and, financially speaking, it was becoming more of a chain round my neck than a dream come true, so the prospect of free publicity was undeniably tempting. Even so, the thought of having people I didn't know round for dinner felt like a big ask. I thought of the pants and bras currently drying on my radiators, the mountain of crockery, lamps and pictures I'd bought for the cafe currently stored in boxes in my hallway, making it difficult to get out the front door.

'What about all the crap in the flat?' I asked. 'I'll have to spend hours clearing it up.'

'Don't bother, it's all part of your incredible charm,' he said breezily. 'So, do we have a deal?'

In the background, I heard the voices of Joe's colleagues, a peal of laughter, then the muffled sound of his hand over the receiver while he talked to them.

'What the hell will I cook?' I asked in exasperation, not knowing if he was listening or not.

'You'll think of something,' he said. 'Sorry, got to go, there's a meeting. Thanks for doing this for me. I . . . I do . . . appreciate it. I think it's a good idea, really. In the long run I'm convinced you'll be pleased.'

Joe sounded so grateful, I softened. There was no way I could let him down. Maybe it would be good fun. Maybe I'd win. Whatever, it wasn't going to change my life in any way, and if it would help Joe out, I didn't want to say no.

'I love you, Eve,' Joe said, suddenly serious. 'More than you know, I really do. Thank you. Bye.'

There was a clattering as Joe put down the receiver, and I was left feeling slightly bemused, panicking about what to cook.

'Me too,' I said to the dialling tone.

And so, after flicking through recipe books and devising a menu – fresh asparagus for starter, fisherman's stew with homemade bread for main and a chocolate and strawberry meringue for pudding, I braved the Saturday morning crowds at Borough Market and spent a small fortune I didn't have on fresh ingredients. But finding that photograph of me and Ethan stopped me in my tracks. It had been taken a couple of days before Ethan left and felt like another life entirely. My hair was longer then, and brown – now it was a red bob. I looked incredibly happy. We were at Reading Festival sitting in the awning of our tent, both grinning, his arm draped over my shoulders, my head turned towards him. Typical. I had never been able to drag my gaze away from Ethan, because he was so annoyingly good-looking. A jobbing actor, Ethan could have been a character in a 1940s Hollywood film noir. As it was, he'd played a drug dealer in *The Bill* and a corpse in *Silent Witness*. Tall, chiselled, dark, with unreadable eyes, Ethan seemed to have stepped right out of one of those smouldering Jack Vettriano paintings, positively oozing virility. Even when he had been up all night and had dark crescents under his eyes, which was often – he liked to party – he could've been on a photoshoot for Yves Saint Laurent. But it was much more than aesthetics. I loved looking at Ethan, because for the two years we'd been in a relationship, I had loved him with every cell in my body. I'd mistakenly thought he loved me back. I shook my head, bit my lip and scrunched my toes in my sandals.

'Don't even *think* about crying,' I instructed myself with a loud sigh, moving away from the strawberries, my bags of shopping banging against my legs as I walked to the bus stop.

'Bloody Ethan,' I sighed. 'Still gets to me.'

After nearly three years apart, following two years together, the thought of Ethan shouldn't still have upset me. But the truth was, it did. Losing him had left a void in my life that, at the time, felt nothing short of cataclysmic, leaving a hollow in my heart reminiscent of my mother's death. Even now, when I remembered how he left, so abruptly – without a word of warning – I felt physically sick. I'd been certain, absolutely certain, that Ethan and I would be together my whole life. But I'd been proved horribly wrong. I sighed. I'd thought I'd had my quota of sadness when my mum died, but I now knew that life didn't work like that. While some people lived without a care, others were magnets for miserable luck.

I boarded a number 40 bus headed for East Dulwich, found a seat and stole another look at the picture. I studied Ethan's face for clues of him being unhappy, because he must have been secretly unhappy. I searched for a hint of what he was about to do. Just as I thought, there were none whatsoever. He was holding out a plastic pint glass of beer to the camera, as if to celebrate. I rested the picture on my lap and closed my eyes. Perhaps that was the hint.

'Ethan Miller,' I muttered. 'What happened to you? Not that I care.'

As the bus roared along Borough High Road and through Camberwell Green, past King's College Hospital and Denmark Hill station, images of Ethan flashed into my mind: smoking a cigarette in his concentrated manner; the easy way he slipped into Italian when talking to his parents; watching a gig in a darkly lit venue with a whiskey in hand, turning to beam at me like only we really understood; stretched out on the grass in the park staring up at the sky, laughing so hard his whole body shook; the tears I'd seen him cry, just once in two years, when he described the recurring nightmare that kept him from sleep. I curled my fingers around the picture and considered screwing it up. I'd loved Ethan with everything I had, but I needed to put him in the past and leave him there.

Five minutes later, glancing up out of the bus window at a row of three-storey Victorian terraced houses, their doors painted red or green or blue, I realized we were at my stop at Goose Green in East Dulwich, now touted by wanky estate agents as home to artists and creative types, driving up the prices even more. Photo still in my hand, I held my finger down on the bell and the driver swerved the bus to a halt, bundling everyone standing in the aisles forward and onto each other's toes.

'Sorry,' I said to the man near me, as I shoved my way to the exit door, the photo slipping out of my fingers and onto the floor of the bus. 'Oops, oh shit, I've dropped . . .'

The doors shut behind me, a whisker of a second after I stepped out onto the pavement. I banged on the glass with my palm but the driver took no notice. Resting my bags on the ground, I took a deep breath. I'd lost the photograph of Ethan. I told myself I didn't care. Ethan was the past. I had

Joe now and he was all that mattered. It might sound sappy, but Joe had galloped into my life and flung me onto his white stallion when I was at my absolute lowest. He deserved my complete and utter devotion. What did it matter if that picture was trampled on and ruined? My heart had suffered the same fate at Ethan's hands. I watched the bus chug up the hill and then out of sight, leaving behind a great furl of black exhaust.

'Forget about it,' I told myself. 'OK, I really need to hurry up.'

I checked my phone. It was four p.m., which left me just three hours until my Saturday Supper Club dinner-party guests were due to arrive. I had so much to do. Sweat burst onto my brow. The thought of cooking dinner for strangers, against the clock, felt terrifying.

'You owe me one, Joe,' I muttered, my mind drifting to the lost picture of Ethan as I walked. I'd shredded most of our photos in a drunken rage soon after he left, then, of course, immediately regretted it and tried, pathetically, to stick them back together. That wasn't the worst of it, either. I cringed at the memory of the reams of poems I'd penned in my diary, furiously dark and angst-ridden. Thank God I'd never sent them to him or shown them to a living soul. I still had them – a stark reminder to be careful with my heart.

I heaved the bags up into my arms and turned into Elsie Road, where I lived in a very small garden flat in a Victorian conversion, which reminded me of a dolly mixture, because the previous owner had had the wherewithal to paint the exterior a charming shade of pale blue and the window frames white. I say garden, but really it was more of a postage stamp

11

with two flourishing pots of lavender in it and a solitary apple tree, but I loved living there, with my cat Banjo. In the last two years, from the window boxes planted with mint, chives and thyme, to the brass Deco doorbell with 'press' embossed on it, I had made it my home. Unusually for London, I knew several of the neighbours, too, mostly young families whose living rooms were stuffed full of baby paraphernalia. I held my breath as I passed an overflowing dustbin that never seemed to be emptied, its contents stinking in the heat. Finally, boiling hot, my bare arms speckled with horrible black thunder flies, I arrived at my flat and unlocked the door.

'Hello!' I called out to Joe, kicking off my sandals and pushing open the door of my kitchen, heaving my shopping bags up onto the counter. 'Joe? Where are you?'

I looked around the kitchen and my spirits instantly lifted. My favourite room in the flat, it was very small, but perfectly formed and stashed with all my favourite things. Today it was refreshingly cool, with clean white walls and a built-in dresser, shelves bowed under the weight of my beloved cookbook collection, cupboards groaning with kilo bars of the finest chocolate for those moments I felt like making a stash of chocolate chunk cookies, copious bags of flour and sugar for baking and a fridge bursting with ripe, melting cheeses for swiping on crackers and guzzling with a glass of red wine late at night. Then there was the beaded curtain that I liked to burst through in the style of Beverley from *Abigail's Party*, which led through to my walk-in larder. That larder had sold this flat to me. Cool and dark, it was now lined with jars of jams, pickles and condiments. I liked to stand in there, just looking. If I could choose where to spend my final hours, it would be in there, alone with a freshly baked, warm, soft French baguette stuffed with crisp, fine, dark chocolate.

'Joe?' I called, stepping into the hallway, tripping over a box of crockery and into an enormous bunch of white lilies that was taking over the entire telephone table. Must have cost a fortune. I frowned. I'd never much liked white lilies. Their overwhelming smell reminded me of my mother's funeral. At the time I didn't know what lilies represented and couldn't understand why people had chosen white flowers for such a colourful person.

'Joe?' I said again, pushing his shoes out of the way with my toe.

Since I'd started going out with Joe, his possessions had popped up in the corners of my flat like wild mushrooms, the edible ones. He had his own place in Kentish Town, but his guitar was a permanent fixture as was his uniform of Worn Free T-shirts, Lee jeans, white Vans and his vintage mustard-coloured MG Spider that lived on the street outside and attracted blokes like bees to honey. My older sister Daisy had vowed to save up for one herself, convinced it was a great way to meet and bag an eligible bachelor.

'I'm here,' I heard Joe shout from the garden. 'Outside.'

I smiled as I walked out and saw the blond, skinny, six-foot man that is Joe up a ladder, twisting fairy lights around the branches of the apple tree. He took off his dark-rimmed glasses, closed his eyes, rubbed them briefly, then climbed down and kissed me full on the mouth. His body, pressed up against mine, was baked warm from the sun. I put my arms around him and leaned into his chest, glancing up at the tall, dark, puffy clouds forming in the sky.

'Are those lilies for me?' I said. 'I've never seen such an enormous bunch.'

'They're to wish you luck for tonight,' he said. 'And to thank you for helping me out at such short notice. You'll be glad when I'm an international media tycoon.'

'I like you how you are, thank you,' I said, holding Joe tight. 'You know, you don't have to buy me so many flowers. I could open up a florist instead of a cafe. Actually, maybe that would be a wise move, considering the mess—'

'If I stop buying you flowers that florist near the Underground will go out of business,' he said. 'I couldn't be responsible for their downfall. Besides, I'm buttering you up so that you'll marry me. It's all emotional blackmail. I'm not totally selfless.'

Joe asked me to marry him, or alluded to it, almost every day. But it was always done like this, in jest, flippantly, never seriously. I'd got used to not reacting or saying something sarcastic in reply. It was just part of our parlance; a joke we shared, though I'm not convinced either of us found it particularly funny.

'I'll check my diary,' I said playfully. 'There might be a window in 2020—'

I looked up at him to smile and Joe, a grin on his lips, narrowed his eyes, plotting something. Suddenly, he grabbed me by the waist and hoiked me up over his shoulder into a fireman's lift.

'Joe,' I screamed, laughing and kicking my legs. 'Put me down!'

'No way,' he laughed. 'I'm taking you to the bedroom right now.'

I wriggled down out of his grip, laughing. Back upright,

with my feet on the ground, I shook my head and raised my eyebrows.

'Sorry, Joe,' I said, pinging the elastic of his pants that was sticking out of the top of his jeans. 'There isn't time. I've so much to do. Later, though?'

I kissed his cheek and hugged him again.

'Later,' he said with a sigh. 'OK.'

I sensed his dissatisfaction. I'd been so busy with the cafe lately, working late nights and early mornings, I knew our relationship had suffered as a result. I was knackered and stressed, that was all.

'I've got an idea,' I said, mentally vowing to make more effort after tonight. 'Maybe we can have breakfast in bed tomorrow morning?'

'Yeah,' he said, visibly cheering up. 'Definitely.'

I didn't want Joe to feel unappreciated. I chewed the inside of my cheek, hoping that he didn't.

'Thanks for putting those lights up,' I said, looking at the lights carefully twisted around the leafy branches of the apple tree. 'I would never have had time to do that.'

'No problem,' he said kindly.

I held on to Joe tightly and squeezed his arm gratefully, leading him back indoors. Nothing was a problem for Joe. He was Mr Capable, adding some semblance of order to my chaotic existence, and I loved him for that.

'I should put those lilies in water,' I said. 'I've so much to do. They're coming at seven, aren't they?'

Joe nodded.

'Yes,' he said. 'Dominique, the girl from the paper writing the story, said she'd arrive then with the others.'

'Did she mention their names?' I asked.

Joe shook his head and scratched his chin.

'No,' he said. 'She said she'd email, but I haven't heard anything. I can text her? Actually, I have a feeling it's policy not to give out names before the group meets . . .'

'That's OK,' I shrugged. 'I'll find out soon enough.'

We walked back inside, my arms goose-bumping in the cool, eyes readjusting to the contrasting darkness. Joe stopped me, held me in his arms and kissed me again, before picking up his car keys and mobile phone from the lily table.

'I'd better get going,' he said. 'I promised your dad I'd go to that folk club with him while you do your thing tonight. Fuck knows what that will be like.'

He raised his eyebrows and gave me a quick smile.

'Maybe I'll get to do some Morris dancing,' he said.

'You need bells on your shoes,' I said, then hugged him. 'Thanks for looking out for my dad. You really are properly wonderful.'

'No, I'm not,' he said. 'I just like your old man.'

Joe looked downcast for a moment and I smiled brightly at him. I knew he was thinking of his own dad, whose permanently drunk and disorderly personality left a lot to be desired. My dad, in sharp contrast, was absolutely adorable. Everyone loved him, but no one more than me.

'Have a good time,' I said, hugging him. 'I do love you, you know?'

Joe squeezed me. I breathed in his smell. Mint. Joe always smelt of mint lip balm. This is a very teenage confession, but when Joe had gone away for two weeks on a press trip a couple of months previously, I bought a pot of the stuff, just so I could slather it on my lips. I'd hated those weeks, not because I couldn't enjoy life without Joe. I could. No, I hated that time because it brought home how much I loved having Joe in my life, which made me feel sick with dread about the possibility of losing him. I knew that people could disappear at the snap of a stick. Each goodbye could potentially be the last. I shivered at the thought.

'Knock 'em dead,' he called from the doorway. 'Actually, maybe don't kill anyone, though that would guarantee publicity. See you tonight, Beautiful.'

'Hardly,' I said, pulling a disapproving face at him, feeling about twelve years old. I couldn't help grinning insanely. He was the only person in the world who could get away with calling me 'Beautiful' as if it was my birth name, without sounding like a testosterone-pumped jock. Perhaps it was his accent. When you've a voice like his, you could say pretty much anything and still sound good. He waved goodbye and closed the front door, leaving me alone in the quiet of the flat.

'Not long left,' I said, moving into the kitchen and locating my frilly red-and-white gingham apron on the back of the door. 'Oh-my-God-look-at-the-time.'

I thought about my menu. I was aiming for seasonal, simple and delicious. I'd bought fresh asparagus and hollandaise for the appetizer, mussels, haddock and clams to make fisherman's stew for the main course, for which I would also bake rosemary and thyme bread, plus boxes of sweet, wild strawberries and pots of organic fresh double cream to use in my meringue dessert. I needed to make the meringues first. They had to be absolutely perfect, sweet vanilla clouds. Then I had to tidy up.

'Brown sugar,' I said, flinging open a cupboard door and pushing aside packets of flour and a bottle of vanilla extract. 'Brown sugar, where are you . . .? And vinegar, I need vinegar.'

I'd learned the trick about brown sugar and vinegar making meringue crisp on the outside, but mallowy and chewy on the inside, from my mum, who was a brilliant home cook. I remembered my dad's expression when she made it; kind of stupefied, like there was nothing else in the world but his mouthful of meringue. I smiled at the memory, cracked six eggs into a bowl, separating the yolk from the whites, and thought about my dad's sixtieth birthday coming up. Daisy was insisting we throw a party for him, but I wasn't sure it was such a great idea. Much like me, he would rather be lurking in the wings than be centre of attention.

'I'll just have one glass,' I thought, pouring myself a glass of white wine, running through what I had left to do, a nervous bubble floating in my belly. I had a growing sense of unease and I couldn't work out why. Perhaps it was the prospect of having to make conversation with people I didn't know, under a photographer's glare, around my own dinner table. Though I was a fairly confident person, occasionally I felt inexplicably shy and awkward, wishing I could magic myself into invisibility. I hoped tonight wasn't one of those nights. I gulped more wine and broke off three squares of dark chocolate, putting all three into my mouth.

The majority of my menu had to be thrown together right at the last minute, the seafood added at the end, so after a little more preparation I showered and dressed. I carefully applied my make-up. I looked at my reflection and pulled a face. Even though Joe had the nerve to call me beautiful and had once, in a moment of madness, compared me to Audrey Tatou (which I secretly revelled in; who wouldn't?), I thought my bob and big eyes made me look like some kind of woodland creature.

'Welcome to my dinner party,' I practised into the mirror, grimacing slightly. 'What can I get you to drink?'

I returned to the kitchen and stood at the stove stirring the fisherman's stew, feeling a knot tighten in my stomach. Out of the window the sky was darkening with rain clouds. There would probably be a storm later. Despite the heavy heat in the kitchen, I shivered.

Leaving the stew to simmer gently, I melted the dark chocolate for the rich pudding sauce, siphoning some off to 'test'. Heaven. I blew my fringe out of my eyes and poured a glass of water, but drank more white wine instead. I was increasingly nervous. With a shaking hand, I assembled my dessert into a leaning tower of crisp, chocolate-dipped meringues with oozing layers of vanilla-infused whipped cream, sweet wild strawberries and crushed pistachio nuts, stuffing any broken chunks of it into my mouth as I worked. I finished up eating an entire layer. No one would know. Buzzing with sugar, I fought with the funereal lilies until I'd convinced them to sit in two green vases, set the table, carefully laying out cutlery, glasses, spotty candles, napkins and one of the vases of lilies in the middle, then, with minutes to go, I paced the flat, picking things up from the floor. I stuffed a discarded bra into a drawer, shoved a worrying heap of bills onto a shelf and blew the dust off my cactuses planted in Marmite pots. I changed the CD three times and pushed my *Cooking with Keith Floyd* DVD under the sofa. I looked out the window and watched a square-headed pitbull dragging his owner along the road. Then, perched on the arm of a chair in the living room, legs crossed, fingers drumming on my knee, I watched the clock. At a minute before seven, the doorbell went in three short bursts, making me jump out of my skin. I glanced in the mirror by the front door and put my mouth into the smile shape. I opened the door and I stared. And I gasped. And my legs threatened to give way beneath me. My hand shot to my mouth. I could not believe my eyes. I blinked. It was Ethan, my ex, former Love Of My Life, the boy who snapped my heart in two, easy as a green bean.

'Oh my God!' he gasped, rocking backwards, stumbling into the dreadlocked wisteria dangling from the trellis. 'Eve?'

My heart pounded in my chest, blood draining from my cheeks. I held on to the door to keep myself upright. It was him. Ethan Miller. I swallowed, and bit my bottom lip so hard I tasted blood.

'Christ almighty,' he said, his eyes perfect circles. 'I cannot believe this. It's been nearly three years.'

Chapter Two

Joe and I met over a bathtub of pickled onions. He was eleven. I was ten. My mum, intent on making an enormous batch of pickled onions to last the year through, decided to use the bathtub to marinade the pale shallots in two feet of dark brown pickling vinegar and two fistfuls of peppercorns. Her bath. Her prerogative. We were, thank heavens, an exceptionally clean family. I watched in silent awe while she worked, as if her life depended on making enough pickled onions to feed an army. I'd find out later that, in a way, it did.

'Ingenious idea, darling,' my dad had said to her, secretly raising his eyebrows at me. 'Eve, why don't you get the neighbour's boy to come and see the kind of madness that goes on round here? He's out in the garden again.'

I'd heard Joe, 'the neighbour's boy', being screamed at by his father and cried on by his mother too many times, and I'd once seen him hurling stones at the window of their shed until the glass splintered and cracked. Then he got screamed at and cried on again. My parents worried about Joe out loud most days. They said he wasn't having a childhood. That his dad was an angry man and that his mum had given up on life. Daisy told me they were trapped in a loveless marriage, as alien a concept to me as my mother apparently needing a 'quick lie-down' every afternoon, despite previously being incredibly energetic. So even before we became friends, Joe and I had something in common; we wanted to ignore the uncomfortable truths in our own homes.

Calling out the bathroom window, across into the neighbour's garden, I asked Joe if he wanted to see the pickled onions in the bath. He, of course, did. He scrabbled over the fence with the speed of a squirrel, marvelled at the onions and our friendship was born.

'I always knew – and hoped – we'd be an item one day, but I couldn't work out how it would happen,' Joe had said when we got together as a couple, sixteen years later. 'You don't live next to a girl like you and forget her in a hurry. I even tried to etch your initials into my skin with a compass, little freak that I was. Can you remember those glasses I wore? Jesus, what were my parents trying to do to me? Actually, don't answer that.'

It was late one wintry night, the lights were low in Joe's flat in Kentish Town and we were sitting together on his double bed, leaning up against a stack of pillows, listening to Johnny Cash on his record player, drinking cider and sharing the chestnuts I'd roasted and sprinkled with sea salt. Joe, the skin around his eyes crinkling as he smiled up at me, was holding a burning candle, dripping the molten wax onto the back of his hand. He held his hand up for me to see the splodge of wax, which was almost a heart shape, caught my eye and laughed gently. I leaned into him and rested my head on his shoulder, all angles and not a very good pillow.

'You looked cute,' I said, digging him in the ribs. 'But the compass thing is plain weird. You could have got septicaemia or something hideous like that. You know, you hid your devotion very well. I never guessed you were remotely interested. I certainly didn't think you were emblazoning my name across your body.'

Back then Joe was totally gangly, wore National Health-style glasses and covered his clothes with little badges. He virtually lived at our house, where he was smiley and pink and ate well. On the rare occasion that I went to his house, he crept about like a shadow, grabbing us bowls of cereal to eat on our knees in his bedroom.

'I didn't get very far,' he said. 'It hurt too much, and besides, your initials are E. T. Not very cool.'

From the moment we met, Joe and I had been best friends, and when my mother died a year later – and I realized why she had been furnishing us with year-long supplies of pickled onions, jams and chutneys – we barely left each other's sides. As we grew older, people assumed we'd get together, but we never did. Though we lived in different cities, we stayed in close contact through our university years – he went to Liverpool to study art, I stayed in London to do film studies – but afterwards, when I fell for Ethan, we barely saw one another. Not something I'm proud of.

'If it doesn't work out with Ethan,' Joe would sometimes joke when we spoke, 'there's always me.'

But even though Joe hinted at the possibility of something happening between us, nothing did, until we met up again in London, one afternoon almost a year after Ethan had vanished. I was thinner, weaker, paler than before. I had somehow lost sight of who I was, and I didn't know what to do. I was grateful for Joe, who was, by then, working as a trainee reporter at the *Islington Gazette* and coming into his own. He was doing geek chic for real, wearing dark-rimmed glasses, skinny trousers, black Vans and shrunken pullovers. He looked every bit the arty Londoner, was undeniably attractive and not remotely pretentious. He had shaken off his childhood shyness and was quietly ambitious, driven to succeed, talking of his plans to be an editor, while I just floundered around like a jellyfish. I got outrageously drunk and after I'd poured my heart out about Ethan, Joe, who had never had a girlfriend for longer than three months, confessed he'd always fantasized that we would get together. I was flattered, but, even then, still in love with Ethan and didn't want to slip into a rebound relationship with Joe. Our friendship was too precious for that. But despite my good intentions, before I knew it, we were seeing each other all the time. One night, after watching a film snuggled up on Joe's sofa, listening to the sounds of the overground train rumbling by outside Joe's window, we slept together. I'd kept my eyes open because when I shut them Ethan appeared on the backs of my eyelids. But I knew I had to get on with my life now Ethan was gone, and Joe was perfect; he already knew me inside out. We were already best friends. My dad loved him and was delighted we got together. Everyone thought it was a marvellous idea for me to be with Joe. I listened to them carefully. Back then, because I seemed to be making such a mess of things, I thought other people probably knew better than me.

Joe was totally different to Ethan; quieter, determined, considerate, a buyer of flowers. He was a brilliant illustrator and captured the essence of a person with a few strokes of his fine black pen, whether he scribbled on the back of a napkin or more painstakingly in his sketchpad. He had all his illustrations pinned up on a wall in his flat and I remember, the first time I saw them all, being gobsmacked and embarrassed, because there were so many drawings of me. I hadn't realized he'd done most of them.

'I hope you don't mind?' he'd said, worried for a moment, then grinning sheepishly at me. 'I'm not a psycho stalker, it's that you're so naturally lovely. I've always thought so. Ever since we were kids. Can't believe my luck, you know?'

It was wonderful – if embarrassing – to be admired like that, after feeling like the bottom had fallen out of my world when Ethan left. Joe banished my crushing feelings of self-doubt and I tried to repay him by sharing everything I loved. I took him to my favourite cafes and restaurants, introduced him to lazy Saturdays wandering through the food markets and let him in to my secret Sunday brunch: Bloody Mary with grated fresh horseradish and lashings of Tabasco to accompany huevos rancheros at a pub in Clerkenwell, trying to erase the memories I'd made in the same places with Ethan. Because we had known each other for so long I felt comfortable and safe with Joe. But it wasn't just comfort. That makes him sound like a pair of slippers. I respected him and I *appreciated* him. I started to love him more deeply, though occasionally, usually just after we'd made love and were tangled up together in bed, his arm like an anchor across my waist, I had the sensation of needing to fight for air. I would close my eyes and count pebbles on a beach in my mind's eye, waiting for the feeling to fade. It always did.

Ethan crept into my thoughts most days, but I did my best

to ignore them. I believed that if I pretended I didn't miss him then eventually I wouldn't miss him. Denial worked, to a degree. Though sometimes, if I caught the Tube to Shepherd's Bush where Ethan had lived, or heard a loud, infectious laugh, or saw a guy standing outside a pub smoking a cigarette looking like he knew something everyone else didn't, I physically craved him. But even though I sometimes ached to see him again, I never did.

Until tonight.

'Well,' said Ethan, now, closing the door behind him. 'This is awkward.'

I was relieved that Ethan had spoken because I had lost my voice. I looked at him; his crow-black hair, grey-blue eyes and pale skin, those rose-pink lips quivering slightly. I watched him run his hand through his hair repeatedly – his nervous affectation. He cleared his throat several times and I understood that Ethan was as shocked to see me as I was to see him. He hadn't, as I fleetingly imagined, tracked me down for nostalgic reasons, but had applied for the Saturday Supper Club and had, because of the last-minute replacement, been sent to my address without knowing it would be me waiting at the door. I fought the instinct to grab hold of him and press my lips to his. I swallowed at the lump in my throat.

'I'm . . . I'm . . .' I said. 'I'm . . . so shocked to see you, I don't know what to . . . so, you applied for the Saturday Supper Club? Did they not give you my name? You didn't know I would open the door? Christ, what are you *doing* here, Ethan?'

I pushed my hand through my hair, unconsciously copying him. Ethan shook his head and lifted his hands up in the air, before letting them drop down again.

'No; I was just given an address,' he said emphatically. 'Believe me, this is as much of a shock to me as it is to you. In a city of nine million people, I knock on your door . . . wow . . . it's . . . well, it's unbelievable. You didn't know I was coming either?'

Trembling – no, visibly shaking – I stared at Ethan and shook my head. Joe hadn't given me any details of who would actually be coming – he hadn't known – just that three guests and a photographer would arrive with his colleague, Dominique.

'No,' I said quietly. 'I had no idea. I was asked to stand in because someone dropped out. I had no idea you—'

'Right,' he said. 'And you live here? In this flat.'

'Yes,' I said. 'I do. Live here. Yes.'

We seemed to have lost the ability to speak with any intellect. I couldn't stop staring at Ethan. Standing there in the hallway, he towered above me. His height and broad shoulders had always made me feel particularly small and thus feminine, which I had loved. I felt a blush creeping up my neck and spreading across my face. I lifted my hands to my cheeks and patted them self-consciously.

'Are you all right?' he asked now. 'You look hot.'

His eyes widened and he shook his head.

'I mean,' he said, 'you look like you're feeling hot, the weather, it's stifling, isn't it? Jesus, am I really talking about the weather? Please shoot me now.'

He held his fingers up to his head like a gun and grinned. Ethan had now got himself together and was staring at me, looking like he was about to laugh. It was his defence mechanism, to laugh. His black hair was slightly longer, but he looked just as gorgeous as ever. Famous lookalike? A bit like a young Robert Mitchum. Kind of dangerous. His eyes, always the topic of frantic discussion amongst females, were astonishing and, once you saw them up close, you didn't forget.

'I can't . . . actually, um,' I croaked, 'I'm expecting the others any minute. I should be in the kitchen. My chocolate sauce will be ruined. What are you staring at me for?'

Ethan's eyes were all over me. I panicked. I'd always daydreamed that when I saw him again, I'd be looking jaw-droppingly beautiful. Thin as a pin. I'd be breezy and positive, probably entertaining a crowd who hung on my every word, or speeding down the road in an open-top Mercedes. I'd toss my long blonde hair around a lot, throw my head back and laugh. But, in reality, I felt the blood draining from my cheeks and an awful fear chill my bones. My hair felt too short and red, my lipstick too thick. I had a bike chained to the front gate, no Mercedes. I wondered if I'd aged. I was only twenty-eight, but still, I knew I had deep laughter lines. I hated myself for caring. Tears welled in my eyes. I told myself not to cry, but I couldn't help it. I bit my lip.

'Don't cry,' Ethan said softly. 'Please—'

I covered my eyes with my hand and wiped away the tears, sniffing noisily.

'I'm not!' I insisted, my mouth contorting. 'Really, I'm not.'

Ethan touched my arm, suddenly serious.

'Eve,' he said, 'I'm sorry. I know this is a shock and I'm probably the last person you wanted to see. I certainly didn't expect to see you.'

Angrily, I wiped at the tears on my cheeks.

'I'm fine,' I said, my voice breaking. 'It's only that I thought . . . thought . . . I was never going to see you again. You know, you just disappeared in a puff of smoke . . .'

I paused to snap my fingers.

'I know,' he said.

'Just like that . . . you . . . you . . . left me that pathetic note! And still, to this day, I don't know what I did wrong or what went wrong, but it must have been really fucking bad to desert me like that, or else you're a total bastard and . . .'

My voice was shaking. I stopped speaking for a moment, overwhelmed at how angry I felt. Ethan looked taken aback, his face pale.

'What do you mean, you don't know what went wrong?' he asked quietly.

Ethan shuffled from foot to foot. I took a deep breath and forced myself to stop crying.

'I don't know, because you never told me!' I started, furious. 'And you never even bothered to—'

Ethan looked beyond me and chewed his lip.

'Hang on a minute,' he said, lifting his hand to stop me speaking. 'Do you mind if I use your toilet? I need to pee.'

I widened my eyes and a strange strangled laugh erupted from my mouth.

'What?' I said. 'You *need to pee*? I don't see you for three years, after you just walked out of my life without explaining why, and that's your opening gambit? You *need to pee*! Jesus, Ethan!'

'Sorry,' he said. 'I wouldn't have asked. It's just I'm really bursting. You know what a weak bladder I have.'

I gasped in exasperation.

'There,' I said, pointing to the bathroom door. 'In there. The light switch is on the left-hand side.'

Ethan smiled gratefully and, after a moment, walked past me and towards the bathroom, pausing outside the door to turn back and look at me, a confused expression on his face. I watched him there, in a stripe of sunlight beaming through the glass panel above the front door, and I felt a strange sensation of dread tinged with excitement, like when you're standing at the top of a helter-skelter, your legs trembling with fear, your heart racing in anticipation of the ride, your hair flying up in a gust of wind. I had to admit, though I hated him for what he'd done, I was also thrilled to see him again.

'Am I the first here, by the way?' he said, smiling. 'Or are all the other contestants sitting round the table listening in?'

I nodded that yes, I was alone, while he walked into the bathroom and shut the door. I listened, frozen to the spot, to Ethan use and flush the toilet and wash his hands and clear his throat. I picked up a notepad on the table by the phone and waved it in front of my face to cool myself down.

'Shit,' I said, suddenly remembering the food simmering in the kitchen. 'The sauce is going to be burnt.'

I darted into the kitchen and with shaking hands took the chocolate off the heat, turned down my stew, which was bubbling furiously, picked up a tea-towel and opened the oven to rescue the bread I was baking. I took it out with the fish-slice, threw it onto the side and slammed the oven shut with my shoe. I threw open the window over the sink and breathed in the fresh air, hoping to cool down my red cheeks.

'Look,' Ethan said, suddenly behind me. 'Are you sure you don't want me to go?'

I turned quickly to face him, amazed that he was there, in my kitchen. Pulling myself together, I decided I wasn't having Ethan come back for five minutes, then disappear again without telling me why he'd left in the first place. This was my chance to get answers. To defend myself against whatever it was I was supposed to have done wrong. I'd waited three years for this moment.

'So you come in and use the toilet,' I said, trying to sound light. 'Then you bugger off somewhere else. No way. You're going nowhere. I want answers.'

Ethan pulled his packet of Drum tobacco from his pocket and started to roll a cigarette, which he did in about ten seconds flat.

'Mind if I—?' he asked, putting the cigarette, unlit, between his lips. He was looking at me, no, staring at me, in a state of nervous amusement. I didn't know how to stand. I looked OK, at least – that was something. How did he expect me to look? In my mind's eye, I caught a glimpse of how I had been after he'd gone, lying in my bed all day, analysing everything I'd said and done in the previous weeks, replaying every conversation we'd had, searching for clues to why he'd left. 'Something smells good. What's cooking?'

'Fisherman's stew,' I said, waving my hand at the cooker. 'Meringue. Chocolate. Stuff.'

Ethan raised his eyebrows.

'Stuff? Yum. Eve, I have to say it, you look great,' he said seriously. Ignoring him I moved backwards, so I was leaning against the fridge, and wrapped my arms around my waist. I told myself to take control.

'I need to know something,' I said. 'Didn't I deserve some

31

kind of explanation? You just wrote me a note, flew to Rome and that was it. Gone. It was like you'd died, Ethan! I thought you . . .'

Loved me. I let the words hang in the air. They seemed to weigh heavily between us, like sopping wet clothes on a washing line.

With one arm across his chest and the other holding his chin, Ethan looked at me, then away, as if deciding something.

'I made the decision to go very quickly after . . .' he said, letting his sentence dissolve. 'I know I should have stuck around and talked to you about it, but under the circumstances I just wanted to get away. It was wrong, but I needed to run. I couldn't be who you wanted me to be.'

'What circumstances?' I said. 'I don't know what the circumstances were, for God's sake. Was it because I could be jealous at times?'

I cringed at the memory of me flying off the handle when Ethan repeatedly stayed out until three a.m., partying. I was routinely invited to these parties, but, just before we broke up, I started playing the martyr and refused to go. In truth I was jealous of how much time he devoted to everyone else in his life, how much time he spent socializing, and wanted to force him into a position where he would choose me over them. Ethan's life-and-soul personality was one of the major reasons I'd fallen for him in the first place, so why had I tried to change him?

'I wasn't trying to change you,' I said now. 'I mean, I shouldn't have been so . . . controlling. I know I was a bit over the top at that summer party, but I probably just had too much to drink. Jesus, why the hell am I apologizing? It was always like this. I was always your sidekick, always trying to please you—'

My hands flapped against my hips. He covered his face briefly and rubbed his cheeks. I'd spent months trying to work out what had made him go off so suddenly, and settled on it being my fault. I had tried to control someone who could never be controlled. I cleared my throat and stared at Ethan, desperate for him to say something. Anything.

'It wasn't you,' Ethan said hesitantly. 'It was me. I made a mistake.'

I stared at him and almost laughed.

'Oh Christ,' I snapped. 'Don't say things like that! I thought it was all down to me being—'

'No,' he interrupted, his eyes flicking up at me. 'I thought you would be better off without me. I wasn't in the right frame of mind for our relationship.'

'Right frame of mind?' I said, almost laughing. 'What frame of mind were you in, then?'

Ethan rubbed his brow. Questions about Ethan's life fizzed in my mind. Had he thought about me almost every day as I had him, even though many of those thoughts were in anger? What did he think of me now? And why did I care? What on earth did he mean by a 'mistake', and wasn't it a bit late to be regretful? My thoughts were interrupted by the sound of voices outside the front door. We moved into the hallway and, through the stained-glass door panels, I saw the outlines of four people. The doorbell sounded.

'Is this the other guests?' he said, sidestepping my question. 'Or your boyfriend? I take it these aren't yours?'

He picked up one of Joe's Vans in the hallway and held it dangling in the air. I stared at Ethan and shook my head.

'His name is Joe,' I said. 'Actually. Joe Cooke.'

'Joe Cooke,' Ethan said. 'The shy guy with the glasses who was your best pal at school?'

'He's not *shy*,' I said, tutting. 'And he does have other distinguishable features, besides glasses.'

'You were friends, though,' Ethan said, sounding hurt. 'I never realized there was anything more—'

I opened my mouth to answer, then the doorbell sounded again.

'Fuck,' I snapped. 'Christ, I can't cope with this. Look, let's just say we're old friends or something to avoid the questions. I can't cope with questions, I don't even know what I'm thinking . . .'

I moved towards the door, hoping I didn't have rivulets of mascara cascading down my cheeks. I rubbed my face with the back of my hand, probably making it a whole lot worse.

'Wait a minute,' he said, and I turned to face him. 'You know, as stupid as this sounds, since I came back to London a few weeks ago, I kept feeling I was going to bump into you again. It's fate; it must be. This was meant to happen. Truly, it's fated.' Ethan spoke with such enthusiasm, I almost believed him. 'Did you wonder the same about me?' he asked.

I shook my head energetically.

'Ethan,' I said, 'for all I knew, you could have been living in the Tibetan mountains as a goat herder. Please remember, I have not heard from you, *at all*, for three years. I had no idea you were even alive, let alone back in London.'

My lip quivered, but I refused to cry. The doorbell sounded again, followed by an impatient 'Hello!' through the letterbox. I looked from Ethan to the door, my heart hammering in my chest.

'So you didn't get my letter?' Ethan said almost inaudibly, then he stopped and looked at the floor. 'I shouldn't have sent—'

'What?' I said. 'What did you say? You sent me a letter? When?'

I imagined a letter, spilling over with Ethan's apologies and proclamations of undying love, sitting lost on the floor of a Post Office somewhere. Again, the doorbell sounded. I moved towards the door.

'Coming,' I shouted. Then to Ethan, 'What did you send?'

'Doesn't matter, you obviously didn't get it,' he said with one of his impossibly bright smiles that I'd archived in a locked chamber in my heart. 'It was a letter to apologize for the way I left so suddenly, but it's totally irrelevant now. I can apologize in person now, can't I? I can make it up to you. We do need to talk, but later. I know it's going to be weird, but let's just be as normal as we can with each other. Let's start afresh.'

I shook my head. There was another knock on the door.

'OK . . .' I said vaguely. 'I'm just so surprised to see you, I can hardly believe my eyes.'

'Me neither,' he said, curling his lips into a smile, before leaning over to me and kissing my cheek. I lifted my hand to my cheek, angry and pleased, blushing madly.

'The door?' Ethan said, breaking into a lopsided smile.

'I'm getting it,' I said. 'I'm COMING!'

Then, with my confused heart leaping and lurching in my chest, my cheek hot and tingling, I took a deep breath, twisted the Yale lock back with a click and forced myself to smile. I opened the door.

Chapter Three

'Drinks!' I said too loudly minutes later, bursting into the living room, shakily carrying a tinkling tray of glasses and a bottle of ice-cold Prosecco. I was almost hysterical with nerves and hadn't meant to shout. My guests visibly jumped. I hurried in and, with shaking hands, crashed the tray down on the wobbly card table, registering their wary stares. I picked up the first glass and began to pour, unable to keep my eyes off Ethan.

'Still got that tic, I see,' said Ethan with a wry smile. I ignored his comment, but before I turned away from him, I thought how relaxed and unfazed he looked. One hundred per cent sure of himself in social situations, probably more comfortable with other people than without; ever the actor, he clearly hadn't changed. I, on the other hand, was dying. I lifted a glass to my lips, tipped back my head and gulped down half of it. Ethan cleared his throat.

'Have a Prosecco,' I said, putting down my glass, rushing to thrust one into each of their hands, then nervously sweeping a bowl of olives under their noses too quickly for anyone to grab one. 'And olives, there are olives. Millions of olives. Oh, I should put on some music. It's like a library in here.'

When I'd opened the door, Joe's colleague, Dominique, the journalist from the *London Daily* – terrifyingly blonde, bold, six-inch heels and waist to match – had made the initial introductions while I ushered everyone in, giving a garbled explanation of how Ethan was an 'old friend' and had turned up on the doorstep for the Saturday Supper Club, just by chance.

'Complete coincidence,' I said to their bewildered faces, flushing boiling red. 'I haven't seen him for *three* years, you know? That's one thousand and ninety-five days, not that I've been counting, but it's a long time not to hear from—'

I stopped talking and bit my lip, smiling at my bemused guests apologetically. Ethan coughed ostentatiously from somewhere behind me. I took their things: a jacket, cardigan and bag, and quickly looped them onto the branches of the hatstand in the hallway that was swamped with coats I never wore.

'Come in, it's a bit of a squeeze in here, it's hardly a palace, but that's London for you. Apparently we have the smallest living spaces in the whole of Europe, which makes no sense considering we are the fattest people in the whole of Europe . . .' I rambled, rubbing my forehead. 'I suppose it's all down to the greedy property developers. Let me get you all a drink. Sit down, if you can find a seat.'

I pointed at my two-seater sofa and matching set of Art Deco armchairs I'd bought from a second-hand furniture shop in Camden. I picked off the cushions – a mismatched, sometimes threadbare collection – from the sofa and threw them into a heap into the corner of the front room.

'This is cosy,' Ethan said now, squeezing onto the sofa next to Dominique, while the other two contestants took the chairs, their knees virtually knocking together. Paul, the photographer from the *London Daily*, stood awkwardly next to the bookshelf and pulled out one of my favourite Julia Child cookbooks, flicking through the pages.

'It's like an experiment to see how many people you can fit into a shoe,' Ethan said, catching my eye and winking conspiratorially.

'I should check the food,' I said, moving into the kitchen, slamming shut the door and leaning my back against it, resting my hand on my thudding heart, the muffled sound of voices drifting through the door. All I could think about was Ethan. Ethan, Ethan, Ethan. He was here in my front room. I glanced at the picture of me and Joe pinned on the notice board alongside random postcards, takeaway menus and an electricity bill I needed to pay. I swore Joe waved. *Remember me?*

'Oh God, oh God,' I hissed, grabbing a square of dark chocolate from its silver foil and stuffing it into my mouth. 'This is a nightmare.'

Besides Ethan, Dominique, the journalist, and Paul, the photographer, there were Maggie and Andrew. Maggie, who I guessed to be in her late twenties, was short and curvy, with curly brown hair that coiled from her head in party streamers. She was very, very pretty with kohled, knowing dark eyes, high cheekbones and cherry lips. She wore a peacock-feather hairband, a sheriff-style gold brooch with 'Dolly' written on it, ridiculously high heels, a sequinned pencil skirt and a sheer black blouse with a big bow at the neck. Even though I had on my new dress, I felt drab in comparison and self-conscious of my overly bright hair. She was the type of girl who could wear a sack and still look good. I wasn't. Despite being small, she had a voice that would fill a hall and I could hear her now, talking animatedly about when she was a teenager and out for dinner in a Chinese restaurant.

'I thought the fingerbowl was a bowl of soup!' she exclaimed, to appreciative laughter from Ethan.

Then there was Andrew, probably in his mid-to-late thirties: fair wavy hair swept back as if he'd just stepped off the top deck of a ship, bright blue eyes surveying my flat, debonair in a pale linen suit, a bottle in each hand – and, by the smell of his breath, one in his belly – a serious, far-away expression on his face.

'Champagne' was his first word to me, said in a clipped English accent, as he handed me both bottles. 'And not just any old champagne, as this is Champagne Bourgeois-Diaz, from a small artisan winery where every bottle is made by hand. I like to have a glass every day. It's my favourite drink. I *need* a glass every day. Or a bottle, preferably, if circumstances allow, which they do, surprisingly often.'

Taking a deep breath, I dressed my salad, opened the kitchen door and returned to the living room, where Ethan, an unreadable expression on his face, was now inspecting a framed black-and-white photograph Joe had taken of me in my polka-dot swimsuit, sitting on a rock on the beach in Norfolk, holding a starfish in each palm. I wanted to snatch it from him and stuff it down the back of the sofa. Even though he'd seen me naked endless times, a picture of me in my swimsuit suddenly felt too personal. I cleared my throat loudly, just to get his attention. His eyes met mine and he smiled a small smile, loaded with nostalgia. I knew so much about Ethan – his favourite book, the school pictures in his mum's front room, the drunken night he peed in a suitcase in his sleep, his phobia of bats. I pulled my eyes away from his gaze.

'So!' I said. 'What should we do now?'

'Take our clothes off,' said Andrew before tipping his head back and draining his glass. 'It's so bloody hot tonight.'

'Andrew!' Maggie cackled. 'I can see tonight is going to be fun with you.'

Andrew smiled ruefully, a slight blush creeping up his neck. 'Failing that,' he said, 'how about eating? I'm starved and something smells good.'

'Why don't you tell us about your menu?' Dominique said. 'Then I suggest you run the evening as you wish while Paul takes pictures. He needs to photograph the food so will have to hang about, but I won't stay for long. If any of you take pictures, please don't put them on Facebook until we're on sale. I'll give you each a call tomorrow for your review of Eve's dinner party. Then, it'll be Maggie's turn next Saturday, followed by Andrew the Saturday after and, finally, Ethan.'

'Prepare to be amazed that night,' Ethan said, with a grin.

'So,' Dominique continued, flicking her eyes to Ethan, 'I'll let you know who the winner is, based on your overall scores, just before we go to print. This evening's menu, with each of your reviews, will be in the paper every Sunday. The first feature will be three weeks tomorrow, after Ethan's dinner.'

While Dominique talked, I felt fear mushroom in my belly. I wanted to be calm and cool about the evening ahead, but I just couldn't be. I was panicking madly. I didn't know how to act around Ethan. Despite the voice in my head instructing me otherwise, my eyes kept drifting to him. Half of me was desperate to interrogate him, to find out the truth about why he went; the other half didn't want to know, wished he would just go again as quickly as he had appeared. One second I felt furious with him, the next, I was delighted to see him again. And each time my eyes fell on him, I found him already looking at me, giving me an indecipherably intense stare, which made my heart feel ready to burst out from behind my ribs. I wondered if he was feeling this too. I gulped my second glass of Prosecco like water, already feeling light-headed. I made myself think about Joe, right now probably feigning interest in my dad's mandolin, politely tapping his toe along to 'Greensleeves'.

'Right,' I said, rubbing my hands together, realizing that everyone, not just Ethan, was looking at me, expecting something. Food. They were expecting food. I suddenly had the unhinged desire to howl with laughter. Be calm, I told myself, be calm.

'So,' I started and, feeling like I was six years old and standing on stage to sing 'Little Donkey' at a Christmas concert, I recounted my menu to their expectant faces.

'. . . and the pudding is what I'm most excited about,' I finished. 'Golden melt-in-your-mouth meringue, dipped in Madagascan dark chocolate, smothered with whipped Jersey cream, wild strawberries and caramelized pistachio nuts and drizzled with hot chocolate sauce.'

Maggie gasped. I tried not to look at Ethan, though I sensed his satisfied smile. I'd made this pudding for him on numerous occasions in our relationship. We'd sat together, elbow-deep in a shared bowl, beaming at one another.

'I must warn you,' said Maggie, raising a hand up in the air, 'I might have a foodgasm.'

'That sounds exciting,' Ethan said. 'Maybe we can share forks.'

Maggie threw her head back and laughed. I exhaled deeply, all at once reminded of one of Ethan's less desirable traits. He couldn't help himself. He was such a flirt. Even here, in my flat, when he should be the picture of contrition, he was behaving like Don Juan. I bit the inside of my cheek, a remembered feeling of jealousy nagging me. I glared at Ethan, picked up his wine glass and placed it on the tray, still a third full. The drunker he was, the more flirtatious he became. I would have to put a stop to that.

'I'm pudding mad,' said Andrew, patting his pillowy stomach. 'You can probably tell. Only this morning I bought a box of twelve chocolate fudge brownies from the Hummingbird Bakery for my girlfriend, who's pregnant and very, very hungry. By the time I got home, three were missing. Needless to say, she wasn't impressed.'

Ethan laughed loudly, in his actor way, and I remembered that was another of the things he did. He laughed all the time. That was one of the reasons people liked him. Wherever he was, he gave the impression he was having a good time or that everything was hilariously funny. I smiled wanly.

'Pregnant,' Maggie said. 'Congratulations! When's she due?'

'In about three weeks,' Andrew said, then, turning to face me, he held up his glass. 'Could I have another, please? What vintage is this? Last year?'

I hadn't a clue. I opened and closed my mouth, twizzling the bottle around madly, looking for a date to jump out at me.

'Ah,' I muttered. 'Yes, last year . . .' I poured more Prosecco into his glass. I wanted to ask more questions about the baby, but just as I opened my mouth, Andrew's mobile phone beeped. He pulled it out of his pocket, sighed enormously, switched it off crossly, then, changing his mind, turned it back on again, muttering under his breath.

'Are you excited?' Maggie asked, breaking a slightly awkward silence.

Something, fear perhaps, passed over Andrew's face. He nodded slowly and stretched his lips back and down over his teeth.

'Actually, I'm pretty bloody nervous,' he said. 'Alicia has found the pregnancy quite hard. We both have. It's all been rather a sharp learning curve and not at all as I imagined pregnancy to be. I imagined brewing camomile tea for Alicia while she padded around in those denim dungarees pregnant ladies wear—'

Maggie burst out laughing.

'Dungarees?' she said. 'It's not 1974, Andrew. No one wears dungarees any more.'

'I don't know about that – they're timeless, aren't they?' he said with a grin. Maggie laughed again. 'But Alicia is not feeling great. She's pretty miserable, actually.' Andrew sighed.

'Wow,' said Ethan. 'That's a big sigh.'

Andrew smiled ruefully. 'She, I mean we,' he continued, 'have wanted to be pregnant forever, but now that it's actually about to happen, I'm scared. Of course, I don't say that to her.'

His shoulders drooped and he looked defeated for a moment. He opened his mouth as if to say something more, but then shook his head.

'What am I boring you with this for?' he asked. 'We've only just met and I appear to be serving up my life story for dinner. I should really just shut the hell up. Besides, you're all much too young for babies. You're probably all still clubbing the nights away.'

Everyone was silent for a moment. Ethan cleared his throat.

'Now I'm imagining us all brandishing clubs on the dance floor,' Ethan said, breaking the tension.

'Chocolate bar or weapon?' I said.

'Weapon,' said Ethan, smiling at me. 'Anyway, Andrew, you were saying . . .'

Andrew held up his glass.

'Nothing. It's this,' he said. 'I blame grapes. Always make me want to talk. You'd think I would have learned my lesson, after sixteen years in the wine business; you'd think I'd know what grapes can do to a man.'

Andrew, quiet now, looked at his hands.

'What's that saying? In vino veritas. In wine there is truth,' said Ethan, frowning. 'Or something like that, but I don't think that's necessarily true. In fact it's not true. I never speak more bullshit than when I'm drunk.'

I watched Ethan carefully. It was unusual for him to divulge anything remotely self-critical, especially when he knew we'd had rows about that exact same subject, many times.

'I once went for a month without booze,' said Maggie. 'I had to start up again because I began questioning why I was friends with people who talked such bollocks most evenings.'

Ethan laughed. I smiled. Andrew blew air through his nostrils. The atmosphere felt lighter and I breathed a sigh of relief. A smattering of light rain had fallen on the window, the droplets glistening gold in the late evening sun.

'OK, let me get some water for everyone,' I said, realizing that we were already one bottle of booze down. 'I'll put on some different music. Then I'm going to need a few minutes in the kitchen to shave my truffles and spoon up my caviar. Just joking. Right, why don't you . . . why don't you . . . guess what each of you does for a living, or something?'

I shook my head. Where did that come from? I thought I hated the 'So, what do you *do*?' question everyone in London seemed so fond of. What did it matter what anyone did? But it was an ice-breaker, wasn't it? Everyone looked at me. I looked at them, suddenly feeling like my living room was more like an elevator than a room. Without the panic button.

'Back in a minute,' I said, sweeping through to the kitchen that was cluttered with plates, pans and ingredients. I forced myself to take a deep breath and think about what still needed to be done. I pulled a few leaves off the mint plant growing in the window sill and threw them into my dish. Dipping a spoon in and tasting, I burned my mouth and swore. The sauce was too peppery and had caught on the bottom of the pan and burnt. I'd incinerated my stew.

'Oh hell,' I hissed, with a massive sigh. 'I don't even know if I can serve this up. Fuck, fuck, fuck.'

I stood frozen, wondering what to do, while keeping one ear on the conversation in the living room through the open door. Maggie explained that she was a window dresser and Andrew expanded that he was a wine broker of artisan wines, finding wines that you wouldn't otherwise know about, mostly from small vineyards in France and Italy.

'And what do you do, Ethan?' Maggie said. 'You look like you're on the wrong side of the law.'

Ethan, of course, laughed. Hopelessly chopping fresh parsley to sprinkle onto my fisherman's stew – I didn't know what else to do at this stage other than flush it down the loo – I strained to hear his response.

' . . . did actually play a drug dealer in *The Bill*,' Ethan said. 'Yes, an actor, I'm resting at the moment, but I've done quite a lot of . . .'

Steam was billowing from the saucepans on the hob, so I put the extractor fan on, which drowned out Ethan's voice. I knew he'd be recounting his CV at great length. Ethan had trained as an actor at East 15, an acting school in Essex, and had quite decent success working in theatre and low-budget British films for the first few years since graduating. When we first met, through my sister Daisy, he'd been in *The Bill* – isn't every actor? – and *Silent Witness*, but after that he was more often working in his parents' deli than for a director. Besides the stage, his other passion in life was food, just like me. The deli customers absolutely adored him, especially the middle-aged ladies, whose tan tights were always in a twist over the colour of his eyes or the timbre of his voice. I smiled at the memory of him quoting lines from *Goodfellas* to his customers. When I went in to see him, I'd virtually had to set fire to my hair to get his attention. Everyone wanted a few slices of Ethan.

'And you, Eve?' said Andrew, when I stuck my head back into the living room to check I hadn't dreamt that Ethan was there. 'What do you do?'

I stood still and looked at Ethan, who was watching me enquiringly. When he left, I had done all the miserable things heartbroken people do, including having a full head of red, getting that red head stuck in the door and calling the Fire Brigade (I got so drunk on a night out that I lost my keys and stupidly tried to get back in through the cat flap) and eventually handing in my notice at my job as a fundraising officer for a wildlife charity. Suddenly I couldn't make myself care about white rhinoceroses any more, even if their numbers were dwindling towards extinction. I decided that it was time to do something I really wanted to do. My best friend Isabel, who managed a restaurant chain, and I had spent hours dreaming about opening up our own cafe; so, after I spent a year working with Isabel, learning what I could about the catering business, we decided, now or never, that we had to make that dream come true. With the help of her stockbroker husband, Robert, we had signed a year-long lease of a small property in East Dulwich, planning on opening a cafe.

'I'm trying to open my own cafe,' I said, waving my hand through the air. 'But I'm having a few problems, like a rapidly declining bank balance and an absent partner, which is why it would be great if I won this tonight. Guilt trip.'

Everything was coming together nicely until last month – just twelve weeks before we were supposed to open – when Isabel announced she was going to leave London to live in

Dubai with Robert, who had landed a fancy job over there, counting gold bullion or something. Though she had already paid the non-refundable money for the lease and had no intention of making me pay it back, it was left to me to find a new partner and/or a new investor to help with costs. I hadn't found anyone, and with decoration to complete, furniture and stock to buy and our pot of money running out, I was beginning to wonder if it was ever going to happen or whether I was going to have to admit defeat.

'Wow,' Ethan said, standing to make his point. 'Eve, that's brilliant.'

I was bolstered by Ethan's praise. I longed to tell him all about my plans, in minute detail. I knew he'd love some of my ideas.

'Ah well,' I said, blushing. 'I'm yet to actually open and you should see the state of the place.'

'Seriously,' he said. 'Don't do it down. You know how good I think it is to work for yourself. We've talked about it. If anyone can make it work, you can . . .'

I glanced at Ethan and we shared a smile.

'Thanks. So, do you all want to come through to eat?' I said. 'I'm not sure it's edible, though, which kind of scuppers my chance of winning, doesn't it? We might have to get a takeaway. I'm not joking.'

'Well, I'm ravenous,' Maggie said, standing up from her chair and pulling down her pencil skirt with a sensational wiggle. She followed me into the dining room, then called over her shoulder: 'Come and sit near me, Ethan, I want to find out all about you. What's that face for? Am I scaring you?'

'In a good way,' Ethan said, following on behind, the tip-tap of his brogues against the wooden floor reminding me of the sounds of our past.

'Personally, I think you're terrifying,' Andrew said, standing. 'But then, most women are, especially pregnant ones. At least the one I know is.'

In the dining room, Andrew checked his mobile and looked distracted for a moment, then pulled out a chair, flipped open a napkin embroidered with pink cottage roses and stuffed it into his collar. I leaned against the back of the chair opposite him. He noticed me watching him and smiled up at me.

'Am I over-sharing?' Andrew said.

I shook my head.

'I love over-sharing,' Maggie replied, glancing very obviously at Ethan. 'Let's all over-share.'

'You know bridegrooms in the nineteenth century ate great bundles of asparagus on their wedding nights to increase their virility,' said Maggie, when I served generous plates of steaming asparagus, their spears coated in a creamy rich hollandaise sauce and topped with a crunch of black pepper. 'They're blatantly phallic, aren't they? Although a little on the narrow side.'

Maggie winked at Ethan and ate her asparagus so provocatively I couldn't even look in her direction. I glanced up at Ethan, whose eyes were glued on Maggie's mouth. Andrew's too. For the entire appetizer, it was like she was the only person in the room. It was as if her pouty red lips were inflating as she spoke and ate.

'Right, then!' I said, standing to forward the CD on to the next song. 'Everyone had enough?'

I whisked away the plates while Ethan and Andrew were still eating. Then, as Maggie bantered with Ethan about aphrodisiac foods and Andrew talked about the vintage kitchen memorabilia he collected, I banged down clean white bowls on the table. Andrew eyed me cautiously.

'My glass is empty,' Ethan said, pouring himself and everyone else more wine. 'Better remedy that.'

We were all getting hideously drunk, I thought, as I served up the fisherman's stew, spooning steaming ladles of it into their bowls, not at all carefully. I sat down and sighed. My head pounded. This wasn't a good drunk. This was tears before bedtime drunk, I could feel it. The quicker this meal was over, the better.

'Fisherman's stew,' I said, slumping down in my chair, suddenly drained of all energy. 'Enjoy.'

A quiet descended. I drank more wine as Ethan dipped a chunk of bread into the sauce, tasted it, then froze, a look of alarm on his face.

'Do you want to spit that out, Ethan?' I said, only half joking. 'What's wrong with it?'

Ethan shook his head, just smiled and raised his eyebrows, then carried on munching.

'There seems to be something missing from this seafood dish,' said Maggie, poking the food. She looked up at me, a smile dancing on those red lips.

'What?' I said in a panic, tucking my hair behind my ear. 'I know I've burnt it and I've put so much parsley in there I can hardly see – oh shit.'

I dipped the ladle into the pot again and stirred, trawling through the liquid.

'I might be wrong,' said Maggie, 'but shouldn't there be seafood in this?'

'Fuck,' I said, sinking into my seat. 'I forgot the seafood. I don't believe it. What an idiot! I must be drunk. I'm so embarrassed. I was supposed to add it while we were having the starter. God, I just cannot understand why I . . .'

My eyes drifted to Ethan and I stopped talking.

'Let me get rid of this,' I said, standing. I started to collect their plates, Andrew's first, but he held on to his and gently refused to hand it over.

'Too hungry,' he said kindly. 'This looks like sensational tomato soup to me. Asparagus followed by soup and bread is an absolute feast. Thank you, Eve.'

'Absolutely,' said Ethan. 'What a gent you are, Andrew. Man after my own heart. Not many of us left, you know.'

Paul was taking photos, laughing behind his camera. I frowned at him.

'That's nothing,' he said. 'Compared to some of the disasters I've seen doing this job, no seafood is not a biggie.'

I shook my head and tutted.

'I'm so sorry,' I said, briefly covering my eyes with my hands. 'Must have been nerves, or . . .'

Or the fact that my ex-boyfriend turned up out of the blue and has been flirting with a woman I've never met before at my dinner table. I glared at Ethan.

'Well,' said Andrew, 'I think this is delicious.'

'It makes a nice change to just have vegetables,' said Maggie. 'I always order the biggest steak on the menu when I go out for dinner. I love meat. I love staring at the meat in the butcher's window. What do you think that says about me?'

51

'You like meat?' I said.

Maggie looked at me, nonplussed.

'You are really scary,' said Andrew. 'You know, one of the things Alicia has completely gone off is meat. The other thing, unfortunately, is me.'

He delivered his self-deprecating line with a snort of laughter, but there was sadness behind his joke. I watched his hand shake a little when he lifted his glass to his lips.

'It's probably pregnancy hormones,' I said. 'You should have seen my sister, Daisy, when she was pregnant. She was a nightmare! I couldn't say anything to her without a scene.'

'So I'm not alone, then?' said Andrew, with a quick raise of his eyebrows. 'Because right now, I feel it.'

I shook my head and smiled that no, he wasn't.

'Wow,' said Ethan. 'Daisy's a mum? That's cool. How is she?'

'Yes,' I said. 'She's fine, you know. She's Daisy. Benji's a lovely little boy, but I know the whole parenthood thing hasn't been easy, especially because he wouldn't stop crying when he was a baby. It was relentless.'

'Christ,' said Andrew, draining his glass. 'Think I'm going to need another drink now. Hardly anyone seems to have a good news story about having a baby. People with kids just say "Enjoy your last days of freedom" in a resigned voice. Especially women.'

'Well,' said Maggie, lacing her fingers together under her chin. 'Who can blame women for telling the truth? Your body becomes an incubator and your figure gets wrecked and you have to give everything up. No sleep. No spontaneity. I mean, where's the joy in that? I wouldn't be too happy about it either. Anyway, that's not going to happen to me. I want to enjoy my life! Sorry, Andrew, I didn't mean that you won't enjoy *your* life. I just mean *personally*, it's not for me. God, I always stick my great hoof in where it's not wanted.'

'Not at all,' said Andrew generously. He shrugged helplessly, but said nothing more.

Sensing his discomfort, I tried to change the subject, asking, inanely, if anyone had any party tricks, knowing that Ethan would immediately leap up, relishing the chance to be centre of attention. Before I'd finished speaking, Ethan pushed back his chair, put a cushion on the floor in the middle of the dining room and did a headstand, staying up until the veins on his temples were bulging and I pushed over his legs, worried.

'You'll have a stroke or your brain will burst,' I said. 'Be careful.'

'Oh, sshhhh,' Maggie said, annoyingly. 'That was impressive! What a man! I just adore spontaneity in a man. Too many people are so boring. I hate boring men.'

Ethan beamed. His chest visibly puffed up. I wondered if he wouldn't start pounding his pectorals at any minute.

'That's me out, then,' said Andrew drily. 'God, I feel so boring – and old – at the moment. Maybe I should be spontaneous while I still have the chance. You know, do something wild.'

Maggie looked up, a sudden flash of mischief in her eyes.

'How about a sponsored streak down Lordship Lane?' she said with a guffaw. 'I'm sure you could raise enough to cover the fine.'

'Steady on, old gal!' Ethan said in a mock posh accent.

'Talking about streaking, though, I must tell you this. I was driving through Camden and waiting at the lights when this guy came out of a shop wearing a shirt, but no trousers or pants. Shoes on. The lights turned green but a whole line of traffic just sat there staring. I mean, what the fuck? Only in Camden.'

Everyone laughed.

'Shirt and shoes but nothing else?' Maggie said. 'Hilarious! You're a hoot, Ethan.'

I sighed inwardly. Maggie was blatant. But then she was pretty drunk. We all were. The table was dotted with empty bottles – I couldn't believe how much alcohol we'd got through; I'm not sure any of us could even remember why we were together. Paul didn't seem that interested either, his camera now ailing on the shelf as he joined in with the wine drinking. I suddenly thought of Joe, looked through the French doors at the darkening sky and watched the fairy lights that he had put up twinkle and sparkle in the apple tree. I checked my watch. I wondered, with a hot flash of nerves, what time Joe would be home.

'I'm glad you said that about me being a man, though, Maggie,' Ethan said, enjoying centre stage. 'You know, when I was in Rome, my neighbour, a really old guy, kept calling out *"Buona mattina, signorina!"* every time I walked past his window, without a hint of irony. I mean, I did let my hair grow a bit longer, but do I look like a woman to you?'

I swigged the last of my wine, annoyed with Ethan for seeming so relaxed when I felt so completely muddled.

'I've never seen anyone less like a woman than you,' Maggie flirted, then, looking at me, 'Have you?'

'Never,' I said coolly. I moved to the stereo, turned my back to the room and changed the music just for something to do. When I turned back, Ethan was outside in the postage stamp, smoking a cigarette. I went outside to join him. The air was muggy and still, even warmer outside than in. I blew my fringe out of my eyes and took a deep breath. I had to say something while I had the chance.

'Look,' I said, my heart hammering, folding my arms. 'This is really, really weird. I've hardly spoken to you and you seem so not bothered. We need to talk.'

'I know,' he said, blowing smoke rings into the sky. 'I'm sorry, Eve, but there's so much to say. I don't know how much to say. You've moved on, you're with Joe, and we're—'

Ethan turned to face me, cigarette dangling from his fingers, a sad smile on his lips. For the first time that evening I felt he was going to say something meaningful and honest. I glanced inside, at the silhouette of Andrew and Maggie talking together, while Paul turned up the music, making the speakers screech. I frowned, worrying vaguely about the young family next door.

'I don't know what to say . . .' he said again. 'You go first.'

'How was Rome?' I said. 'Really?'

Ethan looked at me curiously.

'Truthfully?' he said. 'Incredible place, it had such a brilliant vibe and so much great food. But to begin with, I pretty much hated it. I didn't know what I was doing and I missed—'

He looked at me sheepishly and smiled.

'I missed you . . .' he said.

'Then why didn't you get in touch?' I said. 'I don't

understand. If you missed me, why stay away? Why not say sorry? Why go at all?'

Ethan shrugged, dropped the end of his cigarette, stubbed it out with his toe and looked at the floor.

'I did get in touch,' he said. 'I wrote to you.'

I shook my head and blew air out of my nose quickly, as if to express doubt.

'I did,' he said seriously. 'But it's not important. I should have phoned you too. Of course I should have done. But there never seemed like the right time. I picked up the phone about ten million times, but when I dialled, I chickened out. I thought you'd be seething, I thought you'd hate me for going off and . . . anyway, there . . . was so much I wanted to tell you about, like when I got mugged and beaten up just for my watch, I really thought that was it, that I was going to die and all I could think about was how much I wanted to talk to you—'

'Oh, Ethan,' I said, shuddering at the thought. I suddenly wanted to touch and hold him. 'That's awful.'

'Yeah, but I survived,' he said, with a smile. 'There were all these things I wished you could see, like this little place I went to most days for a coffee. Not just any coffee. The best-coffee-in-the-world coffee. And I would sit outside and wish you were with me getting drunk on caffeine—'

'But,' I said, tears filling my eyes, 'you left me, not the other way around, and you're making it sound like it was all my decision. I don't get—'

My voice cracked. I stopped talking. I didn't want to cry. It would weaken me even more and I wanted to stay strong. Ethan's face paled and he looked sad. I lifted the cool wine glass up to my cheeks, not looking at Ethan, but watching the couple in the house opposite, who were standing in front of the kitchen window. I looked away when they started kissing.

'I just want to know,' I said quietly, 'why you left.'

I looked him in the eye and waited for his response. When he left, I was paranoid that he'd run off with another woman – even though, in my heart, I doubted it. Plus, his flatmate and best friend insisted that wasn't the case. Failing that, I was sure he was going to say he'd got tired of my petty jealousy, that I had driven him away, even though I did think that unfair.

'I still don't know what it is I'm meant to have done. I know it's a while ago now, but I need to understand,' I said. 'Your pathetic note explained nothing, and really, it's insulting that I'm having to ask at all . . .'

Tears leapt into my eyes, but I blinked them away.

'Eve . . .' Ethan said, his voice low. 'I . . . that note was stupid and I had no right, I was completely out of order to treat you like that when I loved you so much—'

I held my breath, stunned by his words, when Maggie suddenly flew breathlessly out into the garden, grabbing my arm, holding out my mobile phone.

'Eve, your phone's been ringing! I answered and it was someone called Joe. He sounded very nice. I told him to come and join the party. But he's ringing again. Ethan, we're missing you in here,' Maggie said. 'Come in, let's dance!'

I took a sharp intake of breath and held the phone. Was Joe about to come home to this drunken scene, with Ethan here? I shuddered.

'Joe?' I said brightly, answering his call while lifting my free hand to cover my ear. Maggie pulled Ethan inside. He gave me an apologetic stare, leaving me outside under the night sky. I listened as Joe told me he'd be home in an hour, then said goodbye before I had time to say anything at all about Ethan. I tucked the phone into my pocket, folded my arms across my chest, looked up at a bright star visible even in the city, and took a deep breath of air to clear my head. Then Ethan stuck his head out of the door again and the quiet intimacy of a minute earlier was gone.

'You coming in?' he asked. 'Andrew says he needs his pudding, or he's going to give you a big fat zero out of ten. What a fucker, huh?'

Chapter Four

Back in the kitchen, the walls, especially the wall hung with my pots and pans, seemed to be pulsing. I turned on the tap and splashed my face with cold water, squeezing my eyes shut.

'Oh God,' I muttered, feeling amazed about what Ethan had said in the garden. All these years I'd imagined that he had gone off me. But, from what he was saying, he'd missed me as much as I'd missed him. I couldn't work out if that pleased me or made me feel gutted. Drying my skin on a towel, I started to panic. Too much of my brain was thinking about Ethan, too little about Joe, and Joe would be back within the hour. I shouldn't have been so drunk. I had known it was dangerous to drink, but equally, I couldn't possibly have got through the night sober. I made myself concentrate on the pudding while I dusted the meringue with icing sugar and poured chocolate sauce into two small silver jugs. My thoughts, though I tried to control them, went to Ethan and when I'd first met him.

'I like your laugh,' were his first words to me. That was

all it took. I'd known instantly that he was the yin to my yang, the salt to my pepper, the anemone to my clownfish. He was, without a glimmer of a doubt, The One. Up until that point, I'd been waiting for my real life to begin, meandering through the trailers, wondering if the motion picture was ever going to start. But, when we met at a winter picnic in Greenwich Park through my sister, Daisy, it was a Technicolor moment. Daisy and her friends had a Christmas picnic every December where a group of them got together, wrapped up in thermals, hats, gloves and scarves, to eat mince pies with fresh cream and drink mulled wine from flasks, play rounders and football and basically act like fools. Ethan was a friend of one of Daisy's friends and, when I turned up, Daisy introduced me to him and winked. Daisy, a housing manager, in charge of huge budgets and teams of people, never winked. I laughed nervously. Then she had to go to buy a present, promising she'd be back later. When she did return, after what felt like minutes, Ethan and I had spoken only to each other. We liked the same things: deep-fried scallops from Petticoat Lane market, cooking, Murakami's novels, the relentless hum of London life, Jack Rose's music, recipe books, daytrips to Brighton for hot chips on the beach. During our conversation, Ethan made me feel like I was the most interesting person in the world. Within that hour I had picked out my wedding dress, named our six children and engraved a romantic message on our double tombstone. When we played rounders, the winter sun a pink marble dropping low in a pale purple sky, our breath steamy clouds in the cold air, Ethan and I only had eyes for each other. I ran round that pitch like Black Beauty.

'Let's get away from here,' he said afterwards, leaning his hands on his thighs to catch his breath, his beanie hat pulled low over his ears. 'Just us.'

I didn't hesitate.

Going out with Ethan was not like any going out I'd done before. Ethan belonged to another solar system socially. He had more energy and charisma and joie de vivre than anyone I'd ever met. It seemed to me that Ethan's life was one long audition for the role of leading man. That night of the picnic, he took me to a bar where he knew *everyone*. He did his trademark headstand to a round of applause, bought drinks for a huge number of people, delivered anecdotes about his life at the deli, showered people with compliments and invited them to a party at his place after closing time. Later, during a lock-in, he asked the landlord to turn the music up then somehow (and I really don't know how he did it) convinced me to dance on the bar in my high heels while singing a rendition of 'Light My Fire'. I have a vague memory of everyone clapping and cheering while I did high kicks dangerously close to the edge of the bar. When Ethan told me to jump into his open arms, I did it without a second thought, laughing hysterically as I flew through the air, knocking him to the ground. Seen through the eyes of a stranger, I must have looked hideously drunk, unladylike and trashy. But I was incredibly happy, wildly excited. Whizzing. I felt happy to be alive. And when we slept together, I was amazed that sex could be that good. It was like diving into a bowl of melted chocolate and finding a liquid rainbow at the bottom. We couldn't get enough of each other. I couldn't stop smiling. Nothing else mattered but him.

Amy Bratley

'Arrgghh!' I said, grabbing a spoon from the kitchen drawer, trying to erase the memory. 'Get a grip, woman.'

I furiously dolloped the meringue, fresh cream, strawberries and nuggets of dark chocolate and a pool of melted chocolate into bowls, listening to Maggie and Ethan's increasingly loud laughter. Clearly something was hilarious. I hated myself for it, but I felt utterly jealous. I wanted Ethan to myself, just for a few more minutes. I wanted Maggie to leave. Out in the garden, I'd thought Ethan was going to say something important; now Maggie had distracted him.

I wiped the moisture from my eyes and carried the bowls into the dining room, plonking them down in front of Maggie, Ethan and Andrew, who was now slumping down in his seat, looking like he'd lost the will to live.

'The finale,' I said. 'Eve's pudding, but not.'

Ethan whistled and I felt myself blush.

'OK,' said Paul. 'Photo opportunity.'

Ethan jumped up from his chair and stood beside me, while I held out a bowl of pudding. He threw his arm around my shoulder while Maggie and Andrew leaned in behind us. Just as Paul took the first of a series of pictures, Ethan kissed the top of my head. My face blazed with boiling heat.

'Perfect,' said Paul.

I sat down and concentrated on dessert and, when I wasn't concentrating on dessert, the carpet. For several minutes, the room was silent apart from the noises of spoons scraping bowls and contented murmuring.

'Bliss,' Maggie said, setting down her spoon. 'Oh. My. God. That was fantastic.'

'I can do desserts,' I said. 'It's what I'm best at.'

'Oh, I can think of some other things,' Ethan said into my ear so only I could hear, grinning wolfishly at me.

I glared at him, astonished. Was he actually flirting with me now? Joe would be home soon. I took a deep breath, a smile fixed on my lips.

'Coffee, anyone?' I asked.

'I can read coffee cups,' said Maggie. 'It's a Turkish tradition, much like reading tea leaves. Let me read your cups. Then we'll go, shall we? We've probably outstayed our welcome.'

Maggie looked pointedly at Ethan. I left the room and quickly made coffee in the kitchen, after sweeping a pile more washing up into the sink and angrily squirting half a bottle of pink washing-up liquid all over it, while Ethan, Maggie and Andrew talked about Alicia. I walked back into the living room. My eyes bumped into Ethan's and he gave me a small, exasperated smile. The music had stopped and the atmosphere was suddenly too maudlin. I put the coffee on the table.

'Don't worry about Alicia,' Maggie said. 'I'm sure she'll come round. You know, you need to do some cosmic ordering.'

'That sounds a bit hippy dippy for me,' Andrew said, glancing up and smiling at me gratefully.

'You won't know if you don't try,' Maggie said, adjusting her hair so that it fell over her shoulders. 'What you have to do is say what you want to happen and visualize it actually happening, then throw that visualization out into space. Then it'll come good.'

'Positive thinking,' Paul said, 'in other words.'

'Yes,' Maggie said. 'So, let me look at your coffee cup and see.'

Maggie, fluttering her eyelashes and gesticulating a lot, made a big performance of reading the cups. She told Andrew his relationship was going to radically improve over the next few weeks, me that I was going to have a surprise in the near future, and I looked at Ethan, transmitting to him that I'd already had my surprise. Then she turned to Ethan, who wore a disbelieving expression.

'You're going to have a night you won't forget,' she said, gazing at him. 'You better believe it, baby.'

It was embarrassing. Even though Maggie was a pretty, cool girl, she was coming across as desperate, wasn't she? Every other thing she said was an innuendo. I wanted to tell her that men responded better to being ignored, didn't they?

'Really?' Ethan laughed darkly. 'That sounds interesting.'

Maybe not. I shook my head and blew out the candles on the table, stacking up the table mats into a pile. I really wanted everyone to go, so I could get my head straight. As it was, I felt drunk, suddenly depressed from too much alcohol and I missed Joe. Ethan was now acting like nothing had ever happened between us again, and I was tired of pretending to the others that I was feeling fine. I needed Joe to come back to remind me what my life was really like. Give me a blast of normality. I started to stack up the coffee cups, balancing them into a precarious porcelain tower. The music had ended, but I didn't bother to put on more. I felt Ethan's eyes on me.

'I think it might be time to leave,' Ethan said, putting his palms flat on the table and drawing backwards.

'Will you walk me to the station?' Maggie asked Ethan.

'Sure,' he said. 'What about you, Andrew? How will you get home, mate? You live in Holland Park?'

Andrew stood shakily, his hair sticking up from where he'd been leaning on his hand.

'I need the bathroom,' Andrew said.

He staggered through the door of the dining room, bumping into the walls with his shoulders as he went. Ethan, who was standing behind his chair, holding on to the back of Maggie's chair, looked at me searchingly. I sighed.

'Are you OK, Andrew?' I asked, calling after him.

Andrew didn't answer, just crashed through the bathroom door and slammed it shut. He seemed incredibly drunk. I sighed and picked up my phone from the table to check the time. There was a text I hadn't seen from Joe:

I'll be ten minutes.

I panicked. I couldn't have Ethan and Joe meeting each other on the doorstep. That would be awful. Joe would be horrified. He knew exactly how I'd felt about Ethan, he'd witnessed my devastation when he left, and if he thought we'd spent the evening together, no matter if it was an amazing coincidence, he wouldn't be happy.

'OK, everyone,' I said, turning out the lamp in the living room so we were suddenly plunged into darkness. 'It's been lovely.'

'Right,' said Maggie. 'I'm getting that you want us to leave.'

'Sorry,' I said. 'I'm pretty exhausted.'

I ushered a bemused Paul, Maggie and Ethan into the hallway and opened the front door before Maggie had even picked up her bag. It was all I could do to stop myself from shoving Ethan out into the night. The prospect of Joe turning up any second was making me clammy with nerves.

'Bye, then,' I said, holding on to the front door, smiling stiffly, waiting for them to leave. 'I'd better get started on the washing up. See you next time!'

'I'll give you a call,' Ethan said, kissing my cheek. 'Be good to catch up properly.'

Be good to catch up properly. Ethan was talking to me like I was his old football coach, not his former girlfriend. I tutted.

'Fine,' I said curtly, not making eye contact with him, trying to ignore the kiss on my cheek. 'Bye, Maggie.'

Maggie, who'd grabbed her bag herself, swaying slightly, her eyes narrowed with alcohol, her peacock feather a little skewed, waved a little wave at me.

'This has been fun,' she said. 'I'm going to give you a brilliant review when I speak to Dominique. Then you'll come to my house and we're going to do the whole thing again, only this time, with a little more spice.'

Did she ever give up? God, she was one of those women who couldn't relax unless every bloke in the room was drooling over her. I smiled at Maggie wanly and avoided Ethan's gaze as I closed the door behind them, my stomach twisting uncomfortably. They were probably going to sleep together now, probably in the rose bush at the bottom of the front garden. They'd probably fall in love and have ten babies and live in the countryside in a farmhouse, with chickens called Dandelion and Blossom running around in the garden, pecking grain with their sharp little beaks and—

'Stop,' I told myself, putting my hands on my hips. I sighed. Now I had to get rid of Andrew, who was taking ages in the bathroom.

'Andrew?' I said, knocking on the door and, when there was no reply, leaning in to listen for movement. 'Are you OK in there?'

I heard a loud snore erupt from the room.

'Oh God,' I said, putting my hand on the doorknob and opening the door very slightly, dreading a scene of half-nakedness. I peered in gingerly. Andrew, fully clothed, his feet sticking out and resting on my Body Shop natural sponge, was fast asleep in the bath, snoring like a walrus. I moved into the bathroom and tried to wake him up by shaking his shoulder.

'Andrew,' I said. 'Andrew, wake up!'

But, even when I turned and accidentally sent the blue glass bottle of Neal's Yard bubble bath crashing onto the floor, the glass splintering everywhere, he didn't flinch.

'Shit!' I said, watching the expensive liquid seep all over the floor tiles. I leaned down to pick it up and sliced my finger open with a shard of glass.

'Fuck!' I said, sucking my finger, tasting blood. I stood up, Andrew still asleep in the bath, and turned on the cold tap at the sink, running my finger underneath the stream of water. I looked up at my reflection and noticed I had a smudge of dark chocolate from the meringue on my forehead.

'God,' I said. 'Why didn't someone tell me?'

I rubbed at it with my free hand and suddenly, everything I'd had to hold inside all evening overwhelmed me. I burst into tears, yanking toilet tissue from the roll and noisily blowing my nose.

'Wish I hadn't said I'd do this stupid Supper Club thing,' I choked. 'I never would have had to see Ethan again, I never would have even known he was in London, but now . . . now . . .'

Now . . . he was waltzing down the road with Maggie, doing God knows what, saying God knows what. Unless he already had a girlfriend? Perhaps he did. A Latino goddess who silenced crowds with her beauty. Why did I care? I felt an awful sinking sensation in my gut, which meant only one thing. Hard as I tried not to, as much as I loved Joe, I couldn't deny it. I still felt something for Ethan. Averting my eyes from my reflection in the mirror, the tap still on, Andrew snoring, I sat on the toilet lid, my head in my hands, and wept.

'Eve?' Joe said, moments later, appearing suddenly at the bathroom door. 'What's happening? Are you OK? Why is there blood in the sink? The tap's on.'

He walked in and turned the tap off, then kneeled beside me, his hands on my thighs. Then, when Andrew suddenly snored, Joe turned and saw him, his face stricken, his eyes widening into saucers. He put his hand on his heart.

'And who the fuck is *that*?' he gasped. 'Jesus, that scared the shit out of me!'

'That's Andrew,' I choked, grabbing more toilet roll and wiping away my tears, then blowing my nose. 'He got completely wrecked and passed out in the bath when everyone else was leaving. I tried to wake him up, then dropped the bubble bath and cut my finger and . . .'

I swallowed to stop the tears from falling. I had no right to expect sympathy from Joe, when really I was crying about the confusion I felt over Ethan coming back.

'It's been a very weird night,' I said, exhaling loudly and collecting myself together. 'Thank God you're back. How are we going to get rid of Andrew? Should we pour cold water over him?'

Joe shook his head and threw his arm over my shoulder, as we stood staring at Andrew. Then he reached for a towel, folded it up and put it under Andrew's head as a pillow. I squeezed Joe's arm.

'Just let him sleep it off,' he said. 'He'll end up in the gutter if you send him outside now. He's going nowhere.'

I suddenly felt enormously tired and strangely detached. I stretched my arms up and yawned.

'I'm going to lie down,' I said. 'I'll sort everything out in the morning. The kitchen's like a bomb site. I need my bed. Come with me, will you?'

Minutes later, while Joe made himself a coffee, I lay on the bed in my baggy M&S grey marl pyjamas, the ones I normally wear when I've got the flu and feel subhuman. Mascara smudged around my eyes, I leaned up against a mountain of pillows, eating the remainder of my chocolate meringue pudding straight from the serving plate, even though I wasn't remotely hungry. A half-empty bottle of red wine stood on the bedside table next to the Veno's cough mixture, my bottle of L'Occitane hand cream, a stack of books that I had started but never got round to finishing and my iPhone, which I'm never more than two inches away from. I reached for the bottle and took a quick swig, then laughed at how unappealing I must look.

'So,' Joe said, frowning from the doorway. 'Are you OK? Has something happened tonight? Why were you crying?'

As Joe spoke, my brain whizzed and my heart beat guiltily in my chest. I wanted to tell him about Ethan; I knew I should. But something stopped the words from coming out of my mouth. If I blurted it all out now, I'd probably cry and he'd read too much into it. I needed time to sober up, to gather my thoughts and to work out how to phrase it properly. Yes, I'd tell him tomorrow when I was sober and together. I watched Joe pick up Banjo and stroke his head.

'Come on, then,' he said, taking his glasses off with one hand. 'Why aren't you saying anything?'

Joe dropped Banjo down onto the carpet then leaned up against the doorframe as if he wasn't sure he was allowed to enter. I felt mildly disappointed. I wanted Joe to rush in and sweep me up in his arms like he normally would, to squeeze and kiss me and blot out every last thought of Ethan. But perhaps he'd picked up on my peculiar mood. Perhaps he knew something was amiss, because now the air between us seemed awkward, like his shutters were going down. I sat up straighter and shook the crumbs off my chest. I had to get things back to normal between us.

'There's a bloke in the bath,' I said. 'I think that says it all. The fisherman's stew was a disaster because I forgot to put the seafood in and the drinking got out of hand.'

'What about the other two?' Joe said. 'What were they like?'
I frowned.

'They were OK,' I shrugged. 'The girl, Maggie, she's a window dresser and lives in Bethnal Green. She's garrulous and a real flirt. The other bloke was . . . he was . . . boring . . . didn't say much, he's a bit . . . um, how can I put it? A bit blank. A bit of a nothing person.'

I couldn't believe the words were coming out of my

mouth. Nothing could be further from the truth. Ethan was an everything person. Scrap that. Once upon a time he had been an 'everything to me' person. Now he wasn't. Now he was nothing to me, so I was right, I was telling the truth after all. I cleared my throat and smiled at Joe again.

'A nothing person?' Joe said, bursting into laughter. 'You're hilarious! I hope no one ever describes me in such glowing terms. But, the food wasn't good? I bet it was. The pudding looks delicious. Hey, give me a bit of that.'

Joe stepped over the molehills of clothes I'd discarded on the floor and came to sit near me on the bed.

'Have this?' I said. 'I wanted you to have some.'

I held out a spoon laden with chocolate pudding for Joe to try. He ate the pudding, murmuring with pleasure. I reached out and held on to his hand, warm and dry, then pulled him in for a kiss, all the while trying to get back to the feeling of our togetherness that I'd had before Ethan came bursting through the front door earlier that night. Joe put his arms around me and squeezed, but there was something between us, some indefinable, tiny, brittle thing, like a stone in your shoe. I could feel the tension in Joe's shoulders. I cursed Ethan under my breath, held Joe even tighter and buried my head in his chest. We stayed like that for a while, until I felt us both relax. Seeing Ethan hadn't taken anything away from my feelings for Joe, and why should it have done?

'Oh, Joe,' I said. 'I'm tired and I've drunk too much. How was your night? How was my dad?'

Joe lay down next to me on the mattress and leaned on the pillow with his hands linked behind his head. I snuggled in closer to him and felt his warmth.

'Yeah, he was good,' he said. 'He was talking about your mum a lot.'

I pulled a face. Mum had been dead for seventeen years, but he *still* talked about her like she died yesterday.

'He was talking about a cake she used to cook for him when they'd had a row,' he said. 'He said just the taste of it made him fall in love with her all over again, and that I should try it out on you.'

'What?' I said, pulling his arm towards me. 'You can't cook!'

He sat up, moved off the bed and pulled off his jumper, without looking at me. Banjo pulled at the carpet with his claws.

'That's what I told him,' he said stiffly. 'That I can't cook. For God's sake, Eve.'

I immediately felt guilty, knowing I'd responded in the wrong way.

'Oh, Joe,' I said. 'I didn't mean that I'm not in love with you. You know I didn't mean that.'

'You sure?' he said.

'Course I'm sure,' I replied. 'You know I love you.'

Joe visibly relaxed. 'Good,' he said. ''Cos I want you to be sure. Really sure.'

I nodded energetically, my eyebrows raised, and watched him take off his T-shirt, jeans and pants, and laughed as he did his normal joke of standing near the bed and pretending to dive into the bed as if it were a swimming pool. When he was next to me, he rolled onto his stomach, pushed a pillow under his chest and looked at me questioningly.

'I'm sure,' I said. 'You don't need to ask.'

'Good,' he said, rolling onto his back. 'Anyway, your dad was saying he had something important to tell you, but he wouldn't say what it was. Highly suspicious if you ask me.'

'That's weird,' I said, frowning. 'I hope he's not ill. Do you think it's something bad? I keep worrying that he's ill. Daisy says he's always at the GP getting results for tests he won't tell her about.'

'I don't think he's ill,' Joe said. 'He looks in better shape than me. Anyway, come here. Those Primark pyjamas are turning me on.'

'Marks and Spencer, actually,' I quipped. 'Get it right.'

Joe kissed me then moved his hand down onto my breast, but I tensed. He moved his hand away, the tiniest of movements deterring him.

'What?' he said. 'What's wrong?'

Joe began to bite his thumbnail.

'Nothing,' I said in a small voice. 'I'm just exhausted and, you know, it feels a bit weird with Andrew in the bath out there—'

'Fine,' he said, trying not to sound hurt. I sighed. He snapped out the lights and turned away from me. I lay in the dark with my eyes wide open, feeling guilty, listening to Joe's breathing. Occasionally a car would drive past the house and headlights would sweep through the slits in the shutters and light up the room. Joe's breathing became heavier and I knew he would soon be asleep, but my head was still whirring. Before I could stop myself, I was speaking.

'Joe,' I said. 'Do you believe in fate?'

Joe's eyes sprung open. He turned his face to me.

'What are you talking about?' he said. 'I thought you were asleep. But no, not really. Why?'

'Nothing,' I said. 'I have been thinking tonight about whether our lives are predestined, or whether it's all completely random and a matter of chance.'

Joe was quiet for a few moments, then he held my hand under the covers.

'It's comforting to believe in fate,' Joe said. 'Because then you don't have to take responsibility for the decisions you make, do you? But really, I think it's all down to chance.'

'I read this story,' I said. 'About a girl who threw a message in a bottle into the sea when she was seven. That summer she got a reply from a little boy who had picked it up. They never met and she didn't write to him again. But, thirty years later, they met by chance, or fate, and got married. It wasn't until they were married that they found the bottle and postcard and made the connection. Isn't that amazing? Surely that's fate?'

'Maybe,' he said, yawning. 'Maybe there are exceptions to the rule. Good story, anyway. Is it true?'

'Yes, it's true,' I said.

Joe curled his body around mine and I closed my eyes and started to fall asleep. My skin melted into Joe's and our breathing fell in step, and I thought about all the other couples lying in bed together in London, one of them unable to sleep because they were thinking about something or someone the other knew nothing about. I felt suddenly aware of how fragile relationships are and how I should do everything I could to protect my relationship with Joe because, lying there next to him, I realized that this was all that mattered, his body against mine, his beating heart close to mine. We had to look after each other. Joe had saved me when I was down. My whole life, since the age of ten, he'd been there for me. I wanted to be there for him. Just as I was falling asleep, images of the bizarre evening fading in my mind, I heard my phone bleep. Unwrapping myself from Joe's arms, I pulled on my silk dressing gown and padded across the room to check my text. It was a number I didn't recognize.

> You should never have let me in. I can't stop thinking about you. I'm sorry for everything. Is this destiny? E x

Is this destiny? I thought of the girl and boy with the message in the bottle. My cheeks flushed red and I bit my lip. I looked over at Joe, still cradling the phone, its light glowing in the dark. There was no way I could reply to that. I would just have to ignore it. Ethan was messing with my head. He had no right. I was not going to answer. I would not give him the satisfaction.

'Put the phone down and go to bed,' I instructed myself. But, before I knew it, my inner devil clicked on REPLY and I started tapping out an answer.

'You make your own luck,' I tapped, pressed send, then stuffed my fist into my mouth. What was I doing? I longed to retract it.

'Who was that?' Joe asked, making me jump in the dark.

'Maggie,' I lied, amazingly quickly. 'Asking about Andrew. I said he was still in the bath.'

I climbed back into bed and snuggled into Joe's back. I stared at the ceiling, my stomach churning. Why hadn't I been honest with Joe the moment he walked in the door? What was I doing lying to him? I couldn't understand my own actions. I lay awake, worrying, as more cars passed by, their headlights flashing into the room, like torchlight seeking out a runaway. I hid my face in the pillows, to block out light and sound. However hard I tried, sleep would not come.

Chapter Five

Glancing at the handwritten poster I'd stuck in the window, claiming that we would be 'opening soon', I shook my head and unlocked the rickety door of the cafe premises, the early morning sun bouncing off the whitewashed windows. Isabel followed behind, holding a carrier bag of paintbrushes and white spirit. Despite it being early Sunday morning, Lordship Lane, the through road in East Dulwich, half a mwe from where I lived, was already buzzing. Right outside the shop a group of teenage girls left over from the night before were sitting on the kerb drinking water from Evian bottles. A father was grumbling at his toddling son to toddle faster, while having a crafty ogle at the girls. I rolled my eyes.

'Did you see that bloke?' I said, turning quickly to face Isabel while pushing open the door. 'He's old enough to be their granddad.'

'Gross,' Isabel said, her dark eyes shining with amusement. She shut the door behind her. 'Oh my God, look at this.'

We stood together and stared at the scene of devastation

before us. Though the builders had finished their work, they hadn't cleaned up after themselves, because we'd run out of money to pay for any more of their time. The shop floor was covered in planks of wood, buckets, empty paper cups, broken-up old furnishings and electrical cables sticking menacingly out of walls. In a stack near the counter was boxed new shop equipment that we'd ordered but hadn't yet unpacked, paint tins, and several rolls of wallpaper were untouched. On the walls were splodges of different coloured paints, a horrible bubble-gum pink and a pea green that I had tried out and quickly rejected.

'Oh fuck,' Isabel said, pulling her long platinum-blonde hair into a bun on top of her head and removing her gold hoop earrings. 'What are we going to do? There's so much to do. I'm taking these hoops out so I don't rip my ears off in here.'

I'd been there almost every day of the last month, to receive equipment, deal with builders, navigate my way around the tiny kitchen and try to make decisions about crockery, storage and stock, so seeing the state of the place was no surprise. Even so, Isabel's reaction made me panic. We were desperately behind. Scrap that. *I* was desperately behind.

'What am *I* going to do, you mean?' I said, picking up a discarded crust of a bacon buttie a builder had left. I threw it into the bin. 'You'll be thousands of miles away in two weeks sunning yourself on the beach. Joe's going to help me this afternoon, so that'll be a start, if he can tear himself away from his laptop. God knows what he's doing on there this morning, but whenever I go near, he closes all the windows down. Very suspicious behaviour.'

Isabel pulled a face and tucked her earrings into her pocket.

'Do you think he's looking at naked ladies?' she said, half a smile on her lips. 'I remember when I found Robert looking at this website of women with the most enormous bums, I was gobsmacked. Honestly, they were the size of VW Beetle car bonnets. If I'd known he had a preference, I would have eaten more cake. I went ballistic, of course. Poor Robert.'

'Ha!' I said. 'Joe's probably planning something romantic. You know what Joe's like. You should have seen the flowers he bought me yesterday. I think he's having an affair with the florist. She's very pretty. I shouldn't joke. Maybe he is.'

I looked at the reflection of me and Isabel in a broken mirror resting up against an upturned chair we needed to throw out, as she shook her head.

'He'd probably relax a bit if you committed to him properly,' Isabel said seriously. 'You know that's what he wants. He probably feels like he's still trying to win you. You know how determined Joe is. He never gives up. How did he get his first job again?'

I smiled at the memory of Joe's campaign to get noticed by a newspaper editor.

'He wrote to the editor every day for a month,' I said. 'He doesn't give up. I do love that about him. Well, I love everything about him.'

'I've never heard you say you love him so much,' said Isabel, grinning. 'What's got into you? You're either feeling very loved up, or guilty. Which is it?'

I frowned and shrugged, and stepped over a box, looking at the floor, an image of Ethan bursting into my mind.

'Anyway, back to the cafe,' I said. 'Once all this rubbish is out the way, it'll look less like a fly tip and more like a cafe floor. I hope.'

I felt vaguely annoyed with Isabel for making me feel bad, though she was completely unaware, and stood with my hands on my hips, looking around the shop, previously a greasy spoon cafe that was stuck in 1982. It had been in serious need of total refurbishment and modernization. I sighed. Though having my own cafe had been a dream for years, I was terrified I wouldn't be able to do it alone now that Isabel was leaving. More worryingly, I had to find £15,000 from somewhere, to cover the cost of a complete new kitchen, furnishings and some unpaid bills. No mean feat, considering I had used up almost every last penny we had and pretty much exhausted business loan opportunities from the bank. I could ask Robert to increase his investment, but I really didn't want to. I had all this to worry about and so much to do, but there was only one thing on my mind today: Ethan Miller. *Is it destiny?* I exhaled heavily.

'Anyway, I wish I wasn't going away,' Isabel said, peeling a banana and taking a bite. 'I never planned all this to happen with Dubai. I don't even want to go, but I can't let Robert turn down that job opportunity and we can't exactly have a long-distance relationship, can we? Well, I wouldn't mind, but he might complain. You know Robert, he's so unreasonable, loaning us all that money. What a git.'

I laughed and hugged Isabel, who looked gorgeous in a blue sundress and green cardigan, her skin peaches-and-cream perfect, her platinum hair velvet-soft.

'I know,' I said. 'I don't blame you, Isabel, at all. I know it was a tough decision for you both, and without Robert's investment, this would not be happening. Just a shame I under-estimated our costs. Anyway, you'll come back a lot, won't you?'

'Yeah,' she said, smiling sadly. She threw away her banana skin and picked up a bundle of decorating sheets, ripping off the cellophane. I watched her, opening and closing my mouth, trying to think of a way to tell her about Ethan turning up. On the car journey here, I'd promised myself I wouldn't make a big deal out of it, but it was literally all I could think about and I was bursting to tell her. I knew Isabel would be horrified if I seemed even a tiny bit glad to have seen him again. She'd witnessed the full horror of our break-up and pretty much hated Ethan, but I was desperate to tell her. Isabel walked over to the counter, where we planned to display our fabulous homemade cakes and biscuits that I was going to bake every morning, though that fun part felt like a long way off. She knelt down to pick a cloth up from the floor.

'You know I'll do everything I can before I go,' she said. 'We can get a lot done in two weeks, especially if I—'

'Ethan's back,' I blurted out, interrupting her.

'Ouch!' Isabel said, shooting upright so quickly, she bashed her head on the edge of the counter. Her eyes went wide. She stared at me.

'No!' she said.

'It's true,' I said. 'Ethan's back.'

'*Ethan's* back?' she said. 'My God! When? Did he call you?' She looked at me intently and her cheeks coloured a little.

'He turned up last night,' I said. 'You know I did that Saturday Supper Club thing for the paper, that Joe asked me to do because someone dropped out? I can hardly believe it

81

myself, but Ethan turned up at my door. He was one of the contestants. It was a complete coincidence. Don't you think that's really weird? I mean, how often do you hear of that happening?'

Isabel was very quiet. She raised her hand to her lips and covered her mouth, glancing down at the floor.

'I can't . . .' Isabel said. 'I can't believe that. Are you *sure* he didn't know? Why didn't you tell me?'

'He didn't know,' I said, throwing my hands up in the air. 'He couldn't have known. It's a total fluke. Isabel, it was so strange to see him again, like he'd never even been away. It's really confused me. I wasn't going to admit this because I know you despise him, but I've been awake all night thinking about him. I feel awful towards Joe, too, like I've cheated on him or something, and literally all I've done is spoken to Ethan—'

'I don't despise him,' Isabel said quietly. 'I just think he's bad news. But why do you feel awful towards Joe? You don't still *like* Ethan, do you? Please say no.'

She put her hands over her face and dragged her fingers down towards her chin despairingly.

'Of course not,' I said, then, giving Isabel a sideways glance, I nodded slightly. 'Maybe,' I muttered. 'A bit.'

Isabel walked towards the window and stood with her back to me, watching the traffic rumble past.

'He broke your heart,' she said. 'You can't let him affect your life now. You have Joe, you've got this place. Joe's worth a million Ethans. He'd never just abandon you, without explanation. You know that, don't you?'

She turned back to face me, looking, all of a sudden, very tired.

'I know,' I said. 'But I can't help it. I'm already thinking about what it's going to be like to see him again at the next Supper Club.'

'When is it?' she asked.

'Next Saturday,' I replied. 'It's every Saturday.'

'You can't go,' she said.

'I know,' I said.

'You're going, aren't you?' she said.

'Yes,' I replied.

'Have you told Joe?' she asked. 'What did he say?'

I squirmed and began picking up the pile of unopened envelopes from the floor near the door, not really looking at them at all.

'I didn't know how to put it,' I said, dumping the envelopes in the bin. 'But I'm going to have to tell him soon. He knows Ethan. It's not like I can keep it a secret. It's going to be in the bloody paper in three weeks' time, isn't it? Although, if I don't go, that'll probably ruin the whole thing and I won't get any coverage for this place, which is why I feel I should go, really . . .'

Isabel gave me a knowing look and shook her head.

'Seriously, this is dangerous ground,' she said. 'If you go near Ethan, you're going to risk everything. Eve, can't you remember how he dumped you? That note he left? Please, concentrate and remember. He's an idiot. He hurt you badly.'

On the back of an electricity bill, hurriedly scrawled in red biro. That's how Ethan chose to deliver his goodbye note to me after nearly two years together. Not a second thought to the bittersweet romance of fountain-pen ink, quality writing paper or sealing wax. Not a care for the intimacy of the spoken word. He left it on top of the cooker in the kitchen of the flat I shared with Isabel in Clapham North at the time. I was absolutely crushed.

'I know,' I said, remembering Ethan's note:

I'm sorry Eve, but I'm leaving London for Rome. It's difficult to explain why, but I can't see a future for us any more. Please don't contact me. I'm sorry if this is a shock. I've loved you, Ethan x ps. I guarantee, this is hard on me too.

I read that letter more times than Harry Potter books have been sold. I knew it off by heart even though Isabel told me I should shred it. The 'ps.' made me spit feathers. I quoted it, verbatim, to anyone who asked where Ethan was or why we were no longer together. I called him, got his voicemail and read the note back to him, demanding to know if it was an elaborate joke. I never heard back. I called again, but still no answer. I sent him a furious email, but I got no answer. And Rome? I knew he had a cousin out there, but he'd never said he wanted to go there. It had made me wonder if I knew Ethan at all. When I had no reply from him, I stopped trying to contact him completely, finding it preferable to pretend he was dead.

'And it made you feel like shit, remember?' Isabel said. 'You fell to pieces, remember? Virtually had a nervous breakdown. Christ, Eve, I don't want to see you like that ever again and I don't want you to go stirring anything up with him because . . .'

She let her words trail off into nothing. She fixed me with a stare, genuine concern on her face. I nodded in acknowledgement. When he'd left, it was like my world ended. Like we'd been driving along in a really fast car with the music turned up high and I'd been whooping at the top of my lungs, when, without warning, he'd opened the passenger door and shoved me out onto a deserted road. I just stared at his letter endlessly, in case I'd missed a sentence, or a clue. But no. That was it. Four lines of piss. And then came the self-doubt. Wave upon wave of poisonous self-doubt drowning out all rational thought. I started to believe it must have been my fault. I scoured my brain for the times when I'd given Ethan a hard time and decided that my petty jealousy had driven him away, that I was to blame. If someone as vibrant as Ethan thought it wasn't working out and had left in such a hurry, then it was probably because I wasn't good enough for him.

'You've got to keep your head straight,' she said. 'Especially because . . . has Joe said anything about his plans?'

She watched my face, and when I looked confused, she shook her head as if dismissing the thought.

'About what?' I asked.

'Oh, nothing,' she said.

'No, come on,' I said. 'What do you mean?'

'It's just that I think you need to be careful,' she said. 'From what Joe's been saying, I think, you know, he's going to *do* something really special and for you to be playing around with . . .'

'He's going to *do* what?' I said, watching her face carefully. 'And I'm not playing around, for God's sake. I've seen Ethan once, in a room full of other people, completely by chance. Anyway, what's Joe going to do?'

When she didn't answer, I frowned.

'Isabel!' I said. Then it dawned on me. Of course. He'd

been asking about moving in together, dropping bundles of property details on the kitchen table, talking about having our own football team of children, buying bigger and more elaborate bouquets of flowers. He was going to propose, for real this time, wasn't he?

'Is he going to propose?' I said, biting at my thumbnail, looking at Isabel. 'I mean, seriously propose?'

She didn't look at me, just shook her head pityingly.

'Oh, I don't know about that,' she said unconvincingly. 'But he's got plans. He came to see me about something and I'm just warning you, it'll break his heart if he finds out you've been disloyal when he's trying—'

'I'm not being disloyal!' I said.

'I know,' she said. 'I just care about you.'

Isabel wouldn't budge when I pressed her for more details and eventually I gave up, assuming that Joe was actually going to propose. It made sense. He'd been working up to it for months with the jokes and banter. I waited to feel excited, but instead, I panicked. Did I want to get married? I picked up the carrier bag of paintbrushes, took one out and flexed the bristles against my palm.

'I should get on and start with the kitchen,' I said, pointing to the grubby old kitchen, which had seen more deep-fat frying than should be legal.

'Don't see Ethan again,' Isabel said softly. 'Don't go next weekend. It's a big mistake.'

I sighed.

'Sorry, I'll shut up,' she said.

'Yes, shut up, I get the message,' I said to Isabel, stomping into the cafe's kitchen, when my phone rang. I whipped it out of my pocket, hoping it was my dad. He often rang in the morning, just to see how I was getting along, and I needed to hear his reassuring voice to ground me.

'Hi, Dad,' I said, smiling down the phone. 'How are you doing?'

'Hello, love, yes, I'm good. Are you still coming over later?' he said. 'How's your morning going? Are you at the cafe?'

The sound of his voice released something in me. I leaned against the counter and looked out of the small kitchen window, out to the courtyard, currently a dumping site for broken furniture. I sighed.

'Fine,' I said, my voice cracking. 'But, well, actually, I'm not fine.'

'I can hear something's wrong,' he said. 'I can hear it in your voice. What is it, love? Come on, out with it. Tell your old dad.'

My spirits lifted a little. If there was one person in the world whom I couldn't keep my feelings from, it was my dad. It was like he could read my mind, or see into my heart.

'Actually, Dad,' I said, 'you're right, something's happened.'

I pushed open the window with my free hand. Isabel stuck her head around the door, held up an example of the menu we'd had printed up and delivered. She gave me a big smile and dropped one on the counter, then opened the back door to the courtyard.

'Oh God, what?' my dad said. 'Is everyone still alive?'

'Yes,' I said quietly. 'But Ethan's back.'

There was a silence.

'*Ethan?*' he said.

Dad murmured while I told him everything about Ethan turning up to the Saturday Supper Club out of the blue.

'Isabel says I shouldn't see him again,' I said. 'I'm not going to the next Supper Club. It's wrong, isn't it? I haven't even told Joe yet. I don't know how I'm supposed to be feeling, but everything I used to feel, it's all come flooding back. I feel sick to the stomach.'

Dad made a humming sound. I heard the sound of the fridge opening and closing in the background.

'Well,' he said, pouring what I knew would be his usual morning fruit smoothie into a glass. 'Personally, I don't think you should see him again, even if it means giving up on the Supper Club. He broke your heart, love, really mashed it up good and proper.'

'I know,' I said, resting my hand on the back of my neck. 'But I need to know why he went. I want to know whether I still do really have feelings for him. I literally can't stop thinking about him. I know it's reckless, but what was it Mum used to say? Jump off—'

'Jump off cliffs and find your wings on the way down,' he interrupted. 'But your mother was crazy. Mad as a hatter. Saying that, I would have done anything for her, including jumping off a cliff, as you know. God love her. But listen, why don't you come over and we can talk about it? Or you can talk and I'll listen. I'm good at listening. Then we can make sense of this together. How about it?'

My eyes filled with tears.

'OK,' I said, in a tiny, high voice. 'Thank you, Dad.'

'No need to thank me,' he said gently. 'I love you very

much. Your mum did too. Both you girls are everything to me.'

I heard him smile down the phone.

'I love you too,' I said, smiling back.

Chapter Six

The night before my mother died, when I was sitting on a squeaky vinyl chair, keeping a vigil beside her hospital bed, in a perfectly eloquent outburst she told me how to make crème anglaise. I listened to her words like she was giving me the Secret of Life. And, in a way, she was.

'This is the time to say goodbye,' my father had whispered to Daisy and me earlier that evening, eyes red, his entire body trembling, in the hospital corridor next to a vending machine. 'Because when your mum falls asleep this time, she's not going to wake up.'

Daisy, who had just turned fourteen, was furious with everyone: me, Dad, the doctors, Mum. She punched the vending machine, stalked away from the ward we were in, yelling that she hated us all and that she didn't want to be in this stupid 'arsehole' hospital a minute longer. Dad, exhausted from nights without sleep, stumbled after her, telling me to go and sit with Mum, which I did, holding her hand and my breath as I watched her, more quiet and still than I'd ever seen her, waiting for something, anything, to happen, when she opened her eyes and ran through the ingredients (heavy cream, whole milk, vanilla essence, sugar and large egg yolks) and cooking method of crème anglaise.

'It's heavenly,' she muttered, closing her eyes. 'Don't forget.'

'I'll never forget,' I said, my nose pressed to her ear, her hair wet with my tears, to make sure she heard. 'Thank you.'

She didn't say anything else and, despite what my dad had said, I didn't say goodbye because I thought 'thank you' was better, and I didn't want her to think I was planning to go anywhere. I wanted to be with her until she'd had enough. I stayed by her bed, holding her hand gently, willing myself not to cry. I didn't want to make her feel guilty for dying. I didn't want her to feel she had to comfort me, when it was she who needed comfort the most. I knew she feared whatever was to come, whatever death was. I had heard her say to my dad, 'I am scared, Frankie. I am so scared to be without you all . . .'

I didn't want her to be scared. I didn't want her to feel alone. Two hours later, after I had fallen asleep with my head on the side of her bed, Dad told me that she had gone, that her organs had finally stopped working. I crawled under the bed and sat there and I screamed and screamed, until a nurse closed our door shut and Dad pulled me out by my legs and held me so tightly, there was no air left to scream.

'It's the three of us now,' my dad said afterwards, on the car ride home, when each of us sat in our coats, raw, pale-faced and hollow-eyed.

'It's the three of us against the world,' he said.

When neither Daisy nor I replied, Dad pushed a Beatles album into the CD player and turned up the volume. 'This was your mum's favourite,' he choked.

Was. I looked out of the window and watched dawn breaking over London, a streaky pink sky contrasting against the grey buildings, the joggers and dustbin trucks and buses and coffee shops opening up, as if nothing had happened at all, as if it was just another ordinary day, while listening to my dad sing 'Here Comes the Sun' at the top of his lungs inside that small Renault with an empty crisp packet underfoot and mum's CND stickers on the boot, her Chanel No. 19 perfume lingering on the passenger seatbelt. He sang out his heart; sang for her, my mum, his wife, all of our most precious love. *Was.*

When we were home again, we steered clear of the kitchen table, formerly the heart of our family life. Without Mum, there was no vase of freshly cut flowers there on the table, no delicious cooking smells wafting out the oven, no jar of home-baked biscuits or enormous Victoria sponge cake, oozing with fresh cream and strawberry jam, waiting at the table centre, no smiling face encouraging us to sit together, to eat and talk and hug and laugh. We avoided meal times, snacking on crackers and cheese instead, or nibbling on meals that various aunts left out in big glass dishes with a list of cooking instructions scribbled on a pad. Dad couldn't cook at all and didn't even attempt it. I tried to speak to him to coax him out of his misery, but for a few weeks he lost his voice completely and didn't even reply. I tried to talk to Daisy about how we could cheer him up – cheer us all up – but she slammed her bedroom door in my face, leaving me alone with my grief. So, at a loss to know what to do, with advice from those various aunts, I decided to learn how to cook. I made it my mission to learn the recipes my mum had filled our life with. I pulled out Mum's recipe books and studied the words and ingredients and made simple meals for Daisy and my dad. I called them to the kitchen table and pushed plates of food, sometimes inedible, sometimes good, under their noses. Dad would put his hand over mine and thank me, his eyes glistening. Daisy would invariably push the plate away and say she wasn't hungry.

'Our hearts might be empty, but at least we have full stomachs now,' Dad would say. 'Thank you, Eve.'

At those moments, I felt unimaginably proud. I knew that my mother would be pleased with me, from wherever she was watching. I knew that this was her key to life: cooking and sharing good food with her family. I would make it my mission to do as she did. I would fill her shoes the best I could, fill the house with the same warmth she had. At those moments, I could see a future beyond grief, a future where we could all, once again, be sat around the kitchen table, together. And after a while Dad began to make an effort to live again, keeping his grief hidden deep, and my mum's memory alive, by constantly talking about her; so, even though she wasn't there for us to see and touch, it was almost like she was in the next room, just waiting.

And that's how we learned to exist. I cooked and Dad ate. We talked about Mum. We talked about what she would do and what she would say. I tried to tempt Daisy out of her room with cakes cooked to Mum's recipes. But Daisy withdrew completely. She refused to eat the food I prepared. On the rare occasion she did eat, she relished telling me it was nowhere as good as Mum's. When once I put on Mum's favourite apron, Daisy ripped it off me and cut it into pieces with the kitchen scissors.

'You can't be her, you stupid little girl!' she screamed in my face. 'I hate you!'

I was holding a recipe book at the time and I hit her as hard as I could until she stopped screaming at me.

'What do you think your mother would say?' Dad had shouted at us, his whole body shaking. 'How would she feel if she could see you both? Think of that, think of her. Respect her memory!'

But, for a while, whatever I did seemed to anger Daisy. I felt I'd lost her too. It wasn't until she left home, four years later, aged eighteen, that our relationship really improved again. Daisy, three years older than me, enjoyed flaunting her newfound independence and I was a receptive audience. Though she was quite scathing about certain aspects of my life, stuck at home cooking for Dad, I tried hard to make her like me. Sometimes she did, sometimes she didn't. Sometimes I felt like giving up, but I persevered. For Mum, for our family, that *was*.

'What do you think Mum would think I should do?' I asked Dad now.

We were standing in my dad's large bathroom. I'd gone straight over to his house in Clapham after Isabel and I had finished at the cafe. As always, when I opened the front door of the three-storey townhouse where I had grown up, I was greeted with the smell of freshly ground coffee – Dad drank pints of the stuff – mixed with paint – Dad was always redecorating some part of the house. The sound of Radio 2 blasted out hits of yesteryear. As I shouted out hello and threw my cardigan onto the coat rack by the front door, I brushed my fingers over Mum's red wool coat that Dad still refused to take off the coat hooks, even after all these years. If I nestled my nose into the fabric, I swear I could still smell her perfume.

'Your mother would have said what she always said when faced with matters of the heart,' Dad said as I stood, arms crossed, leaning against the bathroom door while he, dressed in shorts and T-shirt, set about shaving off every last strand of his head of white hair for charity. 'Jump in and think later. But I don't recommend it at all, especially not in this case.'

Dad was perched on the edge of the claw-foot bathtub, staring into the mirror on the open door of the medicine cabinet above the sink, his hair falling in puffy clumps like dandelion seeds onto the monochrome tiled floor. A tall, well-built man with tanned skin from all the time he spent out in the garden, Dad's hair had been jet black before Mum died, but without her he said the colour drained straight out of him and into the earth. His eyes, dark blue pools, had never lost their luminescence. They always seemed full of sadness to me, but often when I asked him if he was sad, he'd laugh and tell me how happy he felt.

'Hmm,' I said. 'But this isn't a question of getting back with Ethan. God, no. It's whether I should pull out of the Supper Club and how I should tell Joe that Ethan has turned up. I know I should pull out, but there's a part of me that does want to see Ethan again next week. That's awful, isn't it? I'm a horrible person.'

Dad shook his head. 'Only natural,' he said, pushing shut the medicine-cabinet door and turning on the tap to wash stray strands of hair down the sink. 'You were in love with the guy, but you have to be careful with Joe's feelings here. Your loyalty is to him. I think you should tell Joe the truth and not see Ethan again. I don't want you getting hurt again. I'm an old man. I can't stand any more heartbreak. Besides, surely you have enough on your plate with the cafe. Talking of which, my pal Andy has a load of old school chairs, those wooden ones with a slot at the back for books, going for cheap. Interested?'

'Um, yes,' I said, abstractedly. 'Thank you.'

Dad paused for a moment and put his head to one side. He held out his arms and smiled.

'Come here, love,' he said. 'You look like you need a hug. I'm worried about you.'

I smiled, walked towards him and gave him a hug, leaning into his chest. He smelt of the garden, of soil and flowers and sunshine.

'Thanks, Dad,' I said, pulling away and trying to cheer myself up. I hated worrying him. He'd had enough stress in his life without my petty troubles. 'So, who are you trying to impress with your new no-hair image?'

I picked up a clump of white curls from the floor by his feet. It was so white it was almost blue. I looked up at Dad and knew he was thinking the same thing. We were tuned into each other, Dad and I, often saying the same word at exactly the same time. We both laughed, then he rubbed his hand over his smooth scalp and grinned.

'I'm hoping that if I do enough charity events, God will be pleased,' he said drily. 'I'm hoping He'll let me in through those pearly white gates if I prove my worth.'

From behind me I heard the sound of Daisy's footsteps at the top of the stairs outside the bathroom door, followed by her two-year-old son, Benji.

'Dad!' Daisy said, appearing from behind me, handing me a cup of coffee. 'Don't talk like that. You're only fifty-nine. Careful, Benji!'

I turned to Daisy and smiled as she held her own drink up in the air, while Benji snaked through her legs, so it didn't spill. Dressed in denim shorts and a striped blue-and-white T-shirt, Daisy looked fantastic. She always did. Even when she'd had a sleepless night with Benjamin, she was bright-eyed and bushy-tailed, as if she had just inhaled a pint of wheatgrass juice. Her hair was shiny enough to reflect the clouds, her skin had mother-of-pearl luminescence and her figure was straight and lithe and had the fantastic tone of someone who spent hours in the gym. Mine, on the other hand, had too many curves to keep track of.

'This is for you,' she said, handing me an envelope. 'I don't know if it's important. Maybe you should change your address, since you haven't lived here for nine years. Just an idea.'

She handed me a letter from the Chocolate Society that had been sent to my dad's address. I'd been a member since I was thirteen years old and still hadn't got round to changing that address, much to Daisy's despair. Daisy was much more organized than me, much more of a grown-up. She'd never let a bill go unpaid, or ignore a toothache, or go to the laundrette because the washing machine was broken and getting it fixed seemed like an insurmountable task. When we were little kids she used to walk round my bedroom pointing at toys I needed to pick up and put away, writing me lists of 'chores' for which she would reward me with a gold star. I went along with it, but I couldn't care less for the gold stars. I much preferred the squares of chocolate I stole from the tin of treats she kept under her bed. She caught me once and slapped me so hard the outline of her hand stayed on my arm for hours.

'Thanks,' I said, taking the letter and coffee, sipping and flinching when I burned my tongue, then putting it down and kneeling to give Benji a kiss. 'How are you, little man?'

Benji, his button eyes wide, a shy smile on his lips, put his arms around my neck to hug me. He smelt of chocolate biscuits, which I knew Dad would have quietly given to him when Daisy wasn't looking. I rubbed his back and squeezed him back, before standing to kiss Daisy on the cheek.

'And how are you?' I asked her. 'You look great. How do you manage to look like a supermodel when you're working full-time and looking after a toddler the rest of the time?'

She rolled her eyes but a smile played on her lips.

'No sleep and soaring stress levels help me stay in shape,' she quipped. 'How about you? Getting on OK with the cafe? And how was the Supper Club thing you did? I've always fancied having a go at that. Everyone at work talks about it.'

I glanced at Dad, who gave me a sympathetic smile then busied himself with extracting the clumps of hair from Benji's hands.

'I'll tell you in a bit,' I said, screwing my face up. 'It was, er . . . interesting.'

'Right,' she said distractedly, frowning, concentrating on Benji, who was now trying to eat the hair. 'Hey, Benji, stop that!'

'Nooooo!' Benji screamed as Daisy pulled him up from the floor, where he was now having a mini-tantrum.

'Please, Benji,' Daisy pleaded in exasperation. 'Just give me a break. Please!'

Benji's screams got louder. He kicked Daisy in the ankle and her eyes filled with tears.

'No, Benji!' Dad said, throwing me a worried look. 'Don't kick your mummy.'

We all looked at Benji while he pounded his fists on the bathroom floor, his tantrum in full throttle. Daisy folded her arms across her chest and closed her eyes.

'Can I help at all?' I asked, but Daisy just opened her eyes and shrugged despondently. She had always been like this. Her mood would change at a flick of a switch. She'd go from dynamic to helpless in seconds.

'He's a nightmare at the moment,' she said moodily. 'I just don't know how to handle him.'

Poor Daisy. She was now a single mum to Benji and it couldn't be easy looking after a toddler on your own. In fact, sometimes it looked like a total nightmare. I made a silent vow to help her out more.

'Maybe I can take him for a day next weekend,' I said. 'Give you a break. Or Dad could have him and we can both go to the Sanctuary for the day?'

'Oh,' Daisy said, a smile bursting onto her lips, 'a spa day would be great. But I'll treat you. I know you're broke.'

I leaned in to Daisy and gave her a hug.

'Thanks,' I said and we smiled at one another.

'Benji?' Dad said, clapping his hands together to distract him. 'Benji? How do I look?'

We all looked towards Dad, who stood grinning down at Benji in front of the window, which was open enough to see the early evening sun pour over the roofs of the houses opposite.

'Like an egg!' Benji said, suddenly recovered, jumping up at Dad until he picked him up and swung him round onto his back.

'Gosh, you're heavy. I'm too old for this,' he muttered, puffing out. 'I'm like one of those old greyhounds, ready for the knacker's yard. Come on, let's go downstairs. Enough crying.'

'Don't say that, Dad,' I said quietly.

'What?' he said.

'About the knacker's yard,' I said. 'You're young.'

Daisy and I exchanged concerned looks. Recently we were always having secret talks about Dad: whether he was OK, whether he was hiding anything, why he sometimes refused to be clear about where he was going and what he was doing.

'Oh,' he said, waving his hand at me dismissively, 'I'm almost an OAP.'

I chewed at my thumb. We'd been wondering if Dad had a health problem and wasn't telling us. I was aware it was paranoid thinking, but when you've lost one parent, you can't help thinking the other one is hanging on by a thread, too. He had been behaving strangely – he'd taken part in copious fundraising events for various local charities, above and beyond any normal person's expectations. It had come from nowhere, this philanthropic streak. He'd bathed in a bathtub of baked beans, washed cars, shaken a money box in the driving rain, dressed up as a giant teddy bear and had now collected sponsorship money to shave all his hair off. Whenever Daisy or I approached the subject, he changed the topic or laughingly told us to mind our own business.

'OK!' Daisy said, recovered now that the tantrum was over. 'Look, let's go downstairs and make you a sandwich, Benji.'

'Granddad gave me some chocolate biscuits, so I'm not hungry,' Benji said. Dad pulled a guilty face and mouthed 'Sorry' at Daisy, who sighed, then waved her hand dismissively in the air as she started down the stairs.

'Toast, then,' she said. 'You need something that isn't chocolate. Come on, Benji. Listen to what I'm saying, please.'

Daisy and Benji headed down the stairs while Dad pulled shut the bathroom door behind us, clutching a dustpan filled with his hair. I thought about how I could best ask him what was going on with him, but before I could, he started talking about Joe.

'Anyway, I wanted to say earlier, that Joe's a good man,' he said in a concerned voice. It suddenly dawned on me what Joe had been doing when they went to the folk club night. 'I hope you're nice to him, Evie.'

'Dad,' I said. 'Did Joe . . . has Joe . . . has he said anything about marriage? Is that what you were talking about the other night at the folk club? As well as wooden recorders?'

Dad smiled, tapped his nose and shook his head.

'I can't tell you what we were talking about,' he said. 'It's up to Joe to talk to you. I'm just saying that he's a good man and I know that Ethan coming back must make things difficult, but he's not worth the—'

He stopped, looked up at me, moved towards me and placed his hand on my shoulder. He looked strange with no hair; so much younger.

'Did he explain why he went?' he asked.

I shook my head and pulled a face.

'Not yet,' I said. 'I'm going to find out. That's what I want. To find out.'

He put his arm tight around my shoulders and directed us towards the kitchen door, where Daisy was slicing a tomato and hissing threats of the 'naughty step' at Benji.

'Be careful what you wish for,' Dad said. 'That was something else your mother used to say. Be careful what you wish for.'

Chapter Seven

After I told her Ethan had returned – it seemed I couldn't stop telling everyone – Daisy turned towards me, a buttered knife in her hand, a distracted frown on her face. The air smelt of burnt toast and the dishwasher was going through the noisiest part of its cycle. She pressed the END button on the dishwasher and clicked off the radio so the kitchen lapsed into a dramatic silence.

'Did you just say Ethan's back? You're joking?' she said. 'I thought he was in Italy?'

'Mummy,' Benji said, clamping his arms around her knees. I sat down at the kitchen table, a big old oak thing with years of scars and scratches, and moved a copy of the *Independent* onto a pile of newspapers, stacked up behind a vase of sunflowers cut fresh from the garden.

'Ouch!' Daisy said, wriggling away from Benji and sucking her thumb. 'Benji, stop pulling me! Look what you made me do! You made me cut my finger!'

She dropped the knife on the stone tile floor and Dad knelt down to pick it up.

'Mummy,' Benji said before bursting into tears. I caught hold of his arm and guided him towards me. I lifted him up onto my lap and hugged him. He buried his head into the crook of my arm and sniffed away tears.

'Are you OK?' Dad said, walking towards Daisy with a piece of kitchen towel. 'Here, have this. Come here, Benj, come and sit on my knee instead. We can look at this book and give your mum and aunty Eve a chance to talk.'

Benji slid off my lap and climbed up onto Dad's, throwing his arm around Dad's neck. Daisy sat down on the kitchen chair next to me with a sigh, peering at the cut on her finger, blotting the blood with the kitchen towel.

'Sorry, Eve,' she said. 'You were saying about Ethan. What a nightmare. Have you told Joe? Did he say why he left? Have this toast, Benji. How do you feel about it?'

She slid the plate of toast onto the table near Benji, who totally ignored it.

'No, I don't know why he went,' I said. 'We couldn't talk, but I'm going to find out. Joe doesn't know. I stupidly haven't told him.'

Daisy looked at me and frowned, beginning to shred the paper towel.

'You'd better tell him,' she said. 'Otherwise he'll find out and be really hurt.'

She adopted the tone of voice she used to tell Benji off and I felt suddenly irritated.

'I know!' I said, exasperated. 'I will, of course. The last thing I want to do is hurt Joe. I'm not a complete bitch.'

'I wasn't saying that,' said Daisy softly. 'I was just telling you Joe would be upset if you—'

'I know he would!' I said. 'What do you think I am!'

'OK!' she said. 'I was only saying. Don't freak out!'

The air was suddenly cool between us and I marvelled at how quickly our conversations could go from being completely calm to incendiary in a flash of words. It had always been the same. I knew in a few minutes Daisy would act as though nothing had been said, while I silently fumed inside my head.

'OK, girls, come on,' Dad said, pausing from reading *Where's Spot?* to Benji, who had turned the toast plate upside down. We all fell silent and I hated that Ethan, only just back in my life, was already causing problems. I sighed and looked out of the kitchen window at the garden in full bloom, which looked gorgeous. I thought of the days Joe and I had spent out in the garden when we were kids, before his family had moved away. Now, the neighbours were media whizzkids with buckets of money, who had painted the entire house sage green and who had loud-voiced barbecues in the garden.

'The garden looks fantastic,' I told Dad. 'Especially the chrysanthemums.'

He rose from his chair and, leaning on the windowsill, looked out at the red flowers. He beamed.

'I like to call them summer margaritas,' he said. 'Your mum's favourite, of course.'

Daisy scraped her chair back and stood, moving over to the kitchen counter again. She put the dishwasher back on and it immediately began to whoosh and whirl. Then she walked over to me and put her hand on my shoulder.

'Eve, I just can't believe Ethan is back,' she said. 'Shall we have a glass of wine in the garden and chat? Do you want one, Dad?'

I looked at her face. She smiled. She was over our cross words already. I nodded.

'Yes,' I said. 'I'd really like that. It's a bit of a shocker.'

'I've got to go out in a minute,' Dad said, standing and holding Benji's hand tightly. 'But pop upstairs with me first, Eve. I've got something I want to show you quickly before I go.'

'Now then,' Dad said, dragging a box-file off the shelf and opening it up to reveal a stack of documents. I peered over his shoulder while he flicked through letters from Mum to him. 'I think it will be in here somewhere.'

We were in the back bedroom of the house, a light, calming room, which was always referred to as 'Mum's room' because it contained all of her things that Dad just couldn't part with. The wallpaper, cream with small pink roses, had not been changed since she died, though the rest of the house had been redecorated several times. Nor had the furniture, a mahogany wardrobe and matching chest of drawers, ever been moved from their position. It was as if moving anything in there would break a spell. I picked up a framed photograph of my parents when they were very young and had just met. My dad was bent double, his face turned to the camera, my mum leapfrogging over him, her brown wavy hair flying up in the air, a gigantic smile on her face. I put it down and picked up another, of her cradling me as a baby. Her gaze was one of pure devotion. I sighed. I might not have her now, but at least I'd had her then.

'Ah,' Dad said, pulling out a piece of paper that had yellowed with age, with splodges of grease on the edges. 'This is it. Your mother's "Lovebird Cake". She used to bake this if we'd had a row and she wanted to make up. She used to cook this a lot, which wasn't great for my waistline. I found it the other day when I was sorting through all these things. I feared I'd lost it. But I thought you'd like to have it. Maybe you could even try it out for the cafe?'

I rested the baby photograph on the chest of drawers and moved to where Dad was standing. I peered at the recipe over his shoulder.

'That's lovely,' I said. 'Joe mentioned you'd found a recipe Mum cooked.'

Dad handed me the piece of paper, and just as I started to read, I heard the clatter of a plate falling onto the kitchen floor downstairs, Daisy's raised voice and Benji shouting back at her.

'God,' I said, catching Dad's eye. 'Is Daisy OK? She seems very on edge with Benji.'

He shook his head in exasperation and sighed.

'It's boys,' he said. 'They're hard to look after. Girls are easier, I think. She has a tough time with him, and you know how hard she works.'

He looked thoughtful for a moment, then pointed at the recipe.

'Anyway, concentrate!' he smiled. 'This is an important piece of Thompson history!'

I smiled back at him. Written in blue ink, in my mum's handwriting, were the words 'Audrey's Lovebird Cake', encased by a biro heart. There was a list of ingredients, method and cooking instructions.

'I bet this is delicious,' I said, with one ear still on Daisy and Benji arguing downstairs. 'I wish Daisy had more help from Iain. He's hopeless, isn't he?'

Anger bolted across Dad's face, then he looked sad and sighed. Iain, a Canadian artist with whom Daisy had had a short relationship, was Benji's father, but since the day Daisy had told him she was pregnant, he'd refused to be involved and was now living back in Canada. He shook his head and cast his eyes to the floor.

'What a bastard, deserting her like that,' I said, voicing both our thoughts. Dad didn't reply, just checked his watch. He thrust the box-file into my hands. I knew he hated talking about Iain, because he probably wanted to break his legs. Although he was the gentlest soul I knew, if anyone crossed his daughters, he flew into the most awful rage. I cast my mind back to an incident when Daisy went to university and her landlord was harassing her whenever he collected the rent. After Daisy's tearful phone call, Dad had driven to Brighton at ninety miles per hour, furiously gripping the steering wheel, punched the landlord in the face and made him give Daisy all her money back, before moving her out into alternative accommodation.

'Oops,' he said now. 'Sorry, Eve, but I've got to go to this charity thing. To show I've shaved off my curls.'

He kissed my cheek and gave me a hug. I hugged him back. He glanced at the clear glass vase of hot pink, pale pink and lavender flowers on the window sill, a mixture of carnations, delphinium and larkspur. He was so sweet, always making sure there were fresh flowers, a burst of life, in this room of memories.

'I need to change those flowers later,' he said. 'Anyway, see you soon. And just tell Joe the truth about Ethan. He'll understand. He's a good guy with a big heart. He loves you. I mean really, really loves you.'

'I know,' I said, with a smile. 'I love him too. Bye, Dad.'

'Speak to you tomorrow, darling!' he called as he walked out of the room and quickly down the stairs. I heard him talking to Daisy and Benji – saying goodbye.

'Bye!' I called after him.

Left standing holding the recipe, I folded it in half and put it on the window sill next to the flowers while I found the space on the shelf where the box-file went. Before I put the file back, I flicked through the documents distractedly, wondering what else Dad had kept. There were letters there that Mum had written to him. Some of them had small illustrations underneath her name, caricatures of Dad wearing different exaggerated expressions. My eyes moved over her handwriting and I was struck by how much it said about her: bold and clear, it seemed to leap off the page and burst with emotion, just how I remembered her. I heard Daisy's footsteps on the stairs.

'What are you doing?' Daisy said, pushing open the door and peering in. 'I've got your glass of wine downstairs. Coming down?'

'Yep,' I said. 'Definitely.'

I put the box-file back, picked up the recipe then followed her downstairs and out into the garden, where we sat on deck-chairs in the evening sunshine, while Benji climbed the stump of an apple tree that had been cut down months before. I sipped the wine, ice-cold and delicious.

'Sorry about earlier,' Daisy said with a sheepish smile. 'I'm so worn out at the moment I didn't mean to sound interfering. You must be feeling horrible, now that Ethan is back. I know I can be bossy and moody, but if you want to talk about Ethan, I can be a good big sister sometimes . . .'

I looked at Daisy and we shared a smile. 'You're always a good big sister,' I said. I cast my mind back to when Ethan had left. Daisy had been absolutely amazing. From the moment he walked out, she had supported me, even though she was going through hell herself, in the early stages of pregnancy and breaking up with Iain, who didn't want her to have Benji at all. When I was dying to see Ethan, she kept me from giving in and flying out to Rome to find him. She had basically helped me function, feeding and watering me for a few weeks while I got myself together enough to cope with everyday life. In return, I helped her through the latter stages of pregnancy and was her birth partner when Iain refused to come back. In those few months, I felt we had bonded more as sisters than ever before.

'So how are you feeling?' Daisy asked.

'Oh, I don't know,' I said. 'I love Joe and don't want to jeopardize that at all, but Ethan confuses me. The thought of not seeing him again now he's back seems stupid, but then again, what will I achieve by seeing him? I need to sort my head out.'

I sipped my wine and closed my eyes, feeling the setting sun through my eyelids. I felt for my phone in my pocket, checking for messages, relieved and mildly disappointed that Ethan hadn't replied to my reply the night before. I should never have sent it.

'Let's face it,' she said. 'Ethan can't be trusted. He let you down. You're so much better off with Joe. I'm sorry to be blunt, but seeing him again would be really stupid.'

Stung by Daisy's words, I forced myself to remember that what she said was true. Ethan had let me down.

'I know that,' I said, irritated. Daisy always felt she had to point out the obvious.

'I know *you*,' she said kindly. 'You'll be searching for some kind of resolution, but there isn't any resolution here. The best thing you can do is to forget he exists.'

'Is that what you've done with Iain, then?' I asked.

Daisy sighed and looked sad, but nodded slowly.

'I try to,' she said. 'But it's different with Benji's dad, isn't it? I'm constantly reminded that his dad is missing, aren't I? It's hard to forget.'

'Then why don't you go and see him out there?' I asked. 'Take Benji and introduce them? Then he'll be forced to take responsibility.'

Daisy shook her head vehemently.

'I can't just turn up on his doorstep with Benji,' she said, almost laughing. 'It's not fair on Benji. I think we should wait until Iain expresses interest, then it will all be smoother, but I do feel guilty about the whole thing.'

I poured more wine into my glass.

'Could you send him an email?' I said. 'Ask him. Don't you think Benji should meet him now?'

Daisy pushed her hair back from her forehead, then massaged her temples with her fingertips.

'Yes, at some point, maybe,' she said. 'But what would I say? There's no future for us, is there? Our relationship wasn't working before he went back to Canada, nothing's going to change. God, I hate talking about him, it's too depressing. I feel like such a failure.'

'Sorry,' I said. 'Look, let's just change the subject. Let's talk about what we could have done at the Sanctuary.'

'OK,' she said, reaching over and touching my arm. 'But look, I want you to promise me you won't go to that next Saturday Supper Club. I can't stand to see you so upset again, raking up all those bad feelings. What good can come out of it?'

'None,' I said with a sigh. 'In any case, he was more interested in this other girl, Maggie, than talking about us.'

Daisy shook her head and tutted.

'What a bastard,' she said. 'I mean, you don't see the guy for three years and he's virtually shagging another girl in front of your eyes? You should tell him where to go and refuse to speak to him again, shouldn't you?'

I didn't have an answer to that. I shrugged and fiddled with a thread coming loose in my top.

'I'm definitely not going,' I said categorically.

For a moment, I believed what I was saying.

'Good,' Daisy said, smiling. 'It's all in the past and you should leave it that way, even though it's hard.'

'I won't go,' I said again too quickly, feigning interest in the tendrils of smoke blooming from the neighbour's barbecue. 'I don't want to see him again.'

'Promise you won't go?' she said. 'I'm just looking out for you, Eve. I'm saying what Mum would have said if she were here. Dad's too soft to say what he really thinks—'

'Yes,' I said, staring at the floor. 'Yes.'

I felt Daisy looking at me, but I couldn't turn around and face her. I hated myself for it, but she'd know I was lying.

PART TWO

Maggie's Supper Club

Chapter Eight

'Actually,' said Maggie, raking her hedge of curls into a pile on top of her head, 'I've become even more of a commitment-phobe since the last guy I went out with wanted to tattoo my name onto his neck. I mean, for God's sake, his neck?'

Maggie rolled her eyes, shook her head in despair and handed me a Turin-sized glass of red wine, which smelt like a handful of freshly picked blackberries squashed into a glass.

'Thanks,' I said, swallowing a big gulp. 'I need this.'

We were in Maggie's artfully chaotic living room in her Bethnal Green flat, where I was perched on the edge of a shabby red-velvet chaise longue, surrounded by a fleet of colourful cushions, some knitted, others screen-printed with illustrations of owls. I rested the glass of wine on my knees. Even though it was warm enough to have the windows flung wide open, the sky blue and vast beyond, I shivered with nerves and adrenalin. I was going to see Ethan again. Against my better judgement – against everyone's advice – I was here. I hated myself for it, but I'd made an effort to look good, too, wearing my flower-print shorts and red top, my arm jangling with bracelets. Any minute he would walk through the door, which I eyed as if it were an unexploded bomb.

'So,' said Maggie, moving across her living room in her silver strappy dress and vintage-style silver shoes, 'how's your week been? Just got to check the food. I'll be back in a second.'

I sighed, thinking about my week, as Maggie disappeared briefly into the kitchen. Music was playing – the kind you hear tinkling out the door of a Moroccan restaurant in a Soho side street – and the smell of lamb, cinnamon and cumin assaulted my senses, making me salivate. A selection of dips, eggplant salad and hummus, were laid out on the table in big earthenware pots, sprinkled with paprika and parsley. She came back into the room and raised her eyebrows in question.

'Sorry,' she said. 'So, you were about to say?'

'Good,' I said. 'Yes. Good. Great.'

I put my glass down on the table and sighed.

'Quite shit, actually,' I said, blowing out. 'To be frank.'

I'd spent the week since the last Saturday Supper Club feeling completely tense, avoiding everyone and not being able to sleep or eat properly. I didn't hear anything from Ethan, though I had expected to and probably wanted to. I'd worked at the cafe every hour I could, falling into bed after Joe was asleep and leaving before he woke up. Joe had asked me repeatedly if anything was wrong, but each time I decided to tell him that Ethan had turned up out of the blue, I couldn't find the words. The more time passed, the worse and more difficult it seemed to get, so I'd vowed to myself I'd tell him that night, after Maggie's dinner. I knew it was wrong that I'd come to her meal but the pull of seeing Ethan again was too strong. I justified it by convincing myself that there are some things in life that you have to do, for yourself. I needed to do this, especially if Joe was thinking about proposing. I needed to work Ethan out of my system once and for all. After these unresolved issues were resolved, I'd have a clearer head. And this was less bad, in my mind, than setting up a meeting with him for just the two of us. This way, I wasn't letting Joe down by messing up the *London Daily* competition and I was getting my head straight for when Joe proposed.

'I've actually been wondering if my boyfriend is about to propose,' I was astonished to hear myself say, instantly feeling disloyal. 'He hasn't yet, but something tells me he might be about to, and I'm feeling a bit confused about the whole marriage issue. I love him, Joe, my boyfriend, but marriage I'm not so sure about.'

Maggie, now sitting on a chair, with her legs swung up over one arm, looked up in surprise.

'Have you talked about it, then?' she asked, stretching to the table to reach the bottle of wine and fill up her glass. 'What is it you're not sure about? Most girls I know are mad keen on it, especially when they get to our age.'

I tucked my hair behind my ear and shook my head.

'I'm not sure,' I said slowly. 'What I mean is, I love him, I've known him my whole life, so it's almost like . . .'

'Eeurgh,' said Maggie, looking up. 'I hope you're not going to say he's like your brother. That's gross.'

I shook my head and rolled my eyes.

'No, I was going to say it seems almost inevitable that we'll be together . . .' I said. 'We're the best of friends and I trust him completely, but marriage seems so kind of *final*. And

I want to get it really right, you know? My parents had this amazing marriage, but then my mum died and my dad's never got over her or had another relationship. It just seems like such a massive thing to do. And can anyone be right for you, for life? How do you know what you'll feel like in ten years' time?'

Maggie nodded sagely.

'I know where you're coming from,' she said. 'When marriage was created people only lived until they were about forty years old, so life didn't mean an eternity, like it does today.'

'I never thought of it like that,' I said. 'But, well, I know Joe's parents have an awful marriage and I think he wants to prove to himself he can do better. I sometimes wonder if that's the most important issue for him.'

I realized, as soon as I'd said the words, I sounded like a bitch and I hadn't meant to. I knew that Joe loved me. Why was I throwing it up for contemplation with an almost stranger? It was easier, in a way, to talk to someone I hardly knew.

'That sounded all wrong,' I said. 'There's a huge part of me that does want to get married but . . . I'm just . . . just . . . not sure. And you have to be certain.'

I sighed. I wasn't even sure of what I was saying. I was incredibly nervous, that was all. My eyes skitted around the room. You could tell from her flat that Maggie was an arty person. Everywhere you looked there was something gorgeous and carefully chosen: kitsch porcelain figurines and antique tins on a shelf, vintage fabric throws, an old-fashioned birdcage nestled in the fireplace bursting with dried flowers, a chandelier with tiny spotted lampshades over each bulb, and an enormous wooden dining table decorated with tree branches of small lights at one end of the living room. It was delightful.

'To be honest with you,' she said, 'and I'm sticking my neck out here – I would rather be a mistress than a wife. No ties, much more fun and much less hassle.'

I widened my eyes and watched Maggie carefully. I wasn't that shocked by her statement – Maggie struck me as someone who might say almost anything at any moment – but most of my girlfriends and I hated the threat of the mistress, especially in the form of gorgeous, almost feline, Maggie.

'Really?' I said. 'You don't care if a bloke has a girlfriend? That's a brave statement to make! You'd get lynched if you were out with my friends. There's no one less popular than the "other woman", unless, of course, it's one of us who's the other woman; then it's absolutely fine and totally justifiable, of course.'

I snickered at the hypocrisy of my words, while Maggie, narrowing her eyes knowingly, stood and picked up a bowl of pistachio nuts from the table. She placed them on the arm of the chaise longue, took one and gestured for me to help myself.

'I know it's not a popular thing to say in female company,' she said, looking out from under her mascara-thick lashes. 'But I'm pretty convinced that there's no one out there I want to marry or have kids with. And relationships are so complicated and muddled. People have so many issues tucked into their closets. I just want to have fun. That's why I like Ethan. He seems like a bloke who enjoys life. He's vivacious, extrovert, but he probably has an interesting dark side. We all do, don't we?'

I thought about Ethan's dark side. He was deeply restless, probably frustrated, rather than dark. He couldn't sit still for long. He always wanted to *do* something, was always on the go, not wanting to miss out on life. He drummed his fingers a lot. He hated going to bed at night, because he couldn't see the point in sleeping and only I knew how fearful he was of his nightmares. I'd often thought he was like someone who'd been told he had three months to live and had decided to get the most out of his remaining days. And, of course, deep down, there was his grief, his great sorrow that he carried in his heart, a picture in a locket.

'We went out on Wednesday night,' Maggie said, rubbing a finger around the rim of her wine glass. 'He's a lot of fun but, like I said, there's a certain enigmatic darkness there, too, isn't there? You're old friends, so you probably know better than I do.'

I froze, my glass halfway up to my mouth.

'You went out?' I asked thinly, my stomach turning in on itself.

'We did,' she said. 'There's definitely chemistry there, and we were having a good time, I thought, until right at the end when he got all maudlin and started talking about some relationship he'd messed up, a girl he couldn't have for one reason or another.'

Maggie rolled her eyes and pretended to yawn.

'A girl in Rome?' I choked out.

She shook her head and shrugged.

'I didn't ask,' she said. 'To be honest, I was trying to steer him back on to conversation about me. I like him; I think he'd be good fling material, though I can't quite put my finger on what's going on with him, but he seems to have quite a self-destructive streak, do you think? I thought I could drink, but wow, he can really put it away.'

I gulped, my heart hammering in my chest at the thought of Maggie and Ethan out together. Jealousy crept up my spine. And what of this girl he was talking about? I didn't let myself think it might be me.

'Ethan is a total party animal,' I said. 'But you're right, he does have a self-destruct button. He had a horrible thing happen to him when he was young and I think it explains quite a bit about him. I don't think he'd mind me telling you that when he was six, his twin brother drowned in a swimming pool when his family were on holiday in France. There were no pool alarms and it was only a few minutes, but no one noticed that his brother was gone until it was too late.'

'Oh my God,' said Maggie. 'That's awful.'

I nodded and continued to speak.

'Ever since, I think he's tried to be two people rolled into one to make up for his brother's absence,' I said. 'He feels he owes it to his brother, you know? Perhaps he feels guilty it wasn't him who died. But he doesn't want sympathy about it. God, no. He insists that people are happy, that they celebrate life and that his brother's life is remembered, with joy, by his parents. He's wild, gregarious, charming and funny, always on the go. His mother absolutely adores him, phones him twice a day. He's like a firework going off in your life.'

I probably shouldn't have divulged so much personal information about Ethan, but after Maggie's news that the two of them had been out, I was, quite pathetically, trying to claim some kind of ownership of him. I could, of course, just tell Maggie about our relationship, but I didn't want her watching us later. I wanted to keep it secret, so I could work out how I felt.

'That's so terrible,' Maggie said, shaking her head sadly. 'I feel really sad for him now. I'll have to be extra nice to him tonight. Poor Ethan.'

I blinked, ignoring her coquettish comment. I was desperate to ask if anything had happened between them on their date. Awful images of them together flashed into my head. Maggie the Mistress wearing full dominatrix gear straddling a glow-eyed Ethan – I shook them away. Why did my mind always take me to places I didn't want it to go? It was as if I was actively trying to sabotage my own well-being.

'So, have you been someone's mistress, then?' I said, trying not to sound the vicar's wife, though, on this topic, I was probably with the vicar's wife. I hated the idea of women like Maggie actively *trying* to bed your boyfriend, because she didn't want the commitment of a single man. Men would be putty in her hands. God, I mean, why couldn't she just find another commitment-phobe and have a half-baked relationship that suited them both and didn't hurt anyone else?

'Fuck, yes,' she said. 'Once you start looking, the world is full of married men who want a mistress. They're literally everywhere.'

'That's just miserable,' I said sullenly.

Maggie shrugged.

'Obviously some want more than what I like to give,' she said. 'They want love and commitment and tattoos on necks, but that's not my style. I lay down the rules and if they take that on board, no one gets hurt.'

'Hmm,' I said, narrowing my eyes at Maggie.

I couldn't quite believe how harsh she was being. No one really felt that coldly about relationships, did they? I didn't buy it. Everything about her flat portrayed her as an arty, creative person with soul, not the ice queen she was making out to be.

'And what about their unsuspecting wives or girlfriends?' I said. 'Doesn't it make you feel bad to be helping him cheat and hurt someone's feelings? Fair enough if their relationship is on the rocks and he breaks up with her, but to keep two relationships going? That's a bit ropey, isn't it? And don't you, really, want someone for yourself? Underneath that cool exterior?'

Maggie shook her head dismissively.

'No,' she said decisively. 'It's none of my business to worry about the wife or girlfriend. I'm only interested in good food, good sex and good conversation. All's fair in love and war.'

'But,' I said, my cheeks beginning to burn, 'that's wrong! If you don't respect boundaries, then what hope is there for any relationship? You can't just wade into a marriage and take the best bits and leave the worst for the wife. If it was the other way round, you'd be heartbroken, wouldn't you?'

Maggie put her hand up to stop me speaking. She smiled indulgently. I got the feeling she was well used to this kind of conversation.

'Calm down, Eve,' she said. 'You sound like a Jane Austen character.'

'I am calm,' I snapped. 'And no, I don't sound like anyone else but me . . .'

I stopped myself speaking and shut my mouth. I was a guest in Maggie's house, after all.

'Look,' she said, more gently, brushing something off her dress. 'I should have known not to bring this up. I never get a good reaction. Anyway, Ethan doesn't have a wife or kids, does he? So he's an exception to the rule. I won't be treading on anyone's toes there, will I?'

I shrugged, and for a few moments we sat there in awkward silence, me fuming at Maggie's words, necking back my wine and repeatedly biting the inside of my cheek. Maggie was exactly the sort of woman I feared. Stunning, cool, in control and happy to trample all over other people's hearts. Plus she had an annoyingly coy expression on her face, like everything she'd just said was perfectly innocent.

'So,' I said, sucking in my breath. 'Did anything happen with Ethan the other night after you went out?'

'Well,' she said. 'It was an interesting challenge for me because—'

Then the doorbell rang. I breathed out. Maggie stopped speaking, stood up and moved over to her iPod dock to turn the music up a little.

'Hang on a sec,' she said.

I nodded, but frowned behind her back. I was thinking about something else now. I shivered. My stomach lurched at the thought of seeing Ethan again. I clutched the stem of my glass tighter and knocked back the dregs of my wine in one gulp. Daisy's voice rang out in my head: *Promise you won't go? I'm saying what Mum would have said if she were here* . . .

'Oh God,' I muttered to myself, when I heard Ethan's voice and the sound of Maggie and Ethan's footsteps coming up the stairs to her flat. Grabbing a copy of *Dazed & Confused* from the coffee table in front of me, I immersed myself in an article about a Russian photographer's childhood encounters with bears, though the words were swarming in front of my eyes, like crawling ants.

'Tube trauma,' I heard Ethan say. He was suddenly only inches away from me, pushing his black hair away from his eyes. My cheeks blazed. I peered out from over the magazine.

'Fucking hour it's taken me to get here,' he continued. 'Apparently, there's a good service, except for all the engineering works on all the major lines. It's really fucking great that there's a good service on just one line. Thanks, London Underground! Hello, Eve, you look gorgeous.'

I dropped the magazine and stood awkwardly. I felt Ethan's eyes roll over me as he pulled off his bag. I put my hands self-consciously on my thighs – I was regretting the shorts, wishing I'd opted for a sack.

'Hey,' I said, waving small circles in the air with my palm, like a lunatic.

'Good to see you again,' Ethan said, waving back at me the same way. I caught his eye for a second and we both suppressed a smile. Then I sat back down again and covered my legs with a cushion.

'So,' said Maggie, placing herself between Ethan and me, holding up a bottle of red. 'Would you like a drink? Eve's boyfriend has proposed to her, so we should all drink to that.'

I blushed madly, irritated with Maggie for putting me on the spot.

'No,' I said quickly, glancing up at Ethan. 'No, he hasn't proposed. I just think he might be about to propose. That's all.'

'That's *all*?' said Ethan, sitting down on the sofa opposite me, making a meal of extracting a bottle of champagne from his bag and not giving me eye contact. 'That's a big deal, isn't it? I think we should definitely drink to that . . .'

'Arsenic, perhaps,' he whispered, so only I could hear. My eyes bumped into his.

'Listen, it's not definite . . .' I said, shrugging, feeling guilty for being so horrible to Joe, immediately correcting myself. 'But I hope he does.'

'You don't sound very enthusiastic, Eve,' Maggie said. 'Most girls would have got a subscription to *Bride* magazine by now. Maybe you should take my advice and be a mistress, have meaningless sex-fuelled flings with handsome men.'

I eyed Maggie. I saw what she was doing. Outlining what she could offer to Ethan, in contrast to me, who was 'marriage material'. She didn't know the half of it. She had no idea that Ethan and I used to be so in love we were virtually inseparable. Ethan was acting oblivious, but couldn't have failed to pick up on the vibes flinging round the room. Ethan put his arm along the length of the back of the sofa – and when Maggie handed him a glass of wine, then sat down next to him, it looked like he had his arm around her. Maggie turned to smile at Ethan, twirling a corkscrew curl with her finger. I felt a pang of jealousy shoot through me. Destiny? What a load of crap. What was I doing here? I missed Joe and wished I'd told him the truth. I stared out of the window and wondered whether I should just make an excuse and go.

'Well,' Ethan said, looking at me, 'you're not most girls, are you, Eve? Anyway, let's drink to Joe's maybe proposal. Really, if you're happy, then we should all celebrate.'

We all held our glasses in the air, somewhat half-heartedly, and I drank quickly. I told myself to slow down. Already I felt light-headed.

'I've got a good feeling about tonight,' Ethan said distractedly. 'Mmm, I can smell something tantalizingly delicious.'

It was true. The subtle smells wafting in from the kitchen were making me really hungry. Ethan sniffed the air, then stopped when the doorbell sounded again. Maggie stood from the sofa and half jogged to get it. This was my chance. If I was here, I should get some answers. I leaned forward towards Ethan, folding my arms around my waist.

'Ethan,' I said quietly. He looked at me expectantly. 'We need to talk. I don't believe in destiny, but I do believe in resolution. I need to know what happened.'

I noticed my hands were trembling. I sat on them.

'Ethan,' I carried on, 'why won't you just *tell* me why you left? It's not going to make any difference to anything, but I want to know.'

Ethan's face darkened and he frowned.

'Of course,' he said seriously. 'Of course you do. I'm sorry, I must seem so flippant, but I'm genuinely pleased to see you, I can't help but be happy.'

Walking towards us from the other side of the living room was Andrew, wiping his brow from the heat. He was considerably more sober than the last time I saw him, dressed in another pale suit, clutching yet more bottles of champagne, a linen bag on his shoulder bearing the slogan 'The Lido Cafe'. Behind him was Paul, his enormous camera bag on his shoulder. Paul lifted his hand in greeting and explained that he needed to photograph the food again and that we should speak to Dominique in the morning about how the evening went with our reviews and scores.

'I gave you a ten out of ten,' Ethan whispered into my ear. 'I tried to give you eleven, but Dominique wouldn't let me.'

I smiled but, feeling embarrassed, I kept my eyes on Andrew, as if he were the most fascinating person in the world. He put down his bag, took off his suit jacket, accepted a glass of wine from Maggie, scooped up a handful of pistachio nuts and sat down heavily next to me with a big sigh.

'I must apologize,' he said, leaning back into the cushions and crossing his ankles, 'for last time. I was absolutely wasted. I'm so sorry I slept in your bath. I haven't done that for at least ten years. Not since I was at university.'

Maggie led Paul into the kitchen, where I heard their muffled voices talking about the menu.

'That's OK,' I said warmly. 'How's it going with your girl-friend?'

Andrew shook his head and pulled a face.

'Not great,' he said. 'She wasn't too pleased when I didn't come home last Saturday night and she was having Braxton Hicks contractions. As you can imagine I wasn't in the least bit popular.'

'Oops,' said Ethan. 'You did say you wanted to be wild while you had the chance.'

'Yes, I did,' Andrew said. 'But the woman's having twins. I've got to be there for her all the time, even if she can't stand the sight of me.'

'Hang on,' said Ethan. 'Did you say twins?'

I looked at Ethan, who had paled ever so slightly. My heart swelled. I knew he'd be thinking of his twin. I remembered a beautiful photograph Ethan had of him and his twin asleep on a sheepskin as newborn babies. They were cuddling one another closely, their noses together, arms and legs entwined, as they must have done in the womb. I caught his eye and smiled warmly. He smiled in return. He sighed, looked at his feet then quickly recovered himself.

'Twins, yes,' Andrew said, smiling worriedly. 'They will be born at Chelsea and Westminster Hospital in two weeks' time. We have an amazing obstetrician. Apparently he's a world expert in multiple births. Didn't I tell you this last time? Must have been too drunk. What an idiot I am.'

I sat back in my chair.

'Poor Alicia,' I said. 'No wonder she's a bit tense.'

'Yes,' Andrew said. 'Apparently they're big babies, too.'

'Jesus Christ,' said Ethan, with a laugh.

'Hopefully not,' said Andrew. 'I can't be doing with the Second Coming, especially not two of them.'

'Ta-dah!' Maggie said a little later, presenting her lamb and date tagine to the low table we were all sitting round on cushions. 'A Moroccan feast for you. Ah, wait, I have couscous coming.'

I breathed in the perfumed scent of ginger, cinnamon, cumin and pepper and looked eagerly at the tender lamb, so succulent and perfectly cooked, it was ready to fall off the bone. On another plate lay a delicious-looking artichoke salad.

'Couscous cumin,' Ethan said, leaning over to breathe in the smell of the dish. 'Geddit? How did you cook the couscous? Above the meat?'

'Very funny,' Maggie said, walloping him over the head with her oven gloves, making the flames of the candles flicker and jump in the breeze. 'Yes, in the steam from the meat. Should make it full of flavour. And this is the wine we should drink with it.'

She held up a bottle of red, which Andrew took from her and scrutinized.

'Hang on there for a minute, will you?' said Paul. 'I need to get a photograph. Freeze, will you?'

We all froze, then, when Paul had finished, Maggie picked up a serving spoon from the low table and started to serve.

'Smells fantastic,' I said, pulling a napkin down onto my lap.

'Feed me!' Andrew exclaimed. 'I think you're the winner so far, Maggie. Sorry, Eve.'

Maggie laughed uproariously. I smiled wanly.

'Thanks,' I said. 'I don't mind. I think you're right. This is fantastic.'

Just before Maggie served up huge plates of tender lamb and deliciously fluffy couscous, Paul took more photographs of each dish and then he, too, sat down to eat, claiming this job was making him 'fat as a pig'. While she served, Maggie explained that she'd spent six months in Morocco teaching English and had learned how to cook proper Moroccan food while staying with a host family, the father of whom seemed more interested in her legs than anything else. Not that she would have minded, of course, I thought, but did not say – he was married! Ethan made us laugh with anecdotes about his parents' constant arguments at the deli (they were stereo-typically Italian and were hilariously rude to each other but passionately in love) and a recent audition for a new flavour of crisps he'd failed to get because he couldn't crunch the right way. 'Years of training to be an actor,' he said, 'and still I don't know how to crunch.'

For the remainder of the meal, I forgot why I was there. Maybe it was the perfumed and delicate flavours of Maggie's delicious lamb and couscous that melted on the tongue and made Andrew's eyes literally roll back in his head; maybe the wine had something to do with it, but I forgot that Ethan had turned up out of the blue just a few days ago. I forgot that I should be with Joe, that he might, this very minute, be preparing his proposal to me. I relaxed. I existed just for the moment, enjoying the times when Ethan's eyes nudged mine and we looked at one another like we knew just what the other one was thinking. It was like old times.

'I'm really enjoying myself,' Andrew said, voicing all of our thoughts. 'First time in ages I've relaxed.'

'Oh, Andrew,' Maggie said. 'You do paint a sad picture of your life. I feel sorry for you.'

'Don't,' he said. 'I just seem to annoy Alicia so much, so there's quite a cloud over my existence at the moment. Everything I do sets her off. We've been trying to get pregnant for quite a few years, and just before it happened we were on the verge of breaking up. We probably should have, but anyway, I never realized quite how irritating I was until recently.'

Andrew laughed at himself, but I liked him already and didn't like the thought of him feeling so miserable.

'That's a difficult situation,' I said. 'But all relationships have ups and downs, don't they?'

Ethan deliberately turned away from me and poured himself more wine.

'Alicia must have some annoying traits, hasn't she?' he asked. 'She can't be completely perfect, can she?'

Andrew nodded thoughtfully.

'I think she is pretty much perfect,' he said slowly. 'I can't think of anything bad to say about her.'

Maggie banged her hand down on the table.

'Oh, come on, Andrew!' she said. 'Release your inner bitch. There must be one thing, just one thing about her that's annoying.'

Andrew leaned back in his chair, looked up at the ceiling, then crossed his legs.

'Actually,' he said quietly, 'there is one thing.'

'Ha!' said Maggie. 'I knew it. Out with it.'

We all leaned in to listen to Andrew's admission. He looked around nervously, as if he wasn't sure he should say anything at all. I watched Maggie wink at him encouragingly.

'We won't say a thing,' she said conspiratorially.

'OK,' he said slowly. 'I don't know if it's something to do with her circulation, but when she gets into bed at night and expects a spoons cuddle, her bottom is always freezing cold. It's got quite big since the pregnancy and she reverses towards me like some kind of lorry. I have to brace myself for it every night, because it's like ice. Of course, I can't say a word in complaint. But, bloody hell, it's so cold.'

Wine shot through my nose as I burst out laughing. Ethan, Maggie and Paul creased up. Ethan rested his hand on my forearm briefly, something he used to do when we were both enjoying or appreciating something.

'What are you laughing at?' Andrew said, laughing a little,

looking slightly bemused. 'It's the truth. She's like a bloody freezing-cold lorry reversing under the duvet.'

'That's more like it,' Maggie said, wiping her eyes. 'I knew you couldn't be *completely* soft, oops, if you pardon the pun.'

Chapter Nine

'Maggie says you have chemistry,' I blurted out to Ethan over the table, when Andrew – probably feeling guilty – popped out to phone Alicia, and Maggie disappeared into her bedroom, to change, she said, for pudding.

'Does she?' Ethan said, folding his arms over his chest, eyebrows raised, a smile on his lips.

'When you went out together the other night,' I garbled. 'She said there was chemistry between you, so I was just repeating her words. Is it true? I mean, do you have chemistry, or is she—'

I stopped speaking, closed my eyes and rocked back in my chair. What was I saying? I put my hand on my forehead and shook my head.

'Maggie said you're getting married to Joe,' Ethan replied in a low voice. 'Is that true?'

I snapped open my eyes and stared at Ethan. He gave me a comical look.

'Maybe,' I said, feeling defensive and protective of Joe, hating that Ethan was talking about him. 'Hopefully. Anyway, what do you care? You made your mind up about me three years ago and I still want to know why you left.'

My head was spinning. I'd drunk too much and was feeling way too emotional. I knew the best thing I could do was be quiet. I gulped down a glass of water.

'We need to talk,' Ethan said, pulling a packet of Drum from his pocket. 'But I need a cigarette first.'

I rolled my eyes. What was a cigarette after three years of waiting? I watched Ethan walk towards the French doors, which led onto a small balcony. He lit a cigarette, looking out at the scrub of green space opposite where I could hear the sound of kids playing football in the last light of the evening. I heard him introduce himself to the neighbours, who were having a drink on their balcony. Ethan talked to everyone he met. How many times had I been out with Ethan in the past, hoping for a romantic night with just the two of us, only to hook up with random people we stumbled across? Admittedly, that was part of his charm; you never quite knew what would happen. I had always wished I could be more like him, instead of self-conscious and tongue-tied.

Maggie stuck her head out of her bedroom door. 'I have a surprise for you before pudding,' she said. 'Cover your eyes, everyone!'

Back in his chair, next to me, Andrew covered his eyes. Ethan finished his smoke and sat down. He held a napkin in front of his face and I closed my eyes, reluctantly, until Maggie told us we could look again.

'Wow,' I said, opening my eyes to see Maggie dressed up in an authentic belly-dancing outfit. She looked incredible. Her breasts were barely covered by the bejewelled bikini top, shimmering gold tassels hung provocatively over her thighs and a slim gold chain was looped around her middle. With her curls cascading down her back, she looked drop-dead gorgeous.

'I second that,' said Ethan.

'Good Lord,' said Andrew. 'I don't know where to look.'

Maggie giggled, then changed the music on her iPod, turned up the volume, and started to belly dance, totally professionally, leaving us all open-mouthed. This was one good party trick. She was mesmerizing and oozing with sexuality. When the music stopped, she froze for a moment, before bowing. Andrew began slow clapping.

'Wow,' I said again, stunned. 'That was completely amazing.'

'Maggie,' Andrew said, 'you looked beautiful.'

'I've never seen anything like it,' Ethan said from the balcony doors, where he was now standing, smoking again. 'That was thrilling.'

She looked over to him and smiled. I watched their eyes lock. My stomach turned over. Ethan walked towards her, holding out his arms when he was near.

'Show me how to do it,' he said. 'What do I do?'

'Men don't belly dance,' she giggled.

'Come on,' he said. 'Show me.'

Ethan tucked his T-shirt up and pushed his jeans further down his hips so we could all see his slim, surprisingly tanned torso, and Maggie put her hands on his waist, showing him how to move. He pranced about, making a joke of it, entertaining his audience, as always. Watching them together made me feel sick. Ethan couldn't be more insensitive if he tried. I thought about Joe. He would never make me feel like this. He was aware of boundaries. Ethan, apparently, wasn't. Somewhere in the back of my mind I realized I was being a complete hypocrite. Wasn't I, earlier, talking about marrying Joe? I blinked, confused and disorientated. I didn't know how I felt.

'I'd better get going,' I said to Andrew, who was clapping at Ethan and Maggie. 'I've got loads of work to do on the cafe tomorrow.'

'Go?' said Andrew, frowning. 'But we haven't had pudding yet. You can't go. You won't be able to rate Maggie's dinner properly. If you do, I'll have to go too, because I don't want to be a gooseberry . . .'

Andrew pulled a face and I gulped. He'd noticed their connection too.

'Just need some fresh air,' I mumbled. 'I'll be back in a minute.'

I stood and picked up my bag without looking at Ethan and Maggie. My face was hot and my eyes moist. I couldn't believe how pathetically jealous I felt, when I had no right at all. I had to get out of there, before I did or said something stupid. I moved towards the door, but Ethan suddenly was by my side and grabbed my arm. In the background, Maggie was still dancing, showing Andrew the moves now, while he laughed awkwardly.

'You're not going, are you?' Ethan said, appalled. 'You can't go.'

'Just want some air,' I said, choking slightly. 'I'm really hot and . . .'

Ethan looked worried, his face suddenly serious.

'Come out on the balcony,' Ethan said. 'We were going to talk. I'm sorry. I'm being a dick. Come on. Maggie says she's got a bottle of tequila after pudding. We could do a couple of shots. Remember when we used to go to that tequila bar?'

I shook my head, though of course I did. The last thing I needed was to get completely trashed with Ethan. I wanted to keep a clear head. I wanted to find out why he left three years ago and then get out of there.

'No,' I said. 'I don't want to get drunk. I just want to talk. Maybe here isn't the right place.'

Ethan grabbed my hand and pulled me out onto the balcony, which looked over a square of lawn surrounded by other blocks of flats. I leaned against the waist-high wall and glanced at the other balconies I could see, some with a string of clothes drying out, others stuffed full of junk, one with two bikes with their wheels in the air. I clasped my hands together while Ethan stood next to me. Our elbows touching, he brushed the side of my face with his hand.

'Look, Eve,' he said.

My face burned and I trembled. No one but Ethan had this effect on me. I had no control over my physical response to him. It was almost animalistic.

'Yes?' I said. 'What?'

'There's one thing I want to say. Two, actually,' he said. 'Firstly, I want to say sorry. Secondly, you can't marry Joe. I won't allow it.'

'What are you talking about?' I said, feeling anger surge up in me. 'You've no right to say anything like that. It's been three years since you had any right to—'

Ethan lifted his finger to his lips to silence me.

'Don't be angry . . .' Ethan said quietly. 'I still—'

He closed his mouth as if deciding not to say any more.

'You what?' I said, chewing my bottom lip.

I wondered fleetingly if he was going to say he still loved me, then laughed at myself for being ridiculous. If he really loved me, he would have come to find me before now. I reprimanded myself for letting my mind go down that road. He probably didn't like the thought of me finding happiness with anyone else. He loved to be the centre of attention, whatever the situation, didn't he? No, this was supposed to be about closure, not opening up all those old feelings.

'I want to kiss you,' he said. 'I'm going to kiss you.'

Before I could say anything or do anything, Ethan moved towards me and kissed my mouth. His kiss was gentle and sweet. He tasted of cigarettes and alcohol and how certainty used to taste. My entire body flushed with desire. His lips stayed on mine, firmer now, and I forced myself to remember where I was and what I was doing. Angrily, I pulled my head back and moved away from him.

'Ethan,' I said. 'You can't just kiss me like that. I'm with Joe, remember? A second ago you were flirting with Maggie and this is all stupid. I shouldn't even be—'

Ethan held on to both my hands, while I looked up at the sky, my eyes blurring. I pulled my arms away and wiped my eyes.

'Look,' he said. 'You know there's something still between us. You can feel it just like I can. Now that I've seen you again, I'm more sure than ever that going to Rome was all a big mistake. I should have stayed. I wish I'd been brave enough to stay.'

The French doors behind us suddenly opened and Maggie, grinning, eyed us both suspiciously.

'The pudding is on the table,' she said. 'Coming in?'

Ethan, reverting back to the Ethan of minutes before, nodded enthusiastically.

'Yes,' he said. 'Definitely.'

He rested his hands on Maggie's waist as he passed by her. I shook my head.

'Just give me a minute,' I said, bewildered, fiddling around in my bag for a tissue. 'I've got awful hayfever.'

Maggie's eyebrows shot into her hairline and when Ethan went into the living room before me, she leaned in close and whispered in my ear.

'I saw that,' she said. 'I think you have some explaining to do, Miss Eve.'

As delicious as it was, I could barely swallow Maggie's pistachio and rose ice cream, delicate pastry honey cakes and dessert wine. All I could think of was Ethan's lips on mine, minutes before. I wondered if I'd dreamt it, but every time Ethan's eyes met mine, I knew I hadn't. He was right. There was something still there between us. But what of it? I was with Joe. I loved Joe.

'I put real rose petals in here,' she said, pointing at the ice cream. 'Surely you'll give me a high score for effort? What do you say, Andrew? Taste this bit—'

Maggie, still in her costume, virtually falling out of the bra top, was spooning pudding into Andrew's mouth. Andrew, unsure of how to handle the attention, eyed me pleadingly.

'Where did you learn to dance?' I asked Maggie, trying to change the subject and grab her attention, wanting to get back to some kind of normal.

'I've taken classes for years,' she said. 'Very good for my figure. I know: let's all dance, shall we?'

Maggie stood up and turned out all the lights, plunging everyone into darkness. I froze. She put on the music she'd previously danced to and clapped her hands together.

'Dance, everyone!' she said. 'No one can see you, so you can relax!'

'Come off it,' Andrew said. 'I'll break my leg.'

It was dark, but not completely dark, so we could all still see one another. Ethan stood up and came over to where I was sitting. He held out his hand and after a long moment, I accepted it. He put one hand on my waist. For a few moments, we danced together, him twirling me into his body and out again, like we'd done before hundreds of times. Then Maggie flicked the light back on. I collapsed onto the floor cushions and Ethan then flopped down onto the cushion next to mine, puffing and panting. As he did so, he rested his hand on the back of my neck and gently stroked my skin, just once. I stiffened. I had to get out.

'OK, enough, I'd better get going,' I said, jumping up out of his reach, checking my watch. 'It's so late. I'll just splash my face with water, then go. I've had way too much to drink.'

'Don't go,' said Ethan, looking at me searchingly. 'The party's only just beginning.'

'No,' I said decisively. 'I've got to.'

I quickly walked towards the bathroom, wobbling slightly, and closed the door behind me, muffling the sounds of music and laughter. I looked at my reflection: bright-eyed and pink-cheeked. Despite the guilt I felt, I recognized joy in my expression. I groaned and leaned over the sink, turned on the tap and splashed my face with water, when I noticed a silver locket hanging on a peg just inside the bathroom cabinet. It was open slightly, so I dried my hands and looked at the picture. It was of Maggie, with a dark-haired, dark-eyed, slim man. They were abroad somewhere, sitting on a moped, her arms wrapped around his middle, both beaming. There was a knock at the door and I quickly hung it back up.

'I need the loo!' Maggie said through the door. 'Are you done?'

'Yes,' I said, opening the door, watching the necklace still swinging. It was obvious I'd been looking at it.

'My locket,' she said, looking from me to it, feeling her neck, as if to confirm she wasn't wearing it. 'Thought I was wearing that.'

'It fell off the hook,' I stuttered. 'Sorry for being nosy, but it fell open. Who's the picture of?'

Maggie's cheeks, flushed with alcohol, paled slightly and her eyes glittered with tears.

'I shouldn't have asked,' I said quickly as she wiped her eyes with the back of her hands. She sat down on the edge of the bath.

'Sorry,' she said. 'Think I've had too much booze. That's Sal. He was my childhood sweetheart. We were together ten years, then he went off with another woman. I found them in bed together when I came home from work early one day. They're married now, with kids. I still love him. I still talk to him. We still love each other.'

'Oh God,' I said. 'That's awful. I'm sorry.'

Maggie, in the glare of the bathroom strip-light, suddenly seemed fragile and lost. Her lips quivered.

'We were engaged,' she said, shrugging her shoulders and glancing up at me, as if to acknowledge everything we'd said earlier about marriage. 'But, you know, didn't work out . . .'

Her voice was quiet and her eyes soft. For a second I saw another side to her, but she quickly recovered herself, grinning up at me.

'So, what's going on with Ethan?' she said. 'You should have said I was treading on your toes. Do you two have history?'

I groaned and leaned the back of my head against the bathroom door.

'We used to be a couple,' I said quietly. 'We were together for two years, then he walked out on me three years ago and I haven't seen him since, until he turned up at the door last Saturday.'

'Nooo,' she said. 'What a coincidence!'

'I know,' I said, nodding. 'Ethan thinks it's destiny.'

'Why did he go?' she said. 'What happened?'

I shrugged and frowned, pushing my hair behind my ears.

'I don't really know,' I said. 'I'm not sure that there was a real reason.'

'Perhaps he got scared,' Maggie said. 'I've seen that happen a lot. The man gets in too deep then decides to leg it without explaining why. They're not as good at commitment as women, are they? When I say women, I'm not talking about myself, you understand.'

I nodded and watched Maggie turn to face the mirror and apply her lipstick.

'I don't know,' I said. 'But anyway, it's all too much, seeing him like this. I need to get going. Joe, my boyfriend, will wonder where I am. I feel terrible for him. If he knew what was—'

Maggie shook her head.

'No,' she said. 'Don't feel guilty. It's a pointless emotion. You're working out where your heart lies. That's admirable, courageous.'

I looked up at her questioningly and she handed me a tissue to pat dry my eyes.

'You think?' I said.

'Yes,' she said. 'If Sal had been braver and done that a little bit sooner in our relationship, I wouldn't have found him shagging that woman in my bed. It would all have been a lot more civilized.'

'Is that why you're so anti-relationships, then?' I asked. 'Because of Sal?'

Maggie shrugged and pulled at a loose bead on her top.

'I suppose so,' she said. 'I just know that I don't ever want to be in that situation again where my entire life is wrapped up in one person. It's easier this way, to be in control and have flings with men who are already committed. On the whole they don't want much from me. I'm not prepared to give up on the emotional freedom that gives me. Do you understand, even a bit?'

Maggie's voice became stronger again as she spoke. It felt to me like she'd given herself this lecture numerous times.

'I do understand,' I said. 'I guess we all have our reasons for being the way we are.'

'Yes, just look at Andrew,' Maggie said. 'Him and Alicia have problems and now twins on the way.'

'I know,' I said. 'Poor guy. Maybe they'll work it out.'

'It's all a bit fucked up, though, isn't it?' she said. 'Relationships always are. That's why I like to keep at a distance. Listen, let's have a quick tequila before you go. I'm enjoying talking to you.'

I checked my watch. It was almost one in the morning. I followed her out of the bathroom.

'I'm not sure,' I said. 'Joe will be wondering—'

'That's where you are,' Andrew said, getting up from the sofa, wobbling slightly. 'Is everything OK? Ethan had to go. He said goodbye. And thank you.'

I tensed. 'Had to go?' I asked, thinking he might pop out from behind a chair. 'Where did he have to go at one in the morning?'

Visions of a girlfriend, waiting for him at his flat, filled my mind. Or maybe he was making his escape before I could make him talk again. Andrew stood up, stretched up his arms and pulled on his suit jacket.

'Home,' he said. 'He was talking about Rome and was about to tuck into that bottle of tequila, then went all quiet and seemed to change his mind. I suppose I ought to make a move myself.'

Chapter Ten

'Do you think there was anyone else involved?' Maggie said, after we'd said goodbye to Andrew and she convinced me to have one last drink. 'You know, in my experience, there always is someone else.'

Maggie was sprawled out on one of her sofas, one knee bent and the other leg outstretched, while I sat opposite her, upright and straight-backed on her chaise longue, dipping my hand into a bowl of Kettle Chips she had put near me. Instead of a tequila shot, Maggie had made me a tequila sunrise, topping the drink with grenadine, which sank to the bottom, giving a pretty sunrise effect. I rested the glass on my jiggling knee and took regular sips. A hypnotic chill-out compilation played out of the stereo, but I was far from sleep. I felt completely wired. Why had Ethan gone off like that?

'No,' I said. 'I really don't think Ethan would do that. He's a massive flirt, but loyalty is important to him. It used to be, anyway. Besides, I was with him all the time, or knew who he was with. I think it was something else. I think, like you said, he got cold feet. Maybe I was going on at him too much,

146

trying to make him stay in too often, when he wanted to go out. I admit I got quite clingy towards the end. I'd phone him and ask him to come home when he was out, that kind of stupid thing. But he was terrible for just doing his own thing. Like tonight, for instance. I mean, where's he gone tonight?'

Maggie turned her head to face me.

'Did he come home?' Maggie said. 'When you asked?'

'Yes,' I said. 'He'd come home and try to find out what my problem was. He was always cool about it and listened to me. This didn't happen often, maybe only twice or three times, but I think it pissed him off, really. When I look back, I was quite pathetic. I don't know why I did it. I was testing him, I suppose.'

Maggie gestured to the crisps so I handed her the bowl. I felt weirdly at home in her flat, like I'd known Maggie for ages.

'Insecurity,' Maggie said. 'It's why everyone behaves like that, isn't it? You should have seen me after I found Sal. I turned into a complete psycho, but it was like I could see myself from the ceiling and I was appalled at what I'd become. I didn't want to be that mad woman who was screeching at her boyfriend, begging him to stay. And there was no way I could forgive him. So I had to change. But what's it like with Joe?'

I gulped down the last of my cocktail, registering that I would very soon need my bed.

'Different,' I said. 'I'm very relaxed with Joe, but I've known him my whole life and don't get myself so twisted up about him. But he doesn't go out like Ethan did, not on massive benders. And the balance of power is more equal between us.'

I yawned now and put my glass down, lifting my legs up onto the chaise longue and closing my eyes.

'I'm tired now,' I said. 'It's suddenly hit me.'

'Hmm,' Maggie said. 'Do you think Ethan has a problem with alcohol?'

I'd never even had that thought before and I dismissed it outright.

'No,' I said. 'He likes to drink, but he's not dependent on the stuff. Joe's dad is an alcoholic and there's a big, big difference.'

Maggie pulled herself into a sitting position, raking her curls back up into a ponytail. She looked tired now, her skin pale and eyeliner slightly smudged.

'Joe's dad's an alcoholic?' she asked. 'What's his mum like? Because these people will be your in-laws, you realize?'

I screwed up my nose, thinking of Joe's mum, who seemed continually defeated by life.

'Oh, she's OK,' I said. 'Depressed about anything and everything, so not much fun. I can't blame her, because she's married to his dad, who's a total pain in the arse. But she could have got away from him years ago and made her life and Joe's life better. Actually – and this is a bad thing to say – it pisses me off that his mum is alive and mine is dead, when mine was so much nicer. Horrible, aren't I?'

Maggie let her hair fall across her shoulders. She grinned at me kindly and I smiled back.

'No,' she said. 'I think you're great.'

'Thanks,' I said, lifting my glass towards her. 'Cheers. Here's to the Saturday Supper Club.'

'Cheers,' she said. 'Hey, you know now that Ethan has come between us we'll be fighting over his attention.'

I looked up at her and she winked at me mischievously.

'May the best girl win?' she said.

'What?' I said crossly. 'I'm not interested in Ethan, you're welcome to—'

'I'm joking,' she said. 'Ethan is off the menu. Maybe Andrew might be worth a one-night stand.'

'You're joking, right?' I said. 'He's about to have twins. Doesn't that count as baggage?'

Maggie stood up, stretched and picked up my glass. I lifted my hand to gesture that I'd had enough to drink.

'Of course I am,' she said, laughing. 'I'm not that bad! You must really think I'm a bitch.'

'Not remotely,' I said. 'You're quite fabulous, actually. My friend Isabel would love you, as long as you didn't try to seduce her husband—'

'Give me a break,' Maggie said, with a laugh.

Just then my phone rang. Joe? I almost fell over trying to get to my bag in time before the voicemail clicked in. I pulled it out of my bag and registered that I'd got two missed calls from Joe and that it was Daisy calling. I frowned. It was the middle of the night.

'What's she doing ringing this late?' I muttered, as I lifted the phone to my ear. A tremor of fear ran up my spine. I prayed that nothing was wrong with Dad.

'Are you OK, Daisy?' I said. 'What's up?'

In the background I could hear Benji whimpering. She must have been holding him, or cuddling him in bed.

'Benji can't sleep,' she said. 'I think he heard us talking about Iain in the garden the other day and now he thinks I'm about to take him to Canada and leave him there.'

Amy Bratley

I put my hand to my mouth.

'Oh no,' I said. 'Poor Benji. That's my fault. Sorry, Daisy. Why didn't I think he'd understand?'

'Don't worry, it's not your fault,' she said. 'I'm actually calling because Joe's been on the phone asking if you'd come over to me. He's worrying about you. He said he'd tried you a few times but you haven't answered. I said you might be with Isabel.'

I swallowed hard.

'Oh God,' I said, glancing at a clock on the wall. It was two-thirty a.m. 'I didn't realize the time. I didn't hear the phone.'

Daisy moved away from the phone while she spoke to Benji, then she was back, her voice clearer.

'You're not at that Supper Club, are you?' she said. 'With Ethan? Oh, Eve.'

'I'm . . .' I stuttered. 'Ethan's not—'

Daisy tutted and sighed.

'What's he had to say for himself this time?' she said coldly. 'Put him on the phone and I'll tell him exactly what—'

'He's gone,' I said. 'Ages ago. He went ages ago and I've been talking to Maggie. Look, I'm going home now. I'll send Joe a text to let him know. I'll see you tomorrow, Daisy.'

'OK,' she said. 'Just get home safely. Joe's worried.'

I hung up and held the phone in my hand, looking down at it. I suddenly felt weighed down with guilt. Joe was at home, probably waiting to propose, and I was drunk, talking about Ethan, who had kissed me hours earlier. I was the one acting like a total bitch.

'Are you OK?' Maggie asked, picking up a blanket from the

150

sofa and wrapping it around her shoulders. 'Ooh, I'm cold. Do you want another tequila sunrise?'

I shook my head, feeling more than anything that I wanted to be with Joe.

'I'm going to get a cab home,' I told her. 'I need to go home. I need to talk to Joe.'

Chapter Eleven

I woke up with what felt like a tractor ploughing my brain, overturning acres of muddy thoughts. I immediately remembered the kiss with Ethan and panicked. Had I ruined everything with Joe? Blinking in the sunlight that poured through the gaps around the blinds, I groaned and turned onto my side, tucking my hands under my head. Banjo jumped up onto the bed and, purring like a drill, clawed the duvet near my feet.

'Be still, Banjo,' I croaked. 'I feel sick.'

I opened my eyes wider and saw Joe watching me from his sun-dappled pillow, an amused smile on his face. I sighed quietly in relief and smiled tentatively as he put his hand out and touched my waist. I was home. I was safe. Joe didn't look angry.

'I must have been asleep when you got in,' he said. 'You realize you're still wearing your clothes?'

I looked down at myself and sighed, remembering, in a dream-like sequence, coming home. Yes, Joe had been asleep. No, I hadn't told him anything about Ethan.

'Oh God,' I said, realizing I still had to.

My stomach tied itself in knots. Food. I needed food before anything else.

'I need a bacon sandwich,' I said. 'With really, really crispy bacon and thick white sliced bread and lashings of tomato sauce. And maybe a fried egg and just one slice of crispy black pudding. I know it's wrong, but—'

'It's very wrong,' Joe said. 'Does your head hurt? Let me get you some painkillers and a glass of orange juice. Do you want to get those clothes off?'

'Yeah,' I said. 'I should have a shower.'

He kissed my forehead and I breathed in his comforting smell, warm and earthy from sleep. I rubbed my temples and, after trying to sit up, slumped back down into the horizontal position. Why was I *still* not telling Joe the truth? Why was I jeopardizing everything I had with him? I'd let the lie run for too long now. In my head I was screaming at myself to tell Joe about Ethan, just blurt it out then deal with the consequences. It was going to be in the bloody newspaper in two weeks' time.

'Oh God,' I said again, with a weak smile. 'What have I done?'

'I've been asking myself the same thing,' Joe laughed darkly.

'What do you mean?' I said.

'Oh, nothing,' he said, pushing the duvet back. He sat up, stretched and swung his legs over the side of the bed. He switched the radio on and Johnny Vaughn's voice filled the room.

'Looks like you had a good night,' Joe said. 'Who *are* those people you were drinking with? They must be hardcore. I think I could set fire to your breath. I thought you were just going out for a refined dinner party!'

I raised a smile. Now. I should just tell him now, I thought. Perhaps he wouldn't really care. But I knew he would. Joe was watching me carefully. I knew he was waiting for details. He could sense I was holding something back. I tried not to look guilty. I fumbled for the best way to tell him, then cowardly changed tack.

'Maggie gave me a tequila sunrise,' I said slowly. 'It tipped me over the edge. The food, though, was fantastic. I think she'll win the cash.'

I couldn't believe myself. All this would be in the paper, Joe's paper. Maybe Dominique had already told him about the coincidence. Moving into a sitting position, I reached for the glass of water by the bed and took a sip. I put my hand to my pounding head.

'Joe,' I began.

'Yes?' he said, looking, I thought, slightly fearful. Perhaps he knew I had something big to tell him. 'Let me get you those painkillers.'

'No, Joe,' I said. 'I'll be OK. I want to—'

'It won't take a minute,' he said. 'You look green. Hang on.'

Joe left the room. I closed my eyes and listened to him banging cupboard doors open and shut, much more loudly than was necessary. I clicked off the radio.

'Joe!' I called through to him haplessly. 'Sssshhh.'

'WHAT'S THAT?' he shouted through the wall. 'YOU OK?'

'Urrrggghhh!' I growled.

I put the pillow over my head, blocking out Joe's noise, and groaned. In the hot darkness, I tried to put Ethan out of my mind. I was probably still drunk, so there was no point trying to make sense of my feelings, or what I was thinking of when he kissed me. I touched my lips as I remembered the feeling of Ethan's lips on mine. Nothing had changed there. I still melted on his touch and, though I'd pushed him away, part of me had wanted it to go on and on. God! I blew out angrily into the pillow. This had to stop.

'Here you go,' came Joe's voice from outside the pillow zone. I peered out and smiled gratefully. 'On the bedside table. I've got to jump in the shower. I'm going to be late if I don't get my arse into gear. What about you?'

I thought about the day I had planned for myself, yet another Sunday sorting out the cafe. I had arranged to paint today, with Isabel, but the thought of doing anything that involved movement made me feel sick. I wanted to stay in bed and stare at the ceiling and work out how I felt.

'Cafe again,' I mumbled, as Joe went into the bathroom. 'But, Joe, I—'

Before I could finish, Joe picked up a towel and went into the bathroom. He wasn't making it easy. I heard him switch on the water and start his morning ritual of singing in the shower, really loudly. When, a few minutes later, he came back into the bedroom to change, I watched him self-consciously wrap a towel round his skinny middle, then roll deodorant under his arms. I sat up in bed, propped up by pillows.

'Joe, be still for a minute, will you?' I said. 'I need to speak to you. I'm trying to tell you something.'

He was halfway through pulling on a green T-shirt and paused to look at me, a worried expression on his face.

'That sounds serious,' he said. 'You're not going to dump me, are you? Am I too much of a skinny rake? Look at this body!'

He stretched out his slender arms and curled them into a muscle-man pose, to make me laugh.

'Don't be ridiculous,' I said, pushing a hand out from under the duvet to reach for the painkillers, resting on a stash of cookery books I kept by the bed. 'You're perfect.'

'Good,' he said. 'Because there's something I want to talk to you about, too. It's a surprise, really. So, shall we do all our talking tonight, over a bottle of wine?'

Surprise. Marriage. It had to be.

'Well,' I said, 'I think I should—'

'I can't wait to see your face,' he interrupted, with a grin. 'We can look forward to it all day.'

Deflated, I gave up trying to talk to him. Joe was completely preoccupied. I imagined engagement rings pinging into his eyes, like dollar signs on a fruit machine. I felt momentarily annoyed. Joe knew I wasn't ready for marriage, that we were fine as we were. Why was he so persistent? Wasn't our relationship good enough for him? He walked out of the bedroom to pick up his bag and earphones from the hallway table.

'For God's sake, Joe,' I muttered to myself. 'Why complicate life even more?'

While he rustled around in the hallway, with an enormous effort, I ventured out of bed, my head pounding with the after-effects of alcohol. I staggered to the blind, which I pulled up. I peered out to the street – my eyes narrow in the light – and watched a couple of cars whoosh by, one with its music blaring loud enough to make the windows vibrate. I stepped away from the window when I saw a man, delivering leaflets, dressed in shorts and T-shirt and flip-flops, whistling up the path past the daffodils and into the wisteria. Then I suddenly noticed a big empty space where Joe's car was normally parked. I scanned the street and panicked. Had it been stolen?

'Joe?' I said, moving out into the hallway, where Joe was kneeling to pick up the leaflet advertising pizza that had landed on the mat. 'Where's the Spider? Did you have to park up the road?'

Joe stood, twisted the catch and, with the door ajar, he smiled over at me.

'Sold it,' he said, lifting his hand up into a goodbye salute. 'Got to go.'

'Sold it?' I said, gobsmacked. He loved that car.

'Yep,' he said, with a curious grin. 'See you later.'

When I finally dragged myself into the cafe, I made my phone call to Dominique to give her a rundown of Maggie's dinner party. I graded her with a nine out of ten and talked about the delicious grilled baby artichoke salad for an unhealthy amount of time.

'Say hi to Joe for me,' Dominique said when I'd finished speaking. 'Tell him we miss his coffee run and want him to come in for more shifts.'

'Right,' I said, rolling my eyes. 'I will.'

After I'd hung up, I sat on a chair and looked around the cafe. There was still so much to do, but, most pressingly,

I needed to get on with preparation for the decoration. I wanted people to come here for the coffee, tea and home-made cakes and biscuits, but also for the atmosphere. I'd dreamt of lavender walls, pale mint-green painted tables, colourful glass vases filled with fresh flowers, lace tablecloths, mirrors on the walls, wooden chairs, scratched and scarred with life, cake stands made from chintzy plates. I had it all planned. But as I stood looking at the hideous wallpaper half stripped off the walls, I felt overwhelmed with the enormity of it all. How could I get it done alone? Just then, Isabel burst through the door.

'Sorry,' she panted. 'I'm so late. Sorry. I've been trying to sort out a problem with the couple renting our flat. One of their references was slightly dodgy.'

I smiled, relieved at the sight of her.

'Oh God,' I said. 'Well, you don't want them, then, do you? I'm so pleased you're here. I was just about to lie down and die.'

Isabel squeezed my arm and nodded.

'I think it was just a disgruntled landlord from when they were students,' she said. 'He said they'd broken a window catch or something. Christ, I don't care about window catches, but I had to follow it up. Anyway, so, how are you this morning, apart from wanting to die? How did last night go?'

I rolled up the sleeves of my shirt and breathed out noisily.

'Hungover,' I said. 'Terribly, horribly, miserably hungover. I have no one to blame but myself. Last night was, well, it was a bit of a nightmare. Ethan kissed me.'

Isabel, dressed in a black vest top and polka-dot skirt, rolled her eyes and shook her head. I frowned. I was expecting sympathy. She moved into the kitchen and started noisily pulling things out of boxes.

'Isabel?' I said, following her in. 'Are you OK?'

Isabel turned round and looked at me for a long moment, rubbed her forehead and sighed.

'You know you're my best friend and I love you, don't you?' she said. 'You know that I support everything you do in life, even if it's really bizarre, like buying those hideous platforms last summer.'

A smile flicked across her lips and I laughed, remembering the offensive shoes I'd bought on a whim.

'Yes,' I said. 'I admit those platforms were a mistake, but what's this about?'

'Look,' she said, giving me a sad smile. 'I'm worried about you. You obviously still have strong feelings for Ethan, but I think you need to think about what you're doing really, really carefully. You're treading on dangerous ground and I think you're really close to ruining everything with Joe.'

I blushed, wanting to come to my own defence but suddenly lost for words. I felt like Isabel was telling me off – she never normally said anything so critical.

'I don't know how I feel,' I said, shaking my head. 'I was just a bit drunk and now I'm hungover. Ethan kissed me, but nothing's really changed.'

Reaching for a mug on the drying rack, I moved to the sink and poured myself some cold water and drank it down to try and get rid of the nausea I felt. Was Isabel right? Had I really been that close to being unfaithful to Joe?

'Everything's changed,' Isabel said. 'Since Ethan turned up, you've been in a daze. You say nothing's changed, but I think you are being disloyal to Joe by not telling him about all this. I don't want you losing yourself over Ethan all over again. And I don't want you to lose Joe, just because you're too scared to commit to someone who genuinely loves you and will stick around forever.'

'Losing myself?' I said, though I knew exactly what she was talking about.

She nodded, her eyes wide with concern.

'Yes,' she said. 'When you were with Ethan you lived his life and not your own. All you cared about was him. I know he's a big character and sometimes it's hard to be visible behind those people, but you can't go back there.'

Both of our faces were flushed. I looked at the floor.

'That's unfair,' I said. 'I cared about lots of other things when I was with him. I was just in love with him, that's all. I thought he was my soulmate.'

'I know you felt that,' she said. 'And again, I'm not denying that you were very much in love with him, but don't forget he just disappeared, without so much as a goodbye, and you spent the next God knows how long moping around over him. I can't believe you're even entertaining the thought of letting something happen with Ethan. He's no good for you. You can't trust him.'

'I used to trust him,' I said. 'I would have died for him. I don't have that with Joe, and anyway, I'm not entertaining the thought of anything happening with Ethan! Oh, I'm so confused!'

Isabel shook her head. Her hands were trembling. Wasn't she disproportionately cross? A thought struck me. Before she married Robert, Isabel had confessed to me that he wasn't her

The Saturday Supper Club

soulmate, but that she knew he'd make a good husband. She had been right, he had made a good husband, but perhaps all this with Ethan was stirring up some of those longings inside her.

'But you have so much else with Joe,' she went on. 'You have love and loyalty and kindness, and he's funny, too, and warm.'

'I know,' I said. 'You don't have to tell me that. Isabel, does this have anything to do with you?'

She looked at me in alarm.

'What on earth do you mean?' she said.

'I mean,' I said with a big sigh, 'is it making you question things with Robert?'

As soon as I said the words I wished I hadn't. Isabel looked as if she was going to cry and I bit my lip, cringing at myself.

'I'm sorry,' I said. 'I shouldn't have said that. I'm just thinking of something you told me ages ago. That was wrong of me. Look, I'm hungover. Ethan's history. This is helping me, seeing him again; even if I did feel tempted, it was only in passing. I'm just trying to find resolution. I love Joe, you know I do.'

'I know,' she said, recovering herself. 'But what's going to happen next time you see him? Last time it was a kiss, next time what?'

I opened my mouth and closed it again, before biting my bottom lip again. Then I shrugged a helpless, hungover shrug.

'Oh Isabel!' I said. 'I don't know what I'm doing. Help me! I'm so confused. What will I do without you?'

I opened my arms to hug Isabel and watched tears spring into her eyes.

'Isabel,' I said, taken aback. 'Don't cry. Why are you crying?'

'It's just . . .' she said. 'Oh, I know you'll do what you want in the end, and if you really love Ethan, I know you'll follow your heart. The rubbish thing is that I won't be here to help you pick up the pieces.'

My eyes filled with tears too.

'I'm going to miss you so much,' I said. 'But don't worry about me. I'll be fine.'

I'd known Isabel since university, when we met in a lecture about postmodernist film theory. She'd written: 'Bored out of my tiny mind' on her lecture notes and slid them along the desk to me. I wrote: 'Tiny minds think alike', and we went to the Student Union bar to sink a few pints of snakebite, because when in doubt, that's what we did. After that we became inseparable. Isabel was my best friend. She was completely fabulous. I loved her. And now she was going. What would I do without her?

'We can Skype, I suppose,' she said quietly. 'And I will be back. We won't stay out there forever. Jesus, last thing I heard about Dubai was that a couple were arrested for kissing in public. Doesn't exactly sound like my sort of place. And this cafe could be so good,' she continued. 'I don't want you getting sidetracked by Ethan when you've got this opportunity here that might just be the start of something great—'

'Ethan would love to get his hands on this place,' I said, immediately regretting it.

'I'm sure this place isn't the only thing he'd love to get his hands on,' said Isabel. 'Seriously, though, I might as well say what I think: the guy's an absolute wanker! He hurt you once so I hate his guts. And, FYI, Robert might be a bit of a bore – and I know what I said to you before we got married – but I do, actually, genuinely love him.'

'Good,' I said.

'Good,' she said.

'Right,' I said. 'Shall we get on? We can pause for more emotional wrangling whenever we need to?'

'Yes,' she said, grinning. 'Sounds like a good plan.'

I passed her a dust sheet, which she started to unfold. I turned towards the door as I heard it opening.

'Hello?' said a voice from the doorway. 'Eve?'

'Oh, hi, Daisy,' I said, seeing Daisy standing in her bicycle helmet, pink-cheeked from the ride in the sun. She smiled, unclipped her helmet and rested down her bicycle basket. It was packed with picnic foods and a blanket. I suddenly remembered we were supposed to be meeting in the park for a picnic lunch.

'Hi, Eve,' she said. 'Hello, Isabel, how are you?'

'Yeah,' Isabel replied, wiping a stray tear from under her eye. 'Not bad, thanks, Daisy, not bad. And you?'

Daisy sighed and nodded and shrugged all at the same time, so there was no telling how she was.

'Tired,' she said. 'I was up half the night.'

She shot me a look and I remembered her phone call at two a.m.

'Shit,' I said. 'Daisy, we're having lunch to talk about Dad's party, aren't we? So sorry, I forgot. I shouldn't really leave Isabel because we've got so much to do here, or maybe you'd like to come along—'

Amy Bratley

I looked at Isabel, who shook her head and waved her hand in the air.

'No,' Isabel said. 'You go. You won't be long, will you? I'll get everything ready so we can work all afternoon. And besides, we'd better get used to being apart.'

We pulled sulky faces at each other and Isabel pretended to burst into tears.

'I'll bake a chocolate cake when I get back,' I said. 'To try out the kitchen equipment.'

'Sounds like a plan,' she said. 'We can have half each.'

I smiled. I was going to miss Isabel. London would not be London without her.

Chapter Twelve

'You shouldn't be so selfish,' Daisy snapped at me, out in the street, when I told her how gutted I was that Isabel was leaving London for Dubai.

'What?' I said, open-mouthed. 'How is that selfish? She's my best friend, I'm bound to be upset. She's upset too.'

'Because,' said Daisy, pulling off her pink bicycle helmet and putting it in her bike basket, 'she's the one who's got to pack up and go to a new place where she won't know anyone. She's probably feeling terrified.'

I frowned and glared at her profile, but Daisy continued looking forwards, pushing her bike, an Orla Kiely rucksack on her back, as we walked quickly along the road to the park. I thought, fleetingly, how grown-up Daisy looked, in her smart Jigsaw capri pants and sheer short-sleeve blouse, wooden bangles jangling on her slim wrist. She seemed incredibly together, whereas I felt shambolic in comparison. She was a single mum of a crazy toddler, yet still had an important job working for the Housing Association and was the kind of person who volunteered for Shelter in the winter months, handing out blankets to homeless people. The sort of thing I talked about, but never actually did.

'And, you know, Dubai isn't Paris or New York,' she said. 'She's going to have a massive culture shock. I don't envy her.'

The pavement was bustling with people today, walking out in the sunshine. I stepped out onto the road to avoid a harassed-looking mother pushing a buggy and holding a toddler's hand, shopping bags digging into her wrists. A driver beeped his horn at me and Daisy grabbed my arm and pulled me back onto the pavement.

'For God's sake, be careful!' she said, her eyes shining. 'The whole world does not revolve around you. You know?'

'Daisy!' I said, standing suddenly still in the middle of the pavement, causing everyone around me to tut and mutter in complaint. 'Why are you so mad with me today? I'm sorry about last night. Are you pissed off with me?'

Though I loved Daisy with all my heart and felt I knew her well, sometimes she was a total conundrum. When she relaxed she was delightful, charming, funny and kind. But other times, she was bad-tempered and irritable and hard to work out. Life had not exactly dealt Daisy a great hand and it had always been my role to attempt to placate her, to cheer her up, but today, I didn't feel like it. I had a banging hangover, a million things to do at the cafe and I was going to miss Isabel like mad. I had every right to be a tiny bit pissed off, didn't I?

'No, come on,' she said, steering me by my elbow. 'Let's get to the park.'

We carried on walking to the park in the sweltering heat, with Daisy sighing at the people walking too slowly in front of us, me silently fuming at her criticism of me. I shot her a look, but she stared straight ahead. So many people had had the same idea, to picnic in the park, and were spread out on blankets covering the grass, that there was hardly any room left to sit. I pointed to an oak tree, slightly up the hill, which had space underneath the shade of its branches.

'How about under there?' I said, heading to the spot, my anger mounting. 'By the way, that was unfair, Daisy. I'm not selfish. I'm upset. I'll miss her so much. This will do, won't it?'

I was pleased for the cool shade of the tree, and flopped down on the grass, which was peppered with buttercups, leaning back on my hands. I watched as Daisy pulled the picnic blanket out of the basket and flicked it out so hard, it made a snapping sound. Without speaking, she kicked off her sandals then pulled a selection of Tupperware pots out of her rucksack, yanking off the lids and tossing them into the centre of the mat. She'd gone to a lot of effort; there were slices of homemade tortilla, juicy tomato, fennel and red-onion salad, red cabbage coleslaw and a block of cheese wrapped in brown paper. She broke up a baguette and handed me a wedge, pointed at the plates and cutlery and gestured for me to help myself, then pushed her sunglasses onto the top of her head and rubbed her temples.

'Daisy?' I said, sitting forward. 'Are you all right? You seem majorly pissed off. This food looks amazing, by the way. Thank you. Why did you go to so much effort? You didn't have to.'

She gave me the tiniest smile. I hoped she was softening slightly. I was usually pretty good at reading people, but Daisy was really confusing me. I smiled a bland smile in return, trying to communicate my confusion at her mood.

'Oh, I'm sorry,' she said, with a massive sigh. 'I shouldn't have said all that. I'm just really stressed out. I didn't get any sleep and this new housing project I'm helping on is an unmitigated disaster. I thought we deserved a good lunch, so I spent an inordinate amount of time making it this morning.'

She paused to pour lemonade into plastic glasses. She handed me one and I took a deep drink, feeling the bubbles burst on my tongue. It took me back, immediately, to coming home from school, when our mum was still alive. She'd give us a glass of lemonade, poured over ice cubes, and a fresh slice of homemade shortbread while we changed into play clothes, carelessly casting our uniforms aside on our bedroom floors.

'My boss phoned me this morning – on a Sunday – to tell me that the windows for the bathrooms in an entire block of flats in Stockwell are all wrongly sized,' she said. 'And apparently I signed them off, so I'm the one to blame for a great chunk of wasted budget. Thousands and thousands of pounds. Thing is, I hardly even remember signing the form. I'm so mad with myself. I never fuck up at work and now I'm going to be hauled up in front of the finance director tomorrow, who's a real dragon. I'll probably lose my job over this.'

I spooned some of the tomato salad onto my plastic plate, breathing in the fragrance of basil, unwrapped the cheese then picked up a knife.

'What a nightmare!' I said, starting to cut a few slices of cheese. 'Surely you won't just get the sack for one mistake. Wasn't it the architect's fault really? Shouldn't they have got the measurements right in the first place?'

'Don't cut it like that,' Daisy sighed, pulling the knife from my hand. 'You need to do it at this angle.'

'I'm not a complete moron, I do know how to cut cheese!' I said, sitting back and rolling my eyes. 'Can I have the knife, please? Can't you blame the architect, then?'

'Just let me do it,' she said, not giving me the knife back and cutting into the cheese. 'But no, I can't blame anyone. That's the point of my job; I have to be accountable for everything. Oh God! I'm so angry with myself. Anyway, there's no point talking about it. What's done is done. I'll just have to see what the dragon says.'

Her mouth was set in a grimace, the corners of her lips slightly downturned. I wondered if she was about to cry. I put my hand out to pat her arm gently and she patted my hand briefly in acknowledgement.

'I'm also worrying about Dad,' she said, glancing up at me. 'He's still being really weird. I've asked him about his trips to the GP, but he just laughs. He's being quite secretive, if you ask me. When I dropped Benji off with him this morning, he was on the phone to someone, but wouldn't say who. Anyway, more importantly, what about Ethan last night? Did you talk more? You shouldn't have gone, you know.'

The mention of Ethan's name made a shiver pass through my body despite the scorching midday heat.

'I know what you think,' I said, shaking my head. 'But we didn't really get to talk much. More lemonade? I'm so thirsty today.'

I drank down another whole glass of lemonade and held the cup against my cheek in an attempt to cool down. I was fed up with people telling me I was wrong to have seen Ethan. I thought about what Maggie had said: that I was being brave and finding out how I really felt. Beyond us, a group of friends started a game of frisbee, the blue disc spinning through the air and landing in someone else's picnic.

'I think you should speak to Dad,' she said. 'Will you? You know you're his favourite; he'll probably open up to you, but I could ask him until I'm blue in the face and he won't tell me.'

I watched Daisy, trying to figure out if she was joking, but she was deadly serious.

'I'm not his favourite!' I said. 'Don't be daft.'

'You are so,' she said, quite coldly. 'You're such a daddy's girl. I was much more of a mummy's girl. We did everything together, Mum and I.'

Daisy paused. I saw, quite unusually for her, she had bags under her eyes. That was my fault. A tear ran down her cheek and she quickly, almost angrily, wiped it away.

'Oh, Daisy,' I said. 'Don't get upset.'

'You know, I'm really missing her at the moment,' she said. 'When I stop and think about her dying, I feel this awful emptiness. I wish I'd told her I loved her more than I did. I wish I'd said goodbye. I wish she was still alive.'

'Oh, Daisy,' I said, putting my arm around her. 'So do I.'

Daisy made a humming sound that she always made when she was about to get really upset and I hugged her tight. Though I knew she missed her terribly, Daisy rarely spoke about our mum's death.

'I'd been a real brat to her those last few days of her life,' she said. 'And when she actually died, I wasn't even with her. I was throwing a tantrum in the hospital car park.'

'You were angry and upset,' I said, passing her a tissue. 'We were both just kids, but you understood better than I did. It was hard for you.'

Daisy wiped her eyes, collected herself and stared off into the distance, biting her top lip.

'You know, you're so much like her,' she said suddenly. 'Sometimes when I see you, I have such a strong sensation of her it blows me away.'

'That's what Dad says,' I said. 'I can't see it myself – when I look at pictures, I mean.'

I said that, but I could really. I just never knew what to say in these situations, because, for some reason, I didn't feel I could claim my mother in the same way as Daisy, because she was older and so had known her for longer before she died. I'd always been the person who tried to cheer everyone else up, to try actually to step into our mum's shoes and do as she did. We sat quietly for a while, in slightly strained silence, while Daisy picked at the food. I lay down on the picnic mat and closed my eyes, listening to the sounds of the park all around us; children shouting, music playing and the spooky chiming of an ice-cream van in the distance.

'I wonder what she'd think of us now,' I said, watching a family nearby set up deckchairs and empty out a massive icebox. The mum was handing out sandwiches to the children, smiling brightly.

'I really wanted to live in a way that would make her proud,' said Daisy. 'But I feel like I'm failing miserably, and if she knew what I was like with Benji . . . Sometimes he makes me so tired and irritable, I—'

Tears started to roll down Daisy's cheeks harder now and she choked on her words. I was taken aback. She was normally such a controlled, private person; I'd only seen Daisy this upset once or twice in her adult life.

'Of course she'd be proud of you!' I said, rubbing my hand on her back. 'You've got a great job, you've taken care of me and Dad brilliantly, you're a lovely mummy to Benji. Daisy, don't cry, this isn't like you. You're just anxious about your job and you didn't get enough sleep last night. If anyone's messing their life up, it's me, not you. Mum would be proud of you. I'm not sure what she'd make of me, though.'

I had meant to sound flippant about my own life, but we both heard something catch in my voice and Daisy stared at me, her brow furrowed.

'Why?' she said. 'I've always thought your life is a great big party. Apart from a couple of blips, you've got loads of friends, you're just opening your dream cafe, you've got a fantastic boyfriend who keeps proposing and Dad adores you so much. You seem to be strolling through life, to me. You are, aren't you? Happy, I mean. Or is this Ethan stuff making you miserable?'

I shrugged, half nodded and pulled a face.

'The cafe's great in theory, but I've got to find a load more cash for the kitchen,' I said. 'I'm convinced that Joe is about to propose for real this time and I don't know what to say because Ethan's come back and . . . I don't know. I still have feelings for him, Daisy, I really do. What am I going to say when Joe asks me to marry him? I'm utterly confused. Ethan was a little bit more than a blip, you know that.'

The words gushed out of my mouth and I stopped in surprise at the force of them. Daisy leaned her head back and stared up at the cloudless sky as if utterly exasperated. She blew air out of her nostrils then screwed up the paper the cheese had been wrapped in and threw it into the middle of the picnic mat. She didn't say anything, or crack a smile, just put her sunglasses back on. I eyed her warily. Maybe she hadn't heard me?

'I still have feelings for him,' I tried again. 'There's something between us, despite everything that happened. Part of me still loves Ethan and I don't know what to do about it.'

'Don't be stupid,' she said crossly. 'You're being completely ridiculous. What are you thinking of?'

I felt my cheeks redden, but I tried to stay calm.

'I'm not being stupid,' I said. 'I'm trying to work out how I feel. You know how much I loved him. I love Joe, obviously, but now that Ethan's come back, it's hard to be clear about what I want, especially if marriage is on the cards.'

Daisy shook her head and released a bitter laugh.

'You're being ridiculous,' she said again. 'I can't believe you're even considering Ethan at all. He abandoned you. You're with Joe now. Why don't you start behaving like an adult, instead of a love-struck teenager? Jesus, Eve, you really don't know you're born with Joe and if he proposes you should jump at the chance. Look at the luck I've had with men.'

'Is that what this is about?' I said. 'You're pissed off because Iain was a shit to you?'

I felt suddenly guilty and wondered fleetingly if the family on the next picnic blanket could hear us bickering.

'Let's just change the subject,' I said. 'This is all getting too weird.'

'Oh, I wish you'd just grow up,' she said. 'You need to tell Ethan where to go. He's not right for you. I always knew that.'

Daisy always did this, claimed she knew Ethan really well, just because she'd been friends with him before I met him. I stood up, brushing the crumbs off my clothes.

'Well, you could have done me a favour and told me that, rather than introduce us that day,' I said, my voice breaking. 'And you know, Daisy, you're treating me like a child. You're not my mother.'

I could tell both of us were almost in tears. As soon as the words had escaped my lips I regretted them.

'I know I'm not your mother,' she said, her voice shaking. 'If you'd forgotten, we haven't got one. *I* haven't got one.'

'You think I don't know!' I said, exasperated, grabbing her wrist. 'Jesus, it's dominated the whole of my life! Where's your mum, Eve? Why don't you have a mum, Eve? What did your mum die of, Eve?'

I was shaking now. I had never said these things before. My voice grew thin and high and I wished I would just shut up.

'And there's . . . there's . . . always been this *thing* with you that I can't explain, this *atmosphere*,' I said. 'You blow so hot and cold, I don't know where I stand. Why do you get so cross with me sometimes? Why were you so cross with me when Mum died? Did you not realize I was grieving too? You were the older sister, you could have looked out for me a bit more!'

Daisy's face paled. She was standing now, tucking her hair into her bicycle helmet, keeping her mouth closed, completely withdrawing from me. As I stood there, shaking, she bent to pick up the Tupperware and pushed them into her rucksack, before mechanically rolling up the picnic blanket. She got onto her bike, while tears filled my eyes.

'I'm cross with myself, not you,' she said, her voice trembling. 'That's the whole point. I'm cross with myself. I'm making a mess of life, not you. And I'm sorry I didn't react

174

properly when Mum died, but the way you tried to be her, the way you started cooking like she did, putting flowers on the table, all that. I hated it. I didn't want to pretend like she hadn't died, just pick up where she left off. And everything you did, Dad loved, but I . . . I . . . couldn't do anything right. Just because I didn't know how to be, everyone ignored me.'

Daisy started to cry. I grabbed her hand and held it in mine.

'I wasn't pretending she hadn't died,' I said, also in tears. 'I wanted us to be together, me, you and Dad. And getting a meal on the table was the only way I could think to do it. It was the only way I could get you to sit with me. I was lonely. I was trying. You weren't shunned, at all. I was the one who felt shunned. Daisy, I've always thought you weren't interested in me, that I was your annoying little sister. Daisy, I love you, please, let's not . . . this is horrible . . . don't go.'

Daisy got on her bike, wobbled slightly, then set off cycling down the hill, leaving me standing there, fired up with emotion, feeling half like crying and half like screaming. I called after her, but she didn't turn around.

'Daisy!' I said again, but she was a speck in the distance now, cycling quickly away. Noticing a woman looking at me sympathetically, I wiped my eyes. I stumbled through the park, past all the people enjoying themselves, and back to the cafe. I opened the creaky door and let it slam behind me. The radio was on loud. I called out to Isabel in a weak voice. She appeared in the kitchen doorway, a wallpaper scraper in her hand.

'What's happened to you?' Isabel said, pulling her dust mask away from her face, her eyes full of concern.

'Don't ask,' I said. 'Daisy has just exploded at me. I'm in shock.'

She pulled out a chair, removed a can of paint and gestured for me to sit down.

'You sit and talk,' she said. 'I'll work and listen.'

Chapter Thirteen

When I arrived home that evening, my entire body ached from stripping wallpaper and repairing patches of damaged plaster in preparation for a fresh coat of paint. I had plaster dust in my eyes and hair, bits of wallpaper in my fingernails and felt in need of a long soak in the bath. Isabel had offered to stay longer, but I was exhausted and promised to return early the next day. I sat down at my kitchen table with a large glass of red wine and rested my face in my hands. In front of me was a vase of dusky pink roses, filling the room with their sweet smell, like Turkish Delight dipped in icing sugar. Next to them was a note from Joe, saying he'd be back soon with a surprise for me. I remembered what he'd said that morning about wanting to talk. I rubbed my chin worriedly. An hour earlier, just as I'd left the cafe after telling Isabel about Daisy's emotional outburst, I'd had a phone call from Ethan. When I'd seen it was his number I hadn't picked up, but he'd left a message, saying he wanted to meet before Andrew's dinner party. I'd blushed just at the sound of his voice. Now I couldn't get his words out of my head.

'What am I going to do?' I said out loud, feeling immediately silly, my voice resonating in the quiet room.

I looked around the kitchen, running my eyes over the photographs of me and Joe on holiday in Barcelona pinned on the notice board, at last year's tickets for Glastonbury we had bought at great expense, at the Tandoori Nights takeaway menu with Joe's favourite dishes circled in red pen, mine in blue. I stared out of the window, which was streaked in rain, the sky beyond it now grey and threatening. Ethan was out there somewhere, stalking through London's streets, thinking and feeling. Joe was, too. But he would be home soon and I'd more or less convinced myself he was going to propose. But what would I say? There wasn't really a 'not sure' option to that question. I remembered Daisy's words, telling me I should bite off Joe's hand if he asked me to marry him. I loved Joe dearly; he was almost an integral part of me. But if I really was in love with him, would I still have feelings for Ethan? Why couldn't I let Ethan go? Wasn't it enough to have been deserted by him? I shook my head, annoyed at my contradictory thoughts. If only it could be simple, like when my parents had got together. Their love story was black and white. Their eyes met over a tape measure and they discovered, literally, that they were the perfect fit. She'd measured him up for a suit one morning, in the dressmaking and tailor shop she worked in, and he asked her to marry him that afternoon. I suppose I'd thought my relationship with Ethan was like theirs when we first met – or I wanted it to be, anyway. I sighed and looked around the kitchen. I needed to do something.

'Baking,' I thought. 'I'll bake that cake Mum used to make. Where is the recipe? Somewhere . . .'

Reaching over to a pile of papers wedged into my recipe book, I found the piece of notepaper with my mum's recipe written on it in her youthful loopy script and ran my finger down the list of ingredients. Good. I had everything. Pushing the chair back, I switched on the light because the rain outside made the kitchen gloomy, and pulled the ingredients from the cupboards, placing them onto the kitchen table. I put on my apron, found my favourite pink mixing bowl and wooden spoon. I creamed together the butter and sugar, added vanilla, eggs, folded in flour, ground almonds and melted dark chocolate.

As I worked, I thought about Joe and tried to imagine what he would say when he came home. My heart ached for him now, wherever he was, pacing along the pavement, homeward, with a hopeful smile on his lips, most probably planning his speech. I knew Joe. He would be enjoying his secret, delighting in the anticipation. But I had the most horrible feeling that I was going to hurt him. Even though I loved Joe. Even though part of me really, really wanted to say yes. Even though I knew I'd be happy with Joe, I *was* happy with Joe, I couldn't tear myself away from the tiny red warning flag waving in my heart. Happiness is treacherous. It can be snatched away at any given moment. And now, with Ethan here, was this a sign that I wasn't even with the right man?

I needed time to think. I needed to see Ethan again. I needed to be fair and honest with Joe, even though it would cost me. I poured the mixture into a baking tin, licking the spoon then throwing it into the sink. I opened the oven and put in the cake. There were voices in my head telling me I was being a coward. I was being weak by seeing Ethan again. That I should decide to marry Joe, commit and live with my decision. But I didn't listen to those voices. I slammed shut the oven door, pulled off my oven gloves, threw them onto the counter and reached for my glass of wine. I took a big glug, stopping abruptly when I heard the front door open then close.

'Hey,' Joe said, suddenly behind me. 'Baking again? You look pretty damn hot in that apron.'

Joe stood in the doorway, wet from the rain. He was smiling shyly. My stomach turned over. I felt desperate to hug him. I walked over to him. I loved Joe so much. He kissed me and hugged me tight, but his eyes flicked around the room nervously. I knew he was working out how he was going to propose. My palms felt clammy.

'I'm trying out my mum's recipe,' I said. 'The one she cooked for my dad. Lovely roses, by the way. Thanks.'

'I bought this,' he said, moving away from me, pulling a bottle of wine from his bag and putting it on the table, then getting two glasses from the cupboard. 'I thought we could talk. There's something I want to give you.'

A smile flicked over his lips. I swallowed hard, staring at the bottle of wine, my cheeks flushing.

'Joe,' I said, my heart pounding in my chest. 'Look, before you say or do anything else, I might as well come out and say it.'

My heart was racing and my mouth dry. I knew that what I was about to say was going to change everything, but I couldn't go on being unfair. It wasn't right. Joe must have sensed my distress, because his face paled and he folded his arms across his chest, wedging his hands under his armpits, as if preparing himself for the bullet.

'Yes?' he said. 'What's up?'

'I . . . I . . .' I said, wishing I'd never started, but forcing myself to go on. 'You know how much I love you, don't you, Joe? Right from when we were kids, you were my best friend. I admire you and don't know anyone as kind and sweet as you. I know that I can tell you anything and I always have told you everything, but there's something on my mind that I haven't told you and I can't hold it from you any more . . .'

I paused, staring at lovely, familiar Joe, wondering why I was going to tell him I didn't want to marry him. Suddenly I didn't know any more, but an inner voice drove me to carry on speaking.

'Joe,' I said, with a deep breath. 'I do love you—'

'But?' he said, with a quick, wary smile.

'But,' I said carefully, 'I don't want to get married. I've guessed, from what people have told me, my dad and Isabel, that you're about to propose, which is amazing and I hate to spoil this moment. I'm so flattered. But Joe, I want to say no, before you even ask, so I don't have to reject you, because I love you too much for that.'

I sighed, because I knew what I'd said didn't make sense.

'That's a bit of a head-fuck,' Joe said, frowning. 'You want to say no because you love me too much?'

He let out a strained laugh. I gave him a sad, uncertain smile. In the background my mobile was ringing repeatedly. Ethan. I wished it would stop. The kitchen light seemed too bright. I wished we were in the garden, where I could breathe.

'It's because right now, I'm not in the place to make a commitment like that,' I said. 'I'm . . . I . . . need a bit of space to think about stuff, to sort my head out about how I feel, and I know that this sounds awful but it's really, really important that we're both completely sure, isn't it—'

Awful? It sounded more than awful. The enormity of what I was saying hit me and I felt dizzy. I put myself in Joe's shoes and felt completely gutted that I was hurting him so badly. After everything he had done for me, everything he'd ever said about the importance of his relationship with me. I was destroying it for him. What was I saying? Was I breaking up with him? This was disastrous. Even though he wasn't speaking or moving, I felt Joe withdrawing from me before my eyes. I wanted to grab hold of him and take it all back.

'I'm not being very eloquent,' I said.

I searched my mind for words, but couldn't find any. I felt Joe's eyes on me but I didn't want to look at him, because I felt ashamed. Because being with Joe was safe and lovely and warm, and now that I'd said all this out loud, I didn't want to be without him. I flopped down onto the chair.

'I wasn't going to propose,' Joe said, his eyes glistening with tears. He averted his gaze and pulled something from his bag.

'What?' I asked, eyes wide. 'Isabel said . . . I thought—'

My stomach filled with cement.

'No,' he said, shaking his head defiantly. 'I was going to give you this.'

He handed me a white envelope. I looked up at him quizzically and he shrugged, biting his lip as he did so. I knew him so well. I knew that he was holding back tears.

'Do you want me to open it?' I said quietly.

He nodded, so, with the oven humming behind us, I opened up the envelope. Inside was a cheque for £15,000 and an illustration Joe had done of the cafe, with my name written on the signage. The rest of the money for the cafe. Joe had given me the money. Tears streamed down my face.

'Oh, Joe,' I whispered. 'How did you get this? I can't accept it . . . but, Joe, you're amazing, completely amazing. I'm so sorry, I—'

I was lost for words, completely drained. I held out the envelope towards him, but he shook his head.

'It's yours,' Joe said. 'I sold the Spider, I borrowed some from your Dad, I raided my savings. It's yours for the cafe, so you don't have to fret about getting the kitchen equipment. It's what you've always wanted, your dream. I wasn't going to propose. I just wanted to make you happy, but at least I know now that you're not. I'm going to go back to my place for a while, I've been staying here too much anyway, you should have said . . .'

'No, Joe,' I said, shaking my head in confusion. 'I don't want you to go. Look, I got my wires crossed and—'

'What?' he said, looking at me like I was speaking another language. 'I'm hardly going to stay after your little speech. It's for the best. At least I know—'

Joe's lips were quivering. I felt sick. I wanted to comfort him, but I couldn't. I wanted us to cook dinner and drink wine, like we normally did. I rubbed my forehead with my hand, not knowing what to do, while he picked up a few things: his guitar, his boots and a bag of clothes. He didn't even look at me again, just silently collected his possessions. I started to panic and wrapped my arms around my middle, following him from room to room, to stop myself from grabbing hold of him, begging him to stay. He stood by the front door and glared at me.

'Joe,' I said, holding up the envelope. 'This money—'

'Yours,' he said coldly, our eyes locking briefly. 'Don't fuck it up.'

He opened and slammed the door and I pressed my nose up against the stained-glass panels, watching him walk down the garden path in the rain and turn left towards the train station. He had his head down, his bag thrown over his shoulder. He wiped his eyes. Tears soaked my cheeks and I slipped down to the floor of the hallway, letting them splash onto my thighs. What had I done? I stayed there for a while, just staring at the floor, where my tears were making black circles, replaying Joe's words in my head, still holding on to the envelope. I couldn't believe he'd sold his car to help me out. And how had I repaid him? By being weak and pathetic, by not knowing my own mind, by being tempted. Then the smoke alarm went off.

'My cake!' I said, leaping up to stand.

I clamped my hands over my ears, running into the kitchen to turn off the oven. I grabbed a tea-towel from the back of a chair and flapped it madly under the smoke alarm until it stopped. Coughing, I pushed open the window and, using the tea-towel, extracted the cake from the oven. It was burnt black, a thin stream of smoke pouring out of the top. I slid the whole thing into the sink and turned on the cold tap. The pan hissed in the water. I stood stock still for a moment, clutching the back of a kitchen chair, my knuckles white. I imagined what it would feel like to scream. Then I reached for one of the wine glasses Joe had got out of the cupboard. I threw it at the wall and watched it smash.

Chapter Fourteen

A while later, the broken glass still littered on the kitchen floor, I grabbed my keys, purse and mobile phone and walked out of the flat, into the pouring rain. It was growing darker and I wasn't sure where I was going, but I wanted to be outside, among people, lost in the city somewhere, anonymous. I didn't want to be alone with the sinking silence of what I'd just done to Joe. I felt oddly blank and my hands were trembling. My hair smelt of burnt cake and it wasn't until I reached the end of my street that I noticed I still had my apron on. Nobody I'd walked past had even batted an eyelid. In my pocket was Joe's beautiful illustration. I glanced at it, then folded it up and held on to it tightly, walking quickly through the streets, busy with people coming and going, some with their heads bent under umbrellas, others not caring about the rain. I carried on towards the bus stop, standing waiting while buses squelched through puddles on the road, wanting desperately to talk to Isabel. I wanted to ask her what she knew about Joe's money for the cafe. Why hadn't she told me about his plans? Why had she let me think he was going to propose, I thought furiously. But it wasn't her fault, was it? Not in the least. I sighed. Boarding a bus headed for Brixton, I let myself imagine that I hadn't told Joe I needed time to think, that we were warm and dry in the flat, drinking that bottle of wine, slicing into the cake, planning how to finish the cafe now I didn't have to worry about money. Images of my plans – deliberately mismatched crockery, cake stands laden with home-baked treats, old-fashioned standing lamps, lace doilies, wooden tables decorated with old-fashioned posters, a large chalkboard for children to draw on and a bookshelf of books for them, too – popped into my head. Joe had gone to all that effort to help me realize my dream. No one had ever done anything so generous, and it wasn't just the money itself. It was the effort involved – the thought and the self-sacrifice. He'd sold his beloved Spider! I felt sick. I didn't deserve someone like Joe, I thought bleakly. He was far too good for me. I'd done him a favour. I found my mobile in my bag and keyed in Isabel's number, but her phone was off. For a moment I thought about calling Daisy, but, after our argument in the park, quickly dismissed the idea. Daisy would be furious with me. She would never understand how I could be unsure about making a commitment to Joe. Or why I would be thinking about Ethan again after what he'd done. In her eyes, if someone wronged you, they didn't get another chance. Look at Iain. Since he'd dumped her, she point-blank refused to have anything to do with him, would rarely even speak about him. Anyway, Daisy had been tired and upset about Mum. She was in no place to comfort me.

Mum. It seemed almost ridiculous to think such a thing, but as we reached Brixton I looked up at the big dark rain clouds, moving across the skyline, a backdrop to the black railway line cutting across the busy road, and I felt an old longing open up inside of me like a flower blooming in fast-forward. I never let myself think like this. It was too dangerous. But I was at rock bottom, wasn't I? Everything would come out of the woodwork now. I sniffed, aware that I was being completely self-pitying, but couldn't help thinking: what would she say to me now? What advice would she have? I missed her so much. I wished I could speak to her. I got off the bus, people jostling to and fro around me, and forced myself not to cry.

'Tickets for the Academy?' a ticket tout said, his thin face suddenly too close to mine, invading my thoughts, and I shook my head in annoyance, looked down at the pavement and carried on walking. I turned in to Brixton Tube, where escalators were spitting up hundreds of people and classical music was booming incongruously out of speakers. I pressed the phone to my ear and quickly called my dad, wincing as I watched a little old guy in a dirty yellow coat sit down on the floor, unlace his shoes and remove sodden socks to reveal filthy, unloved feet. I felt the familiar internal tug of war in my heart that I always had when I saw lost souls like this. Should I go and offer my help? I pushed my hand in my pocket and found a pound coin, which I dropped by his side. It meant nothing, really. What would Joe have done? Bought him a coffee. Spoken to him. Given him his own socks. Advised him to see a doctor. I remembered Joe's expression when I told him I didn't want to marry him. I gulped. I didn't know what I was doing any more. All I knew was that I'd gone and ruined everything, all for Ethan.

'Hello, darling,' my dad answered. 'How are you?'

The sound of my dad's voice, soft and cheerful, lifted my spirits slightly. I held my hand over my other ear, to block out Tchaikovsky, so I could hear him properly.

'Can you meet me?' I asked, my voice thin. 'Tonight? I'm in Brixton so I can get the tube.'

'Of course,' he said. 'Hang on a second, will you?'

He was silent for a moment and the sound was muffled, as if he had covered over the mouthpiece of his phone. I thought I heard the sound of a woman's voice in the background.

'Is that Daisy?' I asked, when he came back onto the phone. 'Can I speak to her? Is she still mad with me?'

'No,' he said. 'It's not Daisy, just one of the neighbours popped in. Have you two girls fallen out? What's happened?'

'Oh, nothing,' I said. 'She was in a strop with me for seeing Ethan again. She doesn't think I should.'

'No,' Dad sighed. 'I know she doesn't. Look, don't bother about the Tube. Jump on a bus up to Gastro. I'll meet you there in twenty minutes.'

'That sounded like a cork,' I said. 'Am I interrupting something? I thought you'd be free, but—'

'Of course I'm free,' he said, almost crossly. 'If you get there first, I'll have steak tartare and a bottle of red. Don't let them sit us anywhere near the loo. I hate it when they do that in restaurants. Doesn't make any sense.'

'Bonjour, mademoiselle,' a waiter said, bowing slightly, as I walked in through the creaky doors of Gastro in Clapham Common, the snug, authentically French little restaurant that was in my list of favourite places to eat – and drink – in London. The smell of classic French cooking hit my nose and

Amy Bratley

I breathed deeply, smiling to say hello. The place was already
bursting with customers and the only remaining table was a
rickety wooden one in the window, facing out at the Picture
House cinema, where normally I could happily sit for hours,
pretending to be Parisian, dropping sugar lumps into strong
black coffees, casting my eyes over the French adverts on the
walls, not to mention the smouldering French waiters grace-
fully moving between tables. I sat down, peeled off my damp
cardigan and hooked it over the back of the chair, laced my
fingers together and leaned my lips against them, deep in
thought. Moments later, I saw a man rush by the window
and in through the door. For a second, because of his newly
shaved head, I didn't recognize him.

'Darling girl,' Dad said, kissing the top of my head and col-
lapsing his umbrella. 'Have you ordered? I'm ravenous.'

'Not yet,' I choked, pulling out a chair for him. I felt his
eyes on me. He put his hand on my shoulder. 'I hardly recognized you.'

'Oh dear,' he said. 'Eve, what's wrong?'

I shook my head and opened my mouth to speak, but
nothing came out. At the sight of my dad looking at me with
his dark blue eyes full of concern, smiling warmly, I felt like
a child and could feel my own eyes filling with tears and my
cheeks heating up. I swallowed, reaching for the menu to
wave in front of my face. Dad put his big warm hand on mine
and sighed. He signalled to the waiter, a gorgeously handsome Frenchman, and I listened while Dad ordered in perfect
French. He turned his attention back to me.

'I've ordered you moules frites,' he said. 'I hope that will
do. OK, what's on your mind?'

190

I smiled gratefully. I was quiet while the waiter brought our cutlery and the bottle of wine, with glasses. I waved my hand dismissively when he suggested I should taste the wine, mumbling that I'm sure it would be fine. My dad smiled apologetically at the waiter then leaned back in his chair, waiting for me to speak.

'I know I'm a dinosaur,' he said, grinning madly and crossing his eyes. 'But I might be able to help. Tell me what's wrong.'

With my eyes trained on the salt and pepper, tiny glass jam pots with perforated gingham lids, I told Dad everything that had happened with Joe. I showed him the illustration Joe had done for me of the cafe. I smoothed it out on the table for him to see. Dad's smile was tinged with sadness. He told me he'd known about the cafe idea, since Joe had borrowed £4,000 from him, to contribute to the cost. He hadn't wanted to tell me because he didn't want to ruin the surprise.

'The trouble is,' I said, concentrating on a plastic lobster hanging from the wall, 'I don't really understand why I'm doing all this, throwing my life up in the air like this. Joe's great. He's more than great. He's almost perfect.'

'Why don't you want to marry him?' Dad said. 'Tell me what makes you hesitate.'

I leaned back in my chair, fiddling with my necklace, as a couple on the next table started to kiss passionately.

'Maybe it's marriage as a concept,' I said. 'Maybe I don't want to belong to anyone else.'

Dad frowned and shook his head.

'It's not about that,' Dad said, appalled. 'You know that.'

I smiled at him apologetically and slouched forward in my chair.

191

'I know,' I sighed. 'Perhaps it's the idea of an actual wedding. All the people and fuss and people arguing about where they want to sit . . .'

'You could have a very small wedding,' Dad said. 'What's the real reason? Is it Ethan? Did something happen at the Supper Club?'

I stared at the candle flickering on the table and nodded.

'I wish I could say it wasn't him,' I said, shifting uncomfortably. 'But yes, it's Ethan.'

We were both quiet when the waiter brought over our food, a steaming pile of moules marinière and a heap of frites for me, and Dad's steak tartare: a circle of raw minced beef surrounded by little glass bowls of capers, onion, parsley, mustard, oil and raw egg. We looked up at one another and, in spite of everything, grinned.

'Hmm,' he said thoughtfully now, passing me the basket of bread. 'So haven't you spoken to Ethan about exactly why he left you?'

He looked at me expectantly and I shook my head. I put down my wine, breathing in the tantalizing seaside smell of my mussels.

'I don't think there is a reason,' I said, scooping one mussel out with half a mussel shell. 'From what he's said already I think he panicked and needed time to himself. I'm sure I must have been too clingy or something like that. There is no other reason.'

Thinking that Ethan had left because he was frightened of commitment, which I thought he was, made me feel better about what I'd said to Joe. At least then I would be justified in having feelings for Ethan. He wouldn't be the bastard some people wanted him to be. Dad's expression grew grim. He finished his mouthful of steak tartare, put down his fork and took a gulp of his wine. Then he held my hand with his.

'I know you've said to Joe that you need time, but I'm sure he would come round again,' he said. 'Joe genuinely loves you. I know he does because I once felt the same way for your mother. I recognize it in him. He'd walk to the ends of the earth over hot coals, give you his kidney, slay dragons, all that. But Ethan . . . Ethan's more of an unknown.'

I frowned, annoyed that he wasn't really listening to me properly. Tearing into a chunk of bread, I dipped it into the garlicky, buttery sauce under the mussels and popped it into my mouth.

'But he says he still loves me,' I said.

Dad sighed an enormous sigh.

'Yes,' he said. 'He probably does. Who wouldn't? But that doesn't mean he's better for you than Joe. If I were you I'd let the whole thing drop. Move on. Forget Ethan.'

Dad needlessly picked up the menu and gazed at the drinks list distractedly. I frowned. Surely he realized this was the most important thing to have happened since, well, since Mum had died?

'But I can't forget . . .' I said sadly. 'That's the whole point. I can't.'

Dad put the menu down and looked at me intently. He sighed heavily.

'Then see him,' he said quietly. 'Then jump off the cliff and find your wings on the way down, as your mother would have said. But be warned, darling girl, you might be in for a nasty fall. Oh, I can't bear the thought—'

He shook his head, muttering, and carried on with his food, but wasn't giving it the loving attention he normally did. He seemed to be thinking of something else entirely.

'You've got to let me live my own life,' I said. 'Even if I get it all wrong, you know? I've decided anyway. I'm going to see Ethan this week, before Andrew's dinner party, and I'm going to tell him how I feel, that I still have feelings for him. There's nothing to lose now.'

Dad nodded at me despondently. I could see that, on whatever level, this conversation was painful for him, so I concentrated on eating my big bowl of mussels and changed the subject. Dad visibly relaxed until we came to the end of the meal, when he told me he had news of his own. The family home – Mum's home – he blurted out without warning, was going up for sale.

'I need a change,' he said quietly, draining the last of his wine. 'I can't go on living in the past. I want to sell up and find somewhere smaller.'

I frowned. Dad had lived in that house now for thirty years. I couldn't understand why he would want to sell. The house was part of him. Without it, he would be like a snail without its shell. It held each and every one of his memories of Mum. Was this anything to do with his mystery illness? I had a hateful feeling of dread. My dad wasn't allowed to die.

'You're not going to die, are you, Dad?' I asked, while the waiter whisked away our plates and a large group edged themselves into the restaurant and up to the bar, enquiring after a table. He burst out laughing and rubbed his bald head self-consciously.

'Absolutely not,' he said. 'In fact, I feel like I'm just coming back to life. Just because I'm nearly sixty doesn't mean I'm going to join the heap of people my age who appear to give up on life, shuffling around in bloody boat shoes. I might be retirement age, but I'm not retiring from life.'

I smiled, leaned over the table and hugged him around the neck. He kissed my forehead and patted my back gently. The waiter slipped us dessert menus and Dad ordered two crèmes caramel, our usual dessert.

'You are just like your mother,' he said, his eyes moist. 'Believe it or not, she couldn't decide between me and another chap. Alec, he was called. What an absolutely stupid name.'

He grinned at me and I laughed.

'But I thought your eyes met when she was measuring you up and that was it?' I said.

Dad shook his head. 'That's true, to a degree. We did love one another from the moment we met and I asked her to marry me the same afternoon, but she was with this Alec bloke at the time. She had to break one heart and she couldn't decide which one to break for quite some time. But I persisted. There was no way I was going to lose her, but it wasn't always easy. In fact it was bloody impossible at times.'

My mouth fell open. I'd always seen my parents' relationship through rosy, Hollywood-movie-style spectacles. He'd never told us this before. It was ridiculous, but I felt mildly disappointed.

'So how did she decide what to do?' I asked.

'I have no idea,' he said. 'Probably tossed a coin or threw a dart at a photograph. Something like that.'

He chuckled and grinned at me. Partly due to the silky-smooth crèmes caramel that had arrived in front of us, gently wobbling on the plates, and partly because it was the only thing to do, I smiled in return.

'It's going to be absolutely fine if you listen to your heart and trust your instinct,' Dad said warmly, handing me a spoon and diving into his pudding. 'That's all I can say and I've said enough. Let's eat.'

PART THREE

Andrew's Supper Club

Chapter Fifteen

The following Saturday, the day of Andrew's dinner party, I woke to the sound of the doorbell ringing. I bolted upright in bed, knocking a plate holding the remains of a late-night slice of toast off the duvet and sending it spinning onto the wooden floorboards with a crash.

'Shit,' I said, swinging my legs out of the bed, catching sight of the time. 'Oh fuck, it's three o'clock!'

Ever since Joe had left the flat, I'd spent more time sleeping than ever before. Though I fully intended to work as hard as I could on the cafe all week, I'd slept late almost every day, waking up feeling groggy and incapable of doing anything much. I never felt refreshed. Instead, it was almost like having the flu, but without the symptoms. Maggie, when she'd called in one evening to share a bottle of wine, had told me that all this sleep was my body's way of protecting itself from confronting the changes happening in my life. She was probably right. I certainly couldn't face thinking about Joe and how he must be feeling. Imagining him in his Kentish Town flat, bruised and rejected after my horrible outburst, made me feel physically sick, so I tried the best I could to ignore it. I didn't know what else to do. I had to see Ethan again. I'd tried to arrange a meeting for just the two of us, but he'd told me he was going to be in Italy until the day of Andrew's party. I hadn't a clue if he was telling the truth.

'Eve?' came Isabel's voice through the letterbox as, dizzy with sleep, I staggered to the front door, only realizing just in time that my dressing gown was gaping open, revealing my naked body to the world.

'Coming,' I said. 'Sorry.'

I hugged it around me and opened the door, just a crack. Outside it was a gloriously hot day and Isabel was dressed in tiny shorts and a vest top. Disorientated, I blinked and yawned.

'What are you *doing*?' Isabel said in exasperation, pushing through the front door and into the flat. 'Why are you wearing your dressing gown?'

I closed the door behind her, stretched my arms up and yawned. She gave me a quick hug and rubbed my back briefly.

'I've only just woken up,' I said. 'I'm so tired.'

'What's got into you?' she said. 'I've barely seen you all week. Have you been in bed the whole time?'

I shrugged and shook my head.

'No,' I started. 'I've just slept in later than normal. Without Joe here, it's been strange, I don't—'

Isabel tipped her head back in exasperation.

'This is all about Ethan, isn't it?' she said. 'Even though Joe is, like, the nicest man on the face of the earth and he raised fifteen thousand pounds and you've known him for ever and he loves you so much, you're still chasing after that fuckwit who ditched you like a ton of bricks three years ago because you've got some silly notion that what you had with him was true love. You're one hundred per cent crazy and acting like a victim who can't control herself. Well, I refuse to stand by and watch you fuck up—'

I lifted my hands in the air to beg for mercy.

'Slow down!' I said. 'Isabel, I've just woken up. Give me a break! Why are you so mad?'

'Oh, Eve,' she said, with a massive sigh. 'I think you're making a mistake. You've got to stop this.'

Anger flashed into me. I knew Isabel had my best interests at heart, but this was too much. I was not the victim here. I was being brave, honest, true to myself, however uncomfortable that felt. How could that be a mistake? In my book, being true to yourself was the most important thing you could do in life.

'I'm doing what I instinctively feel I should do,' I said with hot cheeks, staring straight into her eyes. 'It *was* true love with Ethan. I know it, in here. I can't ignore that.'

I held my hand against my heart and exhaled.

'Then why did he go?' she asked more gently, holding out her arms, the palms of her hands raised upwards. She let them fall against her sides.

'Because . . .' I began. 'Maybe he got scared, or I was too full-on. You don't just stop loving someone overnight like that, do you? It's like now, I haven't stopped loving Joe or anything, but right now, I can't be with him. It wouldn't be fair.'

Isabel was shaking her head and muttering under her breath.

'Cut that out, will you?' she said. 'You did nothing wrong. It was not your fault that Ethan was an arsehole who didn't respect you enough to break up with you properly.'

I took a deep breath. Isabel would never understand how I felt about this. I'm not sure I even understood.

'But he wrote me a letter explaining why he left, which I never got,' I said, exasperated. 'So he did at least make an effort. Ethan is not an arsehole. He's the most incredibly charming, most charismatic personality I've ever met. He wouldn't just leave because he couldn't be bothered to talk to me. Anyway, now he's back and he thinks it's fate. He thinks we're destined to be together, and as stupid as it sounds, there's a bit of me that needs to find out if we are.'

Isabel combed her hands through her hair then pressed them over her eyes for a moment.

'I'm sorry,' she said. 'But I think you're wrong on every level. I can't just stand here and watch you mess up your perfectly good life with Joe, in which, by the way, you were perfectly happy before Ethan rocked up, because you're too pig-headed to let me remind you of what your relationship was like with Ethan. Already now that he's back you're not concentrating on the cafe properly and, Eve, the cafe is not just your dream, it's mine too. I know I'm going to Dubai, but I still care about the place, I'm still working my arse off to make it work for you. I've spent this whole week virtually on my own, finishing the plastering. You've popped in a few times and done a few things, but nowhere near enough. Look at my nails.'

Isabel's voice was trembling. She thrust her hands out in front of her, showing me her chipped candy-pink nails. I could see from the contortion of her mouth she was furious with me. I panicked. In our ten-year friendship the closest Isabel and I had come to a row was her telling me she didn't like the ethnic rug I'd bought from Camden market for the flat that we'd shared. In the end I'd thrown it out the window and onto the street. We'd both fallen about laughing.

'I know. I'm sorry,' I nodded, feeling utterly miserable. 'But, Isabel, please try to understand where I'm coming from. I'm going through something really major and it's all I can think about. Joe is looking for a big commitment from me, and I know he's great, but I've never stopped thinking of Ethan. I've never stopped wondering what would have happened if he hadn't got frightened or I hadn't done whatever I'd done.'

'Is that what he told you happened?' she said. 'That he got frightened? Because I'm seeing some parallels between Ethan and you, with you and Joe, just the other way around.'

'What do you mean?' I asked.

'You're throwing away your chance of happiness with Joe,' said Isabel, 'because the kind of happiness you have with him is scary. It needs work, commitment, consideration and sacrifice. It needs you to be a grown-up and responsible. Your love for Ethan was all-consuming; you thought only about him, so you didn't have to think about yourself at all.'

My eyes filled with tears.

'It was like an obsession,' she said, her voice softer now.

Isabel's anger had disappeared. She put her arms around my shoulders and pulled me close for a hug. A tear slipped down my cheek and I angrily wiped it away.

'I don't know what I'm doing,' I confessed. 'I just know

that I was very much in love with him and that's an addictive feeling. I still am, but I miss Joe, too. Terribly.'

It was the first time I'd admitted it out loud. A weight lifted from my shoulders. Isabel dropped her arms, reached for the carrier bag she'd brought with her and pulled out a bottle of wine.

'It was infatuation,' she said. 'Not love.'

For the next hour or so, though I was very aware I should have been at the cafe making up for lost time, Isabel and I sat in the garden propped up in deckchairs, drinking cold white wine. The neighbours were having a barbecue and we were cloaked in their smoke for most of the time, not that I really noticed. I was more concerned with our conversation. With her outburst over, Isabel confessed that she was unbelievably stressed about the move to Dubai and that she didn't want to go. I asked her if she'd told Robert how she felt, but she shook her head, saying that he was excited about the move.

'Part of me is tempted to tell Robert I don't want to go at all,' she sighed, before glancing at me. 'God, I can't believe I said that; but I was excited by the prospect to begin with, now I wonder what will become of me out there. I feel rather like I'm dragging along after him, just because he wants to go. I think you may have been right, before, when you realized something isn't quite right with me and Robert. Nothing major.'

She smiled apologetically at me, squinting in the sunlight.

'You're not dragging after him,' I said. 'You wouldn't go if you weren't excited by the change, I know you wouldn't, and I'm sure Robert must understand it's going to be tough on you both, but you especially. You can always come back, can't you?'

Isabel nodded and shrugged.

'You were lucky with Joe like that. He understood what you needed in your life and was trying to help you achieve it, before . . . Robert is far more selfish. He'd never admit it, but I'm sure he thinks his job is far more important than anything I might do, which of course is bullshit. But let's see what happens. Like you say, I can always come back on my own. All this change is unsettling.'

I looked at her and thought how strange it was that our lives were about to become so different. We'd lived together, worked together, spent years meeting up in bars all over London to dissect our relationships and talk about our dreams, but that was coming to an end. I didn't want to think about that now. The prospect of Isabel being thousands of miles away was awful. I told myself to concentrate on the night ahead instead. I opened my mouth, wanting to ask Isabel to advise me on what to wear to Andrew's dinner party, but stopped myself just in time. Isabel had already made it quite clear she didn't approve of me going. I would have been the same if this were the other way around. She checked her watch and put down her wine glass.

'You can't go in your dressing gown,' she said suddenly, reading my mind. 'So shall we go and rake through your wardrobe?'

'I thought . . .' I said, giving her a grateful smile.

'I meant what I said, but . . .' she said, with a deep breath. 'But you need to look like you're in control of your life, even if you're far from it.'

I grinned. We stood, stretching out our legs, picked up the half-empty bottle of wine and went into the bedroom, cool and dark after the bright sunshine. Isabel flung open the wardrobe door and stared at my clothes. I stood next to Isabel and pointed to my black dress with a white Peter Pan collar.

'How about this?' I said, lifting it out and rubbing the fabric between my fingers. 'Not too showy?'

'Are you going to a funeral?' she said, scraping the hangers along the rack. 'I think this is more like it,' she said, pulling out a zebra-print jumpsuit I'd bought from eBay but never worn. 'If you're going to do this, you might as well do it properly.'

I was dubious. I'd bought that jumpsuit in a mad pre-menstrual Internet-shopping binge, but never actually dared to wear it. Half an hour later, I had it on, my red hair blow-dried into position, my make-up firmly applied. I got ready in a trance-like state. I didn't let myself think of Joe once. I focused on nothing.

'Perfect,' she said. 'There's no way you can be a victim looking like that.'

'I'm not so sure,' I said.

Isabel and I walked to the train station together and at the ticket machines, before parting, she hugged me tight.

'Be careful,' she said. 'Try not to get swept along by old infatuation. Look at him objectively. Listen to what he says with a critical ear. Watch him. Reflect. Think carefully. Please. It's not too late for Joe, you know.'

At the mention of Joe's name, my heart ached. I'd gone through the entire afternoon avoiding thinking about him because, as more time passed, the space and time between us seemed to be taking shape and solidifying into something impenetrable, and that – despite everything I'd made myself think and believe about doing the right thing – made me panic.

'OK,' I told her. 'I hear what you're saying and I know that I'm not sure what I'm actually doing. I just know that it's something I have to do, to find out, either way, how I truly feel. It doesn't mean I don't love Joe.'

'But it might mean you lose him,' Isabel said gently. 'Tread carefully.'

I nodded, sighed heavily and kissed Isabel goodbye. I stepped into the train station, where I had to remind myself where I was going. Andrew lived in Holland Park, so I needed to go to Victoria and then catch the Tube from there. I pulled my Oyster card out of my bag and, as I did so, Joe's illustration of the cafe fell onto the floor. I bent down to get it, but it fluttered away in a sudden breeze and out onto the pavement, where people were waiting in a jumbled queue at the bus stop.

'Excuse me,' I said, elbowing people in the queue to get onto the pavement and retrieve the illustration. Just as I bent down to pick it up, someone in heavy boots stood on it, causing it to wrinkle and tear. I remembered the photograph of Ethan I'd dropped on the bus. When the person moved, I lifted it up and saw that his picture was filthy and creased.

'Shit,' I said, quickly stuffing it back into my bag. 'It's ruined.'

I paced up the steps to the trains. *Tread carefully*, I heard Isabel's voice in my head. *Tread carefully.*

Chapter Sixteen

Walking from Holland Park underground station towards Andrew's address, I felt like my feet were following a well-worn track. There was a nagging sense of déjà-vu in my head, even though I'd never been to this street before. I suspected that was more to do with how I felt about seeing Ethan again. My stomach was in my mouth, my heart bumping in my chest at the prospect. I'd always felt like this, hadn't I? That seeing Ethan was all that mattered, at the cost of all else. A voice in my head was telling me I was being pathetic, but I pushed it away. When it came to Ethan, I didn't feel in control, and that was what had been so addictive. I'd *liked* that feeling. So much else in life, even relationships, felt predictable. Part of me wanted that excitement back. At the very least I wanted to hear what Ethan had to say, to find out if I could be that person I once was back then: so in love I didn't care much about anything else. Aware that I was staring at the pavement, trying not to stand on the cracks – a childhood superstition to avoid bad luck – I looked up to check the house numbers. The Victorian townhouses were cavernous giants, most of them vast properties, single houses, and not divided up into fifty-five flats like just about all the really big houses near me. I glanced at a deli with cured hams hanging in the window, presumably Holland Park's version of the corner shop. I frowned as I remembered reading that some properties in Holland Park sold for over £10 million. Who had that sort of money? And, I thought crossly, as I gawped in through the windows of houses so grand they were like Hollywood film sets, who needed so many *things*? Money. I hated that it dictated so much about life. If only I had £15,000, I could stop worrying about the cafe and make sure that it would be exactly what I wanted it to be. That amount would be nothing to these residents, but where would I get that now? I thought about Joe's cheque and his ruined illustration and was struck by guilt, before I was distracted by the sound of running footsteps behind me. I turned and—

'Hey, zebra legs!' said Ethan, slowing down to a walk and resting his hand briefly on my shoulder, with an amused expression on his lips. 'You're on a mission there. Wow, you look wild.'

He moved as if he was about to kiss my cheek, but thought better of it and stopped. He looked me all over, approvingly.

'Do you bite?' he said, with a wry smile.

'Sometimes,' I said, my entire body trembling. Ethan laughed. My mind raced. Oh God. We were flirting. I had to remember the point of all this: to find out why he had left, to discover whether that *thing* I'd thought was still there – that untouchable, superior, once-in-a-lifetime *thing* that had stopped me from committing to Joe – was real or imagined. I couldn't tear my eyes away from Ethan, his black hair freshly washed catching in the breeze, his cheeks pink from running, his dark blue shirt hanging over dark brown trousers, at the bottom revealing his camel-coloured brogues. I was struck, again, by how handsome he was. Under his arm he carried a bottle of red wine like a newspaper. He shoved his hands into his pockets, the wine staying where it was.

'I've missed you,' he said, 'since the last time.'

'Only been a week,' I said, blushing. 'Doesn't really compare to three years.'

'No,' he said, suddenly downcast. 'You're not wrong. But, Eve, it's so amazing to see you again. I thought you might not come tonight after what you said about Joe—'

What had I said about Joe? I resented the fact that Ethan knew anything about my relationship. That was my private life. This was something separate. Twisted logic, but that's how I justified this to myself. What was Joe doing now? I felt ashamed, thinking of how I'd left things with him. But ultimately, though I hadn't told him about Ethan, I still hadn't done anything really wrong, had I? I wasn't being unfaithful, was I? I shook my head, convincing myself that infidelity amounted to secret liaisons for passionate sex in hotel rooms, not a stroll through Holland Park with an old boyfriend.

'I know you said you love him,' Ethan said, putting one hand up to my arm. 'But you loved me too, *before* him.'

'Does that give you some kind of claim over someone, then?' I asked, disbelieving. 'If you get in there first? Because if that's the case, I've known Joe a whole lot longer than I've known you.'

'Yes, but you weren't in love with him before,' he said. 'We were *in* love, Eve, I know it and you know it. What we had was a one-off. Seeing you again has made me realize that, though I never really stopped thinking it. Are you in love with Joe? Because if you are, I'll shut up and fuck off, but if not, I'm staying put.'

Annoyed with Ethan for finding my weak spot and jumping on it with a pogo stick, I narrowed my eyes and bit my lip.

'It's none of your business,' I said to Ethan. 'Joe is wonderful, he's my best friend and I do love him, of course I do. But . . . it's just that seeing you has confused me and, oh Christ, I've messed up and wrecked my rel—'

I bit my tongue and stopped talking. I hated that I was confiding in Ethan. I let my words trail off into silence. I didn't even know what I wanted to say. Defending Joe to Ethan was a pointless exercise, and why did I care what Ethan thought? I waved my hand in dismissal and started to walk faster, slightly ahead of him.

'Anyway, where did you go after Maggie's dinner party?' I asked. 'I went to the bathroom and when I came back you were gone. Bloody good at disappearing, aren't you?'

Ethan let out a bark of laughter.

'I couldn't stay there any longer with you there,' he said, exasperated. 'I was getting drunk and wanted to be just with you, so I thought I should go, since you told us you might be marrying Joe. The thought of it makes me feel sick.'

Ethan shouted out in frustration and I whacked his elbow to quieten him down, though secretly I was thrilled by his admission.

'Shall we talk about something else?' I said, walking even faster and pointing down the road. 'I think he lives at number fifty-three. I reckon that Andrew will do an amuse-bouche or

Amy Bratley

something for appetizer. He'll pull out all the stops. Did you hear him talking about wine? He knows *everything*. I reckon he knocks it back, too. He looks like a man who has gout in his future.'

I was talking quickly, trying to get our conversation on to a more mundane topic, away from how nervous I felt.

'I know,' Ethan said. 'He was telling me about that wine, called Petrus, I think, which is the most expensive wine in the world. Over twelve thousand pounds a bottle. That's some people's annual salary.'

I nodded, pleased for the change of subject.

'There are probably a few bottles of Petrus nestled in these houses,' he said. 'It's like Millionaire's Row. One day I'll own great swathes of Holland Park and, like Robin Hood, I will turn it over to the poor. Then we can live here.'

Ethan puffed his chest up and laughed. *Then we can live here.* Everything he said was loaded with meaning. I held my breath for a moment then shook my head.

'Ethan,' I said, as we fell back into step side by side. 'What about you? Tell me about you. Do you have a girlfriend? Wives and children in every port? Why did you come back from Rome? Are you wanted by the Mafia?'

Ethan threw his head back and laughed. He had a laugh like a box of fireworks going off.

'Probably,' he said. 'I was certainly drunk and disorderly a few too many times. And in answer to your second question, I came back because I thought I should stop running. Not that I have literally been running for the last three years, that would be exhausting – and now that this has happened with you—'

'What?' I said, gazing up at the enormous white Victorian

212

houses as we walked. 'What's happened? Nothing's happened, Ethan, except words and a clumsy kiss. Nothing's happened at all.'

Who was I trying to convince? Ethan ignored me.

'Basically I want to stop pissing around,' he said. 'I want to make something of my life. I've not exactly won an Oscar for my contribution to the world of acting, but I still really want to *do* something. I'm burning with ambition, me. Burning.'

He laughed at himself, but looked crestfallen. Seeing his disappointment, I immediately fell into the old routine of boosting his ego whenever it showed signs of deflating. I was Ethan's personal set of bellows.

'You're really good,' I said earnestly. 'It's not an easy profession to make a career out of, is it? Anyway, there's nothing stopping you from being an actor now, is there? Why give up when you've got natural talent?'

I didn't even believe what I was saying. I had no idea, any more, whether Ethan was a good actor. He shook his head.

'No,' he said seriously. 'I've given it up for good. I've been trying to prove something to myself for years but I need to change direction completely. You know I've always wanted to open up my own place—'

'I know,' I said, turning back to face him, feeling Joe's illustration burning a hole in my bag. 'Well, you know I'm just in the process of . . .'

I thought about the cafe, waiting for me to breathe life into it. I would so regret it if I failed to get it started, and I'd hardly done anything that week. I silently vowed to myself I would make it work, no matter what.

'Yeah,' he said, not really listening. 'Well, I think my folks are going to hand over the deli to me soon. They're getting tired of working all hours, my dad's ready to hit the golf course and I'm thinking of turning it into a rustic pizza place.'

He was talking animatedly, gesturing with his hands, staring at me intently, just like he used to. All at once I had a sensation of dread. That intense gaze he fixed me with, that I'd imagined was unique to our relationship: did he do that to *everyone*? Had everyone in Rome seen that look?

'Guess you know what's on the menu at mine next Saturday?' he said.

He looked at me expectantly, a smile breaking over his lips, eyes bright and wide.

'Pizza,' I said, with a sigh. 'I'm guessing pizza. I've never really liked pizza much.'

'How can you not like pizza?' he said. 'Pizza is the perfect food.'

'It might be for you, Ethan,' I said. 'But it's not for me. The mozzarella is always stringy, and if you don't eat it immediately, the pizza base goes soggy.'

'You clearly haven't had one of my pizzas for quite a long time,' he said. 'Just you wait and see.'

Pizza. Were we really talking about pizza? I sighed, and while Ethan talked about toppings, I looked up at the blue sky, and at the straight lines of the houses contrasting against the white cotton-ball clouds.

'It's not just any old pizza,' Ethan continued. I rolled my eyes. 'This is pizza to die for. I guarantee you'll be oozing with compliments. Then, if I win this competition, which I think I might, I can emblazon your quotes on my promotional material. I've got it all planned out.'

He tapped his nose and gave me another grin. We were walking close together, close enough for me to smell that Ethan was wearing the Dior eau de toilette I used to buy him years before.

'Is that Dior you're wearing?' I said. 'I hope that's not the same bottle I bought you. I think it has a shelf life, you know? Like our relationship clearly had.'

Ethan laughed again, a firecracker laugh, then put his arms around my waist and, before I could do anything, he lifted me up and swung me round and round in circles. A couple walking past looked up at us, smiling sweetly.

'It's so good to be with you,' he said loudly. 'I think about you all the time. I thought about you all the time!'

'Ethan!' I said, forced to lean my head against his chest, and for a moment I wanted to stay there. 'Put me down! Be quiet!'

Gently, he rested me down on the pavement. I frowned. I could never get the upper hand with Ethan. He would always do something big, outlandish, something like this, to steal the moment.

'Sorry,' he said, as I smoothed down my outfit and tucked my hair behind my ears. 'I think this is fate. I think fate is pushing us together. This is our second chance.'

I bit my lip, wanting to tell Ethan that he was three years too late. If he'd come back straight after he'd left, perhaps I would be more open to his talk of second chances. But I couldn't play hardball. Actually, I wanted to believe what he was saying. He stared at me, his lips slightly apart, moving closer. An unexpected bolt of desire rushed through me.

'I . . . oh . . . this is so . . . Ethan, stop,' I started, blushing all over.

He nodded once, understanding, then pointed across the road.

'Look, is that Andrew's place?' he said. 'What the fuck is going on there?'

I followed Ethan's eyes to the opposite side of the road where, at Andrew's address, number fifty-three, an extremely heavily pregnant woman with long ginger hair pulled back into low bunches, dressed in a billowing floral dress, was lugging a chair out of the front door, dragging it into the front garden and tossing it into the flowerbed. Her bump was very low and I knew from Daisy's pregnancy that meant it wouldn't be long until she 'dropped'.

'What the hell's she doing?' I said. 'She's about to give birth by the look of her. Do you think that's Alicia? Must be.'

We waited for a car to pass before we crossed over. The driver slowed down a little, to see what was going on too.

'Yes, it's got to be,' said Ethan, his eyes twinkling with amusement. 'Blimey, she looks a bit fierce, doesn't she?'

Already in the front garden were two suitcases spilling out clothes, a standing lamp with the dark red shade knocked askew, a wicker two-seater chair, magazines and books scattered about the floor and a selection of men's shoes chucked randomly onto the pile. Ethan grabbed my hand, but I pulled it away. We slowly approached the house, glancing at one another worriedly, the previous moment seemingly forgotten.

'You stupid bastard!' the woman – who I assumed to be Alicia – was shouting. 'You do not understand what it feels like to be pregnant in this heat, so don't ever say you do! Never, ever, never, ever! How can you know what it's like to have swollen fucking ankles and acid reflux!'

Andrew's neighbour, an aristocratic-looking gent out in his beautifully manicured garden, pruning a bush of bright red roses, looked at us and lifted the straw boater hat off his head, holding it to his chest for a moment. He wiped his slightly sweaty forehead with his shirtsleeve.

'Beautiful evening, isn't it?' he said, ignoring the screaming from the other side of the wrought-iron fence. 'If it's Andrew you're looking for, he's under there. In the bunker.'

The neighbour chuckled and pointed to the table that was out in Andrew's front garden. Sitting underneath it and hugging his knees, with his chin resting on them, was Andrew, dressed in pale suit trousers and shirt. He smiled and raised a hand to wave as we tentatively approached through the front gate and up the mosaic-tile garden path. I could feel Ethan, next to me, wanting to laugh. We walked up to Andrew and both knelt down on the grass near him. He shot his hand out from under the table to shake Ethan's hand, then kiss mine.

'Are you all right, mate?' Ethan said.

'Slight problem,' Andrew said, pointing towards the house. 'Alicia has thrown me – and a few of my things – out of the house. Why don't you take a seat? I'll see if I can get past her and get you a drink, though I'm slightly concerned she'll murder me.'

'Would you rather we just left?' I asked, half hoping he'd say yes. But Andrew grabbed on to my ankle.

'Please don't go,' he said. 'I need you.'

Ethan and I shared a look.

'No problem,' said Ethan, patting Andrew's back. 'We'll stay. Eve, why don't you sort the chairs out? There's one there, look, on the roof of that BMW. Is that your car,

Andrew? Looks like it's left a dent. I'll see if I can persuade Alicia into allowing us a few glasses. I've got some wine here.'

'Thank God for the cavalry,' said Andrew. 'I'd suggest we go to the pub, but I'm worried she's going to go into labour at any moment and Paul texted to say he's on his way. Jesus Christ, I'm about to have a nervous breakdown. What red have you bought?'

I left Andrew scrutinizing the label on the bottle of wine, picked up a couple of chairs and stood them on the front lawn, while Ethan started towards Andrew's front door. I watched him tentatively push it open, step into the hallway and call out Alicia's name. Andrew stuck his head out from under the table.

'The food,' Andrew called after Ethan. 'There's sushi in the fridge that I made for tonight. Can you try to get that, too?'

For a few moments, everything was quiet except for the distant whine of a gardener at work with a strimmer and the gentle hum of Radio 4 in next door's garden. Andrew smiled at me and shook his head in dismay.

'The reversing cold bottom is nothing on this,' he said drily.

Ethan came out seconds later, carrying an armful of clinking wine glasses and a bag of crisps.

'Here comes the party,' he said. 'Sorry, but the sushi's gone. It seems Alicia suddenly felt starving and ate the whole lot. She said we could have these, though. Your kitchen is out of this world, Andrew. I expected Gordon Ramsay to pop out from behind the door. You should see it, Eve. Everything totally top of the range. There's no fish slices from the 99p shop in there.'

He looked at me, bubbling with enthusiasm, and I raised my eyebrows in acknowledgement.

'Wow,' I said lamely.

'Oh, a bag of crisps, that's generous of Alicia,' Andrew broke in. 'She can't have eaten the whole lot. That's half a kilo of raw tuna. I'm sure she's not even allowed to eat raw tuna.'

A window of a first-floor room flew open. Alicia stuck her head out, her cheeks boiling red.

'DON'T EVEN THINK ABOUT TELLING ME I'M NOT ALLOWED TO EAT RAW FISH,' she shouted, before slamming the window shut. The old man next door chuckled.

'God,' Andrew said, his lips quivering. 'It's a disaster. Sorry. Perhaps you should get off to the pub and leave me here. I'll have to call Dominique and Paul, maybe we can postpone or I can be disqualified or ...'

He held his head in his hands.

'I'm just not cut out for dealing with women,' he said. 'I should have realized that years ago.'

'Don't worry,' I said. 'We can just have a drink and wait for Paul, then we can go ...'

'It's sorted,' Ethan said, pouring us all a glass of wine, handing Andrew his first. He gulped it down. 'I phoned Maggie and she's bringing a stash of fish and chips from that gourmet fish place near the Tube. You can get skate wing, squid, huss and haddock from there. Alicia said she wanted three pickled eggs. Is that normal? Oh, look, here's Paul now. We'll all give you a decent score, don't worry, though I'm dubious about whether you need the prize money as much as I do.'

I kept one eye on the house behind us, half expecting Alicia to hurl a hand grenade out of the window. Paul walked towards us, a confused expression on his face.

'Is this your own house, Andrew?' I asked. 'It's enormous.'

'Yes,' Andrew said, slightly guiltily. 'My father was a wine merchant, much more successful than me. He was very well known in the trade and so I've tried to work only with artisan wines. I wanted to avoid the bigger names. And yes, I inherited this place when he died a few years ago. I felt ridiculous living in it alone, so when I met Alicia, I moved her in pretty quickly. Big mistake. Hello, Paul. I'm afraid things have taken a turn for the worse here. There's nothing to photograph because my girlfriend has eaten it all. Should I phone Dominique and postpone?'

Paul shook his head, grinned and didn't look remotely fazed, like this kind of thing happened all the time.

'Don't worry, pal,' he said. 'This makes it all more interesting, to be honest. Plates of food don't do much for me, really. I prefer reportage, and Dominique absolutely loves it if something interesting happens.'

Ethan handed Paul a drink and they both sat down on the wicker chair, Ethan watching me, a smile tickling his lips, as we all pretended everything was normal.

'Where did you meet Alica?' I asked Andrew.

'In a wine bar in Kensington,' he said. 'I recommended she try an oyster; she did, then was sick in the street afterwards. I offered her my bed to recover, since we were near to my house, and she slapped me round the face. Not very romantic, but I immediately loved her. She doesn't suffer fools gladly. You should have seen the way she laid into this chap whose dog chose to crap just outside the gate there. Breathtaking.'

Andrew shook his head at the memory, while I imagined Alicia karate-kicking a dog owner before he'd had the chance to locate his poop-a-scoop. I opened my mouth to ask

Andrew what Alicia did for a living, when Maggie turned up at the garden gate, clutching a large carrier bag.

'Fish and chips,' she said. 'Or, a selection of seafood, lightly battered, served with chips. I bought a bottle of tomato sauce and some pea-and-mint fritters too. So, what's the story? What happened with Alicia? Wow, Andrew, is this your house? Are you a member of the royal family?'

Andrew laughed self-consciously, climbing out from under the table.

'Actually, my third cousin is related to the Windsors,' he said, accepting the carrier bag stuffed with greasy paper parcels. 'Thank you for these, but my menu was going to be a Japanese sensation. In answer to your question, yes, this is my house, if I'm ever allowed back inside. Alicia's about to give birth, I can feel it. God, I don't know if I'm ready to be a dad. Even after all this time, especially after all this time. I don't think I'll ever get my head around it.'

Andrew cast his eyes towards his house and quickly screwed the carrier bag up into the tiniest ball, before throwing it on the ground near a heap of magazines that had been hurled outside during the row.

'I wonder if anyone is ever ready?' asked Ethan wistfully, his eyes following a flock of birds making their way across the sky. 'I don't think I ever will be. Not for a long time.'

'That's all very well,' said Andrew. 'But women your age are hearing the tick-tock of the biological clock. If you want to wait you're going to have to aim at least ten years younger than yourself.'

He glanced up at Ethan, caught his eye and winked.

'Not a bad idea, though, is it?' he laughed.

'I couldn't possibly comment,' said Ethan with a laugh, deliberately not looking at me. 'So, Andrew, are you going to dish out the chips? Why don't you tell us what you were going to cook?'

While Andrew reeled off an inspired menu with accompanying wines, I spoke to Maggie, who, dressed in a short floral dress and with her hair down tonight, seemed less convivial than she had been at her own dinner party.

'So,' she said, leaning in close to me. 'How's it going with you? Are you feeling any brighter?'

I frowned and shook my head.

'Not really,' I said. 'I feel really strange. Kind of like I'm burying my head in the sand about everything.'

'Still sleeping a lot?' she said.

I opened my mouth to reply, but Ethan bounded across the lawn to interrupt, a hot chip in his hand.

'Maggie,' he said, kissing both her cheeks. 'Hello. Are you ready to eat? So, what are you girls talking about?'

'As a matter of fact, you,' said Maggie. 'But then you probably guessed that, did you? I'm getting that you like to be centre of attention, Ethan.'

Maggie's tone was playful but Ethan looked hurt. His eyes met mine and, though he laughed, he looked slightly vulnerable.

'Not always,' he said quietly. 'Sometimes I would like to just sit in the corner quietly and observe. That was one good thing about Rome when I first got there. I was pretty much anonymous everywhere I went. Here, all the people that come into the deli know me.'

'And then, of course, there's your fans from when you

were a corpse in *Silent Witness*,' I said, making him smile. 'Swamping you on the street.'

'Food!' Andrew called out. 'Come and get it.'

We all looked towards Andrew, who was holding out plates of fish and chips.

'Exactly,' Ethan said with a laugh. 'It's tough being this famous. I mean, look at this face. It says Hollywood, doesn't it?'

Andrew, now standing, waved knives and forks at us. 'Look, shall we eat while these things are still hot?' he said. 'I ought to check up on Alicia in a minute. Good God, what a shambles. Come and sit near me, Maggie. Food's ready.'

'Thanks, Dad,' Maggie said.

'Oh Christ,' Andrew said. 'I am definitely not ready for that.'

Maggie took a single chair near Andrew, leaving the two-seater wicker chair empty. Ethan stretched out his hand, offering me a place on the two-seater.

'Thanks,' I said avoiding his eyes, sitting and accepting a plate of food from Andrew, though I knew I wouldn't be able to eat a thing. Ethan sat next to me, his thigh touching mine. As he ate, he turned to look at me, or subtly knocked his elbow against mine, as if checking I hadn't disappeared. I played with the food on my plate, pushing the chips into a pile. When I glanced over at Maggie, she was watching me, a sympathetic expression on her face.

'The thing about men,' Maggie started, waving a chip-pronged fork at Andrew. 'Is that they're not as good at adapting as women. Girls adapt and survive, whereas men, despite what they say, don't cope so well with change.'

'I think you might be right,' Andrew said. 'I detest change; I'm hopeless at it.'

Ethan put his fork down on his plate, shaking his head.

'I'm not sure,' Ethan said. 'In my experience, women find it almost impossible to adapt to change. They don't face up to reality, whereas men do; even if they internalize their emotions, they do get on with life. They think they have to.'

Ethan cleared his throat and glanced nervously at me.

'Rubbish,' said Maggie, dismissively.

'I'm thinking about my parents,' he said, bristling at Maggie's tone.

I nodded in acknowledgement. When his brother died, his mum had refused to stop buying two sets of everything for years, while his dad wouldn't speak about his death.

'I lost my twin when I was a kid,' Ethan explained to Maggie and Andrew. 'When we were six he drowned in a swimming pool. It was years before my mother could accept he was gone, but my dad just carried on.'

He put his plate, still mounded with food, down on the grass. A pigeon hovered close by and pecked at the lawn. Maggie and Andrew made sympathetic murmuring noises.

'Christ,' Andrew said. 'How dreadful.'

'Yeah, it's not been great, but I hate to be miserable about his life,' Ethan said. 'I feel I owe it to him not to fuck up mine because I see my life as ours, as belonging to both of us.'

Ethan looked at me and gave a sad smile.

'Not doing such a great job, as it happens,' he said quietly.

It was rare to see Ethan so melancholic and open. He hardly ever spoke about his twin to people he didn't know well. It surprised me, but I liked it. I wanted to hug and kiss him, squeeze his hand. But just as I was suppressing the urge, from inside my bag my phone started to ring. I picked it out and saw that my dad was calling.

'Sorry,' I said, getting up from my place. 'It's my dad. I'd better take it.'

With the phone pressed to my ear, I walked away from Ethan and Maggie, towards Andrew's house, where the front door was open. From somewhere inside, I heard Alicia sniffing with tears.

'Hey, Dad,' I said distractedly, leaning on the outside wall by the front door, next to a rose trellis. 'Everything OK?'

'Hello, darling Eve,' he said, in a serious voice. 'Are you at that dinner party?'

There was a burst of laughter from Maggie and Ethan and I watched them, with one eye, wondering if I should tell someone that Alicia was obviously crying on her own inside the house or if she just wanted to be left alone.

'I am, yes,' I said. 'I know you don't think I should be, but I need to talk to Ethan and he's been away all week, plus I can get publicity for the cafe, which I can't let go because I've been so hopeless with it now that Joe has—'

Dad interrupted before I could finish.

'Eve,' he said, 'I haven't been entirely honest with you about Ethan. I'm sorry.'

I frowned, confused, and put my free hand up to my ear, so I could hear his voice more clearly.

'What do you mean you haven't been honest?' I said. 'About what?'

Dad sighed heavily. I could almost hear him cringe. My heart started to pound in my chest.

'Oh dear,' he said worriedly. 'Let me explain.'

Chapter Seventeen

While the others continued to talk, I turned away and, with my phone clasped to my ear, stared at my shoes, dread gnawing my insides.

'Go on, Dad,' I said. 'Just tell me.'

Sensing his hesitation, I felt the blood drain from my cheeks. There are times in your life that you just know something awful is going to happen. This was one of them. I held my breath in anticipation.

'You remember Ethan told you he sent a letter when he first disappeared?' he said evenly.

'Yeah,' I said quickly, suddenly extremely alert. 'And?'

'You have to understand that I did this because I love you more than anything. You – and Daisy – mean absolutely everything to me. Before your mother died, I promised I would look after you with extra care and love—' he said, his voice breaking with emotion. 'You were the baby and you'd lost your mum, for heaven's sake—'

He stopped speaking and I realized, with alarm, that he was choking back tears.

'Go on, Dad,' I said worriedly, glancing back at Maggie pouring Ethan, Andrew and Paul more wine. 'It can't be that bad, can it?'

He took a deep breath.

'The letter Ethan sent explained exactly why he left,' he said. 'I know that because I opened it and read it and decided you'd be better off not knowing the truth. I'm sorry.'

I just stood there, listening, but not saying anything. Dad had read Ethan's letter and hidden it from me? It didn't make any sense. Anger and fear coursed through me.

'You *what*?' I said. 'You read the letter meant for me from Ethan? *Why*? What did it say?'

In all the years since my mum died, my dad had been very protective and overly cautious of me and Daisy, which I completely understood. But this?

'I thought I was doing the right thing,' he said. 'I opened it by mistake, and once I'd read it, I didn't want you to read it. I thought I was protecting you. I never thought he would come back.'

'But why are you telling me this now?' I asked. 'If you'd hidden it from me, why tell me about it? What did it say?'

All the time we were speaking I was imagining what was in the letter. It can't have been that awful, or else Ethan would have said something by now, wouldn't he?

'Because I know you're getting involved with Ethan again,' he sighed. 'And I want you to know, before you get too carried away, that he's not to be trusted. I hid that letter because you would have been even more heartbroken than you already are. You will be heartbroken.'

227

'OK,' I asked in a level voice. 'So what did he do? Just tell me now. Don't keep me hanging on like this.'

Dad sighed.

'I can't, darling, it has to come from him,' he said. 'Confront Ethan. This news should come from him. Get off the phone and ask him right now. I am sorry, Eve, darling. I love you so much, I've only ever wanted you to be happy. I'm here all evening so come to see me and we'll talk. I'm sorry, darling, I feel awful . . .'

For a moment, I tried to imagine being in my dad's place. It must have been so hard suddenly to be left alone to bring up two girls, to make all the decisions he's made alone. I know that he would never have meant to hurt me, though obviously I was bewildered by his decision. Normally I would have consoled him, reassured him that he'd done the right thing, but now I just couldn't.

'OK,' I said. 'Bye, Dad.'

'Bye,' he said quietly. 'I'm so sorry, my love.'

I hung up feeling numb with fear and, with my phone still in my hand, walked through the front door of Andrew's enormous house to find the bathroom and wash my face. I needed a moment to think, to gather my wits. Then I would confront Ethan. With my stomach in my mouth, I opened a door to a room I thought might be a toilet, but it was a reception room, with Alicia lying awkwardly on a couch.

'Excuse me,' she said indignantly. 'Who are you?'

I looked up to see Alicia, her pregnant bump incredibly low, spread out on the sofa, clearly in pain. She wiped her eyes and glared at me.

'I'm sorry,' I said. 'I'm Eve, one of the Supper Club guests.

Are you OK? I thought I heard you crying. I'm sorry I'm in your house uninvited. I'll get out, but I needed the toilet. Are you OK, you look so uncomfortable . . .'

Alicia rested her head against the sofa, her copper hair blooming out above her head like a halo. She breathed out and turned her head from right to left, as if loosening her neck.

'I'll be OK,' she said, before her face crumpled and she started to cry. 'Actually, I think it's all about to happen. I keep getting these cramps. But you know what? I don't want kids now, I just want my old life back.'

I opened my mouth to tell her it was a bit late, but thought better of it.

'I insisted we had this baby,' she said. 'These babies, I mean. Andrew was never into it and now I understand why. Despite how he comes across, he's still a child. How am I going to cope with three children to look after?'

Alicia put her face in her hands and I went over and awkwardly patted her shoulder. With the thought of Ethan's letter imprinted in my mind, I felt completely lost for words.

'Sorry,' she said, rubbing the bottom of her bump. 'You're a complete stranger and here I am, oh my God, this is really, owwwwwwwwww.'

Alicia gripped her lower back and bent over, apparently in excruciating pain.

'Oh my God,' I said, jumping up. 'Let me get Andrew.'

Leaving Alicia moaning on the sofa, I ran out onto the front lawn. Ethan turned to face me.

'There you are,' he said, lifting his glass up to me. Seeing him sitting there, smiling up at me, I heard my dad's voice clearly and loudly in my mind. My stomach clenched.

'Andrew,' I said quickly. 'It's Alicia. I think it's starting.'

Andrew jumped up, knocking over a chair, and ran towards the house, handing me his wine glass when he passed by. He disappeared for a second then came running out, his skin three shades paler.

'Shit,' he said. 'Phone the ambulance. Quick.'

Chapter Eighteen

Ethan grabbed my mobile phone out of my hand and rang an ambulance, giving Andrew's address and explaining that the twins were on the way. I listened to the alarm in his voice, Alicia's moans in the background, and stood, frozen to the spot, my dad's words playing out in my head. Maggie moved over to Paul, said something to him then looked at her watch.

'Ethan?' I said quietly as he paced towards me, closing up my phone and handing it back. 'Ethan, I need to speak to you.'

Ethan threw his arm over my shoulder and squeezed.

'Isn't this mad?' he said. 'The twins are about to be born. Do you think we should all fuck off? They don't want us here, do they? Hey, Maggie, I was just saying I think we should go? Do you fancy a drink?'

I wriggled free from Ethan's grip and faced him.

'Ethan,' I said steadily. 'I've just spoken to my dad. He told me he read the letter you sent when you left London. He said I can't trust you. I want to know why.'

Ethan backed away from me and shoved his hands in his pockets.

'Your dad read my letter?' he said, confused. 'So he hid it from you? How could he do that?'

I shook my head.

'Protecting me,' I said. 'Whatever you did, must have been bad. I need to know. Now.'

Ethan swallowed hard and nodded.

'Let's get out of here and we can talk,' he said, almost in a whisper.

Tripping over a suitcase, Ethan moved over to Paul and Maggie, explaining that we were going to leave. Maggie glanced at me worriedly and I gave her an anxious smile, unable to stop angry tears from welling up in my eyes.

'Ring me later?' she said, rubbing my arm. 'Are you OK?'

I nodded but couldn't speak. I felt too sick. From inside the house came a huge scream and I scanned the street for an ambulance. It can only have been seconds since Ethan called, but it felt like an eternity.

'Here,' I said, with relief. 'It's coming.'

A paramedic, with what I thought must have been a midwife, parked outside and rushed in through the garden gate. On hearing Alicia's screams, they bolted in through the front door. We all stood out on the lawn, not knowing what to do. I folded my arms across my chest. Ethan lit a cigarette and avoided my eye. Moments later, there was a tiny cry, followed by another tiny cry. Andrew appeared at the door, looking, I thought, about one hundred and fifty years old.

'Born,' he said, his eyes filling with tears. 'We have to get them to hospital now. Alicia's lost quite a lot of blood.'

There was no time for congratulations or to see the babies. In an eerie silence, Alicia white as a sheet and in tears, the new family were put into the ambulance, passers-by trying not to look at what was happening. The doors slammed shut and they were gone.

'You two go,' Maggie said to Ethan and me. 'We'll pick up this stuff and find out what's happening. We'll speak later.'

I smiled at Maggie gratefully, hardly saying goodbye to Paul, before I pushed open the garden gate and waited in the street for Ethan, my heart in my mouth.

As Ethan and I walked along the street in silence, a melting orange sunset ahead, I felt the tension crackling between us. Finally, we were alone. Something bad was about to happen. I could feel it in the sultry evening, the potent perfume of mimosa growing in a nearby garden thick in the air. I sensed it in the pit of my stomach, which lurched with every step of Ethan's deliberate stride.

'All right?' he asked, with a quick smile over his shoulder. He messed up his hair with his hand. 'Wasn't that mad? I mean, that those baby girls were born, while we were sat there, eating chips and pea fritters? Did you see Andrew's face?'

I understood, just because I knew Ethan, that he was leading up to talking to me properly.

'I know,' I said with a flicker of a smile. 'Imagine if you could freeze-frame the world and take photos of what everyone was eating at the exact moment you were born. That would make an interesting collage, wouldn't it? Probably be quite difficult logistically.'

Ethan laughed and pulled out his packet of Drum tobacco.

'That's what I like about you,' he said. 'I can always rely on you to say something weird.'

'Thanks,' I said drily. 'Ethan, are you going to talk to me

233

now? This isn't funny any more. I feel like I'm actually going to be sick.'

He sighed and rolled a cigarette and lit it, the match like burnt toast in my nose.

'Let's find somewhere to sit,' he said.

We continued to walk, a safe distance apart, though occasionally our elbows brushed against one another. He sucked rapidly on his cigarette and I rustled in my bag for a mint. I tried to distract myself by thinking about Alicia. Now she had two tiny lives in her hands, daughters who would, no doubt, completely change her life. I wondered what it must feel like, suddenly to become a mother, to have all that responsibility heaped on your shoulders. How had my own mother felt when I was born? In the pictures I had of her and me, she looked adoring, devoted, bursting with love as I clung to her like a paperclip. She had no idea, then, that she would never see me and Daisy grow up into adults, or know my father as a man in his forties and fifties. I shook my head sadly. Even though I sometimes let myself imagine what it would be like to have children – visualizing impish blondes running along a sandy beach in bare feet, tucking into a home-baked cake under the branches of a willow tree in the garden – I knew I wasn't anywhere near ready and that wasn't what it would really be like. I hadn't *done* anything yet. I felt like a child most of the time. Plus, I was terrified I'd mess it up. I didn't have a mother to show me the ropes, so I was already at a disadvantage. I snatched a glance at Ethan and tried to imagine him as a father, but I couldn't, not for a moment. I never had been able to see him in that role. He was far too interested in enjoying himself, far too self-centred.

'What are you thinking about?' he said as we turned left up another street of grand houses.

'You,' I said. 'I was wondering what you've been doing for the last three years. I was wondering what awful thing you're about to say. My dad sounded pretty bleak.'

'It's history,' he said. 'Do you really want to go there? Bring it all up?'

'I need to know,' I said.

We had veered off the main residential street and up into a side road – still in Holland Park – where we reached a locked wrought-iron gate, beyond which were the immaculate communal gardens of the enormous townhouses, beautifully landscaped into works of art. The tension in the air was unbearable. I had to break it.

'You'd think they could share their wealth a little,' I said. 'Would it really hurt to leave the gardens unlocked, so the local kids could have a play?'

'Well,' Ethan replied, 'if you don't have a key, break in. Or jump in. Let's climb over.'

'What if someone questions us?' I said warily. 'They'll know we don't live there.'

'They won't,' he said. 'This is London. No one talks to anyone else, unless they already know each other. Lots of these properties are probably pieds-á-terre for millionaires who are slurping cocktails in the Caribbean right now. If anyone does talk to us, we'll ask if they've got change for a fifty. They'll think we're locals and leave us alone.'

He caught my eye and clasped together his hands to make a foot-hold for me.

'Over you go,' he said, nodding at his hands and bending

towards me. He was trembling and was obviously nervous, which made me feel so much worse, so I tried to lighten the mood.

'Are you going to drop me over there and just leave me?' I asked, raising my eyebrows. 'Because I will scream and—'

'I won't,' he said, as I struggled into the foothold and, after checking the street for passers-by, I straddled the stone wall, pulling up the straps of my jumpsuit, which were loose on my shoulders, jumping down to the other side and landing in the branches of a hydrangea bush with a small scream.

'What on earth am I doing?' I muttered, pulling a twig from my hair. 'Ethan?'

'I'm off,' Ethan said from the other side of the wall. 'See you later.'

'Very funny,' I said, looking all around me. Beyond where I was standing was an enormous lawn, which each house, or set of flats, backed onto. A couple of properties had French doors on the ground floor flung wide open so I could see inside their opulent homes. There was opera music playing somewhere, and the sound of robust laughter coming from a group of people sitting round a table in one of the gardens.

'Come on, then,' I said to Ethan in a loud whisper. 'Come over and talk to me.'

'I'm not coming over unless you answer this question,' Ethan said, his face poking over the wall, so I could just see his grey-blue eyes.

'What?' I said. 'Come on, Ethan, this is stupid. It's you who has to answer some questions.'

I stepped away from the hydrangea bush, crunching on dry fallen leaves underfoot. Ethan pushed himself up onto the wall, where he sat, his legs dangling down, his heels rhythmically kicking against the stone.

'You feel it too, don't you?' he said quietly. 'You feel that there's something here between us, don't you? Come on, Eve, say it. You do, don't you? I want you to admit it before we talk.'

I'd waited for this since Ethan left. I'd waited for him to come back and tell me he still loved me, but now it was happening, I felt completely thrown. My heart raced.

'I . . .' I frowned and shook my head. 'I don't—'

'I know you do,' he said. 'Admit it, there's something here between us. You can feel it too, can't you?'

I bit my lip. Up until this point, I had played safe. I hadn't crossed that certain line in my head. If I spoke now, I would be taking this, whatever it might be, to another level. I would be stepping over that line.

'Oh God, Ethan,' I said. 'I don't know! It's not that simple. You can't just walk out, then turn up years later and expect everything to be as it was. All I want to know now is what the letter said. Tell me, for fuck's sake!' Ethan was gazing at me. He ignored my words. His smile was wry, knowing. He jumped down from the wall.

'But do you think there's something there?' he said. 'I know I'm not imagining it. You feel it too, don't you? That's the important thing.'

I thought, randomly, about Joe's morning. Most days, I knew what he ate for breakfast, that he didn't like more than a drop of milk on his cereal, that he had a digestive biscuit and a cup of coffee before anything else, that he spent ages coaxing his hair into shape with my hair wax, but pretended he never used any. He suddenly seemed very far away, almost like he belonged to a different life. And Ethan seemed incredibly close, hyperreal. I could feel his breath on my skin as he stroked my cheek and tilted my chin up so I was facing him.

'You do, don't you?' he said, quietly urgent.

I wanted him to kiss me.

'Yes,' I said. 'But that doesn't mean . . . I want to know what you wrote—'

'It means enough,' Ethan said, interrupting me. He leaned forwards, finding my lips with his, and, standing there by the hydrangea bush, we kissed. It wasn't the tentative kiss I'd expected. Ethan was bold, firm. Ethan was telling me something with this kiss. His hands were around my waist now, fiddling with the buttons on my jumpsuit. It was all going so fast, my thoughts couldn't keep up with what was happening. Even though a voice in my head was shouting at me to stop, I carried on kissing him back. It was a release. I thought of nothing. What was he telling me with his kiss?

'Sorry,' he said suddenly, pulling away from me and running his hands through his hair. 'I'm so, so sorry.'

I took a deep breath and rubbed my hands over my face.

'For leaving?' I said, tucking my hair behind my ears. 'Or for this? Because I am too. I should not be doing this, it's . . . God, I don't even know what I'm doing here. You lure me away from Joe and—'

'I didn't lure you away,' he said. 'You came of your own free will.'

The spell now broken, I shivered with cold. I'd done it now. I panicked. Dad had told me Ethan was untrustworthy,

238

that he would break my heart, again. Why was I kissing him? My stomach folded in on itself.

'Tell me what that letter said,' I said. 'Now.'

'OK' he said. 'OK, I'm sorry I left you in such a horrible way. I really, badly fucked up and – shit, I don't know what to say.'

Ethan was dying. I could see this was close to impossible for him to talk about. Ethan didn't apologize very often. He hated to admit he was in the wrong.

'I promised myself I would tell you,' he said, kicking at loose stones with his shoes. 'I promised myself if you told me you still loved me, I had to tell you the truth. I had to tell you what was in the letter I sent, the one that your dad read. Then we could start again, on even footing. Then there would be no secrets waiting to jump out of the dark.'

I didn't like the sound of this. I glanced up the gardens. The people previously sitting out had gone inside and switched out their kitchen light. It must be getting late.

'Tell me what?' I said, my voice thin.

'The reason I left,' he said, taking a deep breath and then exhaling slowly. 'I left because I slept with someone else.'

His shoulders drooped in relief for having got it off his chest. He shoved his hands into his pockets and glanced up at me, his expression guilty.

'Oh,' I said, too utterly stunned to react, but still – even then – wanting it not to matter, desperate for all this still to mean something, for me not to be throwing away what I had for nothing. 'Who?'

'I'll come to that,' he said. 'The point is I felt terrible, I couldn't cope with what I'd done and so I ran away to Rome

239

like an idiot, and now I'm back I want you to know how I feel about you. I never stopped loving you.'

Ethan looked at me pleadingly. He held on to both my hands, but I shook him off.

'Who?' I said.

'Please,' he said. 'That's not important right now.'

'Yes, it is important,' I said firmly, my body trembling with dread, because suddenly it did matter. It mattered more than anything else in the world. Faces of girls we knew and didn't know circled in my thoughts.

'Who?'

Chapter Nineteen

'I wrote you that letter,' Ethan said now, his skin pale and expression deadly serious. 'I explained everything in there. I asked you to forgive me. When I didn't hear back from you, I assumed you hated my guts. That's why I stayed out in Rome. But now, this is fate. I really believe that. There's no other explanation for meeting again like this. It's time to stop burying my head in the sand.'

Ethan was shaking now, as he pulled his tobacco from his pocket. I snatched it away from him and threw it on the floor. He looked at me warily.

'Who?' I said slowly. 'Who did you sleep with?'

He looked at the floor and shook his head. His shoulders rounded, he rubbed the back of his neck. From a road nearby came the screech of sirens.

'It's bad,' he said quietly, keeping his eyes on the floor. 'OK?'

He held my gaze for a few seconds. I felt sick.

'OK,' I said in a voice barely more than a whisper, my stomach tightening into knots.

'I need you to let me explain why it happened,' he said softly. 'You might understand if you just let me explain.'

I breathed out, my cheeks puffing out with air. My heart was pounding so hard, blood whooshing in my ears, I felt faint. I stared at Ethan, waiting. Still waiting. Always waiting.

'Who?' I said. 'Who. Did. You. Sleep. With.'

He squeezed his eyes shut. I grabbed his wrist and shook him.

'Tell me!' I said.

'All right, all right,' he said. 'Oh, fuck, fuck, fuck. I wish you'd got my letter after I left. Bloody hell, I'm sorry.'

He turned and fixed me in the eye. Cringing, he folded his arms across his chest and wedged his hands under his armpits. All at once, I was reminded of Joe. I sucked in my breath.

'I can't believe I did this,' he said, swallowing quickly. 'I wake up in the night, sweating about it. It's pretty much my biggest regret. You have to let me explain, it can all be explained . . .'

My stomach lurched. I stared at him.

'Daisy,' he said, quietly.

Daisy. I shook my head in disbelief. My mouth fell open.

'Daisy?' I said, my eyes almost popping out of their sockets. 'As in Daisy, my *sister* Daisy?'

Ethan nodded sheepishly and cleared his throat. Out of the corner of his eye, he watched me, a grim expression on his face. Taken aback, I blinked. I couldn't understand. A hideous image of Daisy and Ethan in bed together flashed into my mind. I let out a horrible whimper then slapped my hand over my mouth.

'Daisy?' I said again from behind my fingers, beginning to tremble. 'When?'

'At that summer party we had, three years ago, literally days before I left,' Ethan said, the words coming quickly. 'It was a massive mistake and only happened once, foolishly, because, well, I was out of my head. We'd been drinking all day and, oh God, this sounds bad, but she came on to me and I felt sorry for her.'

I cast my mind back to that party, which Daisy had helped organize. She wore a green silk dress. She looked more beautiful than I'd ever seen her, more beautiful than me by far. She also got drunk and danced, which was rare for Daisy. She didn't normally drink much. Perhaps she'd been planning the seduction all along? I wondered if I was going to be sick.

'You slept with my sister because you felt *sorry* for her?' I choked. 'What the fuck? Are you completely mad? What is there to feel sorry about? I don't believe you, Ethan. Daisy would never do that to me; she's my sister.'

I started to walk away from Ethan, my legs liquid. He was seriously sick. Thinking about it, just for a second, made me realize Daisy would never, ever do such a thing. She didn't even like Ethan. Through bleary eyes I looked for the garden gate. I had to get out of there. He was mad. He was sick. Why would he say such a thing? I scrabbled for a reason. Finding the gate, I fiddled with the lock, but it was padlocked. I rattled it stupidly. Ethan stood near me, running his hands through his hair. I turned to face him.

'You're crazy,' I said, my voice shaking. 'Why would you say such a thing? I need to get out of this garden, away from you . . .'

I looked around, desperately, for a way to get out of the garden. I wanted to scream. I noticed a dustbin close to the wall. I dragged it closer still, then climbed up onto it while it wobbled beneath me. I clung on to the top of the wall, trying and failing not to cry.

'It's the truth,' Ethan said from by my feet. 'Let me help you.'

Ethan tried to support my leg as I swung myself up onto the wall, but I kicked him away.

'Don't touch me,' I spat, wiping my eyes with the back of my hand. 'Don't you dare touch me, you liar!'

He held on to my foot and I pulled it away, so he was left holding my sandal.

'Why would I lie about something so awful?' he said, his lips quivering. 'Please. I'm so sorry. Let me tell you what happened. Your shoe?'

'I don't want to know,' I said, sliding down the wall and onto the pavement, tiptoeing on my bare foot. I took off the other sandal and started walking towards the Tube as quickly as I could in bare feet, my heart in my mouth. I heard Ethan jump down from the wall behind me, run to catch me up.

'Your shoes,' he said. 'Put your shoes on. You'll hurt yourself. There's probably glass on the floor.'

'I don't want them,' I said forcibly, facing forwards. 'Go away. Just . . . just . . . leave me alone! You disappeared before, do it again now. Go! Why did you come back? Go!'

Ethan tugged at my arm to try to get me to stop, but I refused to look at him. Then he started talking, his voice low with an edge of anger.

'It happened that night of the party,' he said quickly. 'Can you remember, we had a row about something stupid like how often I went out? Can you remember that Daisy was pretty drunk? I walked her home, just to get some headspace, and she invited me in for a whiskey. When we'd had another drink, she started to cry, telling me that she'd always been secretly in love with me during the whole time she was with Iain. Apparently when she invited me to that winter picnic in Greenwich Park she'd been hoping that something would happen between us, but then I went off with you. I'd had no idea she felt like that.'

I said nothing, too shocked to speak. I told myself: if I keep walking, he'll go away.

'She broke down and said it was torture watching us together,' he said. 'She said she could've made me happy if only I'd let her, if only you didn't exist. She then started throwing accusations at me, saying I didn't find her attractive and Iain didn't and that no one was ever going to love her. She said you had everything, you always got everything you wanted and that no one understood her and that she might as well just kill herself. Then she went into her bedroom and after a few minutes she called me in. I was worried she might be about to overdose or do something mad, she was *that* upset. I went in to see her and she had taken her clothes off, Eve. She was sitting there, naked and crying her heart out. It killed me, seeing her like that. Daisy has always seemed so strong and capable. She was all broken up. I should have left, but I wanted to comfort her and make her feel better. I hated seeing her so sad. She asked me to hold her, so I did. I held her and told her she was beautiful and that of course she would find someone to love. She said she didn't want anyone else and that she wanted me. So I stupidly said, if it had all been different, etcetera, perhaps she and I would have got together. I said it just to make her feel better. But she took me on my word, because she started kissing me and, I don't know, I knew it was the biggest mistake in the world, but I didn't know what else to do. To reject her again felt too cruel. Iain, then me, you know? I justified it to myself as a few minutes of my life that would make Daisy feel better about herself.'

My eyes were bleary with tears. I tasted salt on my lips.

'And what about me?' I said. 'Where do I come into this? Did it not occur to you for one second that I might not be too happy about your grand act of charity? Your screwed-up fucking benevolence? I mean, Christ, Ethan, you can't actually think that's an excuse for screwing my sister? Why couldn't you have just hugged her and given her a therapist's number?'

He shrugged hopelessly.

'I was so involved in the moment that nothing occurred to me other than how I could get Daisy to stop crying,' he said. 'I didn't think properly. It was all so intense and emotional. I know it seems ludicrous, but I can't bear to see anyone in such a state. I felt sorry for her and guilty that it was me, me and you, making her feel so bad.'

I let out a strangled laugh in disbelief.

'You expect me to believe that?' I said. 'That is complete and utter bollocks. You fancied a fuck and you got one, then you dress it up with all this "I felt sorry for her" crap. Saint Ethan saves the day. Great. How long did this go on for? Were you having flings behind my back from the beginning? Anyone else you felt sorry for while we were together, apart from my . . . my . . . *sister*! Nice choice, Ethan.'

He shook his head wearily.

'I'm not making out I'm a saint,' he said. 'It might sound

like a stupid story to you, but it's not. I made a mistake, I admit that, but it was complicated. Daisy was so unhappy, so vulnerable and it was all my fault—'

'I can't believe you,' I said, almost laughing. 'Couldn't you have just perhaps talked to Daisy, or made her a cup of sodding tea or something?'

Ethan put his hands on his face and growled. A taxi pulled in further up the road. I lifted my hand to hail the cab, but it drove off without noticing me.

'Shit,' I said. 'I want to go home.'

'But life isn't always black and white, is it?' he said. 'You have to allow for grey areas.'

'I'm not interested in grey areas,' I said. 'You've just blown my world apart. Could you just leave me alone? God, why did you even tell me? What good can come out of telling me? Now everything is ruined. Joe is pissed off with me, Daisy has betrayed me and you are the biggest wanker that graced the earth . . .'

Tears were streaming down my face. I felt them on my neck.

'I had to tell you because your dad found the letter,' he said. 'And anyway, if we got back together, Daisy would tell you herself. That was always her threat. That was why I left in the first place. She said if she couldn't have me, no one could, and that I should leave, or she would tell you I seduced her. That night, when I left her house, I hated myself so much I wanted to die.'

'Why didn't you tell me that night?' I said. 'Just run the risk that I might hate you but that I might forgive you?'

'Because I thought you'd never speak to me again,' he

247

said. 'And if I didn't tell you but I stayed, Daisy would. I was trapped. I left because I thought it would be better for everyone. You could get on with your life without me. Daisy wouldn't be in pain. If I'd stayed, you and Daisy would have fallen out and we might have broken up.'

'Too bloody right,' I said. 'You were saving yourself, Ethan. You were running away from a shambolic situation that you created to save face.'

Ethan shook his head vehemently. He interrupted me.

'After I'd been away a month, I missed you so much I questioned my actions,' he said. 'I thought about how much I loved you and hoped that we were strong enough to get through anything, so I wrote to you explaining everything. I knew you and Daisy would fall out and I felt terrible about that, but my desire for you was greater. Selfish, perhaps, but I loved you too much not to tell you the truth. I waited and waited for your answer but it never came, so I assumed that was it, you hated me, full stop. I know this is horrible to hear. I wish I could change what I did. But I didn't do it because I'm ruthless and egotistical. It was a mess, the biggest mess, but I love you and always have. I will love you until I die.'

Ethan was crying now, but I didn't care. I wanted him to feel as miserable as me.

'Eve,' he said, tears running down his cheeks. 'I'm sorry.'

We'd reached the Tube now and had paused outside in the busy pavement. People were unashamedly watching us. It was clear we were having a massive argument. Being looked at didn't stop me from crying. I didn't think I'd ever stop. I was utterly dumbfounded. Through the tears, I scrabbled in my bag for my Oyster card and grabbed my sandal from Ethan. I threw it on the pavement and stuffed my foot inside. I took a deep breath.

'You ruined my life once,' I said to Ethan. 'And now you've done it again. Don't come near me, ever again.'

Ethan grabbed my arm. His eyes were red and his skin blotchy. He looked scared and, for a fraction of a moment, my heart softened and I felt sorry for him.

'Don't go,' he said. 'Please. Calm down. I love you.'

I pulled my arm back from him, touched my Oyster card to the machine and went through the barrier. When I glanced back, he didn't look the relaxed, confident, charming man he usually was. He looked hollowed out, panic-stricken. Lost.

'I know you still love me,' he called after me, as I joined the queue of people waiting to go down the stairs to the trains rumbling noisily below. 'Even now, I know you do. I'm not perfect, I messed up, but I love you so much I can't sleep. I talk to you, Eve. I talk to you like you're there with me. You're always with me, in my heart.'

People were looking at me, some with half-smiles of amusement on their faces, as if we were re-enacting a romantic scene from a film. Except in this case, there was no happy ending. I didn't smile. I kept my eyes firmly fixed on my hands, bleary with tears.

'Life is nothing without you!' he shouted again, as I descended out of view. 'I love you.'

I'd waited a long time to hear those three words again. And now they meant nothing. Nothing at all.

'There's only you!' I heard him shout, before I was on the platform and he was no longer in earshot. 'Only you.'

I nearly laughed. You hit the nail on the head, Ethan. It's only me, now. Only me.

I waited on the platform, alongside a boy with a pink Mohican and a group of girls dressed up in tiny black dresses and high heels. They were laughing loudly and sharing a bottle of wine, even though you weren't supposed to drink booze on the Underground any more. No one seemed to care, or even notice. I stared, not really seeing, at the destination sign flashing overhead, trying to work out where to go. A wave of nausea washed over me. Despite the heat of the night and the suffocating Underground air, I shivered. What was I going to do? I tried to make sense of Ethan's words, but every time I imagined him and Daisy together, I wanted to throw up. Folding my arms across my stomach, I sucked in my breath as a train thundered into the platform, blowing my hair up into the air. It screeched to a halt and stopped, the doors flinging open. I decided to get on the train and change at Oxford Circus, then go to see my dad. It was all I could think to do. Dad must know all about this. I stepped up on the train and closed my eyes for a moment. Had Daisy and Dad talked about this? Exactly how much did he know? I shook my head in despair. How could they not tell me about something that affects me so profoundly? I felt blindsided. I found a seat and ignored the people opposite staring at my blotchy, tear-stained face. I focused on a poster above their heads advertising a dating agency. Someone had changed the 'd' to an 'm' with a thick black felt marker pen. I flicked my eyes along to the next advert for around-the-world tickets. Perhaps that's what I would have to do now? Get lost somewhere, on the other side of the world. I couldn't stay in London. The reason my ex-boyfriend had left me was because he'd slept with my sister. She, apparently, had gone all out to steal him from me, then was the epitome of sympathy when he left. I'd treated Joe really badly because I'd thought I was still in love with my ex, probably thrown away anything we had, and what about the cafe?

It's not just your dream, I remembered Isabel saying.

Maybe I should just jack the whole lot in, pack my bags and leave, just as Ethan had done, just as Isabel was about to do. But I couldn't do that to my dad, could I? He'd feel abandoned, blamed. Mum had gone, I couldn't go too. Oh God. One minute life is good, the next, you're slam-dunking into a deep dark pit. With a groan, I leaned forward and rested my face in my hands, replaying Ethan's description of his infidelity in my mind. Grotesque images filtered into my head and I snapped my eyes open instead. The awful thing was, as much as I hated Ethan, even now, the news just sinking into my brain, though I didn't want to, I believed Ethan, that he felt sorry for Daisy on some level. It was just like him to want to make things better. But the fact remained that he slept with my sister. No one forced him to, even if he did feel sorry for her. But Daisy's desperation – her level of jealousy – shocked me. She'd never even mentioned that she liked Ethan before we'd got together, let alone since. And when I'd broken up with Ethan – or rather he had fled to Rome – she'd been loyal and loving. She'd listened to me sobbing about how much I didn't want to live without him. She'd talked me out of flying to Italy to try to get him back.

'It's stronger to stay away,' she'd advised, when I was desperate to contact him.

I shook my head at the memory of her advice, so controlled and self-assured. I'd hung on to Daisy's words. But now, those words seemed loaded with self-interest. Would she really want to destroy my relationship with Ethan because she wanted him for herself? Even though I'd told her on countless occasions how happy we were? I closed my eyes again and felt our entire shared history unravelling furiously quickly, like the rope of an anchor thrown out to sea. If I couldn't trust my own sister, who in this world could I trust?

'Eve,' said Joe's voice from somewhere nearby. 'Are you all right?'

I pinged open my eyes. There was Joe, a look of astonishment on his face, his eyes full of concern, his skin light brown from the sun, standing just down the carriage. He smiled at me and I felt my eyes instantly fill with tears. He moved towards me, navigating several pairs of legs and a suitcase. I didn't trust myself to speak, so I nodded my head in reply, biting down on my lip. I wanted to tell him everything, but I couldn't say a word. He didn't know anything. He didn't know what my life had now become. He knew only that I'd treated him badly and resisted his love. I wanted to shout out that without him, my life had suddenly become a scary, horrible place. That I wanted him to come back. But I couldn't. He deserved better.

'I'm just going to see my dad,' I said in a small voice.

Joe nodded.

'How's the cafe?' he asked, picking bits of nothing off his T-shirt. 'I want you to keep that money.'

'Fine,' I said. 'But I can't accept your money. Honestly, Joe, it's really sweet of you, but it's not going to happen.'

We looked at one another. Joe gave me a sad smile.

'Look at it as an investment,' he said. 'We've been friends forever and despite what might happen, I want you to get on and realize your dreams. Keep it.'

He glanced up out of the window at the platform we were drawing in to. He twisted his body away from me and held on to the bar above our heads.

'I can't,' I said again. Joe looked hurt.

'I'm getting off here,' he said. 'Just keep the cash. Do me a favour.'

'Oh, Joe,' I said, suddenly panicking. 'Do you have to go? I need to talk.'

Joe frowned and looked at me like I'd said something completely outrageous.

'I don't really feel like talking,' he said. 'Goodbye.'

He stepped off the carriage and, without looking back at me, he disappeared into a throng of people pushing their way to the exit. I stayed watching in case he turned round, but the doors slammed shut and the train raced off, with a high-pitched scream, into a dark tunnel.

'Goodbye,' I whispered, my hand pressed against the window.

Chapter Twenty

'Sit down, my love,' Dad said, when he let me in the front door in floods of tears, and led me through to the kitchen. 'Let me get you a very strong drink.'

He pulled out a chair for me at the kitchen table. I flopped down onto it and rested my arms on the scratched table surface, reaching out to the biscuit tin and pulling off the lid.

'I bought those this afternoon,' he said, as I lifted out a pale pink macaroon and sank my teeth into it. 'They're a little brittle. Would you like a hot chocolate with a shot of something in it? That's what I feel like.'

I let the sugar melt on my tongue, nodded and muttered my thanks, my heart drumming so hard I felt sure he must be able to hear it. How could I broach this subject? I knew, once I'd said what I had to say, everything would change. Our little family unit of three would be ripped up by feelings of distrust and resentment. All my dad's hard work over the years, to give our family a heart, despite my mother not being there, the missing ingredient, would be ruined. Was this any way to thank him? I fleetingly entertained the idea of not saying anything about it, but I knew I had to. After all, he'd told me to confront Ethan. He'd wanted me to know the truth. There was no way I could pretend it had never happened, as my dad had done.

'You spoke to Ethan, then,' he said quietly, moving around the kitchen, his shaved head shining under the spotlights, while I picked fallen petals from a vase of white roses. With his back to me, he found a bar of bittersweet chocolate in the cupboard. He set about grating half of it into a saucepan, then pouring over milk, before turning up the heat. I put the petals in a heap and drummed my fingers on the table.

'Yes,' I said. 'I did.'

'Dark sugar,' Dad said. 'Bit of nutmeg and a good slug of rum. That's the way she made it, wasn't it?'

'Yes,' I said, remembering the hot chocolate Mum used to make for Dad, then for Daisy and me, minus the rum. It was always incredibly thick. She was never mean with the chocolate.

'So, what did he tell you?' Dad asked. 'The truth?'

I nodded and he sighed, shaking his head. He heated the saucepan, stirring rhythmically before pouring the hot chocolate into small glass tumblers and handing me one. He pulled a chair out opposite me, placed his own glass down in front of him and smiled sympathetically.

'It's bad,' he said. 'I'm sorry, my love. I'm sorry if it was wrong not to tell you, but I didn't want you and Daisy to fall out over a man.'

He reached his hands over the table and clasped mine tightly in his.

'You should have given me the letter,' I said. 'I've spent three years wondering why.'

'But you would have hated Daisy,' he said in a low, emotional tone. 'And I couldn't bear to see you girls fall out. I know I shouldn't have read the letter. It was addressed to you, care of me, and I had no idea it was from him. I opened it absent-mindedly, but when I flicked my eyes over it, I took the decision to keep it from you. I didn't want you to know what Daisy had done, what Ethan had done, for two reasons. One, because you're my baby girl and I couldn't bear to see you hurt so much and two, because I didn't want you girls to fall out. Your mother would have hated it. Her dying wish was that I made sure we three, as a family, stayed close. I stand by my decision. This family has seen enough sadness. I thought we'd never see Ethan again.'

Dad stopped speaking and took a deep breath.

'But why would you keep that information from me?' I asked, unable to keep the anger out of my voice. 'I'm not a baby. Why didn't you let me have the facts? Then I could have lived accordingly. You might have wanted to respect Mum's wishes, but she's dead! What about my wishes? I'm alive! You've seen how I've felt since Ethan has been back. You've seen how I've behaved towards Joe. Why the hell didn't you set me straight? And as for Daisy! I spend my entire life treading on eggshells around her, and all the time she's been stabbing me in the back.'

Dad sat back in his chair, let his arms drop to his side and sighed.

'I didn't want you and Daisy to hate one another,' he said again quietly. 'You and Daisy are everything to me. Your mum would have been heartbroken if she thought you weren't happy together. God, it's always been difficult to keep

Daisy happy. She's always been jealous of you, but I've done my best. When I found out she'd done this, I was horrified. I was so disappointed, but I sensed she was too, in herself. She's not a bad person, Eve. She's just jealous and insecure. She never really grieved properly for your mum and you know me, I couldn't talk to her about it. I decided to treat her like an adult, let her be on her own, and concentrate on you. That's probably where it all started. We should have talked more but after your mum died I wasn't too good, I kind of fell apart for a while . . .'

Dad's sentence trailed off. He suddenly looked frail and older than his years. His eyes were moist.

'Don't think about that now, Dad,' I said gently, as bravely as I could. 'You'll upset yourself. I'm not blaming you. What's done is done. I just wish I had known.'

'Oh, love,' he said. 'It's all my fault. I know it is. I'm sorry. I've failed you and Daisy. I've failed your mother. The whole thing, I've messed up, trying to do the right thing but getting it completely wrong . . .'

Dad put his elbows on the table and rested his head in his hands.

'It's not your fault,' I said. 'It's Ethan and Daisy's fault. The only thing you should have done differently is to have shown me that letter. I don't want to be kept in the dark about my own life. As for Daisy, I can't even think about her yet. I seriously can't let myself think about how angry, how betrayed I feel . . .'

Dad sat up straight again and pushed back his chair and walked over to the cooker. He picked up the saucepan and poured himself more hot chocolate. I lifted my glass to my lips and sipped, jumping when there was a loud knock on the door. My stomach turned. Daisy? I looked at the clock on the wall. Eleven o'clock. No, it couldn't be Daisy, she would be at home. I noticed a takeaway menu on the table.

'Who's this?' I said, frowning. 'You're not expecting anyone, are you? Have you ordered a takeaway?

Dad shook his head. He put down the saucepan and cleared his throat. He moved through the kitchen, catching his reflection in the mirror as he went. I noticed him grimace at himself, checking his teeth.

'It might be . . .' he said. 'It could be Elaine.'

'Elaine?' I said. 'Who's that?'

Dad said he'd tell me later. He moved to the front door. I stayed at the table, clutching my tumbler of hot chocolate, listening. I sucked in my breath when I heard Ethan's voice, slurred with alcohol.

'Frankie,' I heard him say. 'I need to speak to your daughter. I love her. I've always loved her. Please, let me see her. I know she's here. She must be.'

Shakily, I got up from my chair and tiptoed to the kitchen door. I held on to the side of it and peered around the edge, where I could see Dad's back and parts of Ethan. He was gesturing wildly, begging Dad to let him in. I stayed silent, not wanting him to see me. I felt like I was watching the whole scene from above.

'I think you should go,' Dad said. I hung back in the shadows, my arms crossed. I could see Ethan, wrung out, a man in pain. I didn't feel sorry for him.

'Nothing good is going to come of you speaking to Eve tonight,' he said. 'She's too upset. You're drunk. Go home. Go away. I wish you'd never come back.'

'Stop being so over-protective of her!' Ethan said. 'You always treated her like she's six years old. She's an adult. Let her make up her own mind!'

'I do not treat her like she's six years old,' he said. 'I just don't want a drunken idiot like you in my house at midnight, thank you very much. I think you've created enough drama for one night. I shouldn't let you anywhere near either of my daughters! Not that you care about Daisy.'

'For God's sake, Frankie,' Ethan said. 'Let me see Eve! I don't "not care" about Daisy, I just don't want to be with her. It's Eve I love. You know that. Daisy needs help, therapy or something.'

What was this? Ethan was defending Daisy now? He was portraying Daisy as the victim and not me. My breathing was fast, my heart pounding and Dad, quiet, let his grip slip off the edge of the door. Suddenly his fist was in the air and he punched Ethan on the jaw. I gasped and ran into the hallway.

'Dad!' I said. 'What are you doing?'

Ethan was groaning and holding his jaw, but he was still standing. Dad grabbed him by his shirt and pushed him up against the wall in the storm porch.

'Do not talk to me like that,' Dad said, his voice hard.

'Sorry,' Ethan said quickly, noticing me behind him. 'I'm sorry. But I'm not the villain. It's complicated. People are complicated. Eve, can we talk?'

Ethan's face was bobbing up over Dad's shoulder, his eyes seeking mine. I shook my head and clasped my fingers together.

'Not now,' I said. 'You'd better go. Please, just go.'

Ethan held his palms up.

'I'll go,' he said, staggering. 'But this isn't the end. This is not the end.'

When Ethan turned away, I joined Dad at the door. He slipped his arm over my shoulder and I watched a muscle under his eye twitching.

'Bloody fool,' he said with a grimace. 'Him, I mean.'

I went to close the door when a woman I recognized arrived on the doorstep.

'Hello,' Dad said. 'Hello, Elaine.'

The woman – Elaine – came into the house and closed the front door behind her, leaning up against it like she was being chased.

'Good God, who was that guy?' she said, her accent American. 'What on earth is going on? Do you want me to call the police, Frankie, honey?'

Frankie, honey? I shook my head. I frowned, knowing I knew her, but I couldn't quite place her. Then I realized who it was. My doctor, from when I was at school.

'Dr Evans,' I said, confused. 'What are you doing here?'

My mind raced. Was Dad ill? Was she coming to deliver him medicine or something? No, I told myself, you're just being ridiculous.

'This is Dr Evans, as you know,' Dad said sheepishly. 'This is Elaine.'

Elaine reached out to shake my hand and Dad, who had almost stopped breathing, stood still as the stocks with a tense grin on his face.

'Lovely to see you again,' Elaine said, eyeing Dad curiously.

The tension in the air was palpable.

'Dad,' I said, looking from him to Elaine. 'What's going on?'

Dad rubbed his forehead and steered me back into the kitchen and told me to sit down at the table. Dr Evans followed us, in a cloud of Chanel No. 5.

'Gosh,' he said. 'This is all very bad timing. I wanted to tell you another way but, to be honest, I've been afraid of how Daisy will react. But, darling, this is Elaine. This is my girlfriend, Elaine.'

'Girlfriend?' I said, looking from him to Dr Evans.

'Well,' she said, 'it's a little bit more than that, isn't it, Frankie?'

Dad shook his head to silence her. He stood perfectly still, fearfully watching for my reaction from under his sun-bleached eyelashes.

'Why all the secrets, Dad?' I asked. 'Why not be honest? What are you scared of?'

He shrugged, sighed and slumped into his seat.

'If I can say something here,' Elaine said, putting down her handbag on the table and taking a seat. 'I think your dad is scared witless or shitless, whatever. If he tells people that we are together, it will become more real and that is frightening to him. Just take one look at me, you can understand why. No, but seriously, he's reluctant to let go of the past, even if the past is just memories.'

I looked at Dad and he looked at me, with a sad smile. From his expression, I knew that memories of Mum were suddenly flooding both our minds. We missed her. I hugged him.

'We're not so different, are we, love?' he said, hugging me back. 'Not so different at all.'

Chapter Twenty-One

I was relieved when the sun rose and filled the bedroom with pale yellow light. I'd spent a sleepless night in my childhood room, which had remained pretty much as it had been when I'd left for university, ten years earlier, with its candy-pink striped duvet cover and matching cushions from Habitat and a sticker of Jason Priestley peeling off the wardrobe. Wearily, I pulled on my dressing gown, pale pink and fluffy, that I'd had since I was fifteen years old and pushed my hair out of my eyes. I opened the door slowly, so as not to wake Dad – and Elaine – then padded downstairs to the kitchen. I paused at the bottom of the stairs to inspect Elaine's Kurt Geiger heels, carelessly strewn on the floor next to her expensive-looking leather handbag that was sagging open so I could see a well-thumbed black diary and a blister pack of some kind of tablet. Despite my anxious mood and it being such a surprise, I smiled at the thought of Dad having a girlfriend. He was so embarrassed about the whole thing – his entire bald scalp had turned pink last night when he'd told me about meeting Elaine – but he'd waited a long time for this. He deserved happiness more than anyone, even if it did feel like our roles were reversed. I could understand why he wanted to move out of this house now. My mother had inherited the house, once in a state of disrepair, from her grandparents and she had lovingly brought it back to life to create a gorgeous family home. It was an expression of her. If I had been Elaine, I wouldn't want to live there; just the decoration alone made it feel like there was another woman in the house. I stood in front of a large framed photograph of Mum hanging on the wall in the kitchen. She was holding a pitcher of lemonade and smiling brightly. Daisy held on to Mum's leg and burrowed her face into her skirt, a gingham fabric printed with patterns of watermelons. I imagined Daisy's response when Dad told her about Elaine. I knew she would freak out about it. God. I frowned; just thinking about Daisy made me feel sick. Everything was going to change. I moved to the sink to wash up a cup and stared blankly out of the window into the garden. The early morning sun was steaming the dew from the grass and the big red poppies at the far end of the garden were unfurling their petals. I looked up at the brilliantly blue cloudless sky. It was going to be another scorcher. Not that I could enjoy it. My hands shook as I boiled the kettle, made myself a strong black coffee and sat at the kitchen table, eyes flitting everywhere, quietly sipping. It was eerily quiet. You'd never know this was London, I thought, vaguely aware I was up earlier than I'd ever been before. In the silence, I tried not to think about Ethan and Daisy, though in reality it was all I could think about. I'd been thinking about them all night long, obsessing over whether everything that Ethan had said was true. The pictures he'd painted spun in my head in confused circles. How could Daisy do that to me? Was Ethan genuinely sorry? Why would he have told me if he wasn't? Was one attempt at making amends in writing a letter I never got anywhere near enough? I was indescribably angry with them both. Now that the first feelings of fury had subsided ever so slightly, and if everything Ethan had said was true, I was overwhelmed with a horrible feeling of disappointment. Everything I had believed about my relationship with Daisy had been turned on its head. And, because I'd never known the reason Ethan had left and had been confused by my feelings for him since he'd returned, my relationship with Joe was probably wrecked. I bit my lip, to stop myself from crying.

'Hi,' said Elaine, from the kitchen doorway. 'Are you OK?'

Surprised by her voice, that strong American accent in our kitchen, I turned to face her quickly, nodded and smiled, pulling my dressing gown tighter around my middle. She wore navy-blue and white spotted silk pyjamas and bare feet with her toenails painted dark red. Her blonde hair was held back with a tortoiseshell butterfly clip and her pale skin seemed almost translucent without make-up. I couldn't get the image of Elaine as Dr Evans the GP out of my head. I blushed again, thinking how she knew everything about me; that I had gone on the pill aged sixteen without telling Dad, had suffered repeated tonsillitis whenever I got stressed and refused anti-depressants when Ethan first left and I could hardly get out of bed.

'Your dad told me all the details about your ex and your sister,' she said, pulling a face. 'I'm so sorry. That must really, really hurt, as if it didn't hurt enough already.'

She readjusted the clip in her hair and folded her arms in front of her.

'It does,' I said. I gave a brave smile and shrugged my shoulders sadly. 'What can I do? I feel like a fool.'

'What are you going to do?' she said. 'Have you spoken to your sister yet? If I were you, I'd tell her exactly what I thought of her. Stealing your sister's boyfriend is pretty damn low.'

I shook my head. 'Not yet,' I said, feeling anger rise in me. 'I'm planning on going to see her, though. I need to talk to her, to see if everything Ethan, that's my ex, has said is true, but it all makes me feel really sick. Plus I've messed my relationship up with Joe, my boyfriend. He just thinks I'm the flakiest woman in the world because I've been so non-committal, which I probably am.'

I sighed heavily. Elaine smiled warmly then walked to the sink. She ran the water and took a tumbler out of the cupboard. It was clear she'd been here before plenty of times and knew her way around. I wondered how long Dad had been keeping her a secret for.

'Bloody men,' Elaine said, filling her glass then taking a drink. 'Ah, that's just what the doctor ordered.'

She winked at me, then continued.

'You're better off without men,' she said. 'Except for your dad, of course. He's different. But I know how you're feeling. My ex-husband, my God, he was a shit. I'm surprised I didn't end up in Holloway for whacking him over the head with a frying pan.'

'Really?' I said, watching in surprise as she pulled a packet of cigarettes from her pyjama pocket.

'Don't tell anyone,' she said, sliding a cigarette from the

packet. 'I spend the day telling patients they have to stop because they are decimating their lungs, and here I am secretly
sucking on these death-sticks like there's no tomorrow, which
of course there won't be if I carry on . . .'

She paused to lift up the cigarette and shook her head in
dismay. 'What a hypocrite,' she finished. 'I promise myself
every morning I will stop but, whatever I do, I can't stop for
longer than a couple of months. Anyway, sorry, what was I
saying? Ah yes, my ex-husband was quite nice once upon a
time, he was good at badminton, anyway – that's how we met,
over a shuttlecock on the badminton court. But as the years
passed he became intolerable. He was a workaholic, and when
his business failed he suffered a massive midlife crisis. I tried to
be understanding and help him through it, but then he started
sleeping around with women, like sex was going out of fash-
ion, and that doesn't do much for your self-esteem, does it?'

She raised her eyebrows and rolled her eyes.

'I was a wreck and found myself living in a life I didn't
recognize,' she said with a sigh. 'I had to get out to preserve
what was left of me, so I divorced him. That was six years
ago. Then, when your father asked me out last year, I was
delighted. He is such a gentle, caring, sweet man. But if it's
any consolation, honey, I know what you're going through.
Feeling betrayed makes you question everything you ever
believed, doesn't it? It's the worst.'

I felt tears spring to my eyes and to stop myself crying I
stood to fill my cup with more coffee.

'Yes,' I said, leaning on the kitchen counter, clutching my
coffee. 'I've spent three years since Ethan left blaming myself
for him going and not being able to commit to Joe through

wondering if Ethan really was the love of my life. And as for Daisy, I just don't get it. I would never do the same to her, not ever.'

Elaine opened the back door onto the garden and stood half inside, half outside, to light up her cigarette. She took a deep drag.

'From what your dad said,' she said, 'your sister has some issues, which probably stem from when your mum passed away. It's worth remembering that, when you try to understand what she did, though it's difficult to be anything other than mad. As for Ethan, do you really think he might be the love of your life? Because if he is, perhaps you could forgive the infidelity? You know, in my job, I see so many people who do actually get through an affair – then end up happier because they've had to dig deeper. Anyway, sorry, I seem to be delivering a monologue. My apologies, you were just trying to have a quiet coffee in your own kitchen and some American woman starts spouting off at you. No wonder your dad has kept me a secret!'

She gave me a big grin and I registered how lovely it was. I shook my head and smiled. 'That's fine,' I said. 'It's nice to be able to talk about it. It's the shock, that's the thing. I just can't believe that it happened. As for Daisy, I knew I pissed her off occasionally, but I had no idea about all this resentment she holds towards me. I just don't know what to say to her. And I would never have guessed in a million years that Ethan would do that, which makes me question whether I really knew him. He was always out boozing, too, until three or four in the morning, so now I'm wondering if he's slept with other women. Then of course there's Joe. He has no idea why

I've asked for time out. Thinking about how I've treated him makes me feel sick. I've been such a bitch to him.'

I rested my head in my hands and sighed.

'Quite frankly,' Elaine said, with a quick raise of her eyebrows, 'nobody's perfect. Don't beat yourself up so much. You're not a bitch at all. Just sort things out with your sister for your dad's sake, then decide what and who you want out of life.'

I looked up at her with eyes open wide.

'Easier said than done,' I said.

'Admittedly,' she said drily, 'that might take a few years. I'm only just working it out at, what am I, fifty-nine years old. Ancient as the hills.'

The next morning, after Sunday spent with Dad and Elaine feeding and watering me like I was a dying flower, Dad trying to convince me to leave the whole sorry mess behind me, I was walking to Daisy's office in Battersea, my hair still damp from the shower. I knew, by listening to Dad, I was delaying the inevitable. I had to confront Daisy and I wanted to catch her before work. I had texted her asking if we could grab a quick coffee, not explaining why. This way, on a work day, Benji would be at nursery and wouldn't be there for Daisy to use as a shield. This way, it would just be the two of us, face to face, with nowhere to hide. I waited at the traffic lights and stared distractedly at the buses and cars speeding past. It was rush hour. People jostled all around me on their way to work, plugged into their iPhones and iPods. I walked determinedly, trying to match their stride, despite the terror gnawing at my gut.

All I wanted to do was speak to Daisy. I hadn't seen her

since our row in the park and I guessed she thought this requested meeting was about that. I was almost desperate to hear her say that Ethan had made the whole thing up, outraged that I should even think such a thing. The sun was bright so I fished in my bag for my sunglasses, feeling safer behind their Jackie O dark frames.

'Please don't go,' Dad had panicked earlier that morning, just before I left, almost blocking my way as I opened the door. 'You'll ruin it, Evie, our family, just think of that.'

He was guilt-tripping me. In my eyes, it was already all ruined. It was hard to go against what Dad wanted me to do, but I had to. Elaine knew. Elaine had nodded approvingly in the background when I gave Dad an emotional speech about why I had to go, right before I left.

'Trust your instinct,' she'd said to me when I extracted myself from Dad's pleading stare and made it out onto the street. Instinctively, I liked Elaine. 'I'll talk to your dad.'

'Thanks,' I'd said. 'Thank you for listening.'

As I pounded the pavement, I practised in my head what I would say to Daisy. Even though the larger part of me knew I had no choice but to confront her, to release the fury and hurt brimming over in my heart, I also felt an awful sense of loss, like part of me would die as soon as I told her what I knew. There would be no going back. Our relationship would be changed forever. If she admitted everything that Ethan claimed, how could I ever trust her again? Could I ever forgive her? Looking up, I glanced at the green frontage of the Magnolia Cafe where I'd arranged to meet her. My heart hammered loudly in my chest. My hands were sweating and as I approached the cafe door waves of nausea washed over me. I stood in line, light-headed with nerves.

'Iced coffee, please,' I asked the girl behind the counter as I swept my eyes over the tables. Daisy hadn't yet arrived. With trembling hands, I paid then carried my coffee over to a table in the corner of the cafe, under a canvas print of blue, pink and green circles, where I could see the door. There was World music playing and I tried to block it out. I fiddled with a discarded leaflet about yoga, sipped my drink and waited grim-faced for Daisy to come. She was the eighth person through the doors. Rushing in, she pushed her sunglasses on top of her head and gave me a brief wave before waiting to order. I watched her as she walked towards my table, her simple coral-coloured sundress clinging to her curves, her long brown hair swinging over her shoulders. I felt the blood drain from my head and gripped the side of the table to keep steady.

'What's this all about?' she said, pulling out the chair opposite me, thudding down in the seat and banging her work pass on the table. 'I can't be late today, I have so much to do. If it's about what I said in the park, I was just in a bad mood.'

She drank her coffee and looked up at me impatiently. When she saw the serious expression on my face, something that could have been fear flashed into her eyes. Sitting forward, she tucked her hair behind her ear and cast her eyes down to the table.

'Eve?' she said, flicking up her eyes. 'What is it? Is this about Dad? You know I'm getting tired of being the one worrying about him all the time. Why am I the one who has to worry about him? You know, you're closer to him really. You should ask him what it's all about.'

I looked at her steadily, my fingers rubbing the base of my iced coffee glass.

'It's not about Dad,' I said, taking a deep breath and wondering for a second if I was going to be sick. 'Daisy, I know . . . I know . . . you slept with Ethan.'

Alarm crossed Daisy's face. She took a sharp intake of breath. She didn't deny it. After a few moments, she nodded once, but said nothing, looking at her hands. She lifted her hand and covered her mouth, biting down on her finger, gnawing at the knuckle.

'Why?' I said, my knee jiggling furiously and voice shaking with anger now. 'Look at me, Daisy. Face me.'

Daisy lifted her eyes to meet mine. Hers were pooling with sudden tears, her cheeks pink with embarrassment. She wrapped her arms around her waist and leaned forward in her chair. A man pushed past my chair asking if I could move in a little. I ignored him, so he shoved past me.

'Hey!' I said angrily.

'I'm sorry,' Daisy whispered.

'But why?' I asked. 'Why would you do that? Daisy, we're sisters. To do that . . . is . . . is . . . it's just the lowest of the low . . . I never thought you'd do anything like that . . . I can't understand why . . . I mean, do you hate me or something? I thought you didn't even like Ethan. And when Ethan left, you—'

I gulped at the memory of Daisy coming to my flat with a bag of ingredients, forcing me to get up and cook pancakes and bacon and maple syrup, just to get me to do something I loved and to eat food I loved. She had stayed with me all night long, her arms around me, listening to me talk and cry about

271

Ethan. She had been such an amazing comfort, it had seemed like she was enjoying the role, enjoying my vulnerability because then she was in control. Then, I needed her.

'When he left you comforted me and pretended you knew nothing about why he'd gone,' I said. 'How could you lie like that? How could you sit there, listening to me sobbing, knowing it was all your fault? And that you'd seduced him?'

My stomach twisted with the painful memory. Daisy was shaking her head now, tears falling down her cheeks. A girl on the next table turned her head towards us, then looked away.

'It wasn't like that,' she said softly. 'I was drunk. I didn't know what I was doing. It wasn't like I planned it. I didn't intend to seduce him.'

I shook my head, leaned in closer.

'But Ethan told me what happened,' I said, my voice pleading. 'He told me you'd taken off all your clothes and waited for him in your bedroom. Daisy, I know what happened. Don't try to deny it, just tell me the truth, please. Don't try to make yourself look better, because from where I'm sitting, you've played really dirty.'

My voice was wobbling all over the place. I gripped the edge of the table and told myself to keep calm. Something I said struck a chord with her, because her body seemed to go completely rigid. She stared at me sternly.

'You have no idea,' Daisy said, an edge of chilling anger in her voice. 'You have absolutely no fucking idea.'

How dare she, I thought. How dare she turn this around like this?

'What are you talking about?' I hissed. 'You seduced my boyfriend then threatened him to end our relationship or you'd tell me what happened. Why would you want to wreck my life like that? Daisy, I thought we loved one another. I have always loved you so much. I know we're different people, different personalities, but I don't get this. What was it? Were things going a little too well for me? You jealous bitch!'

I was shaking with anger now and the girl on the next table couldn't stop looking at me. I felt like shouting at the top of my voice, telling the entire cafe exactly what Daisy had done. Mostly, I felt like crying.

'What are you doing?' I said, as Daisy began collecting her things up from the table, pushing on her sunglasses. I grabbed her wrist. 'Don't you dare go! You owe me an explanation.'

She ripped off her sunglasses and wiped her eyes, now pouring with angry tears. Her lips were white round the edges and tiny beads of sweat had collected between her mouth and nose. Guilty as hell, I thought. Guilty as hell.

'OK, you can have your explanation,' she said, her voice cracking with emotion. She stood up, pushed her chair back and picked up her handbag. 'But let's walk.'

Chapter Twenty-Two

Outside in the street, the heat was stifling. I clung to the shops' cooling shadows, while Daisy walked near the kerb in direct sunlight. You'd never know we were going anywhere together, or indeed that we were sisters.

'Over there,' Daisy said, pointing to a small park across the road from her office, with a playground and area of grass where a couple of drunks sat on benches nursing cans of lager, a bin next to them spilling over with rubbish. When she lifted her arm, I smelt her perfume, Chanel No. 19, the same our mum had worn. I walked closer to her, struck by the ironic significance of that. I nodded once.

'Let's walk round there,' she said dully, glancing at her watch. 'I need to get to work. I have a Monday meeting . . .'

Her words were half drowned in the surrounding din of traffic, but I nodded again in agreement. We walked in tense silence for a few seconds, then, after turning into the park, Daisy stopped dead. Her jaw tightened while she seemed to think of what to say. She faced me while holding on to the strap of her handbag, like she might get mugged at any moment.

'I was in love with Ethan before you ever met him, OK?' she said quietly. 'Totally smitten, if you must know. I had the future all planned out.'

Stunned, I stared at her but didn't speak.

'I met him at his parents' deli,' she continued. 'I went in there every day for lunch, when I was at my old job. Spent a small fortune. We became friendly and went out for coffee a couple of times. I thought he liked me, so I invited him out with my friends and they all loved him, so he became part of our gang. Nothing physical ever happened between us, and I never admitted how I felt, but I assumed he must have known. Then, at the winter picnic, I invited you too. I went off to the shops and when I came back, something had happened between you. Something unstoppable. I knew you'd get on, because you both loved food, but I had no idea that you'd fall in love. From that night you were locked together. What could I say in the face of your togetherness? I saw him first? Give him back? He's mine, for fuck's sake? What?'

Daisy's eyes brimmed with angry tears. I racked my brains for memories of Daisy expressing any interest in Ethan, but couldn't recall a thing. Yes, she'd introduced me to him quite proudly, but I'd stupidly mistaken that for her sisterly pride in me.

'You never said anything,' I said. 'I mean, before I even met him. You never even mentioned Ethan. Then you started dating Iain. How was I supposed to know?'

I looked at her face. She was frowning and trying hard not to cry.

'I didn't have a chance to say anything,' she said. 'You were busy with your life, I was busy with mine. I liked the thought that people would be able to tell that me and Ethan were attracted to each other. I wanted you to spot it at the winter picnic, that he and I had a connection. Anyway, what was happening in my life was never a priority for you.'

Daisy folded her arms grumpily across her chest.

'Don't be ridiculous,' I said, pulling a face. 'You were always a priority, but I'm your little sister, three years behind you. You've never really told me about your love life. Anyway, I didn't think we had to be that formal with one another. We're sisters. We love each other. It's an unwritten rule, isn't it? That we put each other first?'

Daisy shrugged.

'You took Ethan from under my nose so you hardly put me first then,' she said. 'But I convinced myself you couldn't be right for one another because I thought he was *my* destiny. You messed it all up for me, OK?'

I exhaled loudly and pushed my hair away from my forehead. I didn't know how to react. I was angry, but confused. Daisy was turning the blame around and now I was feeling somehow guilty. I couldn't believe that I was about to apologize.

'I'm sorry,' I said reluctantly. 'But I had no idea. You didn't say anything and clearly nothing was going to happen between you, because nothing ever did.'

Then I remembered the reason why we were there. Daisy turned to me and caught my eye.

'Hmm,' Daisy said, with a lift of her eyebrows. 'But something did happen, didn't it? Which proves what I had begun to believe. That he was no good for either of us.'

I shook my head in astonishment, amazed, in a detached

way, at what an impact you can have on other people's lives without even realizing it.

'Nothing happened until the night of our party, though, did it?' I said crossly. 'But Ethan seemed to think he was doing you a favour by sleeping with you. He said you were a wreck and that he felt sorry for you. That should tell you something.'

I wanted to hurt Daisy for hurting me, but I immediately felt ashamed of the cruelty in my words. Disappointment crossed over Daisy's face. Her eyes narrowed.

'You took him away from me,' she said. 'You knew what you were doing.'

I let out a bitter laugh and a homeless guy drinking cider looked over at us.

'Are you joking?' I said, exasperated. 'I would never, ever do something like that. Ethan and I fell in love. I had no idea you even liked him. In fact, when we were together, you actively disliked him. You never turned up for nights out when I invited you. When he came to Dad's for Sunday lunch you made excuses most of the time . . .'

Daisy rolled her eyes and took a deep breath.

'Why do you think I did that?' she said. 'It was torture watching you two together, all over one another like a rash. Imagine how I felt, will you? Just imagine for one second. It should have been me sitting there hand in hand with Ethan.'

I started to think Daisy had completely lost the plot. She had imagined an entire relationship with *my* boyfriend. I felt slightly spooked.

'But, Daisy, you're being insane,' I said. 'You didn't actually have a relationship with him, did you? It was all in your head. It was Ethan and I who actually had a relationship and you ruined that by throwing yourself at him. You wrecked it for me because you couldn't have him yourself, and, to me, that is pretty fucking vindictive and weirdly obsessive. How could you do that to me, your own sister?'

Daisy's eyes filled and she started to cry. She scrabbled in her bag for a tissue and blew her nose, which turned bright pink.

'I have always tried to be there for you,' she said, openly crying. 'But since Mum died, everything has always been about you. Dad was obsessed with the way you tried to keep our family going by learning how to cook just like Mum. It was disgusting the way you behaved. You even put her clothes on and used her perfume. You freaked me out.'

I grabbed her wrist.

'I was a child!' I half shouted. 'I wanted her back! And *you're* wearing her bloody perfume now!'

She shook her wrist free, dried her eyes and started to walk away. I followed her, feeling so angry I wanted to grab her and shake her.

'You and Dad were so close,' she continued. 'I wanted in on the act too, but no, it was all about you and how hard you were trying and how well you were doing. It made me sick, so I decided to get my own life together. To go to university, to get a good job, to get out and do it all myself because that was how it was always going to be. Me, all by myself.'

My eyes widened as Daisy spoke. I saw my entire history as a deflating balloon. The efforts I'd made, not even consciously, to keep the three of us close-knit had sickened her. Couldn't she have seen that I was trying my best?

'But . . . but . . .' I said, walking faster to keep up with her. 'I did all that because I missed her, simple as that. I wanted to make you and Dad feel better. I couldn't stand the misery in our house. It was oppressive. Anyway, this is about Ethan. You ruined my relationship. Couldn't you just have been happy for us?'

Daisy stopped walking suddenly and sat down heavily on a bench. She pushed her sunglasses on top of her head and blinked in the sun.

'I just wanted to have something for myself,' she said wearily. 'You've always had everything on a plate. I've spent my life working hard, being sensible, missing Mum and wishing you and Dad liked me more. But then I got fed up. I wanted Ethan. Or just the knowledge that he was attracted to me. That was enough, and I justified it to myself as a test. He was no good for you if he'd be seduced by me. I was doing you a favour.'

'That's insane . . . and twisted and stupid!' I spat. 'And I haven't had everything on a plate! What are you talking about? Jesus, Daisy, this is a head-fuck. This is all because you were jealous.'

She went to stand up so I grabbed her arm, but she shrugged me off, almost violently.

'I just wanted something . . . someone . . . for myself,' she said. 'I had Mum but then she died. Is that so difficult to understand?'

'Yes,' I said. 'It's difficult to understand when it's my boyfriend you're talking about. Christ! What about Iain? You had him, didn't you? Why couldn't you just get on with that?'

Daisy looked up at the sky for a second, as if remembering something, then checked her watch. Her face hardened.

'I need to go to work,' she said. 'Iain was a wanker. Don't even talk about him. I can't bear to talk about him now.'

'I know he was an arsehole about your pregnancy and I can't believe he doesn't want anything to do with Benji,' I said. 'But you had a relationship with him, so what are you talking about, never finding anyone to love you? You must have loved each other for a while.'

I felt suddenly exhausted and my shoulders slumped. I wished I had some water, because my mouth was dry. Daisy pulled her bag higher up her shoulder, stood up and began to walk away from me.

'I have to go,' she said. I followed her, feeling completely deflated.

'But, Daisy,' I said, lifting my hands up in the air and letting them fall to my sides. 'This . . . it's . . . it's all a massive mess . . . what are we going to do?'

'I don't know,' she said, chewing her lips.

We walked towards the exit together, Daisy's words racing through my mind. I followed her a little way, then stopped and lingered by the bus stop outside her work, while she stomped off through the main revolving doors, not turning to speak or wave goodbye. I felt sick and leaned against a wall, took out my mobile phone, intending to call Isabel, when my own words struck a dark chord deep in my heart.

I can't believe Iain doesn't want anything to do with Benji, I'd said.

I'd never been able to understand why Iain hadn't wanted to know Benji. Iain had been friendly, warm and kind. Maybe he was a bit flaky and non-committal, but Daisy's description of his reaction to Benji's birth suddenly seemed unbelievable.

A lie. It dawned on me that there was another reason Daisy never wanted to speak about Iain. I stood still as the stocks, while a woman barged past me, tutting in frustration. I thought of Benji's birth. I ran through the dates in my mind. I did the maths. I pictured Benji's shock of soft black hair. I sucked in my breath and stopped breathing. I put my hand on my heart, feeling my heartbeat pounding in my teeth. My head ached and I flushed boiling hot, breaking out into a clammy sweat. The bus approaching blurred into a fuzzy red splodge and, though it was a brilliantly bright day, the world became dark as granite as my legs gave way beneath me. Now it all made sickening sense.

Benji was Ethan's son.

Chapter Twenty-Three

Still on the pavement by the bus stop, I came round seconds later, while a middle-aged woman I didn't know, with very short bright blonde hair, helped me put my head in between my knees.

'It'll help the blood rush back to your head,' she said, gently holding my shoulders. 'Something like that. I'm not a nurse, but it's common sense.'

The contents of my bag were strewn across the floor: lipstick, pocket mirror, wallet, scissors, phone, cafe keys and a tube of mints. And I thought, that's how I feel now: all emptied out, scattered about.

'Just stay like that for a few minutes and breathe,' the woman said. 'And here, I've got a new bottle of water in my bag. I got it free on the Tube. You should have some water and be in the shade. It's pretty hot. Do you want me to call an ambulance or your boyfriend or friend?'

I shook my head and blinked, fuzzy spots stretching and shifting before my eyes. I glanced up and tried to focus, seeing a bus full of people staring at me and the lady's peacock-feather earrings close by. I looked down at my knees and closed my eyes.

'No, thank you,' I muttered shakily. 'Just give me a minute and I'll be—'

A picture of Benji as a newborn, attached to Daisy's breast, as she lay in a narrow bed in King's College Hospital, her hair over her bare shoulders, a look of pure devotion in her eyes, was burned onto the back of my eyelids. Daisy had lied. Not only about her affair with Ethan, but that Benji was Ethan's son. How *could* she? I suddenly knew it with such certainty my blood ran cold. Daisy had Ethan's baby and he knew nothing about it. I was dumbfounded. My world was skewed, as if it were a snowstorm globe that someone had picked up and shaken about so violently all the miniature characters had fallen on their heads.

'Are you sure you're OK?' the woman said. 'Do you think you can stand up? You look very pale.'

Gradually, my vision cleared and, with her holding my arm, I stood up, dusting off the back of my shorts, taking a sip from the woman's water bottle and forcing a smile. Her eyes were full of concern as she handed me my bag, which she had stuffed with my things.

'I'm so sorry,' I said, taking the bag. 'Thanks for helping me. I'm going to get a cab. I don't know what happened. Maybe it's the heat . . .'

I let my words trail off, while the woman flagged a cab down for me. I turned to thank her again before I climbed in and sank back on the cool leather seat and asked the driver to take me to East Dulwich. I didn't know where else to go. I needed to think rationally. I needed to feel calm.

With the air con blowing cold air into my face, I forced myself to focus on the cafe, just for a moment. I did not allow myself to think about Ethan and Daisy. I muttered my plans for the cafe under my breath. The figures jumbled in my mind's eye, making my brain ache. I strained to focus, but I couldn't help it. Daisy and Ethan were in my thoughts. I looked out the window and they were everywhere. Each child I saw was Benji, half Ethan, half Daisy. I felt sickened. What should I do? Should I tell Ethan? Did he know? The impossible questions seemed to hang and solidify all around me. I searched my bag and found my phone, then, with shaking hands, I texted Isabel.

Meet me in the cafe? Something bad has happened.

Soon I wouldn't be able to call on Isabel because she'd be thousands of miles away. I shuddered. With my phone resting on my knee, I stared out of the window at the world passing by, not really seeing anything. When Ethan found out about Benji he would want to be in Benji's life. He would want be in Daisy's life. I chewed my cheek, hating the thought, but at the same time hating myself for being so selfish. This wasn't about me any more. This wasn't about my nostalgic longing for true love. This was about a little boy who didn't know his dad, an incomplete family. How could Daisy lie like that?

'Stupid bitch!' I hissed to myself, suddenly hating her.

I banged my forehead with the palm of my hand. Daisy had Ethan's child and I felt jealous of that. Madly jealous. How dare Daisy play with people's lives like that? Mine,

Ethan's, Benji's. Or, was I to blame, really? Had I not listened to Daisy enough? Not paid enough attention to the detail? Had I missed something at that winter picnic in Greenwich Park?

I thought you'd be able to see that I loved him, Daisy had said to me. *You only see what you want to.*

When the cabbie dropped me off he wished me good luck and I smiled vaguely, not even remembering whether I'd picked up the change. Unlocking the door to the cafe, the whitewashed windows glaring in the sunlight, I breathed in the familiar dank smell. If I was going to turn this place around in time for the date I'd set for opening, I was going to have to work like crazy. But, I thought, I didn't even care any more. Part of me felt like running away to the other side of the world. Maybe I would go to Dubai with Isabel. Just go. Like Ethan had done three years ago. Up and go. Leave him and Daisy to it. But even as I formed an image of myself packing a suitcase and standing at Heathrow airport, determined to begin a new life, in a new world, I knew I'd never do it. Wherever in the world I was, my heart and mind would be here, stuck in this moment. I pulled a chair down from one of the tables, rested it on the floor, sat down and put my head in my hands. I closed my eyes.

'Eve,' Isabel said moments later, bursting through the door and slamming it shut. 'I got your text. What's going on?'

Glamorous in a white dress, cinched in at the waist with a red belt, she came over to my chair, kneeled down next to me and put her arms around me. In a flood of tears, I told her everything.

'Daisy is unbelievable,' she said into my hair. 'How could

she do that? How could she sleep with Ethan? And as for Ethan, well, I think he's . . .'

'It gets worse,' I said, pulling away from her. 'Much worse.'

Isabel listened open-mouthed as I told her that Ethan was Benji's father.

'I've worked out the dates,' I said listlessly.

'But she still was sleeping with Iain, wasn't she, before he left?' Isabel said, frowning. 'It doesn't necessarily mean that Ethan is the father, does it?'

'But Iain would never have reacted like Daisy pretended he did,' I asked. 'She pretended to me that he told her he didn't want anything to do with her, that he wasn't going to pay Child Support or even talk to his son, because it was all a massive mistake and she should have had an abortion. I couldn't believe he'd ever be like that, but at the time I didn't question it. God, the sympathy I gave her about it all and there she was, all the time, lying.'

'Have you asked her, though?' Isabel said. 'Have you asked her if that's definitely the case?'

I shook my head and sighed, getting up to pace the cafe floor.

'Not yet,' I said. 'But I'm going to. I think I might just phone her and ask her. I don't want to see her again yet. I don't think I could be in the same room as her, fucking stupid cow.'

'Does your dad know, too?' Isabel asked.

'I don't know,' I said haplessly.

'Right,' she said. 'You need to phone one of them now. They need to start telling you the truth. Call now and ask them straight out, cut the crap.'

Isabel picked my phone up off the table and handed it to me.

One of the things I'd always liked about Isabel was that she was unafraid. She didn't spend hours debating what to do, in fear of offending or causing trouble like me. Isabel was decisive, direct and a woman of her word. She didn't bow down to other people without putting her opinion forward first. Whereas I would have a good cry when life was spiralling out of control, in a pathetic tantrum, which didn't get me anywhere, Isabel would take a practical approach to the problem. Like now.

'Why is this all happening?' I asked her, resisting the temptation to ask, 'Why me?'

Isabel pulled out a bottle of Pimm's from her bag and put it on the table.

'I have no idea,' she said. 'But there's no point in anguishing over that, is there? What you need to do is leave the dead wood behind and move forward. You can't do anything about the way Daisy or Ethan behave, but you can change your own behaviour. If I were you, I would throw myself into getting this place open and then you will have something to be proud of, something that is all yours.'

'I know you're right,' I said. 'But half of me wants to give up on this place altogether. It's all too much without you.'

Isabel shook her head energetically.

'Speak to Daisy about Benji,' she said, gesturing at my phone. 'Then you'll have all the cards on the table and you can work out how to play your hand.'

'Nice analogy,' I said with a quick smile, the first genuine one of the day. 'But I'm hopeless at games.'

'I know,' she said, giving me another hug. 'But you have to phone.'

*

It was lunchtime now and I stood outside in the shade at the back of the cafe in the small courtyard that I envisaged being a sunspot for customers to drink their coffees in peace and quiet, away from the merciless bustle of the main road. At the moment it was a cracked concrete slab, cluttered with plastic chairs from the previous owner's careless attempt at closing down and clearing out. I squinted in the sun at my phone and opened a text message from Ethan, asking me to call him. I quickly deleted it, then, with a beating heart, I phoned Daisy. After a few rings, it went to voicemail. Of course she wouldn't answer, I should've realized that. I hung up and dialled the reception of her office. My hands were clammy with nerves.

'Daisy Thompson, please,' I said.

'I'll put you through,' the receptionist said. 'Who's speaking, please?'

'Ethan,' I muttered suddenly, my mouth dry.

'Okaaay,' the receptionist said, doubtfully. 'I'll put you through.'

'Hello?' Daisy said, almost immediately. 'Ethan?'

In her voice, the way she said Ethan like it was a question, I heard something that struck a chord deep in my heart. I heard hopefulness so raw and delicate that for a second I was speechless. My eyes rested upon a sparrow landing on an upturned orange chair and balancing there.

'Ethan?' she said again, softly, her voice catching. 'Is that you?

'It's not him,' I said quietly. 'It's me. Daisy, listen, I want you to tell me the truth. Just say yes or no. Please stop the lies now. Tell me, is Benji Ethan's son?'

There was a long pause, where I could hear the background

noise of Daisy's office; a woman laughing, phones ringing, a fax machine buzzing, Daisy's breathing.

'Daisy?' I said. 'I'm your sister. You can tell me, really.'

Daisy's breathing was shallow. I heard tears in her voice when she told me what I'd suspected was true.

'Yes,' she said. 'But he doesn't know. I don't want him to know.'

I hung up the phone. I walked inside and gave Isabel a nod.

'Benji is Ethan's son,' I said, sitting heavily on a hard-backed chair opposite her. 'I'm so shocked I don't know what to say.'

'Fucking hell,' Isabel said, raising her eyebrows. 'Does Ethan know?'

'No,' I said.

'Then someone has to tell him,' she said. 'He might be a shit, but he has a right to know he has a son, for fuck's sake.'

I could feel her eyes burning into me.

'Yes,' I said half-heartedly. 'I guess he does.'

PART FOUR

Ethan's Supper Club

Chapter Twenty-Four

'But I'm really not feeling well at all,' I lied to Dominique on the phone. 'I think I have serious gastric flu. I'd better pull out of Saturday's dinner party. I don't want to make the others ill.'

Clasping the phone to my ear, standing in the kitchen of the cafe, two days before Ethan's dinner party, I tried to sound pathetically ill, though in reality I had just helped Isabel put up shelves in the kitchen's storeroom.

'But you can't just pull out,' Dominique snapped. 'Seriously, you can't. The first feature is coming out on Sunday and if you don't go to Ethan's party, the whole thing will be screwed. We won't be able to run it and the editor will be left with a big hole in her paper. My life won't be worth living and Joe probably won't get shifts again because he put your name forward, plus that amazing free publicity for your cafe we promised you will not hap—'

Dominique's voice was getting higher and higher, faster and faster.

'OK, OK,' I said, interrupting her. The mention of Joe's

career at the paper he desperately wanted to work on made me feel guilty, plus the publicity I would get on the cafe was too good an opportunity to turn down.

'Can you just go for the photos?' Dominique said, more gently now. 'Then make your excuses and leave? I don't mind if you make up your scores for the food Ethan cooks. I just need you to go and be in the pictures so we can run the piece.'

I'd picked up the phone to speak to Ethan one hundred times since the weekend, but I couldn't go through with the call. Neither had I spoken to Daisy. She had sent me an email, asking me not to tell Ethan about Benji, but, though I had drafted various replies, I hadn't sent one. I didn't know what to say, I felt too confused. My dad, beside himself about my stand-off with Daisy, had called me every day, worried sick, but I convinced him I was fine and just wanted to concentrate on the cafe. In truth I was a wreck. The only person I really wanted to see was Joe – he'd always made me feel better in the past – but how could I? Now, instead of sleeping too much, I couldn't sleep at all. I wasn't eating either, and had already lost weight. I knew I should face Daisy and Ethan, but the thought of actually seeing Ethan again turned my stomach.

'Yeah,' I said, deflated. 'I guess I can do that, if it's only for the photos. But I won't be able to stay long, I'll be too weak.'

Dominique breathed a sigh of relief.

'Thank you,' she said. 'I'll make sure your cafe gets a really good plug. Email me the details over again and I'll make sure it goes in.'

I remembered that conversation with Dominique now, as I walked with Maggie – beautiful in a bright green dress – to Ethan's cousin's flat, in Hackney, where he was staying. I didn't want to go to his place – at all – but I felt trapped. If I didn't go, at least for half an hour, I'd be letting everyone down and doing myself out of publicity. Ethan had messed up my life in so many other ways, I didn't want him to ruin my chances of making the cafe a success, too. I had to go.

'How are you feeling?' Maggie asked warily.

I hadn't told Maggie about Benji – it wasn't fair to Benji or Ethan – but I'd confided in her about Daisy when she'd come over to my flat for a drink earlier in the week. Maggie had been really lovely to me, promising that she would do all the talking at Ethan's and that she'd go along with my story of feeling ill, so I could escape.

'Not too bad,' I said, giving her a sideways glance. 'Actually, I feel awful.'

We were standing just outside The Dove, a high-ceilinged, dark-wood pub in the too-cool-for-school Broadway Market. Ethan and I had been to The Dove several times together that first winter we'd got together, holding hands in the candle-light, sipping golden pints of Belgian beer, smiling in that glowing way people in love smile.

'Shall we have a glass of Dutch courage?' she said. 'Doesn't matter if we're late. Ethan can wait. You waited long enough.'

Desperate for a drink to calm my nerves, I nodded and pushed open the pub's door, immediately submerged in other people's noisy conversation. I remembered the feeling of excitement I'd felt on meeting Ethan in there, seeking him out amidst tables of young people who seemed so hip and confident and full of promise, feeling a thrill that I, with my carefully chosen outfit and slash of bright red lipstick and fabulous boyfriend who would make friends with complete strangers so effortlessly, could, perhaps, belong. Now, though, I felt none of that energy. Instead I felt restless and jumpy and desolate. In my heart I carried a secret that seemed so fragile, so life-changing, the importance of it made me feel dizzy. As we walked in, I felt everyone's eyes move to Maggie – she really was gorgeous.

'Everyone looks at you,' I said, nudging her. 'How do you manage it?'

Maggie was grinning, obviously loving the attention. I was the opposite, feeling like I wanted to curl up and hide under my duvet.

'I'm a window dresser, aren't I?' she said. 'So I just imagine I'm a window that hundreds of people walk past. My aim is to turn heads, preferably encourage people to stand and gawp, or at least smile.'

'Hopefully not graffiti or smash-and-grab,' I said.

Maggie ordered drinks and we found a table close to two bearded chaps who couldn't keep their eyes off her. She turned her back to them.

'Can't be bothered with them tonight,' she said. 'I've had some shit news of my own, actually.'

'What's that?' I said in concern.

Sunlight from the early evening shone through the big window near our table, making dust particles dance and spin. I took a deep drink from the Belgian beer Maggie had ordered, feeling the alcohol hit the back of my throat.

'I just got made redundant,' she said. 'So maybe I'm not such a great window dresser after all.'

I looked up, surprised. Maggie raised her eyebrows disconsolately.

'Oh God,' I said. 'What happened?'

I listened as Maggie told me how half the window-dressing team at the store she worked at had been made redundant with only two months' salary as a pay-off and that now, with a massive rent on her flat, she needed to get a job within weeks to survive. She told me the ins and outs of the store politics and, after a while, though I was concentrating hard on her words and I could hear her perfectly clearly, another voice in my head, shouting out in alarm about Benji being Ethan's child – and that I was about to see Ethan – was drowning her out. I rubbed my forehead, willing that voice to go away. I'd spent the whole afternoon in a state of nervous panic, picking through bits of broken crockery we planned to use for a mosaic in the cafe courtyard. Already my shoulders were tense and my stomach hollow with dread. I drank more beer.

'And I just don't know where to go from here.' I tuned in to Maggie's voice for a moment. 'I mean, I suppose I'll go freelance to begin with, but—'

I nodded and murmured and thought about Daisy's emailed plea not to tell Ethan about Benji. There was no way I planned to tell him tonight, but I was torn. Didn't Ethan have the right to know that he had a child? Of course he did. Hadn't I always advocated the telling of truth, no matter how hurtful it might be? But I was a hypocrite, wasn't I, because I hadn't told Joe the truth about any of this. No. Joe was still in the dark and now, ironically, more than ever before, I wanted to talk to him, ask for his advice. I shifted in my seat as Maggie stopped talking and was staring at me, waiting for me to speak. I plucked at something randomly.

'If I had the money,' I said as breezily as I could, 'you could work at the cafe with me. Now that Isabel is going away, you could come in with me and make everything look amazing and we could both do some cooking. Could be great, what do you think? Maybe Andrew could stump up the investment money. He's rich enough. It could be a Supper Club joint venture, that'd probably be a first.'

A Saturday Supper Club joint venture, without Ethan, I thought. I was just saying something for the sake of saying something, but Maggie's face was breaking out into a grin.

'That's not a bad idea, you know,' she said, her eyes sparkling. 'I could definitely make it look amazing. Despite the redundancy, I am bloody good at my job. Didn't you say you wanted to recreate the feeling of a kitchen table in your cafe? We could dress the whole place up like an old-fashioned kitchen, even have the cooker and sink as part of the cafe and you could bake there, in front of everyone, at a kitchen table. We could both wear lovely little frocks, and what about food, the food would be—'

'Cakes, biscuits and bakes,' I said, feeling a glow of enthusiasm despite my mood. 'I've got an idea about a signature cake that I think could really work. My mum used to cook this amazing chocolate cake called Lovebird cake, and that's going to be the cafe's name – Lovebird – and I thought I could have a wall for pictures of things that people loved. Wouldn't have to be another person – in fact, the mood I'm in, I'd rather it wasn't. I'd keep a Polaroid camera there and people could take a picture of what they love, then I'd stick them up on the wall.'

Maggie nodded enthusiastically.

'And I want to sell whole cakes, not just slices,' I carried on. 'Big enough for three or four, and serve them on a cake stand, with a knife, for customers to cut themselves, so it feels like they've just taken a cake out of the oven. And it has to be really child-friendly, so—'

I paused for breath, smiling apologetically at Maggie. With everything that had been going on with Ethan and Joe, my enthusiasm for the cafe had waned. But inside, I realized with relief, I was still as keen as ever.

'Fantastic,' said Maggie, clapping her hands together. As we talked more, she infected me with her alcohol-fuelled enthusiasm and, for a while, my spirits lifted. We were talking animatedly now, loudly enough for the people on the next table to turn and glance at us. The beer was helping. I tried to shut out everything I was feeling about Ethan, but I knew it was still there, ghoulishly glowing in the depths of my mind.

'We could leave a bit of the window free for the kids to dress,' Maggie said. 'Or have a mini-kitchen in there with balls of dough, so they can make their own biscuits. We could bake them while they wait. You have a nephew, don't you? Maybe we could try the idea out on him first or get him to help with the promotional material. How old is he? Too small?'

The mention of Benji made my heart stop. I didn't want his existence to be a stark reminder of such unhappiness, but how could I deny it? I veered from hating Ethan and Daisy for what they'd done they were as bad as one another – to feeling sorry for Ethan and fearful for Daisy. Ethan didn't want my sister. He'd made that pretty clear. What was he going to say when he discovered he had a child with her? If I told him the truth, would Daisy and I ever speak again? As furious as I was with her, I didn't want our relationship to be completely over. We were sisters. We didn't have a mother. We should be there for one another, somehow. That's what our father had drummed into us all these years. That we should stick together, no matter what.

'Two,' I said. 'He's two.'

I looked at the table and concentrated on the glass in front of me.

'Bless,' she said, her voice soft. 'Hey, what's wrong? I'm not seriously going to jump in on your business, you know. I'm just talking, trying to forget about work crap.'

I shook my head, glancing up at the ceiling.

'It's not that,' I said, with a sigh. 'It's just tonight, I'm nervous about seeing Ethan—'

I blew out and closed my eyes for a moment.

'You'll be OK,' Maggie said. 'Honestly. It won't be so bad. And you'll get over him in time. I know, I've been there.'

We arrived at Ethan's forty-five minutes late. His cousin's red-brick Victorian conversion flat was a large ground-floor space that, because of its sparse but elegant decoration, with a glass chandelier hanging majestically in the hallway, felt to me like a property featured in *Homes and Gardens* magazine and not a real home that people actually lived in. I couldn't imagine Ethan feeling at home there at all. His old flat was a cross between a second-hand record shop and a hurricane scene.

When Ethan opened the door, my heart leapt into my mouth and I almost turned and ran. I couldn't really look at him, so I focused on the scene behind him. He had covered the expansive table with cream candles, already lit, and filled green glass vases with poppies. He'd made a huge effort, but that was typical of him.

'I was worried you wouldn't come . . .' he said, visibly shocked to see me. Then, recovering himself, he stepped backwards into the flat and invited me and Maggie in.

'Welcome,' he said. 'Come in and have a drink.'

We stepped over the threshold and despite the heat I shivered. Maggie closed the door behind us. From the living room Ethan's favourite Love album was playing loudly.

'We've already had a few,' Maggie said, pulling off her cardigan and handing it to Ethan. 'But there's room for another.'

'And another and another,' Ethan said with a nervous laugh, delicately laying her cardigan on a chair in the hallway, glancing over at me. I averted my eyes and breathed in the delicious smell of melting cheese and of peppers and pancetta browned to perfection, but the thought of actually eating anything made my stomach constrict. Ethan cleared his throat.

'Anyway,' he said, clasping his hands together in a very un-Ethan like way. 'It's really great to see you both.'

He kissed Maggie's cheek then leaned in close to me. I stumbled back slightly, knocking into the telephone table on which balanced a vase of purple and pink sweet williams. He steadied me with his hand on my elbow, but I shrugged it away. Maggie threw me a glance, her mouth turned down at the edges in a small sad smile.

'Andrew and I were getting worried,' Ethan said too loudly, hastily moving away from me. 'Paul's hitting the bottle and we've polished off the antipasto. So, how are you both?'

Just great, I thought. Absolutely amazing. But I didn't say anything, just followed him and Maggie inside the flat and into the living room, a very large open room decorated in autumnal colours with a black stone statue of Buddha sat peacefully on the mantelpiece.

'Hi,' I said, lifting a hand in greeting to Andrew and Paul, who were sitting either end of the dark red sofa holding glasses. Ethan, suddenly by my side again, handed me a cocktail glass filled with pink liquid.

'Strawberry and basil margarita,' he said, smiling. 'I think you'll like it. Taste it, tell me what you think.'

Ethan watched me as I drank. It was beautiful and smooth and fruity and delicious. I finished it in three mouthfuls.

'Thank you, but—' I said. 'Not really my thing.'

Ethan looked crushed.

'Let me get you something to eat. I know you're going to like these canapés—' he said, but I shook my head and rested the glass down on a table, next to an enormous russet lamp.

'It's fine,' I muttered. 'Thank you. I'm actually not feeling hungry.'

Ethan frowned, concerned, then something like recognition passed over his face. He looked at me knowingly and I cast my eyes to the floor. He knew I was lying. I was notoriously hopeless at it. My stomach churned noisily and I wrapped my arms around my waist protectively.

'What are you talking about, woman?' Andrew said from the sofa. 'How can you not be hungry at the Supper Club? That's not allowed. I'm starved. You know, the roasted garlic and marinated green bell peppers were out of this world. I've given him a ten out of ten for those.'

I gave Andrew a wan smile.

'Oh, by the way, Alicia insisted that I must apologize

again for my dinner party,' he said. 'Having twin girls on the kitchen floor was never part of the plan.'

Andrew was sitting forward on the sofa, leaning his drink on his knees. Still dressed in a suit, he looked dishevelled and exhausted. He hadn't shaved for a couple of days and had dark smudges of tiredness under his eyes.

'How are the twins?' Maggie asked, holding her head to one side. 'How are you and Alicia coping? Shouldn't you be at home?'

'Guilt trip!' cried Andrew. 'I'm working as hard as I can. It's exhausting, you know. Alicia and I are both like zombies. You'd never think that two tiny beings could be so totally demanding on . . .'

I tried to listen to Andrew, but was only really aware of Ethan, who was in and out of the room, banging around in the kitchen, finishing off his dinner. When he was in the room, he repeatedly glanced at me, smiling tentatively. I couldn't smile back. All I could think about was Benji. He didn't know anything about Benji. How could Daisy have not told him? It was cruel and wrong and I felt guilty for knowing when he didn't.

'So, what's it like to be a father?' Ethan asked, now by my side, offering me a bowl of fat green olives. 'Is it as tough as it looks?'

I gulped at Ethan's question, so innocently asked.

'It is utterly life-changing,' Andrew said, flopping backwards in the sofa so he was almost horizontal, clutching his glass to his chest. 'They're only a week old, but it's so much harder than anything I've ever done, harder than cooking a soufflé, even – something I've never managed to do.'

'Oh, that's easy,' Ethan said. 'The secret's in the amount of whisked egg white you add. The more, the higher it rises. I'm sure you're doing a fine job with your girls. Hey, my pizzas are ready in five minutes. Let's all sit. Eve? Will you come through?'

I nodded and followed Ethan into the kitchen, listening to Andrew, Paul and Maggie continue a conversation, collecting their glasses to bring through. Ethan quietly pushed the door to behind us, turned and grabbed my hand.

'Eve,' he said urgently. 'I meant what I said the other night. I know I made a terrible mistake, an awful mess, but Daisy means nothing to me. You know that. It's you I love. I know this hurts, I know it's not going to be easy, but I want us to be together. I'm certain we can put the past behind us.'

He pulled me towards him and made to kiss me. I felt the heat from his chest. His lips brushed against mine, so with my hands on his chest, I pushed him away.

'Ethan,' I said. 'No, we can't put the past behind us.'

'Please,' he said fervently. 'You have to believe me. I don't care about Daisy. Christ, do you really think I do?'

He held on to my wrist, tightly now.

'Get off!' I said, shaking myself free. 'Ethan, leave me alone. You have no idea.'

Ethan stepped back and leaned against the sink, rubbing his jaw with his hand.

'I do know how you feel,' he said. 'I can imagine perfectly how you feel, but I will do anything to convince you that I love you. Absolutely anything . . .'

His eyes searched mine for softness, but I stared stonily at him, the secret I knew boiling up inside me like molten rock. I felt desperate to tell him the truth, to rid myself of the burden. But how could I put it into words?

'Can we come in?' Maggie said from just outside the kitchen door.

'Course,' Ethan called out. 'Sorry, must have closed on its own.'

I looked towards the door and watched the handle turn as Maggie came through, followed by Andrew and Paul.

'Everything OK?' Maggie said, standing suddenly still, her eyes darting from Ethan to me. I shook my head very slightly and hung my head. 'I'm so hungry. This looks bloody brilliant, Ethan. Very posh.'

'Smells good,' said Andrew. 'Very rustic.'

I took a deep breath and smiled up at Maggie, grateful that she had quelled the tension in the air. Andrew, Maggie and I took our seats around the table, while Ethan, pale-faced and obviously upset, brought out his pizzas, placing them in the centre of the table. Paul began taking pictures, mostly concentrating, I noticed, on Maggie. In the candlelight, with her flawless skin and dark shiny eyes, she looked like a film-star.

'What am I going to do with bloody David Bailey here?' Maggie laughed. 'Stop taking pictures of me.'

Andrew filled up my glass with white wine and while he worked his way around the table, I drank deeply, realizing that with the beers and cocktail I'd had, I was already feeling drunk.

'Just make your excuses and go,' I silently instructed myself. I'd done everything I told Dominique I'd do. I was in the pictures, I could describe the food. I should just go. I took a deep breath.

'OK,' I said, standing, pushing back my chair. 'I'm not feeling that great. I think I should—'

Before I could finish my sentence the doorbell sounded in four long angry bursts. Everyone looked at Ethan, who stood still, holding a bowl of salad leaves, and frowned in confusion.

'Don't know who that will be,' he said, placing the bowl on the table then moving towards the door. 'I'll be one minute—'

The doorbell rang out again, this time in one endless burst.

'Whoever it is,' said Andrew, 'they're pissed off about something.'

Hearing a female voice from the hallway, I paused to listen. It was Daisy. My heart pounding, I scraped back my chair and walked out into the hallway to see Daisy on the doorstep opposite Ethan. She was white as a sheet, her mascara smudged around her eyes as if she'd been crying and she leaned up against the doorframe, obviously drunk.

'Daisy,' I said. 'What are you doing here? Where's Benji?'

Ethan stood awkwardly by the door. All the colour had drained from his cheeks and his eyes were wide.

'I've been phoning you,' she said, slurring her words. 'I've been phoning and texting you all day, telling you not to come here, but came. Did you want to get in there first? Be the one to tell him?'

I shook my head, my eyes flicking to Ethan, who looked increasingly bemused.

'Don't lie to me,' she said. 'Why else would you have come tonight, you bitch?'

Ethan, frowning, looked at me intently.

'Tell me what?' he said. 'What's going on? Look, Daisy, I think you should leave. Really, we've got nothing to talk about.'

Daisy shook her head and stepped over the threshold and into the flat.

'I'm not going anywhere,' she said, swaying on her feet.

'It's me who should leave,' I said. 'You two should talk. I'm sorry, Ethan, this isn't why I came tonight, but you and Daisy need to talk. She has something important to tell you.'

Ethan, pulling his bottom lip nervously, wedged one hand defensively under his armpit.

'Shut up,' Daisy said to me. 'Just shut up.'

'What the fuck are you two talking about?' Ethan said. 'You're not making any sense. What do you need to talk to me about? In my view, we've got nothing to talk about, nothing at all.'

'Where's Benji?' I asked Daisy again.

Daisy narrowed her eyes at me.

'You fucking bitch,' she said.

I shook my head, tears filling my eyes.

'I just meant that,' I said. 'Where is he?'

'Can someone please tell me what's going on?' Ethan said, his voice shaking.

Daisy stumbled past me and sat heavily on a chair.

'Nothing,' she said wearily, bending down and rubbing her eyes. 'Oh fuck, I feel sick.'

Shaking with anger, I moved towards her and lifted her chin up with my finger.

'Come on,' I said, looking her in the eye. 'Daisy, just tell him. If you won't, I will.'

'Tell me what?' Ethan said, pushing his hair back from his face. 'Will you just fucking well tell me whatever this is?'

His raised voice brought out Andrew and Maggie, who

hung back, their arms folded, worried expressions on their faces.

'Can we help at all?' Andrew said quietly. 'Are you OK, Eve?'

'Not really,' I said. I reached past Ethan and picked up my bag. My heart hammering in my chest, I turned to Ethan, then looked back at Daisy, who was slumped in the chair, crying.

'Benji's your son,' I said. 'Daisy had your baby.'

I was aware in the background of Maggie's hand shooting up to her mouth. Andrew gasped and pulled Maggie's shoulder, trying to get her back into the kitchen. Daisy's cries suddenly stopped and she stood, holding her breath, staring at Ethan.

'What?' Ethan said, staring down at the floor. 'Benji is my son? You didn't tell me?'

His face was flushed now, his mouth set in a ruler-straight line, jaw jutting forward. He leaned against the wall.

'Daisy,' he said, 'is this true?'

Daisy nodded once and stared at her hands.

'Daisy,' he said. He stared at me desperately, his eyes brimming with tears. 'Daisy's son is my son, too?'

I nodded, feeling like I might throw up at any moment. I watched Ethan slide down onto the floor, where he covered his head with his hands. He started to cry and I suddenly panicked about whether I should have told him the truth. I bit my lip, tasting the salty tears pouring down my own cheeks. Daisy stayed silent, her hand curled into a fist and pushed against her mouth.

'Sorry,' I whispered, before opening the door and letting

myself out of his flat. I closed the door quietly and walked down the street, my legs feeling like liquid, tears still streaming down my face. *Sorry*.

It was almost dark. I stood still for a moment and looked back towards the flat and saw Andrew leaving, pacing up the road in the opposite direction. I sighed heavily. I knew what this news would do to Ethan. I knew that he would be completely blindsided. Was it really the best thing for the truth to be out there? I shook my head in confusion. I didn't know any more. I didn't know anything. All I knew was that I wanted to talk to Joe. I wanted Joe to hold me, to kiss me and tell me that everything was going to be all right. But I'd dug my own grave. An image of Ethan sinking to the floor flashed into my mind. I'd never seen him so genuinely pathetic. Daisy's voice, drunk and accusatory, echoed in my head. I thought about going home, but didn't want to be alone. Banjo had enough food. I watched a bus trundling down the road towards me and knew it would go fairly close to Isabel's flat. With shaking hands, I fished into my bag for my Oyster card, got onto the bus and found a seat by the window. I sat among strangers, chattering and laughing or listening to their iPods. People who knew nothing of the turmoil inside my heart.

Chapter Twenty-Five

'It's up to them now,' said Isabel after I told her about the evening at Ethan's. I lay on her bed, in a quivering state of shock, my head banging with the evening's alcohol, watching her sort through clothes to take and clothes to give away. Her platinum hair fell over her eyes as she spoke, and in one dramatic motion she swung it from one side of her head to the other.

'It's best everything's out in the open,' she continued. 'Daisy and Ethan need to talk and think about what's best for Benjamin. This isn't some plot in a soap opera. This is a little boy's life, for God's sake. That's the important thing to remember here. You know, this might even be good for Ethan. If anything's going to make him grow up, this will.'

I propped myself up on my elbows and sighed. I was drowning in gut-wrenching regret for telling Ethan about Benji. Now, I felt frozen with cold fear, fretting about what Ethan would do and what he'd be feeling. His life had just been changed forever, just because of one 'mistake' that, in his words, had lasted less than five minutes. If I were in his shoes, I'd be incredibly angry that Daisy had never told me. And what about Daisy? Benji was her son. She would hate me for telling Ethan about something that was her business. I didn't know if she'd ever speak to me again. Oh God. Despite what had happened between her and Ethan, I hated the thought of that more than anything. What would Dad say? What would our mum have thought? I heard Dad's voice in my head: *It's us against the world now.* I buried my head in the pink mohair blanket on Isabel's bed for a moment and let out a muffled scream. It was all such a mess.

'What about these?' Isabel said, trying to distract me, holding up a pair of Hawaiian-print hot pants. 'Dubai or Oxfam?'

I looked up, my hair prickling with static electricity and my cheeks hot.

'Come on,' she said. 'Help me. Eve, come on. Focus.'

'Oxfam,' I said. 'Unless Robert would like to wear them to work.'

Isabel laughed and I managed a hopeless smile. She moved over to the almost empty wardrobe – a huge old oak thing – that was about the only piece of furniture in her bedroom that remained standing. The rest had been dismantled and packed up, ready to be stored while she rented out her flat. I hated seeing Isabel's home like this. In the years I'd known her, this flat had become a second home to me. When we weren't out drinking or dancing, much to Robert's chagrin, we'd spent countless evenings on the sofa, tucking into a plate of freshly baked cake, plotting our escape from normal life into being our own cafe bosses. I sighed. We'd almost got there. Almost. I wondered fleetingly if that would be etched on my grave stone. *Almost got it right, but ballsed it up in the end.*

'You never know,' she said. 'Despite the fact he likes to think he's James Bond, he's got quite a feminine side. Can you remember that time he put a dishwasher tablet in the bath because he thought it was one of my Lush bath bombs? That was funny.'

I smiled at Isabel, remembering Robert's red face when she told our group of friends about his itchy rash, while we were in the pub one lazy Sunday afternoon. It was about the only time I'd ever seen him blush.

'Come on,' she said, pausing to sit down on the bed for a moment. 'I know you're worried, but Ethan did need to know about Benji. It's stupid to think otherwise. Maybe it didn't happen in the best way, but it's out there. Just got to let the shit hit the fan now.'

'Thanks,' I said to Isabel. 'Thanks for always cheering me up. You're always so level-headed. I'm going to miss you so much. Are you sure I can't convince you to stay and bankrupt yourself working in the cafe with me? What if I beg? London won't be London without you in it. It'll be quieter, uglier and ten times more boring.'

Isabel stood and closed the wardrobe door, picked up a rolled-up pair of socks from the floor and threw them at my head.

'I can't hang around here forever,' she said. 'Dubai needs me.'

'I seriously hope they weren't Robert's socks,' I said, throwing them back at her. 'Please, Isabel, please stay? I don't know if I can cope without you.'

She didn't do sentimental, it just wasn't her thing, but her eyes flashed with moisture.

'Don't say anything else,' she said, glancing at me with wide eyes, in a mocking threat.

'Sorry,' I said with a sad smile. 'It's just with everything going on I wish you were going to be around. I feel like everything I touch at the moment is turning to shit and you're the one sane person I know. I don't know what I'm doing. I feel like I'm stumbling from one disaster to the next.'

'You know what I think?' she said, perching on the end of the mattress again, resting her hands on her lap. 'I think you should go and see Joe and sort things out with him. You're missing him. I think you need to leave Daisy and Ethan to sort out the mess they've made and make a life for yourself with Joe. Commit to him, Eve. He's waiting for you. I know he is, but he probably won't wait forever. How would you feel if he got another girlfriend? You'd hate it. You can trust him. You're the oldest friends. Before Ethan turned up again, you were really happy with him, you were just beginning to thaw.'

Isabel gave me an apologetic look.

'By that I mean you were just beginning to relax into your relationship,' she said. 'Not that you're an ice queen.'

'I know,' I said, exhaling suddenly, frowning at the horrible thought of Joe having another girlfriend. 'I *was* happy and I do love Joe. The thought of him with someone else is awful, but I can't deny that there's still something there with Ethan, even now, even after everything that's happened. When he was in Rome, I told myself that he was a bad person and that Joe is a good person, but I realize that just isn't true—'

'Not true?' said Isabel. 'Of course it's true. Look at what Ethan has done.'

'I know,' I said. 'But Ethan isn't a *bad* person at all. Yes, he'd done something unthinking and stupid, but if he's a bad person, that makes me a fool to have fallen for him and to have missed him all this time. I don't believe that I was a fool; I think what I felt was genuine love. Whatever he's done, I still love the essence of Ethan. Sometimes we do mad things, don't we? Say things we don't mean? Give the wrong idea to people? And I've never stopped thinking about him. At night, when I was in bed with Joe, as I drifted off to sleep, I would often visit Ethan in my head, in an imaginary room that he was sleeping in, so I could check him. I still held him in my head and heart, in a secret place. That's not normal, is it?'

'What are you talking about?' Isabel said, jumping up from the bed, her face suddenly stony. 'You're a sentimental lunatic. Look at the facts. Ethan slept with your sister and he has a child with her. Sorry to be harsh, but a child with your sister after a one-night stand is serious baggage. He might profess to still loving you, but he's a nightmare on legs. You should run for the hills. Joe, on the other hand, has been the constant in your life. He's gorgeous and interesting and sweet and loving. You two have always been dead close. So your sex life might not catch the world on fire, but that's not everything, is it? He'll support you in whatever you want to do, rather than distract your attention by being so dominating, like Ethan. When you've got a bloke like Joe, you can feel much more free because of the stability he offers you. You can get on with your cafe, have a social life and be loved, without having to worry.'

'I'm not so sure,' I said. 'Ethan apart, I worry a lot about Joe because he wants so much more than I'm giving. Sometimes I feel like our relationship is not at all equal. He is the adoring one. I am the one with the power that I don't even want or like. I want us to be equal. It wasn't like that with Ethan.'

'Maybe you should stop comparing them,' she said. 'Be wise. I think with Ethan you're chasing a dream. You're putting your first love on a pedestal like everyone does. Christ, when I think back to my first love, Aidan Jones he was called, I can remember how fabulously dizzy I felt when he turned up to collect me from my parents' house in his dad's old jag, smelling of Eau Savage, with an armful of roses and roaming eighteen-year-old hands. Wonderful. If I compare that to endless nights sharing takeaway curries with Robert, him farting and burping in between each course, sucking every morsel off the chicken bones like Henry VIII, there's no competition.'

'Robert wins every time?' I said, raising my eyebrows.

'Exactly,' she said. 'But seriously, what I'm trying to say, not at all clearly, is that love isn't always heart-stoppingly exciting, is it? Real love is not just about lust. Anyway, you know this, don't you?'

'Of course I do,' I said. 'I'm not just talking about sex, I'm talking about a connection. I want to talk to him. I want to tell him everything. I want to know everything he's thinking and discuss the world with him. Oh God, I know it's a disaster area, but I do believe that the kind of love I had with Ethan comes once in a lifetime. I guess I'm just sad to give up on that.'

'So does death come just once in a lifetime,' she quipped. 'And on the whole that's not much to write home about, is it?'

*

315

That night I stayed in Isabel's spare bedroom. Curled up in her duvet, I waited for sleep to come, but it would not. I tossed and turned, thinking about the day as if it were a film I was watching, picturing each person now left alone with their version of events. I imagined Andrew with his baby girls, cradling them to sleep, wondering what life held for them both, hoping they would do it all better than we had done. I thought about Ethan and Daisy and what they would have said to each other. I wondered if he, true to character, would take his time to look for the best in Daisy's decision not to tell him. While some people looked for people's flaws and found their weak point, Ethan found the best in everyone. Perhaps he would see in Daisy a brave person who had looked after his son quietly and proudly, without disrupting too many lives. Perhaps he would try to love her for the sake of Benji? They were, after all, once friends and had been before I ever came along. The more night-time, lonely hours, that passed, the more I convinced myself that was what was happening – Ethan and Daisy were going to get together, for Benji's sake. I fidgeted in Isabel's spare bed, casting my eyes over the boxes of her belongings, labelled 'Books' and 'Kitchen' and 'College stuff' waiting to go into storage. Soon she would be gone from my life, too. I thought about what she'd said about how much Joe loved me and I felt suddenly humbled and embarrassed that I had talked of Ethan in such glowing terms, when he was just too complicated for words. Remembering my life with Joe, just two weeks ago, felt like another time entirely. Though it felt, just a little bit, that I was sacrificing something by being with Joe, I knew I would be gaining a whole lot more. I suddenly missed the way he could never decide what to wear. He was worse than a girl. I smiled in the darkness, remembering him standing at his wardrobe, in his pants, staring helplessly at his clothes. I missed the sound of his voice and the feel of his hand on the small of my back as we walked together. In the half-light of morning, though I hadn't slept at all, the confusion I'd been feeling started to lift. I had to be rational. I made a decision. Ethan may have come back and turned my life upside down, but his own life was a mess. I didn't want to be involved. I couldn't be involved. Not now. I wanted to get on with my own life, not be a part of Daisy and Ethan's complicated affair. I decided I would tell Joe I needed him, as soon as I could. In the morning. Yes. Wasn't this what he wanted, all along? I glanced at my watch. It was four-thirty a.m. and finally I felt sleep coming. My eyelids grew heavy. I felt relieved about my decision to get my relationship with Joe back on track. Daisy would get what she wanted. If I didn't see Ethan again, I could try to convince myself to forget about him almost completely, in time. You could do anything if you put your mind to it. Finally, I closed my eyes. I forced myself to relax into my decision to let Ethan go. I loved Joe. I needed Joe. Joe's love was simple. Our relationship would be easy. I would go to his flat tomorrow and tell him I loved him. And then, just as sleep was about to snatch me from my musing, I remembered something Dominique had said to me on the phone when she reminded me that the first instalment of the Supper Club would be in the paper tomorrow. *I'm not sure you're going to like the photos much.* I remembered the hug and kiss with Ethan, at my dinner party, the smile on Paul's face as he lowered his camera and checked the image on the back. I sat bolt upright and blinked in the half-light of dawn.

'Fuck,' I said, swinging my legs out of bed and pulling on my clothes as quickly as I could. 'I bet they've stitched me up.'

Chapter Twenty-Six

'Can I talk to you?' I said to Joe, nervously, when he answered the door to his ground-floor flat. 'I was awake all night thinking about you. There's something I've got to explain, something horrible, before anyone else does.'

We stood on the doorstep of his flat in Kentish Town in the pale early morning sunlight. The air was warm and the streets already buzzing. From somewhere nearby came the smell of bacon frying. I'd left Isabel's place ridiculously early to pick up the newspapers from the newsagent, then, after reading, sat in a coffee shop working out how to explain it away. Joe, in dark blue jeans and an old green T-shirt I hadn't seen him wear in years, bare feet, with his hands pushed deep into his jeans pockets, looked pale and dishevelled, like he, too, hadn't slept. I felt sick with shame. His misery was about to get a whole lot worse. The article was just as I'd feared it would be – a complete misrepresentation of what had actually happened. With a headline of 'Proof Is In The Pudding' under a lead image of Ethan hugging me close to his chest, kissing my forehead, a plate of meringue in my hands with Maggie and Andrew raising glasses as if in toast, the picture caption read: '*Cafe owner Eve Thompson, 28, from south London, knows that the way to a man's heart is through his stomach . . .*'

If it had been any other man hugging me like that, it wouldn't have mattered. But whichever way I looked at the feature, I seemed guilty as hell. When Joe saw it, he would have every reason to hate me.

'Come on, then,' he said flatly, pushing open the black-painted door and angling his head down the hallway towards the kitchen. 'I'm just charcoaling some toast. Ever the chef.'

I followed Joe, letting the door slam heavily behind me, stepping over a pile of post he'd left untouched on the door-mat, aware of the magazine lying like a grenade in the dark of my bag. My eyes flicked around Joe's small kitchen. There were dirty plates stacked up by the sink, a few half-empty bottles of booze on the kitchen table and a bowl of prawn crackers and a large greasy brown-paper bag on the oven, left over from a takeout. By the sink there was a carton of milk, a packet of Wagon Wheels and a pile of this morning's news-papers that he'd clearly just been out to buy. I started to sweat when I saw the *London Daily* at the bottom of the pile. Had he already seen it?

'Home sweet home,' he said, with a lift of his eyebrows. 'I haven't exactly been whizzing around in my Marigolds and apron this last week. I've been working nights on the *Guardian* news desk and days at *Time Out*. The editor there, Martin, says they need a news editor and I'm going to go for it. I really want it, they're a good bunch to work with.'

'Wow,' I said, approaching Joe and holding out my hand

to touch his arm, then, when he backed away slightly, letting it drop. 'That would be fantastic.'

'Or there's a job going at the *London Daily*,' he said. 'Senior, but I reckon I stand a good chance.'

There was the sound of the toilet flushing and taps running in the bathroom at the back of the flat. Joe looked anxiously at the kitchen door then closed it quietly. I assumed that Jimmy, Joe's brother, was home.

'Dad's staying here,' he said, suddenly looking exhausted. 'Turned up three nights ago, totally wrecked. I reluctantly said he could sleep on the couch until he sorted himself out. Mum's thrown him out again. She told him not to come here, but of course that's where he came, and I can hardly turn him away.'

I searched Joe's face. He had an awful relationship with his dad. He tried hard not to dislike him, but the years of irrational rages and drunkenness had taken their toll. I knew having his dad to stay would be putting Joe under incredible strain.

'Jesus,' I said, full of concern. 'Are you coping? I'm sorry, Joe, I didn't realize. You should have told me. How's he been?'

Joe shrugged, his eyes downcast.

'Oh, you know,' he said. 'Same. Doesn't know the difference between night and day right now. It's all just one big drinking binge. He's full of remorse one minute, crying about how much he loves us. Then telling us we're useless and worthless the next. He likes to tell me I'm a crap journalist. You know how he is. Jimmy's sharing the shit, though.'

He sighed deeply, collected himself and gave me a small smile.

'He just looks for ways to undermine you both,' I said. 'He's jealous that he let his career slip, his whole life slip. He must look at his sons and feel constant guilt. You're a fantastic journalist!'

Joe rubbed his arm, clearing his throat.

'Anyway,' he said, flicking his eyes up to meet mine. 'So, how are you? How's the cafe? And how did your Supper Club thing go? Did you win? I was thinking it must be in the paper today, but I haven't had a look yet.'

Joe was being falsely casual, so I felt I had to match him. He didn't want to talk about his dad at any length – he never did. His dad had always been there, in the background, causing havoc. That was just the way it was. I waved my hand in the air dismissively at the same time as catching sight of Joe's open wallet on the kitchen table. Tucked on the inside was a photo-booth snapshot of us kissing, wearing antler headbands, taken at London Bridge station one drunken Christmas. I longed to be back there, perched on Joe's knee, my arms around his neck, carefree.

'Oh, I don't know who won yet, and I don't care,' I said. 'I wish I'd never taken part. It's um . . . um . . . um . . .'

I couldn't find the words. Joe looked at me quizzically and turned to the toaster, pinging out a wafer-thin slice of toast, burnt black, lifting it up and then immediately dropping it onto the breadboard.

'Shit!' he said, shaking his scalded fingers in the air. He smiled at me.

'I don't do very well on the culinary front without you,' he said. 'In fact, my diet of Wagon Wheels and Pret a Manger sandwiches is getting very boring.'

'Pret a Manger sandwiches, eh?' I said with a small smile. 'What's wrong with Gregg's?'

'There's one by work, so I pop in there for a croissant at breakfast, then a sandwich at lunch,' he said. 'Then another sandwich at tea. They must think I'm incredibly unimaginative, but I just can't be bothered with food right now.'

He leaned with his back against the kitchen counter, the stack of papers behind him, with one arm folded across his chest, the other gripping a mug of coffee. He moved to turn down the volume on the Roberts radio I'd bought him, on which a woman was laughing raucously. He looked at me expectantly.

'So,' he said, clenching his jaw as if preparing himself for a punch. 'What did you want to talk to me about?'

I rummaged in my bag, dropping my lipstick and house keys on the floor. He picked them up and handed them to me, and I stuffed them back into my bag before pulling out the copy of the paper and flicking it open to the Saturday Supper Club feature. I gulped. Beyond the kitchen door came the noise of Joe's dad banging on Jimmy's bedroom door, shouting at him to get up. Anger crossed Joe's face.

'Oh, Joe,' I said, cringing horribly. 'I've been stupid, really stupid, and I'm so sorry about how this looks, because it wasn't like that. It wasn't like that at all. I just haven't known what to say.'

Joe's eyes were as hard as stone when I showed him the feature. Watching him read and absorb the photograph of Ethan and me was like waiting to be beheaded.

'He just turned up out of the blue,' I garbled. 'And the whole thing threw me into a state. But that picture and that headline, they make it look like there was something going on, which there wasn't at all. It was just Ethan, he's like that, you know he is, throwing himself at everyone, and seeing him again, well, it threw me a little bit, too, if I'm honest.'

As I spoke, anger flickered across Joe's face in waves, but he said nothing. He didn't take his eyes off the pages. When I'd finished speaking, I sat down on a chair at the table and waited there, holding my breath, wringing my hands together, searching Joe's expression for a clue about how he felt. I picked an apple from the fruit bowl and passed it nervously from hand to hand.

'Is this why you said you didn't want to get married?' Joe asked, angling his head towards me slightly.

'Ethan told me he still loved me,' I said quietly, putting the apple down. 'And that confused me. You know I never really knew why we broke up, so when he came back, saying he'd never stopped loving me, it was a complete head-fuck, even though I loved you, of course. I've moved on, haven't I? But even so, it was a shock and that's why I said what I said about not wanting to get married. I needed time to think.'

'He said that, did he?' Joe asked. 'That he'd never stopped loving you? Then why did he go? Did you find out?'

I stood up slowly and walked over to the sink. With my back to Joe, I turned on the cold tap and poured myself a glass of water. I didn't turn to face him.

'It's all a bit grim, really,' I said, taking a sip. 'But I want to put it behind me, behind us, now, and get back to how we were. Can we? Nothing's changed, has it?'

Joe looked at me, his mouth set with anguish.

'What's a bit grim?' he said, scowling. 'Why did he leave you?'

I sighed and put the glass down on the draining board, on top of a mountain of cups and plates and bowls. I turned round and leaned against the counter.

'He slept with Daisy,' I said, my voice breaking. 'And, this is awful . . . he's . . . he's Benji's dad. Can you believe it? Oh, Joe, even though he's ancient history, it's been awful. Ethan's Benji's dad! You have to admit that's a lot to take in. But I don't want to think about it any more. I just want it to be how it was between us, without this mess thrown in making everything ten times more complicated.'

Joe was silent for a few moments. He tapped his front teeth with his thumbnail, then looked at me, his expression cold.

'So,' he said. 'When you found out that Ethan had slept with Daisy and fathered Benji, you decided to come back to me? And what if you hadn't found that out? Would you be here now? Or in his arms?'

I was taken aback by Joe's cold response; I'd thought that news would provoke some kind of sympathy. He flicked the paper shut, stood from his chair and began to pace the kitchen like a caged tiger.

'Would you be here now?' he said. 'Or with Ethan?'

'No!' I said in exasperation. 'I don't want anything to do with him. He's a nightmare. This just goes to prove what I already knew, doesn't it? Please, Joe, can we forget he ever came back? I really, really want to forget he ever came back. It makes my head hurt. I want it to be us. You and me. I want us to get on with things.'

My words were rushing out of my mouth in an attempt to convince Joe I wasn't a disloyal, unfaithful person. I flushed red.

'I don't know,' he said moodily. 'In that picture you look so . . . so . . . excited.'

His voice was flat, hurt, disappointed. I closed my eyes briefly. I couldn't deny what I looked like in that photo, but I had to make Joe understand I'd been swept up in a moment.

'I was in shock,' I said. 'It's that picture, I can't believe Dominique let it go, she must have known that you would be upset by that. Isn't she meant to be your friend?'

It felt good to be blaming someone else, but I knew I didn't have a leg to stand on. Of course Dominique would pick that picture. Far better than an image of my blackened fisherman's stew. Joe picked up the article from the table where he'd put it and chucked it into the rubbish bin with disdain, staring down at it for a long moment, his back to me.

'I've never trusted Dominique,' he said without turning round. 'I can't believe she'd do this.'

I didn't dare breathe. I wasn't sure who he was trying to convince – himself or me. My shoulders relaxed just a tiny bit. Was he trying to say that he believed me? That he had decided to believe me? Was it easier for him to think it was all Dominique's fault?

'I know,' I said quickly. 'What a bitch.'

Joe gave me a wary look, as if to tell me not to push my luck. I hated that the article existed. Even though Joe was putting on a brave face, I knew he must be gutted inside.

'Look,' I said. 'I'm so sorry for all this, it feels so "not us" to have to deal with something like this. I'll do anything to make you realize that I love you, that I feel awful to have put you through this . . .'

'Anything?' Joe asked.

I breathed out. Was he going to ask me to marry him, even after everything I'd said?

'No,' Joe said, reading my mind. 'I don't mean getting married. You've made it quite clear you don't want to get married and after this, well, I think we need time. I need time, too.'

Just then, the kitchen door swung open and Joe's dad stomped into the room. He collected his jacket from the back of a chair and stomped out again, without so much as a hello.

'Eve's here, Dad,' Joe called after him. 'It would be polite to say hello to her, you know?' Then he muttered, 'You old git,' under his breath. 'God, I wish he'd just leave.'

'She'll break your heart, you fool!' his dad called. 'Just look at those eyes!'

He slammed the front door and Joe looked at me, crushed, yet trying not to show it. I wanted to make him feel better.

'Let's move in together,' I said quickly. 'It's stupid us both having flats when we spend all our time together anyway. Why don't we just have one place?'

'Really?' Joe said, a grin breaking out over his face like a sunbeam. He laughed suddenly, joyously. 'You know I'd love that. God, I'd love that.'

'Great,' I said, laughing too, with relief. 'That's the best news I've heard in days.'

'There's just one condition,' Joe said, suddenly serious.

'What's that?' I said.

'You don't see that arsehole again,' he said. 'Ever.'

'OK,' I said, nodding. 'OK.'

Joe put his arms around me and kissed me passionately. I kissed him back, ignoring the small voice in my head asking me what the hell I was doing. Just yesterday I'd been talking to Isabel about how I needed time, how I'd had something with Ethan I couldn't find with Joe. But I wanted, so badly, to make things right with Joe, I told myself I was doing the best thing. I wanted to make him happy and we were virtually living together already. What was the big deal? When all this had died down, we'd be fine again. Better, probably, because I wouldn't be wondering why Ethan had deserted me those years ago. Finally, I'd have resolution.

'Oh, Joe,' I said, smiling at him, feeling the warmth of his arms around my waist. I was amazed at how easily and quickly he'd forgiven me for not telling him the truth from the start. 'I was frightened you'd never speak to me again. I'm glad you're happy.'

'Do you know what I'm going to do?' he said. 'I'm going to go to the shop and buy a bottle of champagne.'

I pulled my mobile phone out of my back pocket.

'But it's not even ten o'clock yet,' I said, a smile on my lips.

'We can chill it and take it to the park later for lunch?' he said, checking in his wallet and pulling out a £20 note. 'I'm so happy. I've hated these past few weeks. Absolutely hated it. I've missed you.'

Joe held me and gave me a lingering kiss. He walked out of the flat and the front door slammed shut, leaving me in silence. I pottered around the kitchen for a few moments, then picked up Joe's copy of the paper, stuffing it into the dustbin along with the other one.

'Stupid article,' I thought. 'How dare Dominique let that picture go?'

I needed to forget about all that now, forget that Ethan had ever turned up like he had. Fleetingly, I thought of Ethan and Daisy together, but I pushed them from my mind. Then I noticed Joe's laptop on top of the fridge, open with the screen glowing. I walked over to it and pressed the space bar. It was open on his Yahoo mail, which he used for work stuff. My eyes ran down the list of names in his inbox and I saw Dominique's name. I decided to send her an email and tell her what I thought of her antics. When I'd signed up to take part in the Saturday Supper Club, I was doing her a favour by stepping in at the last minute. What thanks did I get? She knew I was with Joe. I wanted her to know exactly how she'd made Joe feel by using that picture. I clicked on her email and my eyes flitted through the email conversation between her and Joe. The first had been sent when he had been freelancing on her desk. It was entitled Saturday Supper Club. I opened it and read.

Hey Dominique, I've picked three contestants for this month's Saturday Supper Club, from the pile you gave me to sort through. They're Andrew Evans – a wine merchant, Maggie Mitchell – a window dresser, and Ethan Miller – an actor. Photos attached I thought my girlfriend, Eve, could be the fourth contestant if you approve? She really wants to do it. Her picture is attached too. She's a great cook, is about to open a cafe so will be grateful for a plug. Will these do? They're all free on the dates you suggested. I'll do the article about money laundering after lunch. I only have tomorrow left in the office, so will get it all finished before I go. Cheers, Joe.

I frowned and read the message again. I read the message for a third time, then, with my heart beating rapidly, read the rest of their conversation, disbelieving. I gasped. I was amazed. I rubbed my eyes and read the email again. It didn't make any sense, but the truth was slowly dawning on me. I screwed up my face in disbelief. Joe had lied to me, lied all along. He'd known all about Ethan. Worse, he'd set this up. He'd *arranged* for Ethan to come to my house. He knew. Joe *knew*. My stomach turned over and I felt sick. I stared at the computer screen until my eyes hurt, at Joe's words to Dominique, not hearing the door open and close behind me.

'Eve?' Joe said quietly, from behind me. 'I've got the champagne. What are you—'

Suddenly he was there, at my shoulder, where I was still reading the email to Dominique. Bleary-eyed with tears, I turned and lifted my chin, searching his stricken face.

'You set this up?' I asked stupidly. 'You knew all along about Ethan? What? Why?'

'Fuck,' Joe said, throwing his keys on the table. He placed down the carrier bag, twisted round the bottle of champagne. His skin was the colour of mist.

'Why?' I said, incredulous. 'I can't understand how you . . . did you really do this? Why would you do such a thing? I would never, in a million years, expect you to do anything so conniving, so deceitful, so treacherous. You bloody hypocrite, watching me apologize like this, letting me sweat . . . and you, all the time, you're sitting there, trapping me, my God, I feel sick!'

I pushed my hair back out of my eyes and held my hands over my mouth. Joe didn't look at me. He sat numbly on a chair, his head bent, eyes closed, his thumb and forefinger pressing on his eyelids.

'How dare you!' I shouted, trembling, kicking his foot. 'Answer me!'

When Joe looked up, tears were trickling down his cheeks. He rarely cried. The sight shocked me. The radio prattled on behind us.

'I shouldn't have done it,' he choked. 'God, I wish I hadn't! But . . . but . . . when I was freelancing, Dominique asked me to sort out four contestants for the Supper Club. When I saw, just by chance, Ethan had entered, I felt sick. You told me he was in Rome but I knew he'd come back. I've always hated that you loved him so completely, absolutely hated it. When we first got together you spent so long talking about him, I wondered if I could ever get you for myself. Every time I propose, you put me off. I know it's because of him. It's been driving me insane, because I can feel this distance between us, no matter what I do. I thought, if I threw you two together, you'd sort out how you felt once and for all. You'd see that I am the one for you. You'd put his memory to rest. A risky strategy, but it would get results fast. I'd *know*. I wouldn't spend my life fearing you leaving.'

I stood still, as the words rushed out of Joe's mouth.

'I can't believe that you'd do . . .' I started, incredulous. 'It's so controlling, so . . . so manipulative—'

'I regretted it straight away,' Joe said forcibly. 'I didn't know what to do. Part of me just wanted to tell you what I'd done, but I couldn't find the words. And all the time, I told myself that this way I'd find out if it really was Ethan holding you back from loving me. I'm a fool, I know, a massive eejit. I don't deserve you.'

He stood up from the chair and walked across to the radio, which he switched off. His hands were shaking. I watched him pour himself a glass of whiskey from a bottle that probably belonged to his dad. He gulped it down.

'I know I don't deserve you,' he said, pouring and gulping down another before emptying the rest down the sink and clanking the bottle in the bin. 'Maybe I've known that all along.'

Joe moved to the open kitchen window and leaned up against the wall and looked out. The sky was clear blue. He bit his bottom lip, turning to face me. His shoulders slumped forward. He seemed so vulnerable. He was fourteen again. A kid with a hopeless dad. I saw Joe as my oldest friend, my sweet Joe. I had to try to understand him.

'Don't say that,' I said. 'It's not about whether you deserve me, or vice versa. This is about being deceitful, about not trusting me, when I've never given you any reason not to.'

I was aware of the hypocrisy behind my words. I thought of everything that had happened with Ethan, which I hadn't told Joe. My eyes drifted to the dustbin. I suddenly felt deflated.

'Look,' he said. 'Whatever you think about this stupid little scheme, I was doing it because I love you and I wanted to find out if you really loved me too or if you're with me because we're old friends and it's easy.'

'This isn't easy,' I said, shaking my head. 'In fact I can't believe how difficult this is becoming.'

'I've always worked hard to get what I want,' he said. 'But with you, no matter how hard I work, I can't quite get you. Even when I'm lying next to you in bed, you're somehow out of my reach. I want to know why. I thought, this way, I might find out.'

'I think I'm just like that,' I said vaguely. 'Maybe I'm just like this. Maybe I keep something back for myself, that's just how I am. Can you not live with that?'

'Yes, yes,' he said, his whole body seeming to wilt. 'Of course I can . . . it's just . . . oh, I don't know, I feel like such an idiot.'

'I'm sorry I made you feel so insecure,' I said. 'I should have realized how I've made you feel. I know how that feels and it's not nice.'

Joe looked up at me in surprise. I smiled. I hated him looking so defeated. Joe was usually such an ebullient person, so in control. I couldn't believe that he had orchestrated the whole meeting with Ethan, but I knew Joe. He wasn't trying to hurt me. He was trying to get an answer, to move his life along, to get what he wanted. Moving towards me, he took my hands in his.

'I should never have done what I did,' he said. 'I can't force you to love me as much as I love you. But, ever since I was a kid, I've had this safe place in my head and heart where I imagined a perfect relationship, with no betrayals, distrust or jealousies. I've been trying to make you and me into that fantasy, but it's ridiculous. I'm sorry. All I want to do is get life right and to do a better job than my dad has done. When

I look at his life, I want to do everything I can not to be like him. But this, this is probably the kind of paranoid, bizarre thing he would do, isn't it?'

I hugged Joe tight, looking over his shoulder at the computer screen still glowing with his email to Dominique. My heart ached.

'You *are* getting it right,' I said. 'You're nothing like your dad and you don't have to apologize for wanting commitment. We all have pasts that make us who we are, don't we?'

'Yes,' he said. 'I just wish I could leave mine alone and move on without it.'

'But I think that's impossible,' I said. 'We're a product of what's happened to us, aren't we? Maybe that's why I'm slightly standoffish. Maybe because my mum died and because Ethan deserted me, I'm scared of people disappearing like that, so it's easier to keep them at a distance.'

'Well, I'm not going to disappear,' Joe said. 'Unless you ask me to. Do you want me to?'

'No, Joe,' I said. 'I don't want you to disappear, of course not.'

'Good,' he said, pulling me into his body.

I wrapped my arms around his middle and held him tight, pushing my face into his chest, feeling the slight vibration of his heartbeat behind his ribs. For a moment, we were quiet and our hearts beat together. Then, when Joe's dad knocked on the front door, swearing and shouting that he didn't have a key, we parted again.

Chapter Twenty-Seven

In the bright light of the midday sun, I sat on a park bench near the bandstand in Clapham Common, in the shade of an oak tree, with Ethan. In my hand I held a bottle of iced tea, which I sipped from nervously, repeatedly screwing the lid on and off. True to form on a sunny day in London, the hundred-odd acres of grassland around us were carpeted with people sunbathing, eating, drinking, smoking, kissing and talking.

'So,' Ethan said moodily, taking off his sunglasses and resting them on the large area of bench we'd left between us. 'You called.'

I'd expected this. I'd expected Ethan to be playing victim, despite how shocking all this business with Daisy and Benji was for me too. He had always considered himself the centre of the universe. I concentrated on a man rollerblading backwards through the park, his dreadlocks flying in the air.

'If I had a body like that,' Ethan said, nodding at the roller-blader, 'I'd go around completely naked at all times.'

Ethan smiled, then looked at me seriously.

'So,' he said. 'Here we are.'

I bit my top lip and exhaled. I took another sip of my drink, then put the bottle down beside me.

'I wanted to apologize about . . .' I faltered, my attention grabbed by a toddler climbing the precarious steps of the bandstand. 'Actually, I don't really think I should be the one apologizing at all, but I'm sorry for how you found out about Benji. It wasn't the best.'

Four days after smoothing things over with Joe – in which we'd spent the whole time treading on eggshells around each other – I'd called Ethan, asking him to meet me in the park to talk. I still hadn't seen or heard from Daisy, despite me ringing her, so I wanted to see Ethan and attempt to resolve the tension between us, finally assigning him to history; then I could work out what was happening with Daisy. I thought one final meeting might help me put a big black full stop after Ethan's name, once and for all. Now that I'd made it up with Joe, I didn't want any concerns over Ethan getting under my skin. This, I decided, would be the best way forward.

'Oh, that,' he said sarcastically. 'That was nothing.'

I looked at him, pursed my lips and narrowed my eyes. I'd forgotten how completely infuriating he was.

'Seriously,' I said, swinging one leg under the bench. 'I'm sorry. I still haven't heard from Daisy. I take it you've talked since the other night?'

Ethan leaned back on the park bench, his legs stretched out straight, his ankles crossed. He rubbed his eyes and sighed, folded his arms across his chest.

'For hours,' he said, staring forward at a group of lads playing football. 'That night, it was awful. She was pretty bloody angry. We were up all night talking in circles.'

'I see,' I said, desperately wondering what they discussed, in turn irritated and worried that Daisy had been angry. How did she think Ethan or I felt? Ethan rolled and lit a cigarette – in under ten seconds – and took a drag.

'We talked about everything,' he said, reading my mind. 'But mostly we talked about Benji and about what to do. Just saying his name is so surreal. I cannot believe I have a son. I mean, an actual, living child that is half mine. It's mind-blowing! This is why they teach you about contraception at school. So you don't end up like this. I was never very good at school.'

My stomach turned. He shook his head, annoyed with himself, then faced me.

'I'm sorry. I shouldn't have said that,' he said. 'This must be really horrible for you.'

'Just a bit,' I said bravely. 'But the bigger issue is that you've become a dad and that Benji can know his dad. That's what matters.'

'Can you believe it?' he said, an astonished expression on his face. 'I mean, do I look like a dad to you? Do dads wear clothes like this? Do dads have less than a fiver in their pocket? I should stop this, for starters. Not exactly a role model, am I?'

He looked at his cigarette and threw it down onto the floor, leaned forward and stubbed it out, then he rested his head in his hands for a moment, briefly defeated, before addressing me.

'You must hate me. Fuck, I'd hate me,' he said, his grey-blue eyes searching mine. 'Do you? Hate me? I'm sure you do, but I hope with all my heart that you don't, because you

337

know how I feel, don't you? I think about you all the time, and I mean *all* the time.'

'Don't,' I said, putting up my hand to stop him talking, my voice raised. 'It's not about what *you* want any more, OK? For Christ's sake, stop being so selfish! Everything has changed. Why can't you see that?'

A girl on the park bench opposite, eating a sandwich out of a brown-paper bag, was clearly listening in, making our lives her lunchtime viewing, so I gave her a glare and spoke more softly.

'Some things have changed,' Ethan said, determined to get the last word in. 'But not everything.'

'Anyway, I've been talking to Joe,' I said, talking over him. 'And we're going to move in together. Since you turned up, I've treated him horribly, but thankfully, he has forgiven me. I hadn't realized how I've been making him feel.'

I felt pleased with myself for bringing Joe into the conversation. It somehow proved my loyalty to him, despite the fact he didn't know I was there in the park. Ethan didn't even seem to hear me, just sat still and said nothing. I sighed heavily. I hated the way that Ethan didn't even acknowledge the fact I had a relationship with Joe. It was as if my life didn't count for anything. The least he could do was show that he cared, whatever he felt. I hugged my waist.

'So did you and Daisy decide—?' I said. 'I mean, are you going to be a part of Benji's life, then?'

Ethan opened his eyes wide. He creased his brow.

'Of course I'm going to be a part of his life,' he said loudly. The girl opposite looked up at us curiously. 'What kind of shit would I be to just walk away now? OK, don't answer that. But yes, I am going to be a part of his life, if Daisy will let me.'

'Have you met him yet?' I said, trying to imagine what it must be like for Ethan suddenly to be in this position. He must still be in shock.

'Yes,' he said with a smile. 'I have met him, but only briefly. I made him an ice-cream sundae, which he refused to eat. Daisy introduced me as a family friend, then told him I was his dad. He cried. Don't blame him. But it's so hard to know how to feel, you know? I don't know him, I never, ever wanted to have a son with Daisy, but now he's here I want to do the best for him. I want to love him, be there for him and I want him to like me, as much as I like my pa.'

'And what about Daisy?' I said. 'How is she?'

Ethan rubbed his face and groaned.

'Daisy wants us to have a go at being friends,' he said. 'Well, actually, she wants more than that, but I've told her that isn't going to happen.'

My mouth fell open. Daisy still wanted Ethan. She was still trying to get him. I laughed bitterly.

'She doesn't give up!' I said. 'You'd think she'd give up. God, I don't believe her. I hope you set her straight.'

'Yes,' he said. 'Calm down, of course I did. But I have to be careful not to offend Daisy, because I really don't want to jeopardize things with Benji. I couldn't live with myself if I knew I'd messed it all up before I even had a chance at getting to know him. So I'm being as civil as I can to Daisy. We're going to have dinner tonight at hers.'

'How snug,' I said, shifting in my seat. Ethan darted me a look.

'It's anything but snug,' he said. 'You have to understand I'm trying to do the responsible thing. I can't float around not taking this seriously. My whole life has been turned upside down!'

'OK, OK,' I said, waving a hand at him dismissively. 'Just do whatever you want to do. I'm not interested any more. You live your life and I'll live mine. That's what I came here to say, so I might as well say it.'

I started to stand, but Ethan grabbed my hand and pulled me back down to sitting.

'I know this is all hard on you,' he said, still gripping my hand. 'I do know that. If I could change everything, I would, in a flash, but the fact is, Benji exists. I've got to make it work. I've got to help take care of him.'

'I know, and you're saying all the right things,' I shrugged, scuffing the floor with my toe. 'It's just all a bit of a mess, isn't it?'

'It's a complete mess,' he said, rubbing his jaw. 'Part of me does want to run away, back to Italy, carry on being carefree. But I can't carry on letting people down. I let you down badly and I'm sorry about that. The only consolation is that you say you're happy with Joe now, well . . .'

I sat silently watching people on the common, while Ethan talked. He rested his hand on my knee.

'If you really are happy with Joe and if you want to be with him,' he repeated, 'I guess I'll have to let you go. But no one could love you like I do, nobody . . .'

He stopped talking and cleared his throat. I looked at him for a long moment. I took in his dark hair, grey-blue eyes, pink lips and perfect jaw. He gave me a small smile.

'If I had my way,' he said, 'you'd be on my bed, right now, naked and eating one of my finest pizzas.'

I raised my eyebrows. Ethan gave me a sideways grin.

'Nice image,' I said.

'It's a perfect image,' he said.

I shook my head and looked up at the trees.

'You and I can never work,' I said, almost to myself. 'It's too difficult, too complicated. You've hurt me too many times. And now there's Benji. Everything is different. Not to mention that I love Joe very much. I just want us to forget about . . .'

I looked at the floor, trying to find the words, wondering how I was ever going to be able to forget Ethan, when he was being 'friends' with my sister and being a father to my nephew. But I had to. I'd made the decision, or rather the decision had been made for me. Now I had to stick to it.

'I just want us to say goodbye properly,' I said resolutely. 'Like we should have done the first time you messed up, so that we can both move forward, get on with our lives and try to be happy. What's the point in anything if we don't try to be happy?'

I stood up and dusted down the back of my skirt. Ethan's eyes swept over me appreciatively and a blush crept into my cheeks. I pretended not to notice.

'I've got to go,' I said, pointing towards the exit of the common and the Underground beyond. 'Bye, Ethan. Good luck with Benji. I suppose I'll probably see you some time, but you know what I'm saying when I say goodbye, don't you?'

He stood up and faced me. He lifted his hand, resting it briefly on my shoulder and pressing down slightly.

'Let's run away,' he said, smiling now, letting his hand fall by his side. 'We could fly to the States, change our names, grow beards, dye our hair . . . well, I could grow a beard.'

I grinned, grateful for Ethan's change in mood. He was trying to make it easier on us both.

'I've already done the dye thing once, and look,' I said, pulling a face and pointing to my hair. 'I suppose I could get my beard dyed to match. Anyway, I'd better go. Goodbye, Ethan.'

I started to walk away from him, then, after a few yards, I threw my empty bottle of iced tea into the bin and turned back to wave again. I stopped walking for a moment.

'Goodbye,' he said, his voice suddenly horribly, desperately serious. 'I'm going to miss you. I already do. I never stopped.'

I didn't turn around again. I carried on walking, my eyes cloudy with tears. This is ridiculous, I told myself, wiping angrily at my wet cheeks. This was supposed to draw a line underneath this mess with Ethan, not make me more miserable. I marched past all the people in the park enjoying the sunshine, walking away from Ethan, away from the past, away from the hurt. I was waiting to feel lighter as I moved towards the future, one with Joe, who deserved to be loved, who I knew I could be happy with. Towards a future without Ethan in it, complicating everything. But as I walked, my legs grew heavier and heavier until, right by the exit, I had to sit down on the grass. I stayed there for a few minutes, sunning my face and forcing myself to concentrate on the future, on what I was going to do next. I took a notepad out of my bag and started to write a list of things to do to get my life back on track. I wrote three points down before I put the pen back into my bag.

Joe's car
Dad's party
Cafe

After a few more minutes had passed, I looked back to the bench where Ethan and I had been sitting, but he was long gone. I folded up my list and stuffed it into my pocket. I looked around the park, in case he was there, somewhere. There was no sign of him now. He had gone.

Chapter Twenty-Eight

Finding the Spider was relatively easy and took just a few days of investigation. Persuading the new owner, a hard-nosed city boy who could have been on *The Apprentice*, to sell it back to me was more difficult. Eventually, after much wrangling and haggling, he reduced his mark-up of £400 to £300 and sold it back to me. I drove it to Joe's flat, parking it right outside his front door. I sounded the horn. Moments later, the door flung open, and there was Joe, a confused then happy expression on his face. I turned off the engine and dangled the keys out of the window, grinning. He jogged down the wide concrete steps to the kerb, a massive smile on his lips.

'Got it back for you,' I said happily. 'Returned to its rightful owner.'

Joe took the keys from me. He broke out into a laugh, running his eyes over the Spider. He patted the roof affectionately.

'Thought I'd never see this again,' he said. 'That money was for you, though, for the cafe. What will you do without it? What about all the kitchen equipment you need?'

He opened the driver door and I stepped out. I looked up

at Joe and he put his arms around me. I moved into his body and he hugged me tight.

'Thank you,' he said, kissing the top of my head. 'You're wonderful.'

'No, I'm not,' I said, pulling away slightly. 'It was your money in the first place. But I know how much you loved your car. I've had an idea about getting the fifteen grand for the cafe anyway. I'm going to ask Andrew if he'd like to invest. He has more money than he knows what to do with. Those are his words.'

Joe stopped smiling and rubbed his jaw. He slung his arm over my shoulders.

'Are you sure that's a good idea?' he said. 'He doesn't seem the most reliable bloke in the world. Last time I saw him he was off his face, passed out in the bath. Do you really think he will make a good business partner? You don't need anyone to make it more difficult for you than it already is.'

'Needs must,' I said cheerfully, wriggling out from under his arm to pick up my bag from behind the car seat, hiding my annoyance that Joe was being negative about my idea. 'He can be a silent partner. Anyway, Robert can put together a contract for me, so it won't be like he can demand his money back immediately. Besides, he's completely loaded. You should see his house.'

I slammed shut the car door and leaned over Joe's front wall to smell a bloom of pink roses.

'These are lovely,' I said, holding one between my fingers.

'Maybe you should try for an extension on the bank loan first,' he said, ignoring me. 'That might be a better idea. I could always look over your business plan with you?'

345

'No,' I said firmly. 'I've decided to ask Andrew. This is my project, so leave it to me, OK? Just concentrate on your car, will you!'

Hearing the annoyance in my voice, Joe smiled apologetically. Though we had been treading on eggshells with each other since we'd both been honest about the Supper Club, I could feel tension boiling beneath the surface.

'Sure,' he said. 'You know best. I'm interfering. This is so great.'

He opened the driver door again, climbed inside and I stood on the pavement, gazing into the distance, thinking about how I could approach Andrew. I had a business plan I'd shown to the bank manager, which I knew Andrew couldn't find fault with, whatever Joe said.

'I'll do it now,' I muttered, sending him a text, asking if I could come over to see him with a business idea. He replied instantly, telling me to come that afternoon and that he was looking after Ruby and Bella on his own.

'It's brilliant to have the car back,' Joe said, grinning out at me. 'Want to go for a spin?'

I walked round to the passenger seat, opened the door and got in.

'Actually,' I said, 'could you run me to Holland Park? Might as well strike while the iron's hot. I've got everything I need to show him in here. Andrew said he's free this afternoon.'

I patted my bag, with my laptop in it, which held all my business plans.

'I thought we were going to work on the cafe?' he said. 'With your dad and Isabel?'

'We are,' I said. 'But we can nip to Andrew's first. If I can secure this few grand, I'll feel so much better about it all. We'll go to the cafe after that, OK?'

'OK,' Joe said. 'Just let me get my wallet and stuff.'

Joe jogged up the steps to the front door of the flat and disappeared. While he was inside, I sat waiting in the car feeling irritated that Joe had doubted my business acumen. OK, so I might not be the most organized person in the world – or the best haggler – but Isabel and I had done our homework. He knew that. Why throw doubt onto the table when I was just about to open? There was no reason to believe we – I – couldn't make a go of it. Yes, it was going to be hard work, yes, it was a risk, launching a business in the midst of a recession, but I believed that the combination of footfall, area, relatively low rent and my homemade cakes was a winning idea, not to mention the personal touches I had up my sleeve that I knew would appeal to the crowd that lived down there. For a second I let myself think about Ethan's reaction to my cafe plans. 'Perfect,' he'd said excitedly. 'That is so *you*.' But Ethan always said what you wanted to hear, I thought. That was one of the reasons why people liked him. Joe was just looking out for me, wasn't he? Perhaps he was feeling last-minute nerves, just as I was. I sighed and chewed my thumbnail, watching a girl on the opposite side of the road lock up her bicycle and go into a flat. She was tall and blonde and looked a lot like Dominique.

Moments later, Joe appeared again. He walked towards the car, then got in, wound down the window and turned on the radio. On the way, Joe tried to convince me that I should speak to the bank again, but the more he pushed, the more resolute I became.

'I'm just thinking,' he said, 'that if it all goes wrong, you won't feel so bad if it's the bank you owe money to. If it's an actual person you know, things can get messy.'

'I think it's a sound investment for Andrew,' I said. 'I know I can make it a success. Why are you so down on the whole thing? This really isn't much cash for him.'

Joe lifted his hands up off the steering wheel, as if in mercy, then put them back down again.

'It's not that,' he said. 'I'm not down on it at all, and I don't doubt you for a minute. Like I've said before, it's just that the recession is hitting small businesses hard. People are much less likely to spend money on going out for a coffee these days. Look at Starbucks. They lost millions last year.'

'But Starbucks are a massive chain with zero personality,' I said. 'And people don't want chains any more. People like independent cafes, with a unique personality that they can relate to. People want a local place that they can call their own, that makes them feel more at home in the big city. Plus, East Dulwich is crammed with yummy mummy types who are desperate for coffee and cake. I have researched this, you know, Joe, I'm not a complete airhead. We've been through all this, months ago. I'm meant to be opening soon, so why are you being all jittery now?'

'I'm not being jittery,' he said, giving me a look. 'I'm just trying to think of us as more of a unit now, so what you do affects me too. Anyway, if it doesn't work out – I'm not saying it won't – but if it doesn't we can always get started on having a family a bit sooner. Once I get a better job – and I'm going to, whatever happens with the cafe – we'll be all right. I'm not putting on any pressure, I'm just saying, OK?'

I sighed heavily, wound down my window as far as it would go. The smell of bitter exhaust hit my nose.

'Please, Joe,' I said, as he swung round the roundabout at the bottom of Holland Park Road. 'Stop talking about the cafe as if it's not going to work out. I haven't even opened yet. And I don't want children yet. I mean, I do one day, but it's the cafe I'm excited about now. You know that.'

'OK!' Joe said, swerving suddenly left. 'Bollocks, I've gone the wrong way now.'

'Just turn round then,' I said huffily, staring out of the window with my arms folded. 'Just go back.'

'That's easier said than done,' he said, looking left and right, trying to work out which way to go, before indicating right and joining a stream of heavy traffic.

'Maybe you should get one of those satnav things?' I said. Joe scoffed.

'I have a brain, there are maps and signposts,' he said. 'I don't need a computer to tell me where to go.'

'OK,' I said, resting my hands on my lap. 'I'm sorry I spoke.'

We drove the rest of the way in silence.

I spent half an hour over coffee going through the business plans with Andrew, but he couldn't really pay attention, with Ruby and Bella crying one after the other on loop. Anyway, he seemed sold on the idea the moment I walked through the door.

'This sounds rather brash,' he said. 'But fifteen thousand is so little to me, I won't notice it. Of course I'll invest in your business. You seem to know what you're doing and you're opening so soon, I wouldn't dare say no. As long as I can come in occasionally with these two for some moral support? They're quite demanding! Much like their mother, who is having a spa day today, God love her. Oh, good Lord, Ruby needs her nappy changing and I think Bella's bottle is still half full. Would you mind feeding her for me? If she doesn't drink it all, she'll never sleep. Exactly the same for me with champagne, of course.'

Andrew, his hair sticking up all over the place, dressed in a tracksuit top with baby sick splattered on one shoulder, handed Bella to Joe, followed by her bottle. The living room, where Andrew was camped out, was a bomb site. Moses baskets, feeding bottles, Babygros, cartons of formula, nappies and wipes lay in a general state of disarray on Andrew's Persian rug. The French doors, leading out onto the garden, were propped open and the TV news was on with the sound muted. Joe and I sat on a leather sofa so enormous my feet were high up off the ground. Above my head was an original Banksy, probably worth a hundred grand, on the wall opposite a framed black-and-white photograph of Alicia wearing a big sunhat and standing in an apple orchard. I thought how lovely and gentle she looked, not at all the fierce creature Andrew described.

'What do I do?' Joe asked, looking awkward, holding Bella out at arm's length. 'God, I'm hopeless. I should get some practice in if I'm going to be doing this one day.'

I put my cup down on the table and helped Joe hold Bella properly.

'Oh yes?' Andrew said, looking from Joe to me. 'Is there something I should know? I ought to warn you, expect never to sleep again.'

'There's nothing you should know at all,' I interrupted, frowning at Joe. 'You need to tilt the bottle a bit, Joe.'

'I didn't mean anything by that,' he said, glancing up at me. 'Just saying I haven't a clue what to do with babies and hopefully, one day, I'll be a dad. Don't worry, Eve, I don't mean today.'

I forced out a laugh, but I detected irritation in his tone.

'Yes,' Andrew said, laying Ruby down on a changing mat to change her nappy. 'You're wise to have kids while you're fairly young. I'm almost forty and this is the most exhausting thing I've ever done! Alicia insists I do all the night feeds since she was the one who gave birth. I thought my job was hard work. Turns out I was wrong. It's a breeze in comparison. Anyway, I should get these girls to sleep in a minute. Think I'll join them if you don't think me rude. It's the only way I'll get through the day. I'm supposed to be going for dinner tonight with a client.'

When Joe finished feeding Bella, he passed her back to Andrew who, with one baby in each arm, looked at us and yawned, clearly waiting for us to go.

'We'll go,' I said hurriedly. 'Of course we don't mind. Thanks for the loan, Andrew, you won't regret it. You don't know what a difference you've just made to my life. Thank you.'

We stood to leave and Andrew shook Joe's hand and kissed my cheek.

'As long as you don't serve fisherman's stew in your cafe,' he laughed. 'Then all should be well.'

Back in the car, Joe and I sat in stationary traffic on Holland Park Road. Though I'd just been given a fantastic break by Andrew – and wanted to be celebrating – the atmosphere in the car was tense. Joe hadn't said a word since we'd left Andrew's house. I clicked off the radio and shifted in my seat, so I was facing Joe full-on.

'Are you all right, Joe?' I said. 'You seem really pissed off today. What's wrong?'

'Oh, I don't know,' he said, looking forward. 'I just feel strange about the whole Andrew thing. I wanted to forget all about that stupid Supper Club, put the whole thing behind us, and I guess that included the people you met. It's all too linked with Ethan. Everything seems to be linked with Ethan – your sister and now this . . .'

'That's rich,' I said crossly. 'You set the whole thing up! If you hadn't done that, none of this would have happened. Don't forget that.'

'I know, I know,' he said, inching the car forward. He glanced at me. 'I'm being uptight. Having my dad stay isn't helping. He's a bloody nightmare. You know what it's like. Last night he stumbled in drunk and left the front door wide open, swinging on its hinges all night long. I woke him up this morning and was greeted by a half-eaten battered sausage and a glass of apple juice with about thirty cigarette butts floating in it by his pillow. He's horrible, but I can't tell him where to go, because he's my dad. Christ, I'm being a pain in the arse today. Sorry, Eve. You got me my car back, too. I'll get over it. Let's do something good later and forget about all this. I hate moaning, it's very dull.'

Joe's dad was a constant blight in his life, bringing his mood down at every available opportunity. I thought back to when we were teenagers and it was Joe's thirteenth birthday. His dad was supposed to be driving a group of us to Alton

Towers for the day, but had been arrested for drink-driving the night before. My dad had stepped in and taken us instead, but Joe had been gutted.

'Well,' I said, 'why don't you come back to mine? Jimmy can put up with your dad for a while, can't he, since he's always out. Come back to my place.'

Joe nodded and gave me a smile.

'Or we could look for somewhere new?' he said. 'I thought Battersea might be a good place to look. I've actually found a couple of flats on Rightmove.'

'Yes,' I said. 'We will do that. But just let me get the launch of the cafe out of the way first. In the meantime, come to mine?'

Joe squeezed my knee.

'I know things have been strange between us,' he said. 'And I know it's mostly my fault. But I know I can make you happy. Don't forget my ultimate goal in life is to get a ring on your finger.'

He was trying to be sarcastic, but the joke fell flat. I shook my head in despair. Joe just did not get it.

'Come on,' he said. 'I'm not being serious. Well, I am, but not really, oh Christ.'

He banged the steering wheel. I tried hard not to show him the annoyance that I felt, because I had no reason to feel annoyed.

'You're obsessed,' I said before I could stop myself. 'Why are you obsessed with getting married? What difference does it make to anything?'

'I could ask you the same question,' he said. 'What difference *does* it make?'

'None to me,' I said.

'Then why won't you?' he asked. 'Just theoretically? If it makes no difference to you, but it's important to me, then why not? This is my issue with you. It's the principle of the thing. Each time you say no, you're rejecting a future with me. I want to know why. I thought we were back on track. I thought you loved me.'

'We *are* back on track and I *do* love you!' I said, exasperated, wishing that someone would tell Joe that if he stopped asking me to marry him, I would probably want him to. 'I don't know what else to say. Can't we just enjoy ourselves, just live for the moment and have a bit of fun? We're still really young.'

I took a deep breath. I saw the disappointment pass across Joe's face and I felt utterly exhausted.

'I do love you, Joe,' I said softly, resting my hand on his arm. 'Please, please, please stop worrying.'

'OK,' he said, with a shrug. 'I'll take your word for it. Because that's all I've got.'

'That's all you should need,' I said quietly. 'My word should be enough. Anyway, let's change the subject?'

'Yes,' Joe said. 'Let's.'

Chapter Twenty-Nine

Half an hour later, Joe pulled up outside the cafe, where the door was slightly ajar. Maggie had offered to help out, so I'd arranged for her to meet Isabel there earlier that morning. Through the window, I could see the outlines of both of them.

'Look,' I said. 'Maggie and Isabel are here already. Dad and Elaine will be here soon, to do the courtyard. Finally, it's all coming together!'

'You jump out,' Joe said, the engine still running. 'I'll park up and join you in a minute.'

I opened the car door and stepped out onto the pavement. It was incredibly hot now and the sun beat down on my head like a metal sheet.

'OK,' I said, slamming the door. 'See you in a minute.'

The rest of the journey from Andrew's house with Joe had been awkward, with both of us not saying what we really felt. Neither Joe nor I was particularly good at confrontation, so any disagreements between us fermented like rotting fruit. At least we had settled on him bringing some of his stuff and coming back to my flat that night. I thought that would help put Joe's mind at rest and push any thoughts of Ethan out of mine. It was worth a go, anyway. I crossed the pavement and pushed open the cafe door to find Maggie and Isabel inside chattering conspiratorially. They both turned to face me when I walked in and stopped talking. I rolled my eyes and smiled.

'Hey,' I said. 'Sorry I'm late. What are you talking about?'

'Hello,' Maggie said. 'We were talking about Ethan.'

'Oh God,' I said. 'Well don't. Joe's about to walk in.'

'Hi, love,' Isabel said. 'Look at these lovely walls.'

I put my bag down and admired the illustrations of lovebirds, with their beaks touching as if in a kiss, that Maggie had stencilled in black paint onto the lavender-painted wall. I burst into a smile.

'Wow,' I said. 'That looks so fantastic!'

Maggie straightened up and stood back from the wall to look at her work.

'Glad you like it,' she said. 'The walls should be done by the end of the day, then I'll work on the window tomorrow.'

'Thanks, Maggie,' I said.

Isabel moved towards me and grabbed my hand. Her bare arms were tanned from the sun and contrasted dramatically with her platinum hair that fell over her shoulders like a velvet cape.

'Come and see these chairs that were dropped off this morning,' she said, pulling me towards the back of the cafe. 'They are so gorgeous.'

I nodded and followed Isabel to a collection of chairs stacked up against the back wall. There were thirty oak chairs we'd got when a local school closed down for renovation and beside them were ten that had been reupholstered in bright floral fabrics. I glowed with happiness. They were perfect.

'They're so good,' I said. 'I can't believe this place is actually coming together at last. I'll definitely be ready for Dad's party, too. You know the sign came? They delivered it to my flat. I'm going to unveil it later, when Dad gets here.'

The door opened and closed behind us as Joe walked into the cafe and said hello.

'Come and see these chairs, Joe,' I said. 'And look what Maggie's doing to the walls. Joe, this is Maggie, Maggie, this is Joe.'

Joe and Maggie nodded to each other and Isabel gave Joe kisses on both cheeks, pointing him over to the chairs.

'Just the small problem of not having a decent oven, dishwasher, or second fridge,' Isabel laughed.

'I have a solution for that,' I said brightly. 'Andrew, you know the guy from the Supper Club? He's going to give me the money, as an investment. I know exactly what we need so I'll order it this afternoon. So, unbelievably, we might actually open on time and we can have Dad's party here, too.'

The mention of Dad's party made me panic. It was Daisy who'd wanted us to organize the party in the first place and who'd suggested we have it here, but she hadn't been in touch with me, so I'd decided to go ahead and sort it out with Elaine's help. But the prospect of Daisy turning up, after everything that had happened, when we hadn't even seen each other since, was terrifying.

'Fantastic!' Maggie said. Isabel clapped her hands together and cheered. Joe smiled at me half-heartedly, so I handed him a paintbrush and tin of white paint.

'Let's make a start on the woodwork,' I said, nudging him playfully with my elbow. 'Come on, Joe, be happy.'

Isabel glanced up at me quizzically, but I avoided her gaze. Joe took off his glasses and smiled.

'I am happy,' he said, brushing my nose with his paintbrush. 'Very.'

An hour later my dad and Elaine arrived to sort out the courtyard. Elaine, being much smarter than I am at thinking ahead, had brought a load of deli sandwiches and bottles of drinks, which she laid out on a table. All I'd managed to provide was a never-ending stream of questions about what should go where, and I could tell everyone was getting sick of me. Maggie, Joe and Isabel tucked into the sandwiches with gusto, while I sipped a bottle of orange juice and pulled the corner off a baguette.

'Not hungry?' Isabel asked me.

'Too nervous,' I said, shaking my head. 'It's all feeling very real now. I wish you were going to be here for the opening.'

'Me too,' Isabel said, moving a crate of teapots off a chair, so she could sit down with her lunch. 'I can't believe I'm going next week, I really can't.'

'I need a strong man,' Dad said from the doorway, 'to help with the bath.'

'That's me, Frankie,' Joe said, putting down his sandwich. 'Let me help.'

Maggie, Isabel, Elaine and I watched Dad and Joe attempt to carry the bath, bursting with beautiful flowers, through the cafe and out into the courtyard. Dad had brought it from his garden, along with several other massive plant pots.

'Looks beautiful, Dad,' I said. 'Thank you.'

Dad jokingly put his hand on his heart and staggered about the cafe.

'Stop,' said Elaine, laughing raucously. 'I'll have to do CPR.'

'Bloody hell,' he said. 'I'm too old for heavy lifting. Joe, son, you'll have to do the rest on your own, or get one of these beautiful girls to give you a hand. That Elaine, she's as strong as an ox.'

'My American blood,' she said.

'You know what?' Dad said, looking round at the stencilled lovebirds on the walls and the old-fashioned glass chandelier hanging from the ceiling. 'This is going to look very good.'

'Thanks,' I said, smiling. 'Are you happy to have your sixtieth party here, too? Daisy thought we should have it here, what with the house up for sale, so if you're OK with that? I know you don't like fuss, but you're only sixty once, aren't you? I haven't managed to speak to Daisy for a few days—'

At the mention of Daisy, everyone in the room tensed slightly. I watched Dad's eyes sink to the floorboards.

'But I'll call her later,' I said hurriedly. 'After we've finished here.'

Dad tipped his head back and rubbed the back of his neck with his hand.

'She should really be here helping out,' he said quietly. 'But, yes, this will be perfect for my sixtieth gathering. Absolutely perfect.'

While Maggie set to work on making an amazing set of cake stands, by drilling holes through the centre of different-sized vintage plates she'd instructed me to get from eBay and screwing them together with a metal rod set she'd got from a catering shop, Joe and my dad worked out in the garden together, pruning the borders and reorganizing the pots he'd brought in. Elaine, continually surprising, was putting up shelves behind the counter, like a pro.

'Makes a nice change from looking down swollen throats and checking scrotums,' Elaine said. 'Maybe I went into the wrong profession.'

Isabel unpacked pretty packets of hot chocolate, coffee beans, chocolate ganache and handmade biscuits that would be on sale, and I decided I should make a Lovebird cake for us all to share. The cooker was on its last legs, but it still worked well enough. After buying the ingredients from the shop opposite, I found a bowl, spoon and cake tin in the boxes of supplies I'd ordered, and got to work. With the cake in the oven, I stuck my finger in the mixture and licked the bowl clean.

'Hope you're not going to do that when you've got customers,' Elaine said. 'Environmental health will be down on you like a ton of bricks.'

Elaine checked over her shoulder and moved closer to me, a concerned expression on her face.

'Eve,' she said quietly. 'Can I have a word?'

'Of course,' I said, patting the seat in the kitchen. 'Are you OK? Is Dad OK?'

Elaine fiddled with the butterfly clip in her hair and adjusted her necklace. She cleared her throat. I set the timer on the oven clock and smiled at her.

'I wanted to talk to you about Daisy,' she said. 'I know this isn't really any of my business, but I thought I should tell you that she's going to bring Ethan to your dad's party.'

At the mention of Ethan's name my stomach turned over. Since I'd seen him in Clapham Common, I'd tried my hardest to put him out of my mind. I knew he and Daisy would be in contact, seeing one another, but I didn't let myself imagine it. The thought of actually seeing him and Daisy together, in the flesh, made me feel sick. Why would she do that to me? Wasn't it rubbing it in my face? I bit my lip hard.

'What do I care?' I said curtly. 'Daisy obviously doesn't care, so why should I?'

'I just thought you should know,' Elaine said. 'Apparently she thinks it would be a good idea for Benji to see Ethan at a family function, so he realizes that Ethan is part of the family. This must be so hard on you. Are you OK?'

My eyes pricked with unexpected tears and I took a deep breath, dumping the mixing bowl and spoon into the sink. Suddenly Joe was standing behind Elaine.

'Everything all right out here?' he said. 'Your dad wants to see the sign, but I said it's all still packaged, isn't it?'

'We're fine, Joe,' I said. 'Just taking five minutes. I'll come in and find the sign in a minute.'

Joe lifted his hands up and let them fall again, turning without saying anything else. Elaine put her hand on my shoulder.

'Do you think you and Daisy can be civil to each other next week?' she said. 'I know your dad is worrying about it. He's not sleeping. He thinks it's all down to him, all this trouble. He worries about what your mum would have said . . .'

I nodded and tried to smile.

'Of course we can be civil,' I said more curtly than I'd intended. 'There's no need to ask.'

The cake baked, I put it out onto the counter, and called everyone in for a slice. Cutting it open, I breathed in the wonderful smell of chocolate and almonds, handing everyone a plate.

'Fantastically delicious,' Maggie said after taking a large bite. 'You should have won the Supper Club, not me.'

I widened my eyes at her. I hadn't even congratulated her. When I received the email from Dominique telling me that we'd all voted Maggie's Supper Club the best, and that she'd won the £1,000, I'd deleted it and not given it another thought. I was far too busy thinking about Ethan and Daisy, or Joe, or the cafe.

'Fisherman's stew,' I said. 'That's all I'm saying. Anyway, well done on winning. It was a dead cert, really, wasn't it? What are you going to spend the money on?'

'Rent, probably,' Maggie said. 'Rent, shoes and macaroons. Or maybe just macaroons.'

Noticing Joe's eyes flickering from Maggie to me, I smiled at him, trying to transmit that just because I was talking about the Supper Club, it didn't mean I was thinking about Ethan, though in reality, Ethan was in my mind, especially after what Elaine had told me.

'This is really something,' said Elaine. 'Oh my God, I'm going to get so fat now that I know you.'

'Will you send some over to me in Dubai?' Isabel asked, after polishing off her slice. 'I actually don't think I can live without this cake!'

'Sounds like everyone approves,' Joe said, licking his fingers, beaming at me. 'Well done, Eve.'

I smiled at Joe and put my arm around his waist. He was sweaty from all the hard work he'd been doing in the garden. He kissed the top of my head.

'Come on, then,' said Elaine. 'Tell us what you're going to call this place. I'm dying to know!'

'Well, it was going to be Isabel and Eve's,' I said. 'Until Isabel decided to do a bunk. Only joking,' I said, glancing at Isabel. She raised her eyebrows comically. 'It's very simple,' I said. 'This cake, this is the one that my mum used to cook for Dad when they'd had a row. I remember it was around a lot, wasn't it, Dad?'

Dad burst out laughing and Elaine folded her arms, shaking her head. An image of my young self, standing in the kitchen doorway, watching my parents, their arms entwined, my dad's nose resting on my mother's hair, both laughing gently, flashed into my mind. I could still remember the sound of her laugh, just.

'That doesn't surprise me,' she said warmly. 'I take my hat off to Audrey. She must have had the patience of a saint!'

'Hey!' Dad said, squeezing her waist. 'I'm the perfect gentleman!'

'You are,' said Elaine. 'Yes, you are. Anyway, so, Eve, you were saying?'

I moved across the cafe to where the sign for the shop was propped up and wrapped in brown paper. I'd had a sneak peek earlier. I started to rip off the paper.

'Anyway,' I said, 'she called this cake her Lovebird cake, so, when Dad gave me this recipe I thought that would be the

363

perfect name for the cafe. I will bake this cake every day, too, so it's always on the menu. What do you think?'

Unwrapping the last of the paper, I held up the sign for everyone to see. Painted on a lavender background was an outline of a teacup, with two lovebirds, their beaks together, emblazoned on the side. Above that were the words Lovebird Cafe.

'Your mum would have loved to see this,' he said. 'Sorry, Elaine, to talk about the past.'

'Not at all,' she said. 'I'm sure she would have been immensely proud. I am too.'

Dad fished in his back pocket, then pulled out the black-and-white picture of him and Mum on the beach when they'd first got together that showed Mum leapfrogging Dad, her arms and legs spread out in a starfish, joy splashed across her face. He handed it to me.

'I thought you could put this on your "Love" wall,' he said. 'To start you off. I'll put one up there of Elaine, too, of course, so I can display my harem of women!'

Elaine laughed and shook her head in mock horror.

'Thanks, Dad,' I said. 'I love this picture.'

'I just wish Daisy was here too,' Dad said. 'Then everything would be just fine.'

'I don't,' said Isabel quickly. 'I'm enjoying myself.'

I gave her a hard stare and turned to Dad to check he hadn't heard. Sadness crossed his face. Joe draped his arm over my shoulders. I leaned into him, grateful for his support.

'Don't worry, Dad,' I told him. 'We're sisters, we'll stick together; we'll be fine, I know we will.'

Isabel raised her eyebrows at me and Maggie looked down into her tin of paint. Joe squeezed my arm.

'Honestly?' Dad asked, his face full of hope.

'Honestly,' I said, as convincingly as I could, helping myself to another slice.

Chapter Thirty

'The big day,' Joe said, as I opened my eyes, early the following Sunday morning. 'Good weather for it.'

Big day. For a nanosecond I thought I'd agreed to marry Joe and we were about to get wed. An image of an out-of-control bridal horse and carriage, galloping straight past a church and disappearing over the horizon flashed into my mind. I blinked it away and smiled up at Joe. Though he'd only been back in my flat a few days, he had relaxed considerably, but I'd had a repetitive dream about us standing at the altar taking our vows. I didn't feel either ecstatically happy or desperately unhappy in these dreams, but was hyper-aware of being watched by the congregation. Everyone staring, their eyes bulging like peeled baby shallots. And each time, just before I could say, 'I do,' the buttons would ping off the back of my dress or the zip would break and the dress would drop to the floor, leaving me naked and hideously embarrassed. I hadn't told Joe about it; I knew he'd read far too much into it.

'Great,' I said, realizing it was Sunday and he was actually talking about my dad's sixtieth party. I propped myself up in bed, next to Joe, who was drinking from a mug of coffee. 'We should get ready. I need to iron my dress. Is there any more of that stuff? I need caffeine. And croissants.'

As soon as I was vertical, my head filled with a million things I needed to do before everyone arrived at the cafe at lunchtime. Though it was now looking beautiful and the kitchen was fully equipped, I had food to prepare and decorations to put up. I rubbed my face with the palms of my hands. I lifted my legs out from under the duvet, preparing to get up.

'Yes, but where are you going in such a hurry?' Joe said, putting down his mug and leaning over to pull me back into bed. 'Come here for a minute.'

I tensed. Joe and I hadn't made love since before the whole Supper Club episode and it was beginning to become an issue between us. Though we'd cuddled up in bed, it was as if neither of us wanted to take the lead and initiate sex. I knew Joe had now reached the end of his tether – he never normally left it this long – and he was giving us a chance, that morning, to get over the hurdle. All I had to do was relax, I told myself. It was easy, really. And when Joe started kissing my neck, I closed my eyes and instructed myself to empty my head of all the stupid anxieties that instantly filed into my mind, like soldiers standing to attention. We'd done this hundreds of times before, so why did this feel like such a big deal? I cleared my throat. Then my phone, next to the bed, beeped. Joe pulled away from me and looked from me to the phone in irritation.

'Well,' he said grumpily, 'who is it?'

Reaching out of the bed, I grabbed the phone and checked. When I saw Daisy's name, my stomach flipped over. I still hadn't seen or spoken to her since Ethan's dinner party. Even though I'd now left three messages, she hadn't said anything about Dad's party, leaving me to plan the whole thing myself, even though it was her idea in the first place.

'Daisy,' I said, glancing worriedly at Joe. 'Let me read her message.'

With Joe peering over my shoulder, I read her text out loud.

'We'll be coming later. I'll bring a cake. Sorry I haven't been around, had things going on. I guess you know what they are.'

We'll be coming later. By that I knew she meant Ethan too. I tried to process the fact that other people at the party would assume they were a couple. I swallowed hard.

'God!' I said, throwing the phone down on the bed. 'What's she talking about? I can't believe she says she'll bring a cake. She knows damn well that's what I'll be doing, since that's what I do! And what does "I've had things going on" mean? Haven't we all had things going on?'

I shook my head in annoyance, while Joe tried to placate me, but I felt furious. He lifted the hair from my neck and kissed the top of my back.

'Don't stress over her,' he said, but I shook him off.

'I'm going to have a shower,' I said. 'I'm too angry to speak, let alone have sex.'

'Super,' said Joe, instantly pulling away and flopping back on the bed. 'That's fantastic.'

By two p.m., the sun high in the sky and baking hot, I was on my fourth glass of Pimm's with not much lemonade and absolutely no fruit, teetering around the cafe courtyard in too-high heels, serving up plates of homemade cheese straws to the thirty party guests, all busy eating, drinking and laughing. People had been drifting in since one o'clock, making all the right sounds about the cafe, bringing Dad gifts including a very random life-size wooden pig and several bottles of champagne. With all his favourite people around him, he was in his element. But Daisy was yet to arrive and I couldn't keep my eyes off the door. I twisted the buttons on the front of my dress, a gingham tea-dress, nervously, until Elaine slapped my hand and told me to stop.

'Eve,' said Antonia, a friend of Elaine's, taking me by the elbow. 'This really is a gorgeous place. I adore the "Love" board. I've taken a picture of my shoes and stuck it up there. I'm sure you're going to be swamped when you open. When do you open?'

I looked down at her shoes, bright red heels with a big red bow on the front.

'Next Saturday, allegedly,' I said, with a little grin. 'There's lots to do, but thanks, I'm really glad you like it and I love your shoes—'

Out of the corner of my eye, I caught sight of Daisy coming in through the cafe door. I gasped as I watched Ethan and Benji follow on behind. My heart racing, pounding in my ears, I stopped speaking.

'Excuse me for a minute,' I said to Antonia, giving her the plate of cheese straws. 'Can you hold this?'

Joe, who was topping up glasses with the jug of Pimm's and watching me like a hawk, followed my eyes to the door, clocked Ethan and Daisy, then glanced back at me, anger flashing across his face. Ethan – bold as brass – came straight towards us, holding out his hand to Joe, to shake. I felt myself begin to tremble.

'Good to see you again, Joe,' Ethan said, smiling broadly. 'Who would have thought life would turn out like this, eh? I certainly had no inkling.'

Ethan, in actor mode now, kissed both my cheeks and complimented me on the cafe, but I saw his lips quivering. He was clearly nervous. I watched Daisy, who was pushing a sunhat on Benji's head and hadn't yet made eye contact with me. My mouth was dry with nerves.

'I hope you don't mind me being here,' Ethan said quietly into my ear. 'Daisy insisted I came. It's not going very well. At all.'

Before I could reply, Ethan saw my dad and went to shake his hand. Joe came to my side and slipped his arm over my shoulder.

'OK?' he asked, gripping my arm and squeezing.

'Fine,' I nodded, listening to Ethan in the background congratulating my dad on turning sixty. I had to take my hat off to Ethan. This must be hideous for him, but he didn't run scared.

'I'm going to speak to Daisy,' I told Joe, slipping out from under his clutch and pushing through a group of Dad's friends, one man talking loudly about a recent trip to Hong Kong, the others politely nodding.

I walked in from the courtyard and saw Daisy pushing a white cakebox onto the counter. I flashed with sudden anger. She was wearing a black maxi dress and platform sandals, her hair held back by a simple headband. She looked beautiful, but when she saw me, she didn't smile.

'Why did you bring a cake?' I hissed. 'You KNEW I'd bake one! That's what I do. And why didn't you answer my calls? I've left loads of messages for you. Do you know how difficult this has been for me?'

Daisy handed Benji a present and told him to go and give it to Dad. She crossed her arms and waited for him to go.

'You told Ethan,' she said crossly.

I sighed and looked at the floor.

'I'm sorry,' I said. 'But, Daisy, you have to admit he needed to know. You can't hold secrets like that away from people, it's not fair on Ethan or Benji.'

'I know, but what about me?' she said. 'What's fair on me?'

I shook my head and exhaled slowly.

'I don't know what you want,' I said. 'I have no idea who you are any more, Daisy. You know Mum would have hated this, that we are like this with each other. Can you remember that time, when she found out that she wasn't getting better, that she sat us down under a tree in the park and made us promise to stick by each other? We've pretty much failed her, haven't we?'

Daisy shrugged and took a glass of Pimm's from Maggie, who was circling the room with a tray of glasses.

'Oh God, I'm sorry,' she said, a tear sliding down her cheek. 'Everything is going wrong. Benji's not taking well to having Ethan around and I know that Ethan isn't interested in me. I think he should go back to Italy. He's thinking of it anyway. I think that's what I want, for us all to get back to normal. For him to go, for us to be talking again. What about you?'

'But what about Benji?' I asked. 'It's a bit soon to expect

him to welcome Ethan with open arms. These things take time, don't they?'

'Yes,' Daisy said. 'But I think he can pick up on everything that's in the air, you know, this tension between us. It's not doing him any good. Look, I know there's a lot of bad feeling between us and I'm sorry for my part in that, but I do, genuinely, want to be friends. I think the sooner Ethan is out of the picture again, the better. He's bad news. I don't know why I brought him today, I shouldn't have bothered. It's clearly not going to work with him being around.'

Daisy looked at me and dropped her hands down by her side. In my peripheral vision I saw Ethan talking to Elaine. He glanced round nervously and I suddenly felt desperately sorry for him. He was never going to be able to do anything right with Daisy, because at the bottom of all this, she still wanted him to want her. Just then, Elaine banged the side of a glass and so Daisy and I walked out into the courtyard, standing by one another, closely watched by Joe.

'Attention, please,' said Elaine, who was standing on a small step at the back of the courtyard and waving at me and Daisy, beckoning us over to the table where I'd laid out the birthday cake, studded with sixty candles.

'I think Frankie would like to say a few words,' she said. 'All ears this way, please. But just to run through a few health and safety issues. This magnificent cake here, with these millions of candles on it, could be a fire risk, so hold on to your hair . . .'

There was a ripple of laughter from the crowd and Dad kissed her cheek. I felt Daisy's arm against mine as she stood with Benji clinging onto her leg.

'Thanks, Elaine,' he said, holding his glass against his chest. 'Yes. Well. Thanks for coming to celebrate me becoming an old man. Sixty! That's quite something, isn't it? Funny thing is, I feel like I did when I was nineteen and I met my wife, Audrey, Daisy and Eve's mum. That old photograph up on the wall inside the cafe, of Audrey leapfrogging me on the beach – that was taken when we first met. Gosh, I was over-whelmed with joy that day. I thought I was going to explode with love and joy and possibility and excitement.'

Listening to Dad talk, I felt like I might cry. I took a large gulp of drink and watched Dad's eyes blear with tears. He pulled a handkerchief from his trouser pocket and wiped at his eyes. Daisy touched my arm, briefly and gently, in ac-knowledgement.

'Oh dear,' he said, holding out his glass to a gentle peal of laughter. 'I think I've had too many of these. But what I'm trying to say, in my inarticulate way, is that today, thanks to my daughters and my beautiful new love Elaine here, I feel some of that joy, love and excitement all over again. And that is a wonderful thing for a man of my age. A wonderful thing.'

Someone in the courtyard clapped and everyone joined in. Dad shook his head and held up his hands to silence every-body.

'Please, don't get me wrong,' he said. 'I'm not being smug. I'm nothing but grateful. I recognize how difficult life can be and I know that both my daughters have had hard times, but I want to stress to them, to you all, the importance of sticking together through the shit. Pardon my French. But I hope you catch my drift. I love you girls with all my heart. You are my everything.'

Dad looked over at Daisy and then at me. I turned to give Daisy a small smile. She raised her eyebrows and reached out her hand and took mine briefly, before letting it fall. I couldn't speak. I was too choked with emotion.

'Come on, you old fart,' Dad's friend Barry called out. 'Cut the cake.'

There was a burst of laughter and Elaine lit the candles on the cake, which Dad blew out, with the twinkling happiness of a four-year-old. We all broke out into a raucous rendition of 'Happy Birthday' before he cut the cake, picking off the candles as he worked.

'Are you all right?' Dad mouthed to me and I nodded vigorously. I gave him the thumbs up, smiling brightly. Maybe I wasn't such a bad actor myself.

By late afternoon, people began to drift off, but a hardcore circle of drinkers remained, sitting round on garden chairs in the courtyard, listening to Elaine tell funny stories about the real reason Dad had suddenly become a philanthropist – purely to impress her.

'I was doing some voluntary medical work for the Children in London charity,' she said. 'And I suddenly noticed that Frankie was this prolific fundraiser, who seemed to stop at nothing to raise money. Baked-bean baths, half-marathons and, most recently, the head shave. It was only a few days ago he admitted the real reason.'

'Oh,' Dad said, 'that's not true. I've always been an active member of that charity.'

'Come off it, Frankie!' said Elaine. 'You'd never even heard of it before I mentioned my involvement!'

My eyes drifted to Ethan, who was smoking a cigarette at the bottom of the courtyard, looking out over the wall. Daisy was standing close to him, slapping suncream on Benji's arms, and by the expression on their faces things were not going well between them. When Daisy took Benji inside to use the toilet, I walked over to Ethan and touched his elbow.

'Hey,' I said. 'Are you OK?'

'Hello,' he said. 'Actually, I'm not doing too well with Daisy. She's not at all happy with me. It's not really working, this idea of mine. Benji doesn't seem mad keen on me, either. I think she wants me to disappear off the face of the earth now.'

'Give it time,' I said. 'Maybe you should spend time with him on your own. Just half an hour or so at a time while Daisy is out in the garden or something. Maybe that would work.'

'Yeah,' he said, stubbing out his cigarette. 'Maybe. Anyway, this place is great. Really properly good, you've done so well. I'm jealous. I wish I could be a part of it with you.'

Hearing Joe calling me from inside the cafe, I turned back towards the kitchen. Ethan put his hand on my arm and pulled me to him, quickly. He looked around, to make sure no one had seen.

'Eve,' he said quietly, 'I know we agreed not to do this, but I can't stop thinking of you. It's like you're in my blood.'

I pushed off his hand.

'Get off,' I said sternly, tears pricking my eyes. 'I have to go inside.'

Quickly, I went back in, into the cool, where Joe was inside the pantry cupboard, staring at boxes of unpacked crockery.

'Ah,' he said with a smile. 'I'm trying to find some fresh glasses. Do you know if there are more?'

'Yes,' I said. 'There should be some on the top shelf in there, probably in a plastic box.'

'OK,' he said, switching on the pantry light. 'I'll get those sorted out, then I've got to go to work. I'm doing another night shift tonight. I'll have to catch the bus as I've been drinking.'

'OK,' I said. 'Just let me tell my dad you're going soon. I want him to come inside for a bit so I can talk to him on his own, make sure he's enjoyed himself. Thanks, Joe, by the way, for everything. It hasn't been too bad, has it, with Ethan and Daisy here?'

Joe looked down at his hands.

'No,' he said stoically. 'Not too bad at all.'

Leaving Joe inside, I went out but Dad was busy talking to his best friend. I returned inside, walked into the kitchen to find Joe, but the pantry door was closed. I turned to leave, when Elaine came into the kitchen to find me. Swaying slightly, half of her hair trailing out of her butterfly clip and clutching a folded-up piece of paper, she spoke quickly and softly.

'I was going to give you this earlier,' she said. 'But I wanted to wait until Joe had left for work. He's gone now, hasn't he? It's the original letter that Ethan sent you, the one your dad had the audacity to hide from you. I found it when we were going through all your dad's stuff, sorting out for the house move. I think it's rightfully yours. It's up to you if you read it, but I think you should have the choice.'

I stared at the letter in her hand.

'Thanks,' I said, taking it from her slowly.

Back in the kitchen, I turned it over in my hands a few times, then I took a deep breath, sat down on a chair and opened it. Loose inside, there was a British Airways ticket to Rome, open-ended for the month of August, dated three years ago. I cast my eyes over Ethan's loopy handwriting, my heart knocking crazily in my chest.

Dear Eve

The first time you looked at me that day in the park, I was hooked. When we spoke, I lit up inside. I couldn't stop looking at you. I had to hold you. I had to keep hearing what you had to say, because everything you said thrilled me. From that day, I was yours. I didn't want for anything or anyone else. Only you. On the night of that summer party, I made the biggest mistake of my life. I ruined everything. After we had that stupid row, Daisy told me she was in love with me and that I'd ruined her life by being with you. She took her clothes off and cried and begged me to hold her. She begged me to tell her I thought she was attractive. It was madness but I wanted to make her feel better. I was drunk. I wanted to be the good guy. I slept with her. Just writing the words in black and white makes me want to throw up, because I regret it so much. I wish, with my whole self, I could turn back the clock. It was, literally, a moment of madness. I know what chaos this will cause. I know how your heart will break and that this will smash your trust in me, in our love. I came to Rome because I couldn't stand to see the disappointment in your eyes when I told you the truth. I couldn't not tell you either, because Daisy threatened to tell you if I didn't disappear. In a panic,

I left, thinking it would be better if you never knew what I'd done. Now though I'm confessing the truth because I can't live without you. I have to convince you of how much I love you. I need you to give me a second chance. I want you to fly out to Rome so that we can talk, away from Daisy, so that I can explain. Please come because I love you more than there are words to express. I am so sorry to have let you down so horribly. I have let myself down too. Please come, Ethan x

I read the letter over again, my eyes filling with tears. I held the letter to my cheek. Elaine, suddenly kneeling by my side, put her hands on my shoulders.

'Oh, honey, you read the letter already?' she said. 'Oh, sweetheart, don't cry.'

I slumped back in my chair and gulped, trying to stop myself, but the tears were coming thick and fast now. I leaned forward into Elaine's shoulder and wept.

'It's the missed opportunity,' I croaked, wiping my eyes on the back of my hand. 'If I'd known all this then, if I'd been able to talk to him then, maybe we could have sorted it all out.'

I felt exhausted and shook my head in despair.

'These things are so hard,' Elaine said, stroking my hair. 'But in my experience, love will out. The opportunity to talk to Ethan is still there if you still love him. You just have to be brave.'

Shaking my head vigorously, I folded my arms and turned towards the window, where the afternoon sun was shining through.

'No,' I said. 'The opportunity has gone. It's too late now. I can't hurt Joe again, whatever muddle I'm in over Ethan.'

'Do you really, really want to be with Joe?' Elaine asked.

I didn't answer for a while, just stared at the skin on my hands, which was dry and in desperate need of cream.

'Joe's so great. He's always been fantastic and I do love him,' I said. 'But there's something with Ethan that I can't shake off, something I can't leave alone. The thought of never seeing him again, it just hurts, here . . .'

I pointed to my heart and Elaine nodded sagely. I opened my mouth to carry on speaking when, from behind me, Joe burst out of the pantry door, his eyes glistening with angry tears. I gulped.

'Joe,' I said, panicking and standing up, 'I thought you'd gone to work. Did you—?'

'Were you *hiding* in there, Joe?' Elaine asked, screwing up her face.

Joe's face was white with anger, his jaw set.

'I heard every word of that,' Joe said. 'I should have trusted my instincts. I don't want to be second best.'

I reached out to hold Joe's arm.

'You're not second best,' I said wearily. 'It's me, I'm drunk, it's this stupid letter. I love you, Joe, honestly. Please.'

'It's NOT ENOUGH!' he said, his voice shaking with anger, his body trembling. He grabbed the letter from my hands and ripped it into shreds. I'd never seen him so properly angry. I held my hands up to my cheeks, frightened.

'Now, Joe,' said Elaine, 'calm down.'

'Don't tell me to calm down,' he said to Elaine, shoving past her and marching towards the kitchen door. Just then Ethan came in, followed by Dad.

'And you can fuck off,' said Joe, pushing Ethan in the chest.

Ethan raised his hands as if in mercy.

'Hey,' Ethan said to Joe. 'Watch it, mate. You've got no right to be shoving me around. Are you OK, Eve? Why are you crying?'

I looked at Ethan, his face full of concern, and I felt angry, really full of rage. If he hadn't been such an idiot all those years ago, none of this would be happening.

'Oh, piss off, Ethan,' I said. 'I mean it. Just get out. Get away from me. GO!'

Ethan gave me a long hard look, then shook his head despondently and left the cafe. For a few moments there was silence, then Dad put his hand on Joe's back.

'Listen here, son,' he said, frowning. 'Whatever's happening here can be sorted out. I know it's all a bit complicated, but women are like that and—'

Elaine lifted her finger to her lip to silence Dad and gestured for him to leave Joe and me alone. Joe looked up at Dad, his cheeks wet. His lips contorted as he spoke.

'I'm not your son!' he said. 'I never will be.'

Joe walked out of the kitchen and towards the front door of the cafe, past bemused guests, who wondered what was going on. I followed him out to the door and grabbed his arm.

'Where are you going?' I asked.

He shook my hand off his elbow and stared forward. He pulled his keys from his pocket and headed to his Spider, where he yanked open the driver door and climbed inside. He turned on the engine.

'Don't drive,' I said, stumbling after him in my heels. 'Joe, you've been drinking! It's dangerous!'

I banged hard on the passenger window and gestured for

Joe to turn off the engine and come back inside. He wound down the passenger window slightly, but said nothing. His face was as hard as stone, his lips pressed between his teeth. I was aware of Elaine in the background, with a couple of guests trickling out of the party, looking at us in concern.

'Joe,' I said calmly. 'You can't drive. You've been drinking. Please, come inside. I want to explain.'

Joe let out a loud embittered laugh. He pushed on his sunglasses and turned on the radio.

'I don't give a fuck about what you have to say,' he said, winding the window back up. I tried to grab the door handle, but he put his foot down on the accelerator and sped down the road, leaving me reeling on the pavement.

'What's going on?' said one of Dad's friends, by my side, his hands on my waist steadying me. I swore under my breath, put my hand on my forehead and watched Joe's car at the traffic lights, his brake lights flickering.

'What's not going on?' said Elaine. 'That's the question. Come on, honey, you need a drink.'

Chapter Thirty-One

The following morning, after Joe had sent me a text at midnight, in reply to a dozen pleading phone calls from me, asking me not to contact him for a while, I sat in the car beside Isabel. Her departure day was here and, after a sleepless night tormenting myself with how bad I felt for Joe and with words from Ethan's letter whirling around in my mind, I'd agreed to drive with her to Heathrow, so I could drive her car back to mine and take care of it for a while. I sat beside her feeling nauseous, fiddling with my phone, obsessively rechecking my messages.

'How are you feeling?' Isabel asked, glancing sideways at me from the driver's seat. 'You look terrible.'

After Joe had sped off from the party, Elaine had made me such a strong whiskey and ginger it completely knocked me out. I had to go back to the flat in a taxi, peel off my clothes, kick off my uncomfortable heels and lie down. I'd hardly eaten anything all day and drunk only alcohol since lunchtime so it was hardly a surprise I had such a hangover. Maggie and Elaine had cleared up the party debris and closed the cafe, so I could rest. Even Daisy helped out, but perhaps I shouldn't be surprised. Daisy seemed to like me best – to be able to cope with me better – when I was down.

'I feel like such a bitch,' I said, stretching the seatbelt away from me briefly. 'Imagine hearing what I said. Joe must feel so bad. I wish I hadn't opened my mouth. He won't even talk to me.'

Isabel changed gear and sped onto the dual carriageway away from London. The tower blocks of flats blurred into a grey stream out of the window smeared with red streaks of graffiti.

'You were only saying what you feel,' she said. 'I'm beginning to realize that your feelings for Ethan are still really strong. Whatever I say about Joe, you can't let go of Ethan, can you?'

I brushed my fringe from my forehead and blew air out of my lips.

'I don't want to be involved with anyone any more,' I said. 'I'm too confused to know my own mind.'

'I think you do know your own mind,' she said. 'But it's going to take balls to admit what's in your heart. Ethan's not an easy prospect and you'll lose Joe's friendship. Daisy will not be happy either.'

I shook my head emphatically. The thought of going down that road with Ethan was too much of a nightmare. I wouldn't even let myself think of it as a possibility.

'Seriously,' I said. 'I don't want anyone. I just want to concentrate on the cafe and keeping in touch with you. I hope you realize I'm going to be Skyping you every night and our phone bills will be huge.'

'That's OK with me,' Isabel said. 'I can't be happy unless I've got you in my life, even if I can only have a fuzzy picture of you on the laptop. Maybe you can have yourself on Skype continuously, so I can keep checking in to see what you're doing?'

Glancing at one another, we smiled warmly. I felt my throat constrict. I was going to miss Isabel so much, but I didn't want to drag her down.

'I'll come out and see you as soon as I can scrape the money together,' I said. 'I might have to sell the new oven, which would make things tricky. Oh well.'

I shrugged my shoulders jokingly. Isabel shrugged hers too.

'Oh well,' she said.

For the rest of the journey we talked about everything Isabel wanted me to help out with while she was away. I was the point of contact for her new tenants and I had to get the car into the garage for an MOT. The time flew by. Suddenly aeroplanes were in the sky above us.

'Christ,' she said, as we neared Heathrow. 'We're almost there.'

'Oh God,' I said. 'This is really it. I think I might climb inside your suitcase and come with you.'

'I'd love that,' Isabel said, heading towards the short-term parking area and into a car park. 'I really would.'

Inside, the airport was bustling with people. Isabel's seven-hour flight was at two p.m., so we'd arrived in plenty of time for her to check in and for us to have a farewell drink. With her suitcase dragging bumpily behind her on wheels, Isabel searched for her check-in gate, while I walked next to her, feeling like I wanted to grab her and bundle her back into the car so she couldn't go anywhere. I checked my phone again for messages, but there was nothing, so I threw it into the bottom of my bag. Joe had asked me not to contact him so I had to respect his wishes. As for Ethan – I had no idea where he was. I didn't care. Well, I did, but I pretended to myself I didn't.

'Oops, sorry,' I said, as I bumped into a couple clinging on to one another for dear life bang in the middle of the corridor. They were both in tears of joy – at being reunited, I assumed – and I envied their blissful intimacy. Isabel and I smiled at each other in acknowledgement.

'I'm just going to get some magazines quickly,' she said, outside WHSmith, checking her wristwatch. 'And a couple of bottles of water, then we can find the check-in. I've got plenty of time.'

I stood outside WHSmith, guarding Isabel's bags, when I glanced over at the Ticket Information desk and did a double take. With his back to me, a black sports bag at his feet, was Ethan in conversation with the lady wearing a red uniform behind the desk. I swallowed and looked into WHSmith for Isabel. I couldn't see her. My heart racing, I stayed frozen to the spot. I kept my eyes on Ethan. He leaned down to pick up his bag and ended his conversation with the woman. Slinging his bag over his shoulder, he turned in the direction of where I was standing. I sucked in my breath, waiting for him to clock me. When he didn't, I wanted to call out his name. I opened my mouth to say something, but no sound came out.

'I've got *Grazia* and *Glamour*,' said Isabel, suddenly back next to me, rustling a plastic carrier bag of goodies. 'Plus a couple of newspapers. Are you all right? What's up? You're as white as a sheet. Do you feel sick?'

I nodded my head towards Ethan, who was studying the departure boards, his bag on his shoulder, his hands shoved into his jeans pockets. I watched a red-haired girl admiring Ethan and felt a stab of jealousy.

'Noooo!' Isabel half shouted. 'I don't believe it! What's *he* doing here? Going back to Rome, do you think? Loser. Has he seen you?'

I shook my head, opening and closing my mouth in shock. Isabel picked up her suitcase and grabbed my arm, starting to pull me in the opposite direction, when Ethan turned towards us, noticed me and, looking completely taken aback, slowly lifted his hand in the air to wave.

'Eve!' he called over a crowd of passengers waiting in a queue. 'Isabel!'

'Oh God,' I muttered to Isabel. 'Hang on a minute.'

His hair flopping into his eyes as he half jogged towards us, Ethan was saying something, but I couldn't hear what above the public announcements bellowing over the speakers. There were too many people and I wished we were somewhere quieter.

'I'm going to wait in the queue,' Isabel said to me, nodding briefly at Ethan and pointing to the British Airways desk. 'Come and find me over there.'

Ethan and I looked at one another and smiled, despite everything. I remembered the things he'd said in his letter, the aeroplane ticket falling to the floor. We looked into one another's eyes.

'Why are you here?' I asked quietly.

Ethan's eyes glistened for a second, then he frowned and sighed.

'I'm going back to Italy,' he said. 'I was finding out if there were any cancellations. Everyone is so pissed off with me here, I need to get away. I've made a mess of everything.'

'So you're running away,' I said, sudden anger coursing through me. 'Again.'

'I'm not running away,' said Ethan. 'I'm—'

He looked around, floundering for words. The departures board glittered with yellow letters and numbers.

'That's what cowards do,' I said. 'Run. So go for it, Ethan. Run.'

Ethan looked at me seriously for a long moment, as if he was about to say something, then he leaned towards me and kissed my cheek once. He smelt faintly of cigarettes mingled with Dior.

'Maybe,' he said with a shrug. 'Bye, Eve.'

I didn't speak. I couldn't speak. My eyes pricking with tears, my stomach aching with anger and sadness and regret and love, I watched him go.

Later, after I'd said a tearful goodbye to Isabel, both of us sobbing like mad at the departure gate, I drove to my dad's house. As I parked up outside, I saw Daisy's Raleigh chained to the garden gate and though I considered for a second turning round and running back to my flat, I forced myself to go inside. With Joe not speaking to me, and Ethan leaving the country, I couldn't bear to ostracize anyone else that I loved. It might be painful, but I had to forgive Daisy completely and move on. This was a new era. Dad and Elaine were moving in together. The old house was up for sale. The cafe was opening in a few days' time. I had to be positive. All I could do with Joe was apologize, and as for Ethan – Ethan had proved to be a coward. I didn't want to love a coward.

'Darling girl,' said Dad, opening the door to me. 'We're all at the kitchen table. Come through. How's your head? Mine's awful.'

'Quite bad,' I said. 'I hope you enjoyed it?'

'I had a fantastic time,' he said. 'But I know you didn't. Young men can behave like fools. I have to apologize for my species.'

I shrugged and walked through to the kitchen, where Elaine, Daisy and Benji were sitting at the table, sharing a plate of chocolate brownies that were left over from Dad's party. Elaine offered me a coffee, which I gratefully accepted. Daisy and I smiled warily at one another and she patted the chair next to her.

'Come and sit down,' she said.

I smiled, gave Benji a kiss and a cuddle, then pulled out the chair, sitting down with my elbows leaning on the table. In front of me stood a vase of roses clipped from Dad's garden.

'You know he's gone, do you?' I said to Daisy.

Daisy nodded and put down her mug of coffee.

'I think it's for the best,' she said. 'It wasn't going to work out for any of us.'

I opened my mouth to say that she'd hardly given him a chance and how could she make assumptions about how I felt, but I found myself saying, 'You're right,' instead.

'He was bloody hopeless with Benji,' she said, lifting Benji down from her knee. 'Do you want to play in the garden, Benj?'

I tensed, feeling myself want to defend Ethan. Could anyone be the instant perfect parent when they were in such a state of shock?

'You've got to give the guy a break,' said Elaine, handing me a plate with a brownie on it. 'He only just found out he was a father. Jeez, I'd be in a bad place for a long while.'

Elaine and I shared a look. Sensing the tension in the air, Dad cleared his throat and put his hands on his hips.

'Well,' said Daisy, 'he didn't even know that two-year-olds don't go to pre-school! And he clearly doesn't want to be anywhere near me, despite what happened before—'

Daisy stopped speaking and looked down at her nails, then at me apologetically.

'Daisy,' said Dad. 'Don't go stirring all this up again.'

'I'm sorry, I didn't mean it like that,' she said. 'I'm just pointing out the facts and trying to say that it's no loss, him going. Is it, Eve? No loss.'

'He was a troublemaker,' Dad said.

'Yes, you're probably right,' I said quietly. 'It's a good job he's gone.'

I nodded and took a sip of coffee. Elaine, who had been quietly listening to us, made a 'hmm' noise, readjusted her hair, traced her eyebrows with her fingers, then, when she had all of our attention, she spoke.

'I know you don't really think that,' said Elaine. 'Do you? Jeez, does anyone say what they're really thinking in this family? I mean, Eve, honey, you're majorly pissed with Daisy and your dad, for scuppering your chances with the man you were desperately in love with. Daisy, you're jealous as hell, but have never even admitted liking the guy. What is it with all these secrets? And Frankie, you're no better. You still haven't told the girls we're getting married, have you?'

I looked from Elaine to Dad, whose cheeks were turning pink. He glanced nervously at Daisy and me.

'Congratulations!' I said in surprise. 'That's good, isn't it, Daisy?'

I nudged Daisy, who was staring at Elaine, a confused expression on her face.

'I guess,' she said. 'Though it's a little out of the blue, isn't it?'

'Hoorah!' said Elaine. 'You're telling the truth about how you feel. I know it feels strange for you, honey, but now that I've got my size fives under the kitchen table, I'd really appreciate it if we could all be a little more open with one another? That way, we might actually know what the other one is feeling. How about that? As for Ethan, I personally think there's one person around this table, Eve, who does genuinely love the guy and I think he loves her back. We, as a family, have to decide if we can help Eve in any way. What do you think?'

Huffing noisily, Daisy pushed back her chair and carried her plate to the sink. She dropped it in the bowl of water and rinsed her fingers under the tap.

'I don't know, Elaine,' said Dad. 'I really think we should be a little bit careful with the whole Ethan thing. You know Daisy had feelings for him too—'

'I know, but it's better to address these feelings than sweep them under the rug,' she said. 'If you can't get rid of the family skeleton, you may as well dance with it.'

'I have absolutely no time for Ethan,' snapped Daisy from the sink. 'Honestly, Eve, if you want him, you have him. I'm thinking about becoming a lesbian.'

Just then, Benji came in singing a hymn about Jesus.

'Do you want to say a prayer with me, Elaine?' he said. 'A prayer to God.'

'I'm not sure where he's got all this from,' said Daisy. 'From nursery, I expect.'

'You know, Benji,' Elaine said, 'it's fine if you want to pray, but I don't believe in God.'

'Don't worry,' he said sincerely. 'He will forgive you.'

I caught Daisy's eye and we shared a small smile. Elaine burst out laughing and jumped up from her seat.

'I saw that smile!' said Elaine. 'Great stuff. Maybe there is a God after all. Hallelujah!'

Chapter Thirty-Two

The night before the day of the opening, five days after I'd waved goodbye to Isabel – and Ethan – I stood in the cafe kitchen, mixing up the ingredients for my mother's Lovebird cake. It was still light and warm outside and the air was heavy with the smell of flowers from Dad's courtyard pots mingling deliciously with melting chocolate from the kitchen. The sounds of laughter from a pub garden three doors down drifted across the evening sky and, with my arms and feet aching from hard work, I felt a pang of envy. I wished to be sitting in the pub garden, nursing a cold glass of wine, a packet of crisps on the go, spending my guaranteed wages without a care. That was the problem with being self-employed, with going out on my own. I would always have to be working. I would never be able to let go.

'Hopefully it will all be worth it,' I said out loud, scraping the gooey chocolate mixture into several cake tins and then sliding them into my new oven. I set the timer and stood back, my hands on my hips.

'What did you say?' asked Maggie from the kitchen

doorway, holding in her hand an antique birdcage that she had painted dark purple and decorated with flowers twisted through the bars. It was going to hang in the corner of the cafe. Dressed in blue shorts, white vest and leopard-print ballerina pumps, her hair piled on top of her head in a scruffy topknot, I was struck by how pretty she was. I wondered briefly what Sal's new woman was like.

'Oh, nothing,' I said. 'Are you all done? Shall we have a drink now? I'm shattered.'

I'd spent the last few days working like a dog to get the cafe ready for opening day. Putting out stock and pricing it all up had taken an eternity, plus finalizing the selection of cakes, bakes and drinks I wanted on the menu had left me nearly tearing my hair out with indecision. I'd managed to smash a whole box of plates that I'd hand-picked from charity shops, so I'd had to scoot out searching for more, plus the fridge was making an awful buzzing noise until I kicked it really hard and it stopped. Then I'd flown up and down Lordship Lane, handing out fliers that Maggie had thrown together for me to everyone I passed. Maggie, who had a part-time freelance contract working for Selfridges starting the following week, had helped me out no end and I was incredibly grateful to her. With Isabel in Dubai, it was wonderful to have Maggie to bounce ideas off and she was so much more creative that I was. While I thought a free chocolate with every cup of coffee would be a good idea, Maggie thought a bowl of giant chocolate buttons would be more fun. I'd offered to pay her, but she said the Supper Club prize money was seeing her through and that she was doing me a favour. I made sure she was stuffed full of cake and coffee. It was the least I could do.

'Let's have a glass of this,' Maggie said.

I watched her open the fridge and take out a bottle of white wine. Fishing in the drawer, she pulled out the corkscrew and opened the wine, then poured us two large glasses. We walked out into the courtyard and sat at one of the wrought-iron tables. I glanced up at the pale sky, sipped my cold wine and smiled.

'It's just as good as being at the pub,' I said, breathing in the evening air.

'Much better,' said Maggie. 'At the pub there are too many men gawping at you.'

'Maybe at you,' I said. 'Anyway, I thought you liked that. To be the object of desire, I mean. You once told me you were only interested in men, sex and good food.'

Maggie shrugged, leaned back in her chair and crossed her legs.

'The novelty's wearing off,' she said. 'I still like the food part, though I'm a bit over cake right now.'

She patted her tummy, of which there was virtually nothing.

'Maggie,' I said hesitantly. 'What was Sal like? Why were you so hooked on him?'

Maggie looked uncomfortable for a moment. She sighed and took a large gulp of wine.

'He's an artist, a successful one, too,' she said. 'So he's quite serious and very hard-working. He's soulful, intense, passionate about what he does, a passionate lover.'

Maggie stopped speaking and shook her head. She rolled her eyes.

'Listen to me,' she said. 'I sound like a dreamy teenager.'

We both watched a robin land on another table and peck at invisible crumbs.

'Would you take him back if he asked you?' I said, but Maggie shook her head.

'No,' she said. 'I'm too proud. No way. And anyway, I like being single, with the occasional no-strings-attached fling. My life is my own. I can be completely independent. What about you? How are you doing without Joe?'

I frowned and screwed up my nose. Joe's brother, Jimmy, had been to collect Joe's possessions from my flat and awkwardly told me that Joe was doing fine, but that he didn't want me to contact him at all. Though I had wanted to call him every day, I had to respect his wishes. I missed him terribly, but I knew, in my heart, it was better we were apart.

'I miss him,' I said. 'But I feel less tormented now. Even though I'm lonely and I would love to see him, I'm relieved that he's not asking me to marry him every five seconds and that I'm not justifying my every move. That sounds bad, but it's the truth.'

'What about Ethan?' Maggie asked. 'Have you heard from him?'

I shook my head and drained my glass.

'No,' I said. 'I guess he's back in Rome. I'll probably never see him again.'

Saying the words out loud made me feel depressed, but I knew they were true. This whole episode, since he'd turned up unexpectedly at the Supper Club, should have given me resolution, but instead it had opened up old wounds and made a few fresh ones, too. Perhaps it would never sit comfortably with me. Perhaps my relationship with Ethan was never going to fit neatly into a box to be stored away in my memory bank. More likely it would always be with me, in my bones, as much a part of me as my skeleton. I would just have to live with it.

'Never say never,' said Maggie, twisting her wrist to see the time on her watch. 'It's half eight. I'd better get going because I'm meeting someone at nine. Will you be OK from here?'

'Of course,' I said. 'Who are you meeting? A man, by any chance?'

'Remember Paul,' she said, 'the Saturday Supper Club photographer? He wants to take me to dinner.'

She rolled her eyes, as if it were a chore, a wicked smile stretching over her lips.

'Is he married?' I asked, frowning. But Maggie shook her head.

'Single,' she said. 'But I'm not letting that put me off. Despite being short, he's actually very well endowed.'

'Maggie!' I said. 'Have you slept with him?'

'Of course I have,' she said. 'Where do you think I disappeared to the night of Andrew's dinner? Hey, are those your cakes I can smell?'

After Maggie left to meet Paul and I decanted the chocolate cakes from the tins and placed them on cooling racks, my dad called to say he was going to pop in with the till roll I'd left at his house. While I was waiting for him, I smoothed out the piece of paper with Mum's Lovebird recipe on it and pinned it to the 'Love' wall, alongside the photograph of her and Dad on the beach. I thought about my memories of Mum, most of them of her in our kitchen, mixing up something delicious, or just sitting at the kitchen table having a cold drink. She worked, too, as a dressmaker for a designer – and was no doubt a smart businesswoman – but I never saw where she went. Most of the time we were together, we were at home. She'd seemed happy there in the kitchen, at the heart of our home, but was she? It struck me that I didn't really know. Maybe she was secretly seething with resentment every time she dragged a tray of freshly baked fairy cakes out of the oven. Maybe she just put it all on, for us. I doubted it, though. Even when she'd fallen ill she'd remained positive, never showing me how unhappy she must have been. I sighed heavily. I hoped her life had been everything she wanted it to be.

'Hello, love,' my dad said, coming in and closing the cafe door behind him. 'Big day tomorrow.'

Dad's silver hair was starting to sprout back where he'd shaved it off, which made him look like a catkin. I walked over to him and we hugged. I pointed to the black-and-white photo on the wall and smiled.

'I was just thinking about you and Mum,' I said. 'About her making this cake all the time. She always seemed happy, but the very fact she came up with that recipe makes me wonder what was going on. Did you row a lot? Was she fulfilled? Did you have a good marriage?'

A cloud passed over Dad's face, as he found a chair to sit on. I hopped up onto the tabletop, my legs swinging.

'Of course we did,' he said. 'Very good. Though it was cut short.'

We looked at one another and he smiled sadly. I wanted to make him feel better.

'I knew your marriage was good,' I said, relieved. 'You two

are my standard. I won't ever settle for anything less than what you and Mum had.'

Dad shook his head and sighed. He looked at his shoes, then up to me.

'It wasn't perfect,' he said. 'In fact, just after we married, we almost split up. Let's just say she was a little bit careless with my heart for a while.'

'What does that mean?' I said, confused. 'Did she have an affair?'

I asked the question, but I didn't really believe that my mother would do such a thing. The image I had of her in my mind, of such a homely person, didn't go hand in hand with a woman capable of an affair.

'She had a very short-lived affair,' he said. 'With a friend I used to play tennis with. She was full of remorse and regretted it terribly. That's the origin of that cake. She was trying to win me over.'

'Oh, Dad!' I said. 'I'm sorry, these cakes must bring back awful memories. I had no idea! Why did you give me the recipe?'

'The cake is so delicious, I knew you'd like it,' he said. 'And your mum's affair was a wake-up call in many ways. Audrey needed a lot of attention and I'd become a little bit lazy. It was hard, but I forgave her and we became closer. Marriages are like that. Forgiveness and understanding are very important.'

Dad stretched his arms up into the air and yawned.

'Why am I blathering on like this?' he asked. 'Do you think you should get some rest before tomorrow?'

The news of Mum's affair was still sinking into my brain. Did I really know her at all? Of course I did. She was still the same person, whatever was going on in her private life. She still loved Daisy and me, she must have loved Dad. Perhaps her life confused her, perhaps she made a genuine mistake. I wished I could have a conversation with her to find out what she thought.

'Yes, but I don't think I'll get any sleep,' I said. 'I'm too worried about whether anyone will actually come in.'

Chapter Thirty-Three

By midday the following day, I hadn't had even one single customer in the cafe. I sat on a chair behind the counter, holding a cup of coffee to my cheek, feeling depressed. I hadn't expected it to be an instant success, but I thought at least one person who had passed by and looked through the window might have come in for a measly cup of coffee. A city of cakes was stacked up in front of me and I wondered what I was going to do with them all at the end of the day. I'd have to start running a soup kitchen, but it would be a cake kitchen instead. In the quiet of the empty cafe, my mind drifted to Ethan. I wondered what he was doing in Rome and how he could live with himself for running away from Benji like that. No matter how difficult Daisy had made it, he should have stuck it out. And how was Joe now? What was he feeling? Still hating me, I expected. I imagined him sitting at a desk in the city somewhere, fuelling all of his energy into his job, not allowing himself to dwell on us. My thoughts were interrupted by the buzz of my mobile phone. I reached into my apron pocket to read the text, when the door opened and Elaine walked in, keeping her hand on the half-open door.

'Eve, honey,' she said, pointing at the door. 'Did you know you have the sign turned round to "Closed"? I've just watched three people come and have a look in your window then turn away again. Shall I turn it round to "Open" for you? That would be a good start.'

'Oh my God,' I said, slapping my hand to my mouth. 'What an absolute idiot I am! Yes, turn it round, leave the door open! Come in and have a drink. There's a ton of cake here too. I can't believe I left the sign the wrong way round. God.'

I served Elaine a massive slice of cake and made her sit in a window seat, so people could see that I did actually have customers.

'Oh,' she said, enthusiastically tucking into her cake. 'This *is* good.'

Soon after, a trickle of people I didn't know came into the cafe. I was so excited I phoned Isabel in Dubai to tell her. She screamed. I burst out laughing.

'I wish I was there too,' she said. 'This is the beginning for you.'

And Isabel was right. Though some days the cafe was very quiet and I ended up throwing away the cakes I baked, over the next few weeks, word-of-mouth publicity and the Saturday Supper Club feature meant that I got busier, especially popular with the yummy-mummy brigade who, most mornings, clogged up the entire cafe with their enormous buggies and baby paraphernalia. I didn't mind. They ordered a relentless supply of coffee and cake for their group and could never stay too long before one of their toddlers demanded they leave. The customers were a constant source of fascination to me, especially the people who chose to stick up a picture on the 'Love' board. Already there was an eclectic selection of pictures up there underneath the one of Mum and Dad: Antonia's red shoes, a couple kissing, a bunch of pansies, an empty plate scattered with cake crumbs and a close-up picture of a nose. A lovely nose, I had to admit.

When I'd been open just over a month, Dominique came into the cafe. Dressed in a black dress and high heels, her blonde hair straightened to within an inch of its life, she looked terrifying. In my gingham tea-dress and flats, I felt suddenly childlike, shadowed by her sophistication. I trooped obediently over to her table, a smile fixed on my lips. I was still seething about the write-up she'd done of my dinner party.

'Joe sent me here,' she said. 'He's got a job at the paper. He's now my boss! Did you know? He wants me to do a review of this place.'

My cheeks glowed and my heart warmed. A smile crept onto my lips.

'That's so lovely of him,' I said. 'I must call him. What can I get you?'

Dominique ordered a mocha and a slice of cake, but as I left her table, she grabbed hold of my forearm. I looked down at her long pink talons gripping my skin, then at her face, in alarm.

'What?' I said. 'Dominique . . . will you get off, please?'

I shook off her hand and she gave me a quick, slightly apologetic smile.

'It's Joe,' she said, tucking her blonde hair behind her ears. 'We're . . . well . . . I'm very interested in him. We've been seeing each other. Are you going to make it difficult for me?'

Taken aback, I blinked and opened my mouth to speak, but no words came out. I couldn't believe that Joe could have moved on so quickly. Perhaps he hadn't been so dead keen on me after all.

'N-no . . . no,' I stuttered. 'If Joe is happy, then I'm happy.'

The door opened and I looked up to smile and welcome a couple with their baby trying to decide where they should sit. I gestured to a big table at the back of the cafe, where there was ample room for a buggy.

'Good,' she said, as I backed away from her table. I made her coffee and cake as quickly as I could, plonking it down on her table.

'Don't choke on it,' I muttered under my breath, heading to the other table. 'Hello, right, what can I get you?'

When Dominique had gone – her plate pleasingly clean – I called Joe and, though he was cool at first, he sounded genuinely pleased to hear from me.

'Dominique says you've been seeing each other,' I said, resisting the urge to tell him I thought it was too quick and that she'd eat him alive.

'Yes, it's weird, she lives in a flat over the road, I didn't even know,' he said. 'I like her, but I think she likes me more. It's strange being in this position, I'm not sure I like it.'

'Oh, it's not so bad,' I said warmly. 'Are you OK, really?'

'Yes,' he said. 'I'm getting there. Listen, have you seen Ethan again? Because there's this Saturday Supper Club thing I can set up . . .'

I laughed and told him that Ethan had gone back to Rome.

'That's strange,' he said. 'Because I'm convinced I saw him in the park with Benji.'

'Must have been someone else,' I said. 'Bye, Joe, I'd better go. Come in sometime.'

'I will,' he said, though I doubted he would. 'I definitely will.'

I hadn't seen Daisy since opening, so when I saw her at the door that same afternoon, I thought something must be wrong.

'Eve,' she said. 'I've come to talk to you.'

Daisy asked me to sit down while she explained that Ethan hadn't ever returned to Rome. Instead, he had moved back into his cousin's flat and was trying, really hard, to form a relationship with Benji.

'I had to give him a second chance,' she said. 'He pleaded with me to give him a chance.'

She paused to look at me, but I was too shocked to speak. Shocked, but also pleased that Ethan had done the right thing.

'I know this isn't easy for you,' she said, 'to know that Ethan has been spending time with me, but I came here to tell you that he's still desperately in love with you. I know he doesn't want me. He never has. You're all he talks about. You're all he wants, but he thinks you don't want to see him again.'

'I don't,' I said. 'He should get on with his life and I'll get on with mine, it's not ever—'

No, I thought. Stop pretending. Just be honest.

'I . . .' I said. 'Too much has happened.'

'He's coming in,' Daisy interrupted me. 'At closing time. I got here first, to warn you. I'm going now. I have to go and pick up Benji from nursery.'

'Closing time?' I said, checking my watch. 'That's in five minutes.'

Five minutes. Ethan. Here. I was suddenly reminded of how I felt when he turned up on my doorstep for the Saturday Supper Club. I took a deep breath.

'Thank you, Daisy,' I said to Daisy's back as she left the cafe, her ponytail swinging behind her.

I put the 'Closed' sign in the window and made coffee and cut two slices of cake. I put on the radio and walked out into the courtyard, looking up at swifts dart across the sky. I closed my eyes for a long moment and exhaled deeply, snapping them open when I heard a knock on the front door. My heart in my mouth, I glanced up to see Ethan standing there, a warm, gentle smile on his lips. I opened the door.

'You were expecting me?' Ethan said, looking over at the coffee and cake hopefully.

'Daisy told me you were coming in,' I said. 'Sit down for a while.'

We sat down opposite one another at a small wooden table, drinking the coffee and eating the cake. As we ate and drank, we looked at one another, speaking without speaking.

'Why did you come?' I asked Ethan after a few minutes.

'A leap of faith,' he said. 'And so is this.'

Ethan stood up and pushed back his chair. He moved towards me, took the coffee cup out of my hand, pulled me to standing and wrapped his arm around my waist.

'What are you doing?' I said, but Ethan's lips were suddenly on mine, silencing me.

He kissed me. My shoulders dropped and my body melted into his. I couldn't help myself. I jumped off a cliff and hoped to find my wings on the way down. I kissed him back. He tasted of cake. We broke off to smile at one another then kissed again. We were lovebirds. Destined.

Lovebird Chocolate Cake

INGREDIENTS

For cake:
180g good quality plain chocolate
175g unsalted butter, at room temperature
90g golden caster sugar
3 eggs, yolks and whites separated
100g ground almonds
90g plain flour

For topping:
200g good quality plain chocolate
3 tbsp milk
Raspberries, enough to form a heart

METHOD

1. Heat oven to 170°C/150°C fan/Gas mark 3
2. Grease and line a 7-inch round cake tin.
3. Melt the chocolate in a bowl over simmering water.
4. Separate the egg yolks and whites.

5. Cream butter and sugar together until light then beat in the egg yolks. Add the melted chocolate and ground almonds.
6. Whisk the egg whites in a separate bowl until soft peaks form, then fold the flour and the egg white into the chocolate mixture, taking care not to knock the air out of the egg whites.
7. Pour mixture into the tin and bake for 25–30 minutes or until springy and an inserted skewer comes out clean.
8. Turn onto a wire rack and, when cooled, make the topping.
9. Melt the chocolate above a bowl of simmering water and add the milk, which will thicken the chocolate, stirring all the time. Make sure to keep the bowl over the heat whilst adding the milk and stirring. Spread over the cooled cake.
10. Use the raspberries to make a heart on top of the cake.